Sin

&

Social Workers

Original Artwork by Joe Roth

Norah S. Bernard

Printed in the United States of America

Cover: *La Jeune Martyre* (The Young Martyr)
by Paul Delaroche.
Oil on canvas. France, 1855.
Photographed at *Le Musée du Louvre*, Paris, France.

Bernard, Norah S.
Sinners & Social Workers/ Norah S. Bernard.

ISBN: 978-0-6151-6034-4

1. Heaven—Fiction. 2. Hell—Fiction. 3. Afterlife—Fiction. 4. Death—Fiction. 5. Devil—Fiction. 6. Sin—Fiction. I. Title

10 9 8 7 6 5 4 3 2 1

Other Books by Norah S. Bernard...

Virus 2.0

Clive & Brie

Sinners

&

Social Workers

Photography by Janet Roth

To Rick
With Love,

My best friend, my sweetheart, my inspiration,

Who keeps me grounded, focused and secure,

As I travel along my own path.

Table of Contents

Part I:
The End

Chapter 1: Charlie Miller

Charlie felt a pang of sadness as the crisp leaves whipped around his feet. Fall seemed to have a depressing effect on him. He watched as his son skipped up the walkway to the schoolhouse door, turned around to wave at him, and went in. Charlie walked back to the car, got in, and turned the key in the ignition. He listened to the engine gritting its teeth in a last ditch effort to turn over. The longer it took, the more his stomach seemed to fold in on itself. He was beginning to feel sick, the queasiness waiting for one more failed cough of the engine before initiating the full court press. But the engine turned over, and Charlie gave thanks softly to nobody in particular.

Jamie had just turned six, an autumn-birthday boy, and was going to kindergarten now. He got over his "separation anxiety' very quickly — well maybe he never had any real anxiety at all — and that was good. But somehow it was a little disappointing, too, that his son engaged so quickly with the strangers who would become his mentors. Jamie was nothing like his father had been when he was a child.

Lately it seemed that Charlie found himself getting anxious about everything — more so as he got older. He was forty this year, and it was a time of reflection for him. Why the mirror seemed so dark, he couldn't say. It disturbed him and at the same time, felt ... somehow ... comfortable. You couldn't really see that much in a dark mirror. Perhaps that was good.

Charlie pulled into the parking lot at the insurance company where he worked. He had worked there for eighteen years — it was the first job he had landed right out of college, and had been there ever since. He was an insurance underwriter, which meant that he went over applications and determined what premium would be paid by the applicant. It was a business where you got paid by people who hoped they would never use your services.

Determining the amount of premium was hardly challenging, though — just a matter of checking off the various boxes which together would dictate the premium. Charlie stifled a yawn and wondered how long it would be before he could go to the employee lounge and get a cup of coffee. There were no wall clocks — just prints of watercolors, farm scenes, animals, and other flora and fauna — exactly what they were missing by being in this dull, suffocating building, doing this dull, suffocating work. He had trained himself not to look at his watch more often than once an hour. He recalled the sense of vicarious humiliation he felt once when a new office clerk, a young girl, was berated in front of everyone for looking at her watch too often! The employees here did not even have the privacy of separate cubicles — all desks were spaced out every six feet or so in one cavernous, open office. The poor young thing was fresh out of high school, and already had a toddler at home. It was easy to see that she was on the verge of tears, but being new, she managed to hold them back. Charlie cringed at the recollection.

It had been many years since he himself had been chewed out for anything. And when he was, he recalled having had the advantage of being summoned into the supervisor's office, so the entire staff did not get to hear it. He noticed, too, over the years, that the female staff seemed preferentially to be denied that courtesy. It was pretty consistent. When the boss called one of the guys into his office, you could tell they had been chewed out — either by their pale, grim appearance when they came out — or they might just tell you about it themselves at lunch. But the women were always chewed out in the middle of the office, for all to witness. More than once, over the years, the whole office watched as they broke down in tears, humiliated; some even walked off the job immediately. All that sexual harassment drivel — he used to think it was bogus. Over time he learned it wasn't.

Glancing around the room and stretching to provide some camouflage as he flexed his fist backward, Charlie surreptitiously looked at his watch. Five after ten. He missed five minutes of his coffee break! He got up and walked to the employee lounge, opened the refrigerator and took out his lunch bag to see what Shirley had packed for him. He saw the note, folded up, and Shirley's near-illegible scrawl on it: "Don't forget! Tomorrow is bring-your-child-to-work day! You promised Jamie!" She always punctuated everything with an exclamation mark.

Charlie sat down at one of the metal tables, and slumped down in the chair.

Bring Jamie to work. Why? What was there for him to see here? What was he even doing here himself? What happened to all his childhood hopes and dreams? He sat at the table, thankful that no one else was in the lounge at the moment. His stomach was sliding again, like it did when he thought his car was not going to start after dropping Jamie off at school earlier. Now it was worse, though. He felt like his stomach was sinking into quicksand. Who would throw him a branch or a rope?

The lounge door opened, and two women walked in, chatting with each other. They dropped their voices as soon as they spotted Charlie, but continued to talk, seemingly at the same time.

How can women do that, he wondered — talk at the same time and carry on an intelligible conversation? He didn't really understand women, but he thought that probably placed him with the majority of men. He loved his wife, he thought. Of course, when he really thought about it — if anyone asked him what love was, he was not sure he could give a really rational answer.

Charlie met Shirley in high school. They were both seniors. She was pretty and popular with a nice crowd. They didn't drink or smoke. He was shy, and probably never would have gotten together with her if she hadn't made the first move. Maybe that's why he was recalling it now — he was in the school cafeteria, and Shirley came in with a girlfriend, like the two women who just came into the staff lounge. Shirley and her friend had also dropped their voices when they saw him; then came over and sat down at the other end of his table.

Shirley started the conversation: "You're Charlie Miller, aren't you? You're in Mrs. Randall's homeroom?" That led to some regular telephone conversations, and the next thing he knew, Shirley asked him to the Homecoming Dance. It was in the fall, of course — around the same time as it was now.

Why was his stomach dragging him down again now? He remembered feeling happy about the fact that a girl was interested in him. And she was pretty and popular. Why did he feel so sad recalling it now?

They dated for the rest of the school year, and on the night of the Senior Prom, they stayed out all night and "went all the way." In those days, kids didn't do that! Well ... if they did, they felt horrible about it! Both Charlie and Shirley had been virgins before that night, and although they professed their love for each other, Charlie felt sick for days afterward.

Just like he did now.

They had separated for awhile after graduation — Shirley went off to the state university and majored in art, and Charlie joined the Air Force. He was hoping to obtain money for college, but he also had another reason. His father had been a Marine in the Korean War, and although he had never pressured his son to join the military, Charlie knew it would please his father immensely to follow in his footsteps. And he was right. His father beamed with joy when told his son was going to join the military — valiantly withholding his disappointment that his son joined the Air Force rather than the Marines.

Unfortunately, barely a year into his enlistment, Charlie was hit by a jeep driven by his commanding officer who was returning home from a local bistro (moderately intoxicated, although that did not appear in the report). One knee was badly injured, and Charlie took the option of a medical discharge. He wasn't really happy in the military anyway. He came home and began attending classes in accounting at the local community college.

By the time Charlie was ready to transfer to the state university, Shirley had dropped out of school and had come back home. They switched places then — he going to State, she staying home — getting together when he came home for holidays and for the summer. Shirley was dating other boys, though. She said she just liked going out too much to sit around just because Charlie wasn't there. He said he understood. He went out with other girls, too, but never really got interested enough in anyone to replace Shirley. When he came home, he was most comfortable with the familiarity of Shirley.

Their high school prom night notwithstanding, Charlie avoided having sex with Shirley when they did get together, because he — well, he just didn't feel right about it. He had a roommate in college who was pretty promiscuous — he went after any girl he could get. Frank used to say, "Ugly girls are like medicine: You don't like to take it, but it makes you feel good!" Charlie laughed at that, but he couldn't really understand how anyone could find pleasure in being with someone they were not attracted to — physically or emotionally.

Then it struck him. Was he "emotionally" attracted to Shirley? Physically — well, yes, she was very pretty, he always thought that. But emotionally? He could not recall any such feeling at this minute. He couldn't really feel anything at all at this minute.

Shirley arranged for the wedding without actually asking Charlie about it. She just started talking about it at his graduation from college. It was kind of embarrassing when her mother called his mother and started talking about wedding plans, and his mother didn't know a thing about it! She put the phone down, came in and asked Charlie whether Shirley's mother was a little — oh, irrational? But no, he confirmed that, yes, they really had talked about getting married.

After the wedding, they went on a honeymoon to Disneyworld. Charlie got sick on the Space Mountain ride, staggered out of the place, threw up, and then passed out on the concourse. He couldn't stand up again without throwing up, so they had to call the paramedics. He was okay the next day, though, and they enjoyed the remainder of the honeymoon — except for the fact that he began to get pretty bored by the third day. Now that he thought about it, he didn't really enjoy the honeymoon much at all. And now that he thought about it again — he didn't really enjoy much of anything.

Getting up from the employee's lounge table, Charlie tossed his half-full coffee cup into the trash container by the door, and put his lunch bag, unopened, back into the refrigerator. He went back to his desk and sat down; pulled the next insurance application off the stack and looked it over. He looked at the words and the numbers and the boxes checked and the boxes not checked, and he looked at the signature line.

"Lucille Fern Hellman." *Hellman's Real Mayonnaise. Hello, man! Hell hath no fury.*

Trying to pull his concentration back to the work at hand, Charlie was struck by another association:

Lucille ... Lucy ... Fern ... Fer ... in ... Hellman ... Hell. Lucifer. Lucifer in Hell.

He sat frozen as he stared at the name on the paper. He didn't believe in anything paranormal. He didn't even believe in God. Not really. Well, he went to church with Shirley on special holidays, like Easter Sunday — but he didn't really believe in anything. He wasn't sure why. He was just sure that he didn't. But now ... this!

How could this not be a sign?

A sign from God.

It was too clear not to be! But why would God send him the devil's name on an insurance application?

A message from God.

No — not a message from God.

A message from the devil.

Or, if it were from God, was he telling him to turn to the devil? That was utter nonsense! But somehow it explained why he felt so sick to his stomach lately — for no apparent reason. He knew it now. *This* was the reason!

Suddenly Charlie felt excruciatingly sad. But no tears formed in his eyes. He felt as if a cement weight were tied to his chest, dragging him down, down, and he couldn't move, he couldn't get up, he couldn't do anything. He just sat at his desk, not moving, staring glassy-eyed down at the papers on his desk.

He had no idea how long he had been sitting there like that, frozen, unmoving, when he felt a tap on the shoulder. He looked up to see not only his boss standing there, but everyone in the office turned around in their seats, staring at him.

"Charlie? Are you all right?" his boss was asking him.

That was strange — Sam Browne was never interested in his welfare in the past. He never even spoke to him, except when he wanted some information about his work; he never gave him more than a nod and a "good morning" or "good night" if he happened to pass by Charlie as he came or went from the work day. Now he was tapping him on the shoulder and asking about his health.

As Charlie looked up, first at his boss, and then around the office, at all the faces staring at him, he felt himself coloring, a hot wave rising up his neck and into his face. What was happening?

"Charlie?" Sam's voice was softer and more compassionate — genuinely concerned and sincere-sounding. Charlie would not have recognized his voice if he heard it without seeing him. Now he looked back up at him. He could not find any words to say. He just stared up at Sam, who was bending over slightly, and still had his hand on the shoulder where he had tapped it.

"Charlie, should we call a doctor?"

That question seemed to snap through his paralysis, and he said, "Why?"

"Well ..." Sam responded, taking his hand off Charlie's shoulder and standing back up straight, "Well, you seem ... ill. Is something wrong?"

Charlie looked back around at the others in the office. Sam followed his gaze, and then said, in his more-familiar authoritarian voice, "Okay, everyone can turn around and get back to work now!" Then he turned back to Charlie, dropped his voice again and said, "Why don't you come into my office now?"

The muscles in his legs tensed — he felt weak and feared he might topple over if he stood up too quickly. But they seemed to be working, and he pushed back and stood up, following his boss across the office, threading their way between desks of others who had lowered their heads and pretended to be working, while their eyes still followed the pair.

Once inside, Sam did not sit down, and did not ask Charlie to sit down. He just turned around and asked him again what was wrong. Dropping his eyes toward the floor, he saw how neatly polished Sam's shoes were, even though they had creases which indicated some years of wear. He looked at his own shoes, scuffed, unpolished since the last time that Shirley took out all the family shoes that needed polishing and did them all. He made a mental note to ask her when she was going to do them again.

"Perhaps you had better go on home, Charlie," Sam was saying. He sounded ... strangely ... far away. He did not know how long they had been standing there, nor how long Sam had been talking to him.

"... and I expect you to go to a doctor. Be sure to bring in a note from him when you return."

Charlie looked up at Sam, and opened his mouth to say something, but Sam was already ushering him out the door. He held him by the arm just above the elbow, and walked him out of his office. As they came into the main area, the buzz of multiple conversations abruptly ceased, and heads snapped back to the work on their desks and remained there while Sam walked Charlie back to his own desk.

Sam stood by the desk as Charlie started to put the stacks of insurance papers back into his file drawer — slowly, carefully looking at each one as though it were an old love letter. Sam stopped him.

"Oh, don't bother putting those away — I'll have someone else take care of it."

Charlie stared at him for a moment. Sam's inscrutable smile was more unnerving than reassuring. He returned his focus to his desk and began straightening up a stack of papers — centering them on the desk pad, laying the pencils in a neat row next to the stack — and then patted the stack of papers as though he were saying goodbye. He straightened up and looked at his boss, who remained standing there, expression unchanged. Then he turned and walked to the coat rack by the back door, took his coat and hat — but didn't bother to put them on — and walked out.

Outside, Charlie was struck by the cold wind that blew the remaining leaves, dried and brown, across the tarmac. He pulled one from under his windshield wiper, held it for a minute, then let it go when a gust of wind blew up and took it along. He got into the car, put the key into the ignition, and listened to the sound of a dying engine, coughing a last weak tubercular hack, and failing to turn over. The ignition groaned slower and slower with each effort, until it finally just made a moribund click. Charlie put his forearm across the steering wheel and laid his forehead on his arm. Then he felt a painful pressure behind his eyes, and wetness down his cheeks, and soon his shoulders were heaving as he sobbed quietly.

After awhile — and he was not at all sure how long he had sat there — he opened the door and got out of the car. He started walking, hunched over against the wind, hat pulled down over his eyes, hands in his pockets. He walked for a few blocks, until he saw a bench and sat down. He couldn't have said what he had been thinking, if anyone asked — he didn't really know. But he looked up when the streetlight went on and realized that he must have been sitting on that bench for hours. He looked at his watch: 5:20. Shirley would be worrying.

Would she, though? She had so many interests, so many friends that she met for lunch, chatted with on the phone, went to the movies with (when Charlie wasn't interested, which was most of the time, but he occasionally feigned interest in something that Shirley was exceptionally excited about), and going for her "night out with the girls."

Then there was Jamie — darling Jamie — a good boy, no trouble at all. He was very attached to his mother, though, always wanting *her* to pick him up when he was a baby; looking at *her* when they sat in the audience at his school programs; bringing his artwork to *her* for praise. Dad was very much the second fiddle in his son's world.

He stood up from the bench and turned to go back to the parking lot where he left his car. Then he remembered that it didn't start. He turned in the other direction and started to walk the two miles or so home. He would call triple-A. Or something.

Charlie walked slowly down the street, not looking up at all to see what corner he had passed. When he got to the Second Street bridge, the wind picked up considerably, and it stung his eyes. About a quarter of the way across the wide open span, the wind blew his hat off, and he reached out over the railing to try and grab it, but it blew off into the distance. He watched it, flying in the wind, as far as he could, in the deepening twilight, in the reflection of the lights from the city, until it sailed down toward the water, and he could no longer see it.

He continued to stare at the water, though, and he suddenly found that he was seeing the events of the day flashing before him in his mind: The car not starting, Jamie running into the school with hardly a look back; then the humiliating breakdown at work; the stares of his co-workers; the mandate from his boss to "go see a doctor" and "bring him a note" from the doctor, as though he were a school child.

The feeling of depression that had been gnawing at his gut all day now came over him with a vengeance, as though demons were clawing at him, dragging him, pulling him, down, down, down.

Then he remembered: *a Secret Message* from *"Lucifer In Hell."*

Just as instantly as he thought about it, he threw one leg over the railing, and felt an unfamiliar empowering surge of energy, as though all of his troubles were about to be over. He adjusted his hand hold on the railing and found a toe-hold on the outer side, so he could swing his other leg over.

What was there? Out of the corner of his eye, he thought he spotted some movement at the other end of the bridge. He stopped mid-hurdle.

A small person — a girl? — was holding onto the railing of the bridge, leaning over slightly and looking down at the water — much the same as he was. There was an ominous feeling about the sight — as though he were looking into that same dark mirror — and he found himself leaning back from the railing and pulling his leg back onto the walkway.

He started walking toward the figure, slowly, so as not to intrude on a stranger's personal space — and not to frighten or offend whoever it was.

In a flash, the stranger threw a leg over the railing, just as Charlie had done himself not a minute before. He broke into a run, and the person — a girl, he could definitely tell now — seemed startled at the sound of his footsteps and began to move more swiftly. She pulled her other leg up to swing over the railing and stood up on the thin ledge protruding out over the water. She bent her knees to push off, and he lunged for her at the same moment, catching her by one arm — shocked by how thin it was. He had no trouble pulling her back, wrapping his other arm around her waist and hoisting her back over the railing to safety.

The girl looked to be in her late-twenties. She was dressed in tattered, dirty jeans that hung on her thin frame, and a sleeveless tank top under her too-thin coat. At first, she started to push him away, balling up her fists and pushing against his chest. She was surprisingly strong for someone so emaciated; but as he kept his grip, she stopped resisting, and started to cry. She rested her forehead against his chest, just as Charlie had rested his head against his arm on the steering wheel earlier and cried.

Finally, she looked up at him, and he saw how pretty she was, in spite of the earring pinned through her eyebrow, and another through her lower lip.

"Thank you, Mister," she said, softly.

"Charlie," he responded. Then, after another minute, "Why were you doing that? Why did you try to jump?" He was forgetting his own near-attempt just moments before — and thwarted by — hers.

"I don't know," she said, after a minute, looking to the side. Then she looked up at him again, and smiled a little. "I'm okay now ... How can I thank you for helping me?"

"That's not necessary ... uh ..."

"Penny ... Penny Jackson."

"There's nothing to thank me for, Penny. I'm glad to have helped." Looking around, he said, "I'd like to get you to a hospital, though — so you can get some professional help for whatever it was that ..."

"No, no, really ... Charlie ... I don't need to go to a hospital. Honestly! I don't know what got into me just then. But whatever it was, I feel a great relief that you stopped me before ... before ... I did something so stupid." She drew closer to him.

"Well, then," Charlie said, patting her on the back in a fatherly manner, and feeling strong and competent. The black shroud of despair he had been wearing all day seemed to slide off his shoulders and fall to his feet. "Well, can I take you home?"

"No, that's okay," said Penny, pulling away and wrapping her ragged coat more tightly around herself. "I can get home all right. It's not far. I can walk. Thanks again for …"

"Well, it's not safe for you to walk in this area by yourself," said Charlie, looking up and down the bridge. His car was several blocks away — and besides, it wasn't going to start. He saw a yellow cab coming, and waved his arm.

"I can walk, Mister — er, Charlie — Really! It's not far! I don't need a taxi." She turned and started to walk away.

"Sorry, Penny, but I insist!" he said, stepping after her and taking her firmly by the arm. The taxi stopped in front of them, and Charlie opened the back door and gently pushed Penny toward the seat. But Penny held back strongly, saying, "I can't — Please! If my boyfriend sees you bringing me home, he'll … he'll …"

Charlie just looked at her and sighed. He didn't want to let her go alone. But he didn't want to create more trouble by taking her home and possibly triggering off a jealous boyfriend.

"Okay," he said, letting go of Penny's arm and taking out his wallet, "Okay — I'll let you go by yourself." He handed a twenty-dollar bill to the cab driver, and then added, "But will you call me to let me know that you're all right? Tomorrow morning? Will you please?" He took a card out of his wallet and a pen from his jacket pocket, and jotted down a number. "Will you?"

Penny took the card and nodded her head "yes" as she looked at the number on it. Then she put her hand behind Charlie's neck, pulled his face to hers, and kissed him quickly on the lips. Before he could respond, she jumped into the taxi and pulled the door shut, leaning forward to tell the cab driver where to take her.

He couldn't believe it. He felt high as a kite. He had been … *saved.* He felt like praying, which he never did, since he had not ever really believed in God — but was overwhelmed with an irresistible urge now.

"Thank you," he said, "Thank you," over and over again. He walked back toward his car in the company parking lot, and as he walked, reached into his coat pocket for his cell phone. He always turned it off when he got to work — that was a requirement — but he had not yet turned it back on again.

Three missed messages from Shirley. He called his voicemail, and listened as his wife's voice became more and more anxious, wondering where he was, what had happened to him that he wasn't at work this afternoon — and was he all right?

Another message was from Jamie: "Daddy, I got an 'A' on my handwriting today! Thank you for helping me with it last night. I love you, Daddy!"

Holding back tears — of joy, now — he called home. He explained that the car wouldn't start, and apologized for not calling earlier, and forgetting to turn his cell phone back on. He said he would call triple-A and would be home as soon as it was taken care of. Then he walked back to work, his step feeling lighter than air. And he sent up a few more prayers of thanks.

To think — less than a half-hour earlier he was about to ... about to ... take his own life? *Oh, my God. What is wrong with me?* He thought about Shirley — how kind she is, how loving; always ready to soothe and comfort him; always seeing to his needs before her own. No matter what else she has to do, or wants to do, she always makes sure that his and Jamie's needs are well taken care of. She is really so sweet, and ... and ... he really loves her so much. How could he have ever doubted that for a second? And his wonderful Jamie: How could he possibly have doubted his son's love for him, when he showed it in so many ways all the time?

Charlie walked on, thankful for everything, even finding positive things about his job — the good pay, the close friendships he developed with a few of his coworkers who had been there as long as he had. The bowling league! How could he forget that! He broke 200 a few weeks ago, with a spare on a seven-ten split for the first time ever! What a night that was!

His spirits lifted, his walk quickened, and he held his head high in the crisp night air.

Charlie was lost in as good a mood as he could recall in a long, long time. He was so lost in his happy thoughts that he did not see the eighteen-wheel semi-tractor trailer turning the corner ahead of him, not swinging quite wide enough, the rear of the trailer bouncing up onto the curb, catching his foot at an angle, knocking him down and barreling over him. He didn't know what hit him. But he left the world a happy man.

Chapter 2: Penny Jackson

Penny turned back and looked out the rear window of the taxicab. When Charlie was no longer in view, she turned forward and looked at her watch. She waited until they had traveled for about five minutes, and then she tapped the taxi driver on the shoulder. He looked at her in his rear view mirror without turning around.

"Can you circle around and get me back to where you picked me up?"

"Back to the bridge, Miss?"

"Yes, please."

"He paid me enough, you know? You don't owe me any more money."

"I know — just take me back, please," Penny replied, a little irritated that the taxi driver was questioning her. Then she decided she should say something to satisfy his curiosity, or he might get suspicious. "Well, someone was going to meet me there ... My boyfriend ... I just didn't want to argue with that man."

"Oh, yeah," said the taxi driver, raising his eyebrows, "Okay, I'll take you back." Then he added, "But I don't give no refunds, y'know?"

"Yeah, keep it, just take me back!" Penny sat back against the seat cover, which was torn, and then grabbed onto the door handle as the taxi made a rapid U-turn on what only seemed like two wheels. She nearly hit her head on the side window, and grabbed onto the back of the seat to keep herself upright. Then she laughed to herself at how absurd that was. *I should have opened the door and let myself get flung out of the car!* Then her thoughts became more somber. *I won't go back to that place.*

She was scheduled to go to court the next morning, having "popped positive" on a drug test. Her parole officer had already said that would be the last time she would get away without going back to prison. Penny was angry about the $149.99 that she spent on the internet for a "guaranteed detox kit" that would "cleanse all body fluids and skin of all illicit substances, including tetra-hydro-cannabinol (marijuana), cocaine, alcohol and all opioid narcotics."

Bullshit. They offered a full money-back guarantee. But she would not be around to write back for it.

Penelope Ann Jackson couldn't remember her real mother, even though she had lived with her for five years. She never met her father. She was told that her mother was a drug addict and couldn't take care of her. Her grandmother, Sadie — the only living biological relative she had

— was given custody of her when she was removed from her mother's care.

Sadie kept Penny until she was thirteen years old, when she finally asked the state authorities to take her away. She had warned her many times that she was going to do that — turn her over to the state department of child welfare — but she always backed down. And Penny came to believe she never would give her up. Until she finally, really did.

Things were all right for the first few years of her new situation. Her grandmother was kind and affectionate, but very strict. Penny began stealing from her around the age of nine or ten, for candy money — and later for drugs and cigarettes. Sometimes she would just steal for the thrill of it, when she saw an opportunity. Sadie started hiding her wallet and other valuables, but her streetwise granddaughter always managed to ferret it out. Later on, Sadie would just take most of the money out of her wallet and hide it, leaving only a little, in the hope of tricking Penny into thinking that's all there was. But Penny was on to her game after awhile, and always managed to find the extra cash in her grandmother's bureau drawers, shoeboxes, pillowcases, and anywhere else.

Sadie tried to "negotiate" with her granddaughter, frequently reminding her of how much she loved her and wanted to give her a good home. She offered her a basic allowance, plus generous additional money for completing chores around the house. Desperate to succeed, Sadie asked no more of her than making her own bed and clearing the dishes when she made herself a snack — but even that was too much to ask. Penny did nothing she was asked to do; and still took whatever cash and other valuables she could find.

Sadie had all but resigned herself to her granddaughter's slovenliness and larcenous behavior — until the girl turned thirteen. One night, a school night, Penny called her grandmother around eleven saying she would spend the night at her friend's house. Sadie had a bad feeling about it, and when she called the friend's house, the mother said Penny had never been there. Sadie called the police, but they had heard that song and dance before — teenagers lying about staying with a friend — and told her to "call back if the kid didn't show up by the next day."

Finally, around five in the morning, Penny stumbled in, eyes red and speech slurred from intoxication with drugs and alcohol. Her grandmother started to interrogate her about where she had been, and castigate her for staying out all night — but Penny snapped at her in such a ferocious manner that the older woman actually stumbled backward and sat down in a chair that was behind her. Still, in spite of that frightening incident, she could not find it in her heart to turn her granddaughter over to the authorities; and that lack of initiative only emboldened the unruly girl.

She began smoking in her room, and her truancy from school became more frequent. Sadie found herself making up excuses for her granddaughter's absences when the school authorities would call. Penny began bringing in unsavory-looking characters, going into her room and playing loud music. Sadie was not sure what was going on in there, but she was fearful of a confrontation.

One night, when the partying upstairs went on into the wee hours, a neighbor telephoned and threatened to call the police if the noise didn't stop. Sadie knew she had to confront Penny. She went upstairs and knocked timidly on her door. No answer, but the music was blaring. She knocked more forcefully. Finally, she banged on the door with her fist and yelled for Penny to come out. The door opened so swiftly that she actually took a step backward. There was a man who looked to be in his late twenties, with no shirt on, a hand-rolled cigarette hanging out of his mouth, grungy jeans open at the waist and his zipper halfway down. There was no waistband or anything visible beyond the zipper to suggest that he had anything on under his jeans.

"*WHAT??*" he yelled at Sadie, who took another step backward. She could see Penny sitting on the bed, wearing only panties, leaning forward and hooking her bra in the back. A cigarette was dangling from her mouth, too.

"Y-you need to quiet down ... the neighbors ..."

The man did not wait for her to finish, but turned around and yelled, "Hey, Penny, your granny is some hot old lady, y'know?" Then he turned back to Sadie and said, "Hey, old lady! Sex is quiet, right? Real quiet! Or maybe you wouldn't remember? Or maybe you never had any? Been a long time?"

He moved toward Sadie, who was rapidly turning away from the man, but he grabbed at her breast before she could turn completely away. She swept her arm up forcefully, pushing his hand away, and turned to run back down the stairs, hearing the man burst out in raucous laughter. But most painful of all was hearing Penny laughing behind him.

Sadie left the house and went over to the neighbor's home who had complained about the noise. She asked to use the telephone, and — to her neighbor's surprise — called the police herself.

Penny and her man friend were taken into custody. Both were charged with possession of marijuana, and the man was charged with contributing to the delinquency of a minor, and sexual assault on a minor. He was returned to prison, from where he had been paroled only a few months earlier. Penny was committed to the Juvenile Detention Center.

The J.D.C. was a stark, cold, concrete building, with long, narrow hallways and few windows. Penny was locked into a cell with a metal door that had a narrow window, obscured by some kind of chain link reinforcement, and a food slot just big enough for a tray to slide in. She would stay there until her juvenile court hearing, scheduled one month hence. When Sadie came to see her the next day, Penny cried so hard she nearly started to vomit. Sadie was horrified and overwhelmed with guilt for letting this happen to her granddaughter. She paid for her bond and took her home to await the formal hearing.

Penny was a different person when she came home. She no longer had to be told to clear her own dishes. She set the table, helped prepare and serve dinner, cleared and washed the dishes, and made her bed every day. She was a model child. She went to school and came home and did her homework. She frequently asked her grandmother to help her with her homework, making the older woman feel not only useful, but truly valued by her granddaughter.

Sadie was in Seventh Heaven. She felt that she really accomplished something with the "tough love" she finally employed. When the court hearing date rolled around, Sadie couldn't stop gushing about how wonderful her granddaughter had been since she came home; what a changed person she saw; and how confident she was that she had learned her lesson. The judge was equally happy to dismiss the case with a sentence of probation, a two-hundred-fifty dollar fine (which Sadie was happy to pay) and a recommendation that the girl attend alcohol and drug abuse counseling.

Penny never attended any counseling. She convinced her grandmother that she had been "clean" for a month already since her arrest, and had no desire to smoke or drink at all any more. A probation officer had been assigned to Penny's case, but they never heard from him, except when he sent a letter one time for her to come in and give a urine specimen to test for drugs.

It took about two more months before Penny started slipping back into her old ways. Sadie started missing money from her purse again, and she received a call from the school asking where her granddaughter was. Penny began making sincere-sounding excuses again, but they soon deteriorated into more off-handed efforts, seeming not to care whether they were believable or not. After Penny was caught in a lie a couple of times, she became more arrogant and entitled, sneering openly at her grandmother when questioned about her behavior or whereabouts.

Sadie was getting more and more depressed and desperate. She did not want to send her beloved granddaughter back to that horrible place, the J.D.C. She would have to threaten that, however. Perhaps if she made a decisive, uncompromising stand, Penny would drop her resistance and stop this unacceptable behavior of hers again. After all, it worked once, why not again?

The right opportunity was not long in coming. Sadie came home from shopping one afternoon, and heard loud music coming from upstairs. It was too early for school to have been out, so she knew that Penny was truant — she only hoped that she was not doing drugs again. There were no signs of a relapse to drug and alcohol use, so there was still hope that she could get her granddaughter back on track again.

When Sadie reached the top of the stairs, the music coming from Penny's room was blaring loudly. This time she did not bother to knock. She planned to let herself in and take advantage of the "surprise" factor. She would confront Penny about the probability of going back to jail if she did not start attending school and behaving like a lady. She took out her house key and used the flat edge of the head of the key to snap open the locked bedroom door.

Sadie was shocked to see Penny and the same man who had been there before. He had served out the remainder of his sentence for violating parole, and had been released. The newer charges — drug possession and contributing to the delinquency of a minor — had been dropped. Now both of them were sprawled out on the bed, naked and sweating.

With drug-reddened eyes, Penny lazily looked over at her grandmother in the doorway. She showed no surprise — actually had no expression at all — just a haze of intoxication. The man just broke out into a big, malicious grin. He jumped off the bed, still completely naked, making no effort to cover himself, and staggered drunkenly toward Sadie.

"So you decided you want some after all, huh, old lady?" All the while he kept smiling his venomous grin.

Penny slid off the bed and caught up with him, walking toward her grandmother with her own unsteady pace. Sadie turned and started to run toward the stairs, but the man caught her by the wrist and repeated his question in a loud, gravelly voice:

"Huh? What? I can't hear you, old lady! You want some of this?" He pointed to his limp organ.

Sadie reached for the stairwell railing, hoping to pull herself away from the man's grip. She did not anticipate her granddaughter's interference. But Penny extended her leg behind her grandmother's knee, and when Sadie pulled free of the man's grip, she fell backward over Penny's foot and tumbled down the stairs.

Her neck was broken. She remained where she fell at the bottom of the stairs for three days, before she was found by a neighbor and her body removed for burial.

Penny and the man stayed in a motel at the edge of town, near the rail yard. She could have celebrated her fourteenth birthday there — except that the day passed and she didn't even know it. The man had paid for two weeks, but after the second week, when no one had seen or heard from them, and no one answered after knocking on the door, the hotel manager let himself in. Penny's boyfriend pulled a gun on the manager, and left him tied up in the bathroom while he and Penny packed up, ransacked the front desk, and took off. The manager was able to free himself, and called the police. The two fugitives were apprehended a few miles down the highway.

The prosecutor wanted to charge both of them with murder as adults. But given that Penny was just fourteen years old at the time of her arrest — thirteen at the time of the murder — the judge would only allow her to be charged as a juvenile offender. The man plea-bargained down to manslaughter and received a sentence of five-to-ten.

Penny spent the next seven years in a prison for adolescent girls. She was released on her twenty-first birthday to a room in a halfway house, with ten other parolees from around the area. She went to work in a fast-food restaurant ... until she found a way to make a better living.

Men would pay her for doing practically nothing — a few minutes, some stupid act their wives wouldn't stomach, and presto! Twenty bucks! She rented a room in a motel whose manager steered business her way, for a "cut" of the profits: He took fifteen dollars of each twenty she made — and frequently reminded her that she would have no business and no place to conduct it if it weren't for his help. He also claimed to be protecting her from the danger she would be exposed to if she had to find her own business on the street.

That arrangement worked out for a couple of weeks, until one "client" started berating her for doing exactly what he had paid her to do. After his tirade, he beat her unconscious. He left her on the floor and took his money back from the table where he had put it when he came in.

Penny decided that that profession was not for her. She could, however, still make money from it. Like the motel manager did.

Hanging around the local high school, Penny smoked with the kids who would cut class and light up at the truck stop a few blocks away. She impressed some who were awed by her age and experience. She turned them on to marijuana (if they weren't already). Then, when she gained their trust, she convinced them to try heroin. She bought it herself and supplied it to the kids for free. When they were securely "hooked" she approached the girls about making money; and the boys about supplying their girlfriends. Once they delivered the girls, and they were duly turned on to drugs, Penny found she could make tons of money.

Men would pay a lot more than twenty bucks for adolescent girls. And boys. Penny learned well from her former manager — if she got paid a hundred dollars, she would give the kid twenty. Or ten, if they were really naïve. And once the youngsters realized what they had gotten into — voluntarily or not — they were too ashamed and afraid to tell anyone.

Occasionally, one of the youngsters would come to Penny — tearful, distraught, telling her they didn't want to do this anymore, not for any amount of money. She would put her arm around them and tell them in gentle, soothing tones, how much trouble they would be in if they copped out. She would always arrange to have these little talks with one of her bigger and more intimidating high school "henchmen" in the room. If the kid insisted on leaving, a subtle signal from Penny to the bruiser brought a rapid and painful consequence. They got the message. They stayed.

One fifteen-year-old girl came to Penny in tears because she feared she was pregnant. She missed several periods and had started to gain weight. Her small frame barely showed any signs of pregnancy, hidden under loose-fitting clothes, even though she was several months along.

Putting her arms around the distraught girl, Penny assured her that she would take care of it. She had one of the boys drive her and the girl miles outside of the city. She sat in the back with the girl, her arm around her shoulders, giving soft words of comfort. They drove into a forested area, where they said a doctor would be meeting them. They told her to drink up from the pint of whiskey they brought along, to "prepare" herself until the doctor got there — she had to drink the up the whole bottle, they said.

After the pregnant girl passed out, they stripped all her clothes off and left. They laughed so hard on the way back that they nearly ran off the road.

The girl regained consciousness late that night. Confused, sick and woozy from the whiskey, shivering from the cold, she staggered through the forest and fell into a water-filled ravine. She drowned, and was not found for several months.

The authorities assumed that the abandonment and eventual death of the girl in the woods was related to the pregnancy, which was discovered on autopsy. The girl's boyfriend, who knew nothing of her forced prostitution by Penny and her gang, was arrested and convicted of rape and murder. He spent four years in prison before being exonerated by DNA evidence.

Penny was eventually arrested for pandering, and at the age of twenty-three, was sent to the adult women's prison. She couldn't believe a place could be worse than the juvenile prison facility where she had spent seven years of her youth. Nothing was clean, except the visitors' room, and she only went there twice to meet with her public defender. Some of the correctional officers were courteous, but she would not do anything but sneer at them.

Penny was assigned to a psychiatrist, who met with her to do an evaluation. She looked at him in disgust and made up sarcastic answers to his questions. ("Do you ever hear voices when no one is around?" "Yeah ... Yours! And it sucks!") The doctor did not schedule any more meetings with her.

One prison employee refused to be put off, though. Marion Wilson, a psychiatric social worker, kept coming back, even though Penny refused to say a word to her during several initial meetings. Eventually, with her persistence in returning, her dogged refusal to give up, Penny finally started to share some of her background with Marion.

The recollections were filtered, of course, through Penny's need to excuse her actions. She referred to being "abused" by her grandmother, even though Sadie had never been anything but kind and generous toward her. Penny justified these accusations in her own mind, feeling she had been, at least, "emotionally" abused — Sadie had no right to tell her what to do.

After working with incarcerated women for fifteen years, Marion knew better than to accept these stories at face value. She was well aware that these unfortunate souls needed to defend their actions by manipulating the truth — so much so that they themselves eventually grew to believe their own distortions. As time went on, Penny came to look forward to these therapy visits with the gentle social worker.

The prison cells on the "residential" unit were open during the day, and Penny walked to her assigned detail in the prison kitchen about a quarter mile away in the sprawling compound. There were tall shade trees, and in the spring and summer wild flowers grew along the walking paths. When the trees were thick with green leaves, they hid the high double-chain link fence that encircled the compound with razor wire scrolling around the top. At those times, for the few minutes that it took her to walk to work, Penny could pretend she was not in prison — just walking through the park on a pretty day — like when she was little, and someone held her hand and took her to just such a place.

Who was that? Did that ever really happen?

The kitchen building was always hot — unairconditioned in the summer and overheated in the winter — and the work was achingly boring. Penny's assignment was to clean the cooking equipment and help the kitchen supervisor with whatever else she requested. And she always had other requests for Penny. Since Marion held the therapy sessions in her office, it was a great relief having somewhere else to go besides her work assignment.

Marion's office was in the Administration building about halfway between the kitchen and the residential unit. The buildings were actually very pretty — on the outside. The women's prison was built nearly a century before, and the decorative stone architecture was beautiful — if you did not notice the bars just inside every window, in every building. But the beauty outside belied the deteriorating interiors, and the administration building was no exception. Walls had peep-holes of paint peeling on top of more paint peeling on top of yet more. In some spots, layers of three different colors could be seen, one under the other, one duller than the next — greens and grays and yellows. Brown water marks from leaks in the ceiling and rusty pipes scarred almost every wall; and exposed electrical outlets had covers long gone or dangling by one last pathetic wall plate screw.

Penny liked talking to Marion because she would listen attentively to everything she had to say, and never came back with any kind of judgmental comment or preaching. Marion's contribution to the conversation usually consisted of asking an occasional question to help her client see her problems more clearly — the Socratic method. She used this in an effort to clarify Sadie's motives in taking in her grandchild:

"Did your grandmother get any money — from the state, or from a trust fund — for accepting custody of you?" Marion knew she did not, and hoped that eventually Penny would see that Sadie had truly loved and cared about her.

But her truthfulness was never directly confronted, and that gave Penny the impression that Marion was naïve. She hatched a plan for manipulating her therapist into helping her get out of prison. Penny wrote a letter to one of the drug dealers she knew who was fairly "high up" in the underworld organization; and described the areas of weak security and procedures in the prison that could be possible means of escape (like the laundry and food delivery trucks). She asked the drug dealer to help her with a plan from the outside.

The inmates knew that all outgoing mail was read and censored; moreover, letters addressed to known criminals or other incarcerated inmates were forbidden, and could even generate punitive consequences. Penny had no family at all to correspond with, and no friends other than the drug dealers, many of whom were also in prison. Her only correspondence up to that point had been between her and her public defender; and those letters had long since dwindled to a stop. She knew she could never mail a letter to a known drug dealer through the standard channels.

But Marion could.

At their next session, Penny brought the letter with her into the therapy room, addressed and sealed in an envelope (which was also against the rules — all letters were to remain open for inspection before mailing). She looked around to be sure that they were not being watched by the correctional officers. The two by the door were busy chatting and smoking, flicking their ashes out the partially-open door, only to be blown back inside by an occasional gust of wind. She took the envelope out of her pocket and slid it across the desk and under Marion's palm.

Marion looked at the envelope, and before Penny could say anything, she said, "You know it's against the rules to ask someone to mail a letter for you, don't you?"

Penny's face fell and her lower lip drooped down into a pout. She chided, "I thought you were my friend!"

"I'm not your friend, Penny," Marion answered, gently patting Penny's still-outstretched hand, "I'm your therapist. You don't need for me to be your friend. You can make friends wherever you are. I have something different to offer you — I can help you in a way that friends are not equipped for."

Penny was not deterred. She grasped Marion's hand in both of hers. Marion felt the sensual softness of them and reacted with an almost imperceptible tremble. She hoped it went unnoticed. It did not. Penny sensed that she was home-free, and fortified her plea:

"But this is a letter to my uncle! My aunt wrote to tell me he was ill — maybe dying! I just have to get this to him! Before he dies!"

Marion knew full well that the "aunt" and "uncle" were fabrications; that there was no family at all since her grandmother died. But she followed along with the natural course of the disingenuous story — which also gave Penny an opportunity to back out of her deception:

"Well, you don't need me to mail this for you … Why don't you just register your aunt and uncle's names at Admin and go ahead and mail it through the regular channels?"

Penny was too shrewd to be put off. "I can't write to him directly because he has been in prison himself — for a petty drug bust when he was younger," she said, scanning Marion's face for any signs of disbelief.

The weakness of her own story did not elude Penny — that she had never mentioned any "aunt" or "uncle" before. But seeing Marion's sweet, placid face, and earnest attention, and sensing a deeper vulnerability, she was emboldened to continue the charade:

"I know that you know our letters are inspected, and we are not allowed to send letters to ex-cons — and that's why I *never mentioned this uncle to you before*," said Penny, dropping her eyes downward, "I was *too ashamed!*"

Marion nodded and took the envelope. After Penny left, she carefully opened it, and read it. The following day, she sent a message to the kitchen supervisor that she needed to see Penny again. When she arrived, she handed the opened letter back to her.

"I apologize for opening your letter, Penny — but I wanted to be able to help you."

As Penny's shocked face began to darken into a scowl, Marion kept talking as calmly and sincerely as she could, "You could be put into solitary confinement for a year for writing a letter like this — planning an escape — you know that." She went on, not waiting for a response. "I should — I am *obligated* — to turn this letter over to the warden, did you know that? But I don't want to do that. I don't want to create any more misery for you. I want you to take this letter and destroy it yourself, and ..."

Penny cut off the rest of Marion's comments by spitting in her face. Then she got up and calmly walked out.

It was two weeks before Marion sent for Penny again. She hoped a little cooling-off time would help her to see things more clearly. She still hoped to discuss the letter and convince Penny of how sincerely she wanted to help her. Perhaps she would eventually make a breakthrough with her, and help her see how self-destructive her antisocial behavior was; and how much happier she could be if she found ways to engage with people in positive, healthy relationships. And she really wanted to see her again.

Penny came to the therapy office when she was summoned again after the letter incident. She waited for Marion to finish her spiel; then she spit in her face again.

Marion waited another month before calling for Penny again, and another month after a repetition of the same greeting. Finally, she stopped calling for her.

Alone in her cell, or slaving away in the overheated kitchen, Penny knew in her heart that she missed those therapy sessions terribly. She missed Marion — the only comfortable, friendly, encouraging person she ever really knew, since she never appreciated her grandmother's affection. When Marion finally gave up and stopped calling for her, Penny felt a terrible sense of loss; but at the same time, she felt that Marion had only gotten what she deserved for opening her letter instead of mailing it. Spittle was the least of what she deserved. There was nothing more to say.

Eventually Penny was paroled from prison — free to walk away from the stone walls and metal bars. But also freed was the simmering rage she had had to suppress during her incarceration. Kowtowing to ugly, overweight men and stupid women with tacky badges on their shirts and huge belts weighted down with keys and holsters and handcuffs, left a cyclonic fury in Penny's gut that she needed to unleash. A payback for the whole world.

It had been during Penny's in-processing physical exam, when she was first brought to the prison, that she learned she was HIV positive. She was not sick, though — actually felt pretty healthy. So when the anti-HIV medications made her feel nauseated and dizzy, she refused to take them. And anyway … about death, she felt it would only be … a relief.

The day she arrived at her new residence, a halfway house, Penny began prostituting herself. Sometimes she charged nothing at all; her goal was to expose and infect as many people as she possibly could. Male or female, it didn't matter. It was payback time. She used her wiles to gain intimacy with anyone who so much as asked her for the time of day.

Injecting drugs proved to be an even more effective way to pass on the infection. Intravenous drug use was something she had always avoided in the past, for fear of pain from needle sticks — but then she discovered the relief from pain that she got from the injected drugs.

Eventually she started to show signs of active AIDS — weight loss, chronic diarrhea, fatigue, sores that wouldn't heal. At that point, she became scared and sought out medical care. But the long lines at the free clinics — and even worse, the condescending attitudes and repetitive lectures — were intolerable. She went back to the halfway house and started spending more and more of her days in bed, with only her stash of heroin and needles for comfort.

Penny was standing in the lobby of her parole officer's building when she found herself having a vision from the fairy tale "Beauty and the Beast": The last petal trembled in the darkness before it fell from the rose, which meant the death of the "beast." Her parole officer had warned her last time that she would return to prison if she failed another drug test. Penny knew she was "dirty" and her P.O. would have the report by the next morning.

That was when she headed for the bridge. She would not go back to prison. She would not succumb to the disease. She would take herself out.

Penny thought about all of this as the taxi driver completed his u-turn and headed back toward the bridge. When he let her out at the end of the bridge, he couldn't help but express his concern about the dangerousness of leaving her there by herself; but Penny said she would be fine. When he protested again, she made her signature response. She spit at him. He drove off. She waited until he was out of sight before walking to the middle of the bridge, where the water below was deepest, and climbed over onto the narrow ledge. She looked around one more time. No "Charlie" around to interfere with her this time. She pushed off. The last petal fell.

Chapter 3: *Marion Wilson*

Marion Wilson looked at her desk calendar and the notes she had written down for the day.

> *11:00 Meeting with Mr. Clarkson*
> *11:30 Lunch with Elaine*
> *12:00 Penny*
> *1:00 ...*

It was the 12:00 appointment that confounded her. Penny had been overtly hostile ever since the letter incident. Marion had spent nearly a year meeting with Penny, listening to her stories, her background truths and fabrications (and from her years of experience working with incarcerated clients, she could pretty well tell which was which). She had never confronted Penny about any of it, but she had thought the letter presented a good opportunity to help break down her denial of the problems that undermined her chances for real change. After all, she held in her hand the evidence that could put Penny into solitary confinement for a year. Giving her a break like this should have bought a lot of trust.

If reported, Penny would initially be locked down in the high-security "segregation" unit, completely isolated from the rest of the prison population. She would not be allowed out of her six-foot-by-eight-foot cell except for one hour each day; and that would only be within the confines of a twenty square-foot chain-link fenced-in concrete slab — a prison within a prison — which served as a "recreational area" for the women in segregation. There was a basketball hoop erected at one end of the slab; but no basketballs were supplied. (Well, there was a deflated lump of cracked leather in one corner which used to be a basketball.) The women mostly just stood around and smoked. Many never even bothered to leave their cells for their allotted hour when the weather was bad.

After a month or more in segregation, when the disciplinary committee got around to her case, Penny would have a hearing during which she would be assigned a "legal advisor" to help present her side to the judicial administrator. She could have her own lawyer, of course — *if* she could afford one. After a brief review of the facts, her sentence would be pronounced. For writing a letter planning an escape, she would most likely be confined for more than a year. And for "assaulting" her therapist — if Marion had chosen to report the spitting incident — she would most likely receive an additional six months in segregation.

Being found "not guilty" in these hearings was a rare occurrence. Two inmates involved in a physical fight would both be consigned to segregation while the administrators "investigated" the matter — no matter if there were numerous witnesses reporting that one woman had jumped the other. Ultimately the sentence would be up to the presiding officer, with wide latitude for determining the length of time in solitary confinement.

Many of the women learned to "please" the correctional officers in whatever way they hinted — or demanded — in order to protect themselves from future arbitrarily severe disciplinary sentences.

But Penny did not have to go to the segregation wing, nor even to a hearing, because Marion opened the letter herself and gave it back to her, rather than to the authorities. Nor did she ever report that Penny spit on her. Marion had hoped that would nurture trust and open an honest channel of dialogue between them, since she was risking her own position by giving Penny that break. In fact, just accepting the letter in the first place would have gotten her summarily fired, if any officer saw the handover.

It failed. Penny was unrelenting in her hostility from that time on. Their previously close (or so Marion had thought) therapist-client relationship never recovered.

Marion Wilson had experienced physical hostility before — being spat upon was not nearly as bad as the abuse that was perpetrated on her early in life. She grew up in a semi-rural area with her parents, four brothers and one sister. Her sister was the oldest of all the children; two brothers came after that, then Marion, and then two younger brothers. Her father, Vern Wilson, was Sheriff of the county; her mother was a homemaker and active in the church.

Marion was twelve years old when her sixteen-year-old sister, Rebecca, left home, running away with a boyfriend she had met a few days earlier. Two nights after her sister left, Marion's father raped her for the first time. The first chance she got alone with her mother, she told her what had happened. Her mother responded in the strangest manner — she walked away without answering at all — just left Marion standing in the kitchen, weeping.

That night her father came into her room, took off his heavy leather sheriff's belt and thrashed her back and legs until she could not stand up. Then he raped her again. She was unable to walk the next morning, but her mother still drove her to school, with a note to give the teacher that she had fallen down the stairs, and injured her legs.

Marion never mentioned her father's abuse again, to anyone. Nor did she tell her mother when her two older brothers began to emulate their father. One night, the fifteen-year-old boy passed by his sister's bedroom, the door slightly ajar. The sheriff did not stop his assault on his daughter. But when he finished, walking by the boy, still buckling his belt, said, "Go ahead — it's time you became a man." The boy then followed suit.

Then thirteen, Marion did not put up any fight. She had already resigned herself to this fate. At least she avoided being beaten again.

Studying hard in school would be the way out. Marion made good grades, and was frequently asked to take part in extra-curricular activities, but her parents never allowed it. By her senior year in high school, she was the top student in her class. She was offered a full scholarship by the state "flagship" university, which had a national reputation for excellence. Her father refused to allow her to accept it, however, insisting that she remain at home and attend the local community college. There he could keep an eye on her. And continue to have his needs met.

After one semester at the community college, Marion discovered that she was pregnant. She was terribly fearful and bereft of any support system; so she said nothing until it became obvious that she was pregnant. That was the next time she received a beating from her father. With welts on her back and legs, he pushed her into the car and drove up the mountain about twenty miles, to a small, decrepit shack. A wizened old woman with coarse, frizzled gray hair in knots came out the front door as they pulled up. She wore a dress down to her ankles, an apron, and a bandana around her neck. The woman and the whole scene looked surreal, like something out of an old-time western movie.

The woman made no gesture in the way of a greeting as they pulled up to the house. The sheriff pulled his daughter roughly out of the car. She screamed in pain — two ribs had hairline fractures from the beating she had taken — but her father just continued pulling until she fell out of the car onto the gravel.

"Can you take care of her?"

The old woman didn't answer, but made a slight movement of her head that was suggestive of a nod. Following her into the shack, the sheriff pulled his daughter along by her arm.

There was only one room: a kitchen area with an old wood stove, a wash basin on a table, a rocking chair, and a rickety bed. Jars of preserves sat on bare wooden shelves. A mongrel dog slept on a faded braided rug in the corner, opening one eye and growling softly as the trio came in.

The woman motioned for Marion to sit down at the table, and her father pushed her roughly into the chair. She did not cry. She had long ago stopped wasting the energy of crying, as it only ended in more severe discipline. The old woman brought out a bottle of whiskey and a smudged glass with a small crack in the lip. She poured half the glass full and set it down in front of Marion. She motioned for her to drink it by pointing to the glass.

Marion thought the woman was unable to speak. But when she saw her father slap a twenty-dollar bill down on the woodstove, the woman shook her head, and said, "No, sir! This girl is too far along — six months at least — that's fi'ty." Her father scowled and looked as though he would protest; but he just pulled his wallet back out and put another twenty and a ten on top of the woodstove.

In a way, Marion was relieved to pick up the dirty glass and drink from it — maybe it would kill her. She took a large swig and immediately began coughing and sputtering. Her father started to walk toward her, in a menacing way that caused Marion to pick up the glass again and, still coughing and spilling some down her dress, finished it.

The old woman motioned for her to lie down on the bed. Marion was horrified — she didn't care if she lived or died, but she did not want to lie down here and let this harridan commit her butchery on her.

But the whiskey had begun to do its work, and Marion's head began to feel heavy and started to spin. She felt that she was going to vomit, but it only caused her knees to buckle, and she sat down on the bed to steady herself. She blacked out.

Waking up in her own bed at home, Marion tried to get up, but felt a terrible pain in her lower abdomen. When she looked down, she saw that she was bleeding heavily. A towel had been placed between her legs, and she was lying on top of a plastic trash bag. She was unable to move or even get up to eat, not only from the pain and nausea, but from the dizziness and headache that she felt when she moved her head at all. She didn't know how long she had been there, but she saw a tray with a teacup and a bowl of soup on the nightstand next to her bed. She closed her eyes.

Two days later, Marion's parents drove her to the hospital, when she became too ill to ignore. Her temperature was one hundred five degrees, and her abdominal pain had increased to the point that she could not move at all without crying out. The teacup and bowl of soup remained untouched.

After six days in the hospital, the doctor came in to discharge her from the hospital. Marion had not actually met Dr. Harrison before, as she was barely conscious when she came in; and during her stay she was attended to mostly by the interns and nurses under the doctor's supervision. So when he came in to sign off on her hospital discharge papers, she was shocked that he spoke in a quiet voice that was almost more menacing than her father's yelling. In low tones that could not be heard beyond her bed, he berated her for "whoring around" and getting herself pregnant, and then murdering her own baby. He said that she deserved to have the pain she went through. He said she should be ashamed of herself for bringing such humiliation upon her family, creating problems for her father, an upstanding gentleman and officer of the law, and her mother, a god-fearing and saintly church woman.

Then he turned his back and wrote some notes on her chart.

Marion expected the doctor to walk out with nothing more to be said, but he closed the chart with a loud snap and turned back to her.

"I've seen to it that you won't put your family through this again, *Miss* Wilson."

Marion was dumbfounded by that statement, and started to stammer, "Wh-what do you mean? W-won't put them th-through ... wh-what?"

Dr. Harrison came to her bedside and leaned down so that he was only inches from her face. She could see the tiny red vessels marring the whites of his eyes, and smelled the faint odor of wine on his breath. He poked Marion hard on her shoulder with his forefinger, and spoke through clenched teeth:

"Your good folks won't have to worry about having any little bastard grandchildren. And you won't be tricking any poor boy into knocking you up again. You won't insult the good Lord again by taking another baby's life. You won't have any more children — I've seen to that!" Then he turned and walked out.

Too stunned to cry, Marion looked around the room, gathered up the few items from her side table, and walked out. As she passed the front desk, a nurse was writing some notes, and then looked up at her. Marion started to say goodbye, but the nurse shook her head with a look of disgust and turned away. Marion continued walking, still feeling a pain in her lower abdomen and dull aches from the bruises she got before her father had taken her to the old woman's shack. When she walked outside, her father was waiting in his sheriff's car. He took her home without speaking. When she got home, her mother was waiting by the door. They told her to pack up her belongings and get out.

The Dean of Admissions at the state university looked over the transcripts that Marion had sent in the previous year, on which they had based their offer of a full scholarship. She did not have any copy of her grades from the community college she had attended for a semester since then, but that didn't matter. The Dean did not hesitate in renewing the offer of a full scholarship. That marked the first time that Marion had broken down and cried for joy since she was twelve years old. Tears broke through in a torrent, and the Dean was taken aback. He had handed out good news and bad news to students over the years, but had never seen a response quite like this.

When Marion finally managed to regain her composure, the Dean inquired about her situation. She let him know that her home life was "problematic," but she was ineffably grateful for his generosity in renewing the scholarship; and she asked if he could help her find a job and work to pay for room and board, and other essentials. She did not go into any details about her family, but the Dean had been around long enough to sense the seriousness of her problems. A girl with an outstanding academic record who came to the university, hat in hand, pleading for a scholarship which was previously offered but turned down in favor of a community college — well, there must have been great personal hurdles for her. He did not press her about the details. He said that he would see what he could do about supplying additional grant monies to cover the cost of her living in the dormitory.

Marion majored in Sociology and History. She made lots of friends at college, but never dated anyone special. Oh, she went out on dates occasionally, but always kept it very platonic. She would not know how to tell someone about her past; or that she could never have children. Besides, when the thought of intimacy with a boy crossed her mind, she felt physically ill. So she avoided any kind of close relationship.

Letters written back to her mother and father were never answered. She telephoned, but they never picked up, so she just left brief, cheerful voice messages letting them know how she was doing. She always spoke in a positive manner, and never stopped hoping that they would eventually respond. If they knew how well she was doing, if they could be proud of her...

Marion also tried to track down her sister, Rebecca, whom she had not seen since she ran away from home, when Marion was twelve. But every lead ended in a blind alley. Maybe, she thought, when she finished school and had more time and money, she could locate her sister.

Every night Marion prayed. She thanked God for her good fortune in being able to attend a wonderful university. She asked Him to bless her older brother, who had been so terribly misguided by her father; and the one next to him, and the younger ones, whom she hoped God would lead away from the temptations of following in their father's footsteps. She prayed that her sister was healthy and living a good life, wherever she was; and that they would some day be reunited. She prayed for her parents — that God would reach into their hearts and turn them from darkness to light. She prayed that He would change their way of thinking, and they would become kind, generous, and loving people. She prayed that they would not hurt anyone ever again, and that they would find happiness and prosperity in this lifetime. She prayed that they would be welcomed into Heaven when their time came. She prayed for God to forgive them — and she reminded Him that she had already done so.

So when Penny spit at Marion in her office and refused to resume their previous — positive, she thought — relationship, it was not so much a blow to Marion's self-esteem as it was a feeling that a soul had been lost. At least, for the time being. After Penny was released from prison, Marion hoped that another therapist or friend would eventually help to guide her into a healthier mindset and lifestyle.

Thirty-five women inmates were assigned to Marion's caseload. Too many, as it did not give her enough time to spend with each one every week, and still do all the paperwork, documentation, and attendance at required staff meetings. She tried to see each woman at least every two weeks, but she was rarely able to spend as much time as she felt they needed to make significant progress. Some refused to meet with her — angry, walled-off, and hostile, that was the only way they could exercise any control over their incarceration — *not* talking when someone wanted them to.

Marion had undergone a course of psychotherapy herself while in college. A psychologist was available in the Student Health Center for a very nominal fee, and Marion could afford it easily by skipping a meal here and there. As kind and generous as the Dean and his wife were to her — truly surrogate parents in every sense — Marion still occasionally found herself, alone in her dorm room, sobbing uncontrollably. She did not want to burden the Dean and his wife with any more of her problems, so she signed up for an appointment with the psychologist.

Dr. Henry Joseph helped Marion to see her parents with more clarity — what terribly disturbed individuals they were. He helped her understand the likelihood that their own upbringing was responsible for imbuing their personalities with angry sadism (her father) and fearful, ineffectual hopelessness (her mother).

Marion knew he was right, even though her parents spoke about her grandparents with an attitude approaching reverence. She recalled, around the age of five, meeting her paternal grandparents, after a two-day car ride. She had watched her father — the sheriff, both feared and revered by his townspeople — shrink into a quiet, anxious little mouse in the presence of his own parents. Marion was too young to really understand what was happening, but she recalled wondering why her father was acting like a little boy.

Eventually, Dr. Joseph helped Marion to see her recurring depression as a shroud that cloaked the memories of extreme pain and helpless childhood rage, and concealed them from her conscious mind. What she did not realize, however, was that her path to social work at a women's prison was an unconscious attempt to repeat, and work through, her own childhood trauma. The prison setting was filled with men in law enforcement uniforms — some of whom were every bit as intimidating as her sheriff-father. And the women inmates shared many of the same helpless and ineffectual characteristics as her mother — a virtual prisoner of her husband, shackled by the traditions and moral attitudes of her isolated rural community.

Marion was feeling particularly good one beautiful early fall afternoon. The air was crisp and cool enough to take out her favorite powder-blue sweater, and the blue-green-and-purple hat she made when the Dean's wife taught her how to crochet. A light wind fluttered through cherry red, neon orange and brilliant yellow leaves; brown ones crunched underfoot. It was Marion's fortieth birthday, and she had just received the best gift she could have ever hoped for — a voicemail message from her sister!

Rebecca's voice was older and more mature than she remembered, of course — and yet there was such a recognizable quality that came through the wires and the years that Marion was certain she would have known who it was even without her introducing herself. On the message, Rebecca said that she received a forwarded email message from someone who knew someone else, who knew someone else that Marion had been in touch with some months earlier, and it finally made its way to her!

Her sister's voice was rapid and animated, gushing with information that had been stored up for years, released in sentences that seemed to overlap each other. She "didn't want to go into too much detail" about why she had left home at sixteen — and admitted that she felt "terribly guilty for abandoning" Marion — but avoided any mention of their father's abuse.

Rebecca had left her telephone number on the message, and Marion was so excited about calling her when she got home that she could hardly keep her mind focused on her work for the rest of the day. The telephone call even edged out her excitement of the previous day, when she had picked up the brand new hybrid car she had bought herself as a fortieth birthday present. She tried to re-focus her thoughts, but the sound of that voicemail message stayed in her head like an old song, and she kept looking at her watch, hoping the hands would move faster toward the end of the work day.

Marion was interviewing a new inmate — a woman with a long history of mental illness, who lived in the streets during the brief interludes when she was not incarcerated or hospitalized. She ate handouts from restaurant managers who wanted desperately to get her to leave the premises; otherwise she ate whatever food scraps she could find in dumpsters. Nothing amazed or delighted her more than finding a fully wrapped, hardly eaten sandwich. She thought whoever threw it away was surely crazier than she was!

The woman had been incarcerated this time after jumping on a police officer who told her to "move along" from a trash dumpster she was rooting through. But a restaurant worker had just thrown out a trash bag minutes before, and she knew that presented her best chance of finding fresh leftovers. When she wouldn't leave, the policeman poked her with a night stick, which only served to enrage her, and she turned on him. He underestimated her strength and energy, and she got a few solid punches in, leaving him with an embarrassing black eye. Since she was already on parole for a multitude of petty and annoying infractions such as trespassing, begging, and creating a public disturbance, she was sent back to prison.

Now Marion was conducting the initial psychosocial evaluation, trying to stay focused and stop daydreaming about meeting her sister. But it was obvious even to the mentally ill inmate that Marion was distracted, when she asked her for the third time whether the woman had ever held any regular jobs. Another voice rang out in her head, drowning out Marion, saying, "*She's one of them! She's one of them! She's trying to drive you insane!*"

Years of experience had helped Marion to "tune in" to the mood of the inmates she interviewed, the majority of which had some degree of mental problems. But on this day her intuitive "antennae" were blocked by the repetition of her sister's voicemail running through her head, and the exciting prospect of seeing her again. So when the woman lunged across the table and grabbed Marion by the throat, she was caught completely off guard.

A correctional officer always stood just outside the door of her office whenever an inmate was in there with Marion; but after the first twenty minutes on this particular day, the officer had stepped outside to have a cigarette. He could still see through the doorway to the interview room from where he stood. But when a female officer came by and asked him for a light, his eyes moved to the shiny "Department of Corrections" badge pinned teasingly on the upper curve of one very ample and curvaceous breast. As she leaned over, her glossy red lips pursed on one end of a cigarette while the officer held a match to the other end, he tried not to tremble while gazing at the cleavage exposed by her cant.

It was over in a few seconds. That was all it took for the deranged woman to knock Marion over, slamming her head on the concrete floor. In an instant, the woman was on top of her, pressing on her throat with all of her strength, crushing her windpipe. She really didn't have to do that though — Marion's skull was already fatally fractured. She was declared dead on arrival at the hospital.

Chapter 4: Dr. Harrison

Dr. Harrison polished the brass nameplate as he walked back through his office door:

DOUGLAS M. HARRISON, M. D.
Obstetrics and Gynecology

He did not like any smudges on it. He sat down at his ornate mahogany desk, straightened the photograph of himself on his yacht, and polished that, too. He picked up the telephone and dialed the number for the hospital dictation service. When the automated prompts allowed, he dictated the hospital discharge summary for the eighteen-year-old girl who had been admitted for severe pelvic inflammation following a botched backwoods abortion. Sheriff Wilson's daughter. When he finished dictating, he pressed the "pound" key to "save" the dictated summary. Then he dialed the sheriff's office, and waited until Marion's father came on the line.

"Your daughter is fine, Vern," he said, straightening up the pens on his desk and brushing some lint off his immaculate white coat. "Yes, I've discharged her now. You can come and pick her up. She'll be just fine!"

Dr. Harrison listened to Marion's father for a minute, and then added, "Don't worry about that! I gave her a good talking-to! I instilled some moral values into that little brain of hers, and I don't think you'll have to worry about her getting into trouble any more." Then he laughed at something Marion's father said, and added, "No, I don't recommend that you go out and shoot any boys, Vern ... You might not get the right one!"

They both laughed heartily.

Douglas Harrison had been at the top of his class in college, and was accepted to all the medical schools he applied to. He wanted to attend Harvard, but they did not offer enough in the way of scholarship to pay for full tuition and living expenses. He did not want to settle for the full scholarship he was offered at less-prestigious institutions, either; so he decided to take a military scholarship. That would pay for all tuition, books, fees, room and board, and give him a generous stipend for additional living expenses. But that obligated him to a commitment of a year of military duty for every year of schooling — four years, once he graduated, and more if he continued his deferment for medical residency training. Nevertheless, he heard that he could easily get out of his military commitment once he graduated from medical school. So it was off to Harvard he went.

Douglas sailed through his first two years of Basic Sciences, and his third and fourth years of rotations through Surgery (really fun), Internal Medicine (boring), Pediatrics (parents are a pain in the ass), Obstetrics-Gynecology (total control), Psychiatry (total crap), and other specialties. He was most profoundly struck by one incident at medical school. It was in a neuroscience class — a large class of over 500 medical, nursing, and physician-assistant students, held in an auditorium. The professor addressed the class from the stage, introducing a short, slightly overweight, middle-aged woman, on whom he would demonstrate the signs of neurological damage that she had suffered. She was a patient of the professor's, and he had asked her to volunteer for the demonstration, for the significant educational value it would provide. Feeling both a sense of obligation to serve the needs of future doctors, as well as wanting to please her doctor, she agreed.

After introducing her to the class, the professor asked the woman to disrobe. She removed her robe and stood in front of the class in her pink lace nightgown. Her chin was held high as she looked above the students' heads, whose education she was helping to grow and shape. She followed all of the professor's instructions as precisely as anyone could — walking and bending and turning around, leaning this way and that, picking up this leg, extending that arm, touching her nose with her fingertips, and prancing around on her toes.

Douglas was elated. *What Power these Doctors doth have!* To get an ordinary housewife, who probably undressed in the closet at home, to take off her clothes in front of an auditorium full of complete strangers — my God, what more could any man desire? Besides the money to be made, that is.

The decision was made. Obstetrics & Gynecology was the perfect specialty for him. Not only do you tell women to take their clothes off, but you immediately get them in the most compromising of positions. He wanted to have that monumental power and control over every female. And get paid for it! What a racket. He could hardly wait. Douglas applied for a post-graduate residency in Ob-Gyn.

Mrs. Harrison was a small, slightly overweight woman who absolutely doted on her son. He was her only child, having lost three other pregnancies before this perfect, healthy birth. His father was a tall, muscular man, who ran a construction company, was gone most days from dawn until long after night fell. He was brilliant but completely ruthless in his business dealings. He pursued a network of contacts not only in the business world, but in the law enforcement community and politics. He obtained contracts and skirted regulations with impunity, and taught his son the ways of getting what you want in life. He made a fortune, due in no small part to his connections, political contributions, and effective intimidation when others were not willing to write or repeal ordinances for him. He was awarded massive construction projects, and with clever and subtle corner-cutting — always cautious and restrained — he was successful in his effort to avoid being caught.

Growing up in a gated mansion next door to the city mayor's home, Douglas had everything a youngster could possibly want. He had his own suite of rooms and entertainment center. When his friends came over, they never needed to be told to quiet down or behave — they were too awed by the opulence of the place, and especially by their friend's lavish possessions. His parents always managed to surprise him with something yet more spectacular on his birthday or at Christmas.

At sixteen, even before he passed his driving test, Douglas was presented with a Corvette convertible. At eighteen, he was handed the Neiman Marcus Holiday Catalog and told to choose anything his heart desired. He chose the "Chartered Trip to Space" — *not* a video game — *real* outer space. Six passengers would be sent sixty-three miles above the Earth via Virgin Galactic's SpaceShipTwo, for a little less than two million dollars. His parents refused — the first time any of them could recall their refusing him anything — and blamed not the price but the inherent danger. (But Doug was sure it was really the price.) Instead, he chose "Bonded Activity #55," a one-of-a-kind sculpture, meticulously crafted out of thousands of No. 2 pencils precision-sharpened to exactly the right sizes, which reached a full seven feet into the air. Price: forty thousand dollars. (The catalog also offered a smaller-scale twenty-inch-tall pencil sculpture for six thousand dollars. Doug chose the seven-foot sculpture.)

Although he reveled in his mother's total attention, Doug's personality was much more like his father's. He had no qualms about demanding that his mother do everything he wanted, even getting annoyed with her when she did not anticipate his needs. He once threw his shoes at her because they were not polished. She ducked, and only got slightly bruised on her arm; but she apologized and picked up the shoes, hurriedly stepping out of the room to get the shoe polish.

Not surprisingly, Douglas was less than thoughtful with the girls he dated. He was, at first, a perfect, debonair, generous gentleman. He would bring flowers and bow with a dramatic flourish to his date when he came to her door; listen to her conversation at dinner with his chin resting on his hands, not taking his eyes off of her; turning her questions back to her, so that she would keep talking, giving the impression that he was only interested in her, not himself. Then once he got the girl into bed, he never called her again. But he wrote her name in his journal, numbered so that he could keep count of how many girls he had seduced, and how many dates it took before he had succeeded. He put a "smiley face" next to the ones who had been virgins.

Once, when Doug accidentally left his journal out, his father found it and easily guessed its significance. When his father confronted him, he admitted that it was a list of girls he had seduced. His father then slapped him on the back, took him down to the kitchen and opened a couple of bottles of beer to "congratulate" his son and celebrate his conquests with him. He admonished his son for not sharing the list with him sooner.

Douglas could do no wrong in the eyes of either of his parents.

The only serious rift he ever had with his father was his decision to go into medicine. Mr. Harrison wanted his son to take over his construction business. He would not foot the bill for Harvard, even though he easily could have — and with his connections, could even have finagled a scholarship for his son. But he hoped to force his son to re-think his desire to go into medicine. When Doug took a military scholarship, his father was disappointed, but resigned to the fact that his son would be a doctor. Mrs. Harrison, needless to say, was thrilled with her son's decision.

Neither recognized the devious scheme their son would pursue to take advantage of women on an enormous scale.

After graduating from medical school and completing his residency training in obstetrics and gynecology — paid in full by the military — he decided to get out of his now eight-year commitment. He was sure he could get out of it, since he was brought up to believe he could get anything he wanted, and owed nothing to anybody or any commitment. He had been invited to join a wealthy, high-powered medical group that promised him a huge income and minimal obligation to work hours. He would have "coverage" for any time he wanted to take off; and he would have access to the group's beach houses — one on each coast — and condos in the most glamorous districts of the most glamorous cities in the world.

When Douglas spoke with his father about getting out of the military, his father expressed the concern that leaving the military with a less-than-honorable discharge would put a black mark on his record for life. Besides, he still harbored, deep down, some resentment that his son chose medicine over his father's construction business, and took a military scholarship to pay his way through — essentially thumbing his nose at his father.

Getting nothing but a lecture from his father, Doug went to his mother and literally cried in her lap: "Daddy wouldn't help me."

Normally timid and subservient, Mrs. Harrison now went to her husband, hands on hips, and demanded that he help Douglas get out of his military obligation. She had never spoken to him like that in thirty-two years of marriage. He was so taken aback by her uncharacteristic assertiveness that he agreed to do what he could to help out their son.

Mr. Harrison made a call to their state senator — to whose campaign he had contributed generously over the years, and by whose influence his company had been awarded numerous lucrative no-bid state construction contracts. The senator sent an e-mail to the commander of Douglas's assigned military post. Shortly thereafter a letter arrived indicating that Dr. Douglas M. Harrison was honorably discharged from the military.

The new doctor soon discovered that getting women into compromising positions and taking advantage of them was like shooting fish in a barrel — so easy that it almost lost its fun-appeal. What was amazing was the fact that the patients often did not even realize what he was doing to them. He marveled at how incredibly, laughingly stupid they were. (What Dr. Harrison did not understand was the horrifying shame and embarrassment that the women felt, who knew they had been unspeakably violated during the exam. They also knew that such a shocking charge against a prominent, well-known and highly respected physician would never be taken seriously. Rather, the women were fearful that they themselves would be judged as a "nut case").

So Dr. Harrison continued his medical rape, on selected women whom he judged to be especially timid and compliant, and his patients and colleagues continued to sing his praises. He also made a healthy sum of money on the side by performing abortions in his home office on girls so young that it would have raised too many questions if they were admitted to the hospital. He had no qualms about conducting these procedures in his home. If a twelve- or thirteen-year-old girl was old enough to get herself pregnant, she was old enough to have an abortion, no matter what the law said. And those nubile young things could be very seductive … very capable of causing older, otherwise sensible men to fall victim to their wiles — even their own fathers. Taking the risk of operating on youngsters as he was, shouldn't he be paid handsomely? After all, he was saving them the operating room and anesthesiology fees, wasn't he?

But putting them to sleep without an anesthesiologist in attendance would have been risky — too many problems could arise, both medical and legal. So instead, he would give them an injection of intravenous Valium, strap them into the stirrups, and do the rest without any additional anesthesia. Some of the girls fell right asleep, and were barely roused by the surgery; but a few awoke and started screaming. He would have to stuff a gag in their mouths to keep the screams from being heard. But the great advantage of using that medication was the almost complete amnesia when the girl regained full consciousness. The rare one who recalled the pain and horror was told she had an "anesthesia nightmare."

Afterward, Dr. Harrison would always lecture the girls about their loose morals. Sometimes he knew they had been impregnated by their father or other male relatives — all the more reason that they needed a lecture. After all, pre-teen and teenage girls could be very seductive toward their male relatives as well as toward unsuspecting strangers who may not even be aware of the girl's true age. Around puberty, girls often looked older, and the little nymphs could easily take advantage of unsuspecting men.

But the *pièce de résistance* was the tying of their tubes. He would teach them a good lesson — they wouldn't have the opportunity to get pregnant again. And, unlike Marion Wilson, whom he told, most of the girls would not learn for many years that they had been sterilized. He always got a good laugh out of that.

Dr. Harrison never married. He liked his lifestyle the way it was. Anyway, he didn't really like adult women very much. His real preference — he discovered after examining a five-year-old girl who had a cyst in her pubic area — was children. He liked their soft, smooth, youthful bodies; and their abject fear of him gave him a sense of power that ignited his libido. He found no preference for little girls or boys — he just liked them very young.

So the good doctor started volunteering to lead a youth group at church. He took the children to ice cream parlors, movies, game arcades, and of course, his own home, where he had Playstations, X-boxes, widescreen TV, and every video game imaginable in his basement rec room. He would do the usual thing that pedophiles do — charm the child, then win the parents' trust, and then invite the child for an overnight or weekend outing.

One visit went very badly. The feisty little nine-year-old girl made a sudden dash for the stairs as soon as the doctor began talking about a "game" that required taking off clothes. He ran after her and caught her easily, of course, but even as he felt pressure to make ominous threats — that he would come after her and hurt her family if she told them anything — she still shouted, "No!" and squirmed away from his grasp. This was very disconcerting to him.

When she bolted for the stairs again, he did not try to stop her.

Dr. Harrison went to his garage and started his Lexus (it drew less attention than the Ferrari or the Porsche parked beside it). It was already dark outside, but he cruised down the street without turning his lights on. When he spotted the girl, still running as fast as she could, he looked around to see whether anyone was around. He was in luck. The street was completely empty, and in this wealthy neighborhood of huge quasi-mansions shielded from the street by long driveways and high hedges, it looked as though he had perfect cover. He stepped on the gas and the car swiftly responded, heading straight for the little girl. When she heard the engine, and turned to look at him, she did not realize the danger at first. As it dawned on her, she ran off the sidewalk and onto the lawn of the property she was passing — but there was a thick hedge there, and she could not find a way through it fast enough to get out of the way. The Lexus plowed into her, mashing her into the hedge; then backed up and rammed into her again.

Returning home, the doctor pulled into the garage, immediately got out and inspected the Lexus for any damage. There was blood and some material from the little girl's dress on the bumper and stuck in the grille. He took a bucket of water and soapsuds, washed the car front, and threw the remnants of her dress into the bucket. He decided not to drive the Lexus outside for awhile.

Reports of the little girl's hit-and-run death were all over the news the next day. Dr. Harrison called the parents and said that he felt horrible that he did not wait to see that she got into her house safely after he dropped her off at home last night. He said he was in a hurry, and when she waved goodbye to him on the walkway up to her front door, he assumed she would get inside safely. He hugged the little girl's mother, and cried with her, his shoulders heaving with theatrical sobbing. The little girl's father actually came over and put his arm around Dr. Harrison and tried to comfort *him*, his performance was so believable. He attended the girl's funeral, and insisted on paying for all the expenses. Dr. Harrison was lauded and interviewed on television as a hero of unequalled compassion and generosity.

Father Bryan was the pastor of the church that sponsored the youth group to which the little girl had belonged. The following Sunday, Father Bryan dedicated his sermon to Dr. Harrison for his unswerving sacrifices and selfless volunteer work at the church, and particularly with the youth group. The congregation was brought to tears, and Dr. Harrison was sniffling most loudly of all. After the service, he stood next to Father Bryan and shook hands with all the congregants as they were leaving, hugging him and giving him words of support and affection. They treated him just as though it were *his* daughter who had been killed by a hit-and-run driver.

After that ordeal, Dr. Harrison took a new tack. First he invited the children to play the video games. or whatever they wanted, in the basement. Then he would offer them a drink — sweet fruit punch laced with gin or vodka — and a sour ball candy at the bottom of the glass, that also helped to sweeten the drink. He would tell them that they would have a race to see who could finish their drink and get to the candy first, and they would get a prize.

But it was Dr. Harrison who got the prize. He would often invite two or more children to spend the night at the same time — and after racing to finish their spiked drinks, they quickly passed out. Then he would have his way with all of them.

No one may ever have learned about the true nature of Dr. Douglas Harrison and his child molestation activities. But one Monday morning, Father Bryan got a call from a frantic woman who was anxiously talking and crying in a heavily accented voice that he could not understand at first. Finally, he managed to calm her down enough to learn that she was Dr. Harrison's housekeeper. Father Bryan could not get any more information from the distraught woman, but drove over to the doctor's home.

The woman answered the door, shaking, with fresh tears streaking down her face, grabbed Father Bryan's arm and started to pull him down the basement steps. There, he was greeted by an unspeakably horrifying sight. Dr. Harrison was lying across the day bed, face down. He had suffered a fatal heart attack. He was completely naked. Underneath him were the thin little arms of a small girl, also naked. She had been unable to get out from under Dr. Harrison after he lost consciousness. She had suffocated under his weight. On the floor a few feet away, a young boy was sitting up, also naked, dazed and barely conscious. He was later determined to have a blood alcohol level equivalent to twice the legal limit for an adult. Another little girl, four years old, was cowering in the corner, wearing only a little ruffled top. She was mute, suffering from psychological shock.

Chapter 5: Father Bryan

Father Bryan had seen a great deal of tragedies, man-made as well as those which he considered Divine interventions — but he had never seen anything more tragic than the sight in Dr. Douglas Harrison's basement that day. He would never forget it. A tragedy of those proportions — such egregious child molestation — was compounded by the high esteem in which the community had held the perpetrator. But the worst feeling, that terrible heavy concrete-block feeling in his chest, was for his own part in the tragedy. He could not forgive himself for not seeing it earlier. He scanned his memory over the younger children's faces in his recollection of all those who had spent time with Dr. Harrison — the nervousness they exhibited, the downcast eyes, the reluctance to talk about their visits with him. How could he possibly have missed such stark, obvious clues??

But even that could not match the heinousness of the hit-and-run murder of the nine-year-old girl some years before. After Dr. Harrison was found dead in his basement, the police searched the whole house. They found the shredded remains of the dead child's dress, covered with blood, in a bucket in the garage. They correctly surmised that the little girl must have said she was going to tell her parents about Dr. Harrison's advances. Then she either got away, or he let her run away, followed her in his car and ran her down. Father Bryan cringed at the recollection of having fallen for the man's crocodile tears, and praising his "selflessness" at Sunday services — practically canonizing the depraved animal!

Father Bryan fell to his knees and prayed for forgiveness, for the sin of "omission" — for *not* seeing what was before his very eyes. He took off his collar. He could not continue leading a congregation when he had failed them so terribly — failed to protect the very children whose lives he was ordained to mold, to teach, to save. He mentally flayed himself for having failed to protect the most vulnerable, those most in need of protection.

The rectory office was a simple place, furnished sparsely, befitting one who eschewed ostentation. Yet it was decorated with warmth, beauty and color, and the personal touch of and by his congregants. There were several chairs and a couch, luxuriously plush, because he wanted his visitors to be comfortable. His own chair, in contrast, was an old style wooden swivel chair. His desk was a sturdy oak mission-style piece that he had bought at an Amish farm that he visited early in his clerical career, and towed it back himself in a U-haul trailer. (He observed the 45 mile-per-hour speed limit posted on the trailer, even though cars whizzing around him on the highway at speeds nearly double that spurred him to mentally cross himself almost continually. He could not physically cross himself because that would have entailed taking one white-knuckled hand off the wheel, which, he feared, might counteract the protection conferred by the *signum crucis*.)

When he first came to the office, it was already furnished with a huge mahogany desk, used by the former priest who left under a dark cloud of sorts — something amiss with the parish finances. But the desk, ornately carved in Louis XIV style, with decorative brass inlays and pull tassels on the drawers, and a plush leather swivel-recliner, were not consistent with Father Bryan's taste. He donated them to the annual church raffle, which brought in a good sum for the educational fund. Father Bryan then found the mission style desk when he visited a farm during a trip to Ohio, purchased it with his own money, and hauled it back.

The walls of the office were decorated with photographs of congregants, celebrating weddings and other happy occasions, and postcards he received from faraway places. But most cherished of all were the pictures, paintings, and letters written by the children, which Father Bryan had framed and hung on every wall. Bookshelves were filled with Bibles in different languages, historical and religious tomes; collections of poetry, newsletters, and homilies; a set of Andrew Greeley novels; and clay figures that the children had presented to him.

It was difficult not to look around at all of these precious artifacts now as the priest sat at his desk and composed a letter of resignation. In it, he confessed to all the sins he had ever committed, as far back as he could remember. He cheated on a history exam in high school. He sneaked cigarettes in private — which was another sin of omission — he should not hide his sins, but try to overcome them in the open. He lusted after a pretty girl while he was at the seminary; and almost had intercourse with her! Well, he had long ago confessed that — but he had never confessed his ongoing lustful memories of her that he could never quite put out of his mind with any finality.

Father Bryan enumerated all of these sins in his letter of resignation, and a few others that came to him. Then he sealed it, addressed it to the bishop who was head of the diocese, put on his overcoat and walked down to the post office. He stood in front of the mail drop for a full minute, looking at the letter and wanting so badly to tear it up. A woman walked up behind him, and he quickly dropped the letter into the mailbox.

Bryan Andrew Madigan always thought he would grow up and go into the priesthood. All of his friends thought he would, too. His parents did not, though, since little Bryan was always getting into trouble. They were called by the school principal regularly, with reports of their youngest (eighth) son's antics — putting a frog in the teacher's desk drawer, pitching pennies behind the school building at recess, or telling dirty jokes to the other boys and girls. Somehow, though, he managed to make very good grades, and by the time he was in high school, he knew he was firmly headed for the priesthood. So did his teachers.

Once his formal studies were completed, and he was assigned to a flock of his own, Father Bryan was an exemplary clergyman. He never failed to take the time that any member of his church required when they were sick or in trouble. He had used his own money to bail out an occasional congregant who was in jail for public intoxication, or getting into a fistfight. He was accepting of the many human foibles and peccadilloes of his congregants, and refused to make an issue of them — such as the young man who was seen exiting a known "gay" bar — even though others of the flock were pointing fingers and demanding that he take action to stop or discipline them. He always had a kind word. His sermons always reflected his humility and his encouragement for others to be humble and appreciative of the gifts they were given, and always to share. He encouraged them to be generous, not just to the church, but to everyone around them who needed a helping hand or a dollar or a sandwich. He did not spend Christmas with his family, but instead, he dropped off his gifts and candies at his family's home the night before; and on Christmas day he went to the local nursing homes and hospitals, spending the entire day there, bringing small gifts for everyone, which he had purchased with his own money.

But probably Father Bryan's most selfless act was that of going to the hospital wards and spending time with the end-stage AIDS patients. Many of them were difficult to look at, covered with lesions; or becoming demented, slow in their thinking and responses. Many of their families and friends had long ago stopped coming to visit, and their loneliness was held at bay only by the hospital staff and the other patients in the ward. The smiling priest would sit next to their beds, hold their hands or stroke their foreheads — giving the love and joy of the human touch for which there was no substitute. Often, a patient would break into tears as soon as he felt Father Bryan's hand on his.

He passed judgment on no one. When a stranger came to speak with him, he would always make time to hear his story. Once, an elderly parishioner came to see him with a dilemma. Thomas Quadling was Catholic, but Rachel, his wife of fifty-seven years, was Jewish. She would never convert, but Tom loved her so much that he insisted on getting married even though he was shunned thereafter by his family for many years. He still attended church from time to time, and Rachel would accompany him because she knew how much it meant to him. She could not leave her religion and convert, though, as she felt she had already hurt her own family enough by marrying out of her religion. Besides, she knew she would always be Jewish in her heart, and any effort to give the appearance of being otherwise would be hypocritical. *Adonai* would know.

The Quadlings had no children. Now in their eighties, Rachel was very sick, and the doctors wanted to put her in hospice care. They offered virtually no hope for her survival beyond a few days or weeks. Tom knew that, as a Jew, Rachel was not eligible for the Catholic "last rites" and he was torn between his church's teachings and his fear that he and his wife would go to "different places" after death, and they would be separated for all eternity. His heart told him differently, that his wife was a wonderful person — loving, generous, kind, patient, tolerant of her husband's and everyone else's shortcomings — and that Jesus could not possibly allow her anywhere but by His side. And yet ... and yet ... the church had taught him otherwise for more than eight decades. He was now beside himself with grief and fear of what might be.

Tom had sought out the advice of the priest in the church that he attended with Rachel from time to time, but he was only admonished that his wife "had better convert while there was still time." He had never attended Father Bryan's church, which was in a neighboring town, but he heard that the priest there was an especially kind and helpful man. He went to see him, and told him of his plight.

"Father, can you help me? I don't know what to do ... I don't want to lose my Rachel for all eternity ... " His shoulders slumped down and he made a supreme effort to remain composed, but he could not. Tears flowed down his face. He pulled a balled-up handkerchief out of his pocket, already soaked with tears, and covered his face with it. His shoulders shook with the sobbing of a man bereft of hope, in the most extreme grief.

Father Bryan stood up from his chair and walked around the desk to where Tom was sitting. He placed his hand gently on the old man's shoulder, and waited until he had spent his grief and regained his composure. When his tears were finally spent, he sat back in his chair and looked up at the priest.

"Do you read the Bible much, Tom?"

"Well ... over the years, yes," he answered, wary of where this was leading. He hoped it would not be another lecture about pressing Rachel to convert to Catholicism. "But probably not enough ... At least not recently ... " He sniffled and pulled the hankie back out of his pocket and blew his nose, emitting a long, loud honk. Then he looked back up at Father Bryan.

"You might be more comfortable to read *Matthew* once more," he said, still resting one hand on Tom's shoulder, and reaching over to the Kleenex box on his desk, bringing it as an offering. The older man looked at the soggy handkerchief in his hand, balled it up again and stuffed it back in his pocket, and took a Kleenex from the offered box.

"Take two. They're cheap," said Father Bryan, and Tom could not help but smile. He complied, and then noisily blew his nose one more time, and looked up at the priest again.

"Matthew?"

"Yes. Chapter 7, verse 17: 'Every good tree bringeth forth good fruit,' we are told." He looked at Tom, who appeared to be anxiously hanging on to every word. " And, 'Wherefore by their fruits ye shall know them.' Verse 20." He looked around for another nearby chair, pulled the chair over and sat down next to his parishioner.

"You see?" he went on, since the older man was too astonished to say anything. "The Bible has been interpreted and the laws changed from time to time over the centuries. Abortion is a good example." He got up from his chair and started to pace beside his desk, one hand gesturing as he spoke, the other behind his back.

"In the 4th century, St. Augustine sanctioned abortion of the male fetus up to 40 days gestation, and for some reason, the female fetus up to 80 days." Father Bryan looked at Tom out of the corner of his eye and raised an eyebrow. "Then in the late 16th century, Pope Sixtus forbade all abortions — an edict that was overturned only three years later by Pope Gregory XIV. It was nearly three hundred years later when Pope Pius IX again forbade all abortions — in exchange for Napoleon's acknowledging Papal Infallibility. You see, Napolean had wanted to halt the severe decline in France's population over the previous fifty or sixty years — and he knew that prohibiting abortions would help reverse the trend — so they both got a good deal."

Father Bryan walked back around his desk and sat down next to Tom again. "Unlike our mortal leaders, though, the Gospel is very clear. What Matthew said cut across all religions, and there is no argument to his meaning: *Every good tree bringeth forth good fruit* …" he repeated, " … *and by their fruits ye shall know them.*"

He looked over at Tom, directly in the eyes. "By your works He shall know you … *And by Rachel's works He shall know her.* Do you see?"

The priest reached over and patted the older man on the shoulder again. He was now dry-eyed, and enraptured by Father Bryan's speech. For a moment, he was unable to say anything. Then he grabbed the priest's hand with both of his hands and bent down and kissed it. He held the hand against his face, and began crying again.

Tom went home and sat by Rachel's side, and comforted her until she died, peacefully, in her sleep. And he knew now, without any further doubt, that she would be waiting for him when his time came to join her.

Father Bryan put on his overcoat, preparing to go outside, when the telephone rang. The voice at the other end was gruff and boisterous.

"What do you mean, you resign.??? What is this all about.??" The bishop who was head of the diocese had received the letter of confession and resignation.

Bryan shook off his coat as he switched hands to keep the telephone next to his ear. He sat down at his desk, and when the voice on the other end stopped shouting, he spoke, quietly, and explained. "If I can't protect my flock — not even the children of my flock — then I do not deserve to lead them anymore."

About an hour later, after Bryan had returned from the grocery market, he found a group of ladies from the church, patiently waiting in their car, alighting when he arrived, and surrounding him at his front door. Mrs. Carrie Barley spoke first.

"Father Bryan! We cannot allow you to resign. It is totally unacceptable. Totally." Mrs. Barley looked at the women on each side of her and nodded at them, a signal to speak up in agreement. They all did so, repeating, "Totally unacceptable, Father."

Mrs. Barley was short in stature, moderately overweight, with a large bosom, the cleavage hidden by a white lace handkerchief, and all rather tightly encased in a corset under her purple dress. She wore a matching purple hat with a large brim, a long string of pearls framing a gold cross on a chain around her neck. She had another gold cross pinned to her dress at the shoulder. Below the cross was a ring, and a pair of reading glasses hung from the ring. A wide patent leather belt was buckled around her waist, or the portion of her waist that was available just below her ample bosom. The other women in the group were similarly dressed in full regalia, hats with wide brims, ribbons or flowers, and high heels. Their heads bobbed up and down as they expressed agreement with Mrs. Barley in her admonishment of the priest.

"Ladies, you don't understand," Bryan protested. "There are issues here that I cannot explain ... I can no longer be of service to this flock ..."

"Poppycock!" interrupted Mrs. Barley. "The church needs you! We need you! You cannot abandon us like this ..."

"I'm sorry, but this is something that I must do for God and ... "

"Bullcorn!" she interrupted again, and there was an audible whoosh as the other ladies in the group all collectively drew in their breath in astonishment at one of their own speaking to the priest in such a manner — or anyone, for that matter!

Father Bryan was taken aback, too. He had not yet formulated a response to Mrs. Barley's comment before she started to speak again. But now her voice was softer:

"We need you, Father! You should not abandon your loving flock ... Not in penance for another's sins!"

At that, Bryan knew that the bishop had broken confidentiality and told these church ladies why he was resigning! *How could he do that?* His private confession of gross ignorance, failure to recognize the signs of evil that were being perpetrated on the church youngsters, and even worse, holding Dr. Harrison up to the community as a symbol of selflessness and charity?? How could the bishop do such a thing??

Father Bryan sighed, and he looked at all the women who surrounded him, pleading with him to stay. Perhaps — perhaps they were right. Perhaps he was hasty in his decision to abandon his flock for his sins, and indirectly, for the sins of another. He would be hurting those who depended upon him, who had grown close to him over the years, who looked up to him. There was no clear reason to do that. Perhaps he was only compounding the problem.

He made his decision to rescind his previous decision; and gave his word to the ladies that he would remain on as their pastor. Mrs. Barley and two of the others closest to him grabbed him in a hug that nearly cost him his breath. He turned down their offer to come over for tea and fresh-baked cakes just then, but promised to see them on Sunday. Then he went back into the rectory and made a phone call to the bishop. His news was greeted with a great joyous bellowing howl, the likes of which would have shocked and possibly frightened the parishioners.

Picking up a pad and pencil, Father Bryan went through his entire living quarters, making a note of all items of entertainment: The console television set in the living room, and the smaller portable set in his bedroom; several radios (but not the clock radio by his bed because he got poor reception there and never listened to it anyway, but still needed the clock); Bose stereo and speakers, and all the CDs of his favorite lectures and seminars; all of his old record albums (even the ones he inherited from his parents — Frank Sinatra, Tommy Dorsey, Elvis Presley, *et cetera*); and finally — perhaps most painfully — all of the books he had read and collected over the years. He called for the church maintenance man to help transfer these items into the basement, where they would be itemized and tagged (probably by Mrs. Barley and her gang) for sale at the next church bazaar.

The maintenance man listened to the priest's instructions, and looked at all the items he had tagged for the move. He looked at Father Bryan quizzically, afraid to ask, but the priest second-guessed him.

"No, I'm not leaving, Hernando. I'm moving all this stuff because … well, because I'm staying." Hernando smiled and nodded his head — still mystified, but content with the explanation.

That was his penance. Father Bryan would eschew all forms of personal entertainment forever more. He would read his Bible, and his Bible alone. He needed nothing else. And that is what he did, from that day on, until his ninety-second birthday. That night he had a dream. He was standing in a field of emerald green grass. Wildflowers of every color bounded a path of golden cobblestones, glistening in the sunshine. It was a perfect day, the sky brightly blue and wisps of cottony white clouds drifting off in the distance. Suddenly a beautiful woman, an angel, shining and translucent, fluttered slowly down in front of him. She kissed him lightly on the cheek and took his hand. He felt exhilarated. She turned and took a step, and he started to follow, but soon realized he was stepping into the air, as they lifted together towards the clouds. He never awoke.

Chapter 6: Carrie Barley

Mrs. Carrie Barley was a staple of the church. She was there almost every day, cooking, supervising arrangements of flowers, organizing, categorizing, and preparing for the disbursement of donated items, making phone calls, arranging fundraisers, rehearsing with the choir, and doing just about everything a volunteer could do for a church. She had received numerous awards for her selfless volunteer work over the years, and these hung proudly framed on the walls in her living room, family room, dining room, and ascending the wall upside the stairwell. She also glowed with pride when speaking of her husband and children, who came to every service, too. Well, her children did, but her husband attended major services. Mainly Christmas and Easter mass.

Carrie was thrilled that she and the other ladies of the church were able to convince Father Bryan not to resign. What was he thinking??? That he was somehow, in any way, shape or form, responsible for the deeds of that evil Dr. Harrison?? Ridiculous! She was glad that she straightened him out. Now, if she could just straighten out her husband, Jules. He just wouldn't attend all the wonderful functions at the church, even though he claimed to be a strongly religious person. He knew the score. He was brought up in the church — even considered the priesthood himself at one time. But Carrie would keep encouraging him, and hopefully, eventually, one day she would bring him fully back into the fold.

Carrie Barley was born Mary Carolina Regina Cielo Maguire. She had two brothers, Francis Xavier Maguire and Thomas Aquinas Maguire; and seven sisters who were all named Mary (Mary Catherine, Mary Abigail, Mary Teresa, *et cetera)*. Mrs. Maguire came very close to giving up the ghost when Mary Carolina, her tenth and last child, was born; and since she survived that particularly difficult childbirth on the strength of her prayers to the Virgin Mary, she thought, she added "Regina Cielo" ("Queen of Heaven") to Carrie's name.

Throughout her childhood, Carrie was certain that she was going to be a nun when she grew up. But that resolution flew out the window when she got into high school and discovered boys. She rapidly earned the reputation as a good-time girl, and the boys passed her number around freely. She discovered how good alcohol felt, if not tasted, and was grateful to be the last of her ten siblings so her busy (and tired) parents were unable to pay a great deal of attention to her antics. Besides, for a long time Carrie was unaware of her mother's own attraction to the bottle, which kept her less aware of her children's escapades. Mrs.

Maguire died of cirrhosis of the liver at age forty-two; that allowed for even less supervision of the children's activities.

At sixteen, Carrie was sure that she was pregnant. She went to church every day after school and lit a candle and prayed for as long as she could without getting home too late and arousing suspicion. After doing this for two weeks, her period came. She was so thankful that she promised Jesus she would never have sex again, and would revive her childhood plan to become a nun. She almost kept that promise all the way through her senior year in high school; but did not keep it completely until after she was married.

Carrie met Jules Barley just before her graduation from high school. They met at a church picnic — not her church, but that of a girlfriend from school who had invited her to come along. Jules was a few years older, already in the seminary and well on his way to becoming an ordained priest. He was tall and slender — very handsome, with bright blue eyes, long lashes, and sandy hair that fell across his forehead. He had a long face, high cheekbones, and a deep cleft in his chin. Carrie had set her sights on him as soon as she saw him.

When they were introduced, Carrie dropped her eyes downward in a demure manner, and smoothed out her skirt with a slightly nervous, childlike quality that boys mistook for shyness and naïveté. She had beautiful golden curly hair that she wore in ringlets tied up in a ribbon and cascading down her neck; round pink cheeks; and a figure beginning to show the well-endowment she had previously been so eager to share.

When her girlfriend left them alone to socialize with others at the picnic, Carrie asked Jules to show her around the church grounds. He agreed. They walked around the grounds, and then along a path that Carrie asked about, which weaved around the perimeter of the church cemetery. When they were out of sight of the others, Carrie put her hand up to her forehead and said she felt a little hot.

"Let's get you some water, or some punch," said Jules, concerned. He started to take her arm and lead her back to the picnic, but Carrie took his hand in hers and pressed it against her chest.

"I think ... I think," she said, eyes half-drooping, "I'm ... I'm going to ... to ... faint," and her knees started to buckle. Jules caught her around the waist and eased her to the ground. Carrie straightened her leg out, knocking Jules' foot out from under him, and he tumbled down on top of her. She was still holding his hand against her chest, and lifted her face, brushing her lips against his.

Jules suddenly felt as though an electrical shock went through him. He became erect so fast and so intensely that it was almost painful. Without thinking, he mashed his lips down upon Carrie's mouth. She took his hand that she was holding against her chest and pushed it downward and then up under her skirt. He fumbled for a minute, still in shock, but managed to get her panties down, ripping them off one leg in the process. She tugged at his zipper, until he pulled it open, releasing his hot, turgid manhood. Carrie took hold of it, but had barely guided it in for a few seconds before Jules released with a loud groan.

Jules started crying, while scurrying to pull out and tuck himself back together saying, "Oh, God, I'm sorry! Carrie, I'm sorry! Oh, God ..." He had been a virgin, and assumed she was, too. Even though it felt better than anything he had ever experienced in his life, he also felt horribly guilty and confused.

Carrie patted his head and tried to soothe his conscience by saying, "That's all right, Jules. Men are human, and cannot always help themselves. I forgive you, and I'm sure Jesus does, too."

At the mention of his Lord's name, Jules started crying even louder. Carrie was still patting him, and trying to get her panties back on, until she realized they were ripped and unwearable. She pulled them off the other leg and threw them over the cemetery fence, where they landed on the headstone of a former parish priest.

Jules dropped out of the seminary and he and Carrie were married right after she graduated from high school. He went to work in the same furniture factory where his father had toiled all his life, but planned to resume his college studies as soon as he could save up enough money. Since he was married, and no longer eligible for the priesthood, he decided to go into education and be a teacher, of history or social studies. He did not feel righteous enough to pursue a degree in theology.

Unfortunately, all hope of returning to school was thwarted, as their efforts to avoid pregnancy by careful timing were wholly unsuccessful. Carrie had two babies by their second anniversary. She had been working as a nursing assistant, but dropped back to part-time after the first baby was born, and had to give it up entirely after the second baby came along. Jules took on a second job, which prohibited him from resuming his studies. Two more babies came along in the next three years, and a fifth child was born on their sixth wedding anniversary. That was when Carrie decided to become celibate. She expected Jules would agree with her decision.

Jules was miserable, but he respected his wife's wishes. He still felt so guilty about the sinful, premarital manner in which he ravaged her and took her virginity (he thought), and failed to control his venal impulses, that he welcomed the decision for the two of them to become celibate. Carrie became more and more involved in the church, and they both felt she was doing so much good work for the church, it was worth whatever sacrifice they were making in their personal lives.

That lasted two-and-a-half years. Then Jules told Carrie that he did not think he could keep on like this. He missed having sex so much, he could not keep his thoughts from it. (He had begun to buy the magazines partially wrapped in brown paper on the store shelves. He kept them in his locker at work, read them on his breaks, in the men's room, and threw them away before leaving the factory. He did not mention this to Carrie.) He promised to be ultra, ultra careful about their "timing" sex to avoid another pregnancy — even hinting that he would not be averse to engaging in artificial birth control.

Carrie refused, stating that she felt it would be a sin for them to rescind their vow of celibacy — and using any kind of artificial birth control was an even bigger sin. But she acquiesced when Jules asked her to at least talk to their priest about it. After all, Father Bryan had always seemed so reasonable and understanding. His sermons frequently focused on the sanctity of marriage, always emphasizing compassion and selflessness toward one's spouse — the importance of each putting the other's happiness before their own.

Fully expecting the priest to agree with her, Carrie went to see him and related the problem. She thought he would be delighted with her commitment to celibacy and to uphold the prohibition of artificial birth control. Moreover, she expected Father Bryan to reiterate the church doctrine, as she understood it, that advised about having sexual intercourse *only* for the purpose of procreation — which would effectively eliminate it for the Barleys.

Carrie listened to Father Bryan patiently, as he went on and on in a detailed, impassioned, and — pacing about his office as he spoke — peripatetic exposition of the history of the religious teachings on contraception.

"What does the Bible have to say about contraception?" he asked, and then answered, "Well, in *Genesis* 38:7-10, we find the story of Onan. Judah had two sons — well, three, but the point here revolves around the first two, Er and Onan."

Father Bryan stopped pacing and looked at Carrie, who nodded to indicate that she was, indeed, listening.

"Judah arranged for his eldest son, Er, to marry Tamar. But, the Bible tells us, 'Er was wicked in the sight of the LORD; and the LORD slew him.' Now, the Levirate law of Judaism at the time prescribed that if the oldest brother died, the next oldest single brother would marry his widow to preserve the family line — *and those children would be considered as children of the first husband.* So Onan, who did not want his own children to be counted as his brother's children, 'spilled his seed on the ground' to avoid inseminating Tamar."

Father Bryan looked over at Carrie again. "That is the basis for the proscription of 'withdrawal' as a sin, as well as — well, uh, — self-pleasure. Do you understand?" Carrie nodded again, but averted the priest's gaze. He went on.

"Now, those scholars who interpreted these stories *might have* interpreted them differently. For example, what if God viewed Onan's sin to be that of denying Tamar *her* right to have children — rather than the wasting of his semen? After all, it is safe to assume that Tamar wanted children, and Onan was denying his wife that opportunity for purely selfish, if understandable, reasons."

Now he stopped pacing and looked out the window, rather than at Carrie. He was wondering this himself. *Maybe "spilling semen" was not a sin?* Frankly he had never really pondered the question in depth before.

He looked over at Carrie then, and waited to see if she would say something. Surely she would have a question. She did.

"Why did God slay Er?"

"Uh ... What?" Father Bryan said, somewhat confused by the question for a moment.

"Why did God slay Er?" Carrie repeated. "He was married to Tamar first — why did God say he was wicked and slay him? What did *he* do?"

"Well, actually," Father Bryan began, but Carrie interrupted.

"Did Er 'spill his seed' also? Is that why the Lord slew him?"

"Well, actually," Father Bryan began to answer her again, but again was interrupted.

"He probably used birth control, too! Just like his brother would later do! That's why the Lord slew them both, isn't it? Birth control of *any* kind is a sin ... "

"No, Mrs. Barley," the priest responded in a more authoritarian manner than his congregant was familiar with. He wanted to get her attention, and be sure that his message was understood. "Actually, curiously, there is *no* mention of why the Lord slew Er. None at all. The Bible says nothing about it. Just that Er was 'wicked.' That's all."

He pulled up a chair next to Carrie and sat down, leaning forward slightly to keep a strong eye-contact connection. "The point is," he continued, and Carrie could not look away from him being so close, "that *we do not know* why he slew Er — and we *do not know for sure* why he slew Onan for spilling his seed. Was it because he 'wasted' his seed? Or because he denied his lawfully wedded wife an opportunity to conceive a child? The Bible does not exactly say..."

"Well," said Carrie, drawing her head back slightly away from Father Bryan, which doubled her chin as it flattened into her neck, "I'm sure Jesus had something to say about that!" and before the priest could respond, she added, "After all, I'm sure the Pope would not be calling birth control a mortal sin without good reason!"

"Uh, no, Mrs. Barley," he responded with a sigh. He had hoped to engage her in some philosophical discussion that she could share with her husband, and help to resolve their dilemma. Now it was becoming clearer that she had an agenda with an established goal and consulted the priest with the expectation that he would take her side. "There are no attributions of contraception to Jesus in the Bible."

Carrie raised her eyebrows and looked quizzically at her priest; then knitted her brows in a defiant affect, and said, "Well … There must be *something* about it! Something that condemns all birth control besides … uh, pulling out!"

Father Bryan restrained the impulse to sigh again. "There is mention in a couple of places in the Bible — once in *Galatians* and twice in *Revelations* — about the sins of 'sorcery' and 'witchcraft'; or 'performing magic' or 'mixing up of potions.' Oral contraceptives have been interpreted by some to be in that category. But, in fact, that could prohibit almost *all* medication from being permitted. And in fact, there are Christians who practice…"

Carrie raised up a forefinger, along with her voice, "But, Father, that's not …"

He now averted *her* gaze, and raised his own discourse a few decibels.

"Even before the New Testament was written down, The *Didache*, or *Teachings of the Twelve Apostles,* written around 80 A.D., was considered the church's first manual of morals, liturgical norms and doctrine. It exhorts against 'practicing magic' and 'using potions' and subsequent scholars linked — decided — that those were references to birth control. Yet, nowhere does it say anything about 'mixing of potions to prevent conception.' In fact, 'contraception' or 'preventing pregnancy' are not found anywhere in the Bible."

"Now more recently," Father Bryan continued, speeding up when Carrie took a deep breath in preparation to interrupt, "The subject came up following the discovery of oral contraceptives in the 1960's. At that time, there was great new discussion about artificial birth control in the Catholic community."

Carrie settled back in her chair, and Father Bryan lowered his voice to its normal level and rate, and continued. "In response to this rising tide of public discourse, in 1963, Pope John XXIII established a commission of six *non-theologians* to study the question of birth control and population. After his death that same year, Pope Paul VI expanded the commission twelve-fold to seventy-two members. They produced a report in 1966 stating that 'artificial birth control was *not* intrinsically evil,' and that Catholic couples should be allowed to decide for themselves about the methods to be employed!"

Father Bryan looked over at Carrie, expecting her to respond, but she remained mute. He concluded, "Only four of the seventy-two commission members dissented — yet the Pope rejected his own commission's recommendations in the text of *Humanae Vitae*, noting that the commission had not been unanimous!"

The priest stopped talking. He sat back, too, and when he spoke again, it was in a much softer voice. "All in all, Mrs. Barley, I can tell you from my own knowledge that there is enough debate about this matter — and has been for decades, if not centuries — that completely faithful and dedicated members of the flock may make decisions based on their personal circumstances and consciences."

Carrie's eyes had begun getting heavy and images of swirling potions had tugged her into a twilight of pre-slumber. When Father Bryan finally stopped talking, the sudden silence seemed to snap her back to full wakefulness. She blinked her eyes several times, and then profusely thanked him for his time and excellent counsel. He thought she was going to get up and say goodbye, but she still sat there.

"Father ..."

"Yes?"

"All this confusion about birth control ... Well, it's all very interesting ... But I must tell you ..." Carrie cleared her throat and shifted in her chair, folded her hands in her lap, and then looked the priest straight in the eyes, and continued, "You see, Jules and I ... We made a covenant ..."

"A covenant?"

"Yes," answered Carrie, "Two-and-a-half years ago ... We agreed ... Jules and I both agreed ... to become celibate! We gave our word to the Lord that we would both become pure and celibate!" Now she was sitting up straighter and jutting her chin out in an act of courage and defiance. "And now Jules wants to back out of that promise! I cannot see how we can do that ... how *he* can do that and *drag me along with him* into eternal damnation!"

"Oh, Mrs. Barley," responded the priest, leaning forward, "You cannot do that!"

Carrie slumped back down, shocked. She did not expect this response at all. She was sure he would affirm her glorious effort to move her marriage into a purer, holier state. "C-cannot?" she finally answered, "But ... why not?"

"Well, the Bible is quite specific about *that*, my dear." He looked up at the ceiling. "*Corinthians.* Chapter 7, I believe. Paul states very clearly that a husband and wife should not 'defraud' each other — that is, deny each other's, uh, *physical* needs and desires. Interestingly, he states that neither husbands nor wives 'own' their own bodies — but each owns the other's."

Father Bryan raised up a finger, adding, "There is only one exception ..." Carrie's ears perked up and she sat up straighter to be sure that she did not miss a word, "For a *brief* time for 'fasting and prayer' both partners may agree to refrain from sexual relations."

Carrie sank back into her chair again, barely listening now, as the priest continued, "This evidence highlights the fact that the early Church condemned anything which violated the integrity of marital love."

Carrie sat still, her mouth open, but she made no comment. She was unable to form any response. Finally, she thanked Father Bryan, stood up, collected her pocketbook, and left. She went home and prepared dinner, and waited for Jules to come home from his job at the furniture factory. She made his favorite meal — meatloaf with Italian bread crumb seasoning, baked macaroni-and-cheese, baby brussel sprouts, and homemade applesauce with large apple chunks baked in a brown sugar and cinnamon glaze.

They finished dinner, cleared the dishes and finished the kitchen rituals. But before Jules could retire to the family room to watch the news and Carrie retreated to the bedroom to watch *Desperate Housewives*, she told him about going to see Father Bryan, as he had suggested. She said she pleaded with the priest to give them permission to rescind their celibacy covenant. "But," she went on, dropping her eyes down in a gesture of defeat, "Father Bryan stated emphatically that we would both go straight to hell if we committed the grave and unforgivable mortal sin of breaking our celibacy covenant."

Jules nodded in acceptance of the fiat. Then he went into the bathroom and threw up his favorite dinner.

After that, Jules gradually began to fall away from his routine. The girlie magazines he read in the toilet no longer provided adequate relief; he began visiting the ladies of the street on the other side of town. He felt he had lost his salvation already, with the lusting that was constantly tearing at his heart and mind, so why not act on it? Jules resigned himself to his fate of damnation, and felt it was hopeless to try living a celibate lifestyle that was a hell itself. On the many nights when his wife was attending one or another meeting at the church, he headed for the red-light district.

Carrie felt guilty, too, for lying to Jules about Father Bryan's advice. However, she felt she had no choice. It was the *righteous* thing to do! She felt bad that Jules had fallen away from the church — although she was completely unaware of his dalliances with prostitutes. She thought she was truly saving both their souls by being celibate. She thought it would only be a matter of time before Jules came around and starting attending church regularly with her again. She felt they would both have their heavenly reward some day, and sing along with Jesus and the angels in heaven for such goodness as they were exhibiting in their loving celibacy. Father Bryan was surely mistaken about that.

She worked hard for the church, helping in every way that was needed, and anticipating ways that she could help even more. She took nothing in return — except for a discount on her children's parochial school tuition, which they could not possibly have afforded on her husband's meager income from his two jobs. (Jules had once or twice broached the subject of Carrie possibly going to work for a *salaried* position at the church, but she felt it was far more righteous to be a full-time volunteer. She had, in a way, become the "nun" she had dreamed of being when she was a little girl — her enforcement of celibacy made that more of a reality now.)

Jules passed away at the age of forty-seven from complications of AIDS (which, he told Carrie, he must have contracted from a public toilet seat. She accepted that explanation because she believed that he had been completely celibate for the last fifteen years). His lengthy illness had eaten up what little savings they had, so — after waiting a respectable period of time following the funeral (nearly eight months) — Carrie remarried.

Unfortunately, she now had no choice but to grant sexual favors to her new husband. But she had already "gone through the change" so, even though it was an obligatory chore, at least she no longer had to worry about pregnancy. Besides, as repulsed as she was about sex now, it did serve to make her feel like a true martyr. She kept count of how many Hail Mary's she could silently recite during each encounter.

Christopher Bennington was a wealthy and politically-connected gentleman, who did not expect Carrie to take time away from her church work, but only seemed to require that his physical needs be satisfied once or twice a week. She complied. After all, he would probably have had the marriage annulled immediately if she insisted on celibacy. She couldn't do that and expect him to stay with her. She had to make sure that all his needs were met. At least at first.

After completing the obligatory act, and all the Hail Mary's, Carrie would pray to the Lord for forgiveness for breaking her personal vow of celibacy. (She did not take this into the confessional, since Father Bryan was under the impression that she had taken his advice those many years ago, *not* to remain celibate. He was unaware that she had reported just the opposite to Jules.)

Carrie believed that Jesus, of all people, would understand and appreciate what she now had to do — breaking her vow of celibacy in order to marry a man of substantial assets and give her children a good home. Even though her children were all grown, settled and prosperous in their own right, Carrie felt compelled to marry this wealthy man so that she would have a financial cushion for them to fall back on, if and when they might need it. It wasn't for her own comfort. It wasn't.

The new Mr. and Mrs. Bennington lived very comfortably for the next two decades. Then, after years of donating his time and money to good charities and public works, Mr. Bennington was encouraged to run for office himself. He was successful, and that required him to be away from home frequently, flying all around the state and to the nation's capital. Carrie gradually resumed her celibacy, and it was clear to her husband that she was happier that way. He had many ports of call, and was able to make a few carefully chosen social acquaintances.

The Benningtons also traveled together several times a year, taking political junkets and vacations to exotic destinations. Carrie had a gallbladder attack during their last overseas junket, a sixteen-hour flight from Singapore. They were unable to get her to a hospital in time. She was sixty-eight years old when she died and left Christopher a widower for the second time.

Chapter 7: Christopher Bennington

Christopher Bennington was born with a silver spoon in his mouth, but he did not seem to realize the significance of it. He never acted snobbish, even though the kids in his class — and even his teachers sometimes — would defer to him. His father was a multimillionaire real estate developer whose name was plastered on office buildings and shopping centers, not just in their town, but in major cities all across the country. He was always appearing in the newspapers, in the business section, and also photographed with Christopher's mother in the society pages. But in spite of their wealth and high station, they sent Christopher to public school, and taught him to follow the rules, respect authority, work hard, and be kind and charitable to all.

And that's what he did. It came naturally to him. He helped other students — whether friends of his, or merely referred to him from friends — who needed help with their homework. He shared his lunch if someone had forgotten theirs. He was brave. Once he stood up to a school bully who was grabbing at a smaller boy's books. The victim's glasses had been knocked to the ground. Christopher stepped in front of the boy, causing the bully to turn his attention away from the smaller boy, and threaten Christopher instead, who stood his ground. He struck a "Superman" pose — chin extended, hands on hips, feet apart — and told the bully he should pick on somebody his own size. Christopher was actually about the same height as the bully, but considerably thinner. Most likely it was his commanding presence and intensity — the utter lack of fear — that unnerved the bully, who turned and quickly walked away without looking back. Then Christopher helped the little boy pick up his books and his glasses, and walked with him until they were sure the bully was not coming back.

Christopher was only nineteen years old when his parents died in a bizarre train wreck in an eastern European city, where they were helping to design and set up educational and occupational training programs for the poor. That particular area of the continent had never been considered a target, but nevertheless, the train derailment was considered likely to have been the result of a terrorist plot. Their bodies were flown back to the States, and after the double funeral, Christopher changed his college major from liberal arts to pre-law. He graduated with a double major in history and political science, and planned to change the world.

Eventually he took over where his parents had left off, building low-cost homes and facilities, to help the poor stabilize and improve their lives. He also built magnificent, glittering shopping malls, fabulous resorts, and civic convention centers that provided the profits to pay for the projects in poverty-stricken areas. He rubbed shoulders with the high and mighty, helping their causes, but cautious to get involved only with partners who had proven themselves to be honest, at least, and aboveboard, if not altruistic. He eschewed an opportunity to join in with a group that was a virtual cinch for a gambling casino license, even with its potential for extraordinary profits. He researched others that were less obviously involved in unsavory pursuits, and avoided getting involved with them as well.

Christopher had been dating Dana for six years, although not exclusively. He felt he could not settle down with one woman. With all of his projects, and as much traveling as they required, being married to him would require his wife to make too much of a sacrifice. For the same reason, he did not want to have children. He actually loved kids — whenever he visited one of the many projects he was working on, he would always try to take time to play catch with the younger children and basketball with the older ones. But again, as with marriage itself, he felt he would be unable to give his own children the time and attention they would need and deserve from a father.

The years flew by, though, and when Christopher turned forty, he decided it was time. Dana was thirty-two now, and he felt she deserved more than a part-time boyfriend — and he couldn't bear the possibility of eventually losing her to someone else. Besides, he could look back on all that he had accomplished, following in his parents' footsteps and bringing many of their dream projects to fruition. Now he really could settle down — at least enough to be a relatively good husband and father.

Dana was beautiful, and at five-foot-ten, almost as tall as Christopher. She was thin, but softly shapely, with silky blonde hair caught up in a comb, with wisps that slipped out and curled lazily at her shoulders. Her pellucid complexion was smoother than velvet. Christopher loved her tremendously, and no one else that he ever dated even came close to providing the joy and excitement that he felt when he was with her. When he was away from her on his many travels, he had to force his thoughts away from her and back onto business. (Initially after he had just met Dana it was very difficult, as the recollection of her image and her touch would constantly interrupt the blueprints, accounts or business meetings on which Christopher was trying to concentrate — but he got better at it with time.)

After dinner in the tiny, out-of-the-way Polynesian cafe where they had gone on their very first date six years earlier, Christopher pushed back his chair, moved around the little table next to Dana's chair, got down on one knee, took her hands in his and asked her to marry him. Dana pushed back her chair, lowered herself down onto her knees, and accepted. As they kissed, still on their knees, the other diners began to applaud. When Christopher said that they could go tomorrow and start looking for a set of rings that she liked, she said, "Oh, why wait?" There were two small wooden napkin rings, with carvings of palm trees and tropical birds, still sitting on the table. She picked up one and slid it onto the third finger of Christopher's left hand; and put the other on her own thumb. They both laughed, along with the other diners.

The restaurant manager came over to their table, smiling widely, and congratulated them in his choppy Pacific-island accent. He left the bill on the table in a black leather folder, and when Christopher opened it, was surprised to see that he had added a ten-dollar charge for each of the two napkin rings.

Christopher and Dana flew across the Caribbean and got married in a small ceremony at a chapel in the Lower Antilles islands where he had helped set up a vocational training and public works program. The chapel was overflowing with congregants of all colors, and afterward they threw a feast and celebration that lasted for two days, and matched almost anything seen before on the island. Initially, the Prime Minister was concerned that it might outshine the wedding of Prince Aribondo, the titular (figurehead) authority of the island. He had married his princess, a distant cousin, only a year earlier, and the P.M. was concerned that a huge wedding might outshine the prince's, possibly creating some ill will. But the prince himself took over the planning and arrangement of the wedding, and made it even more spectacular than his own. He hoped to show Mr. Bennington and his new bride how grateful he was for the time, expertise, and largesse that he had shown to his little island and all his people.

Six months later, Dana was sure that she was pregnant. She was not, but instead they discovered that she had a uterine tumor, and she underwent extensive surgeries, radiation, and chemotherapy over the next year. She died one week before their second anniversary.

Christopher was devastated. He stopped traveling, delegating that to his employees who appreciated the opportunities to travel. He only wanted to visit Dana's grave every day. He brought a dozen fresh roses every day, and laid them on her gravestone. He sat on a bench for hours at a time, leaving only when he felt he had no more tears left for that day. The people he worked with tried to bring him back to his "old self," inviting him out to dinner, or a ball game, or even just for a cup of coffee — but he always turned them down with a smile and a prefabricated excuse. Many of his colleagues and friends tried to get him to talk, and occasionally one was bold enough to suggest that he see a therapist. He just smiled and thanked them, and said he "might do that."

One Sunday, a former secretary came by his office. Miss Beatrice P. Evans ("Don't call me 'Mizz' Evans — I'm a 'Miss'!"), now seventy-eight years old, had also worked for Christopher's father. She knew what the younger Bennington had been going through since his wife's death, and she knew that she would find him here, at work, on Sunday.

Five feet tall in sensible shoes, Miss Evans had thin cirrus-cloud white hair that barely concealed her shiny pink scalp; pale crinkled skin with bright pink powder under her eyes, light blue above, and rose lipstick extending just slightly outside of her natural lip line. She stood in front of Christopher's desk and refused to sit down. She insisted that he get on his coat and come with her — and most imperiously demanded that he leave his briefcase in the office! As he had already visited Dana's grave that morning, he felt little reason to refuse her request.

Walking briskly, she led him to her twenty-two-year-old Chrysler convertible, parked in a handicapped spot directly in front of the office building. The car was in pristine condition. Miss Evans carefully tied a scarf around her hair and knotted it under her chin. She put the top down and then proceeded to drive at thirty miles an hour in the left lane of the highway. She did not notice — or simply ignored — the cars whizzing around her, the angry honking and angrier gestures. Eventually they arrived at the destination — her church.

Except for his wedding on the little island, Christopher had not been to church in years — not since his parents died. But when Miss Evans brought him back, he felt somewhat obligated to attend. He began to attend regularly; and then something unexpected happened. He started joining his colleagues again in their social and business activities ... accepting invitations ... laughing ... enjoying things again. But most remarkably was what he *stopped* doing — something that would have frightened anyone who knew him — wondering whether life was worth living anymore. Now he knew it was.

Perhaps it was the beautiful chapel, with its statues of saints carved into the marble columns — one in particular. The first time he saw it, Christopher could not take his eyes off it — a statue that resembled Dana so much, he wanted to run and embrace it. And as he stood in front of the beautiful saint, he did not exactly *hear* the words as much as he *felt* them: "Live and enjoy, my Darling ... Do not waste these years on sorrow!"

He knew it was a message from his beautiful wife as surely as though she were alive and standing right there talking to him. He realized that she wanted him to get on with his life.

When he looked up at the face of the marble statue a second time ... still very beautiful, but ... somehow ... it no longer resembled Dana as when he first looked at it. But the message remained in his heart.

Christopher met the widow Carrie Barley in the church. She had just lost her own husband, Jules, a few months earlier, after a severe case of "influenza." (That was what she told everyone, as she was too ashamed to explain that her husband died of AIDS — even if he did get it from a toilet seat.) At forty-six, she was a few years older than Christopher. Short and slightly overweight, but very pleasant-looking, Carrie had a sweet, round, rather angelic-looking face, and a childlike, coquettish manner that was somehow both cute and seductive. She was totally attentive to Christopher, always smiling in his presence, and hanging onto his every word. They began going to church functions together. Soon she began inviting him to dinners at her home — and she was a superb cook. Eventually, with the feeling that Dana would approve — not because Carrie was neither as young nor as pretty as Dana (as if anyone could ever possibly be as beautiful as Dana, even in her last days of life) but because she would keep Christopher comfortable and happy in his later years, he proposed marriage. Carrie accepted, and arranged for Father Bryan to perform the ceremony shortly thereafter.

It was not apparent at first, but after a few months it became more and more obvious to Christopher that Carrie was not really enjoying sex with him. Her initial enthusiasm faded fairly quickly, and eventually disappeared altogether. Christopher wondered whether — suspected really — that she had only been pretending to enjoy it at first, and couldn't, or didn't want to, keep up the façade. It seemed pretty clear, as time went on, that his new wife was carrying out an obligation rather than taking part in a joyful experience. When he entered politics in earnest, and was elected to a state congressional seat, travel took him away from home for weeks at a time. As he anticipated, Carrie did not seem to mind at all. She had her church work, and never complained about his extended absences. He made it a point to take her along with him on occasional junkets, when appropriate, or just on vacation. But their physical relationship had dwindled to nothing.

Christopher ran for office and funded his own campaign. There were so many people with their hands out — *offering* money! But he was not naïve. Those offers invariably had enough strings attached to open a yarn shop. He felt fortunate to have amassed his own personal wealth, built up on the foundation of the fortune that his parents had left him, so that he could essentially bankroll his own campaign. In that way, he was beholden to no one. He also had great admiration for the internet donation process that Howard Dean had developed for his '04 Presidential bid, as that was truly a grass-roots brainstorm — virtually untainted by special interest or corrupt influence money. It would have been interesting to see how different the "special interest lobby" would have been hamstrung, had Dean actually won.

Christopher ran for the U. S. Representative seat in his congressional district, and that was his first political victory — one of many to come. He was re-elected twice, and then was serendipitously ensconced into the U. S. Senate when a seat was abruptly vacated by its occupant who had been caught on a cellphone camera patronizing a Las Vegas house of prostitution. Most damning of all, though, was that he was dressed as a woman for the occasion. He also stepped down from the church where he was the beloved guest minister on some Sundays — dressed as a male, of course.

Christopher had mixed feelings about it. After all, the Senator was a single man, never married, and it was a legal industry in Las Vegas, in a free country. Besides, Nevada was not even the Senator's home state. But the brouhaha that erupted into an outrageous scandal was clearly detrimental to the party, the Senate, and the people of his home state. So when the governor approached Christopher after the senator resigned, he accepted the appointment. And since there was only one year left in the term, he was easily re-elected for a new six-year term of his own.

Senator Christopher Bennington made a big impression during his first elected term as U.S. Senator, authoring numerous bills to clean up corruption and reform elections. He sponsored a bill to limit credit card companies from charging usurious "default" interest rates — as high as thirty percent or more for being late for a payment! That was printed in tiny, light grey lettering on the back of the credit application, which on the front touted very low or even zero-percent interest rates, for an initial period. But even more egregious was their claim to have the right to increase lower interest rates to these outrageous default levels if a cardholder was late with *any* payment to *any other* credit card company, auto loan, house loan, or *any other kind* of loan reported on their credit history! The word "usury" seemed to have become an archaic relic.

Christopher's bill to stop these abusive practices also included other safeguards for unsuspecting constituents, such as making it unlawful to send out "pre-approved" credit applications and personal checks attached to a cardholder's account — easy prey for the "identity thieves" to pluck out of anyone's mailbox, purchase anything they wished, and have it charged to the unsuspecting victim's account. Finally, he added the provision that credit card companies could no longer "double-dip" by approving purchases that exceeded the cardholder's credit line, and then charging huge penalty fees for exceeding their credit line.

During the heated debates over this bill, Senator Bennington was shocked to discover that there were politicians who were so loyal to their contributors (the credit card and banking industries) that some of them nearly started a fistfight over these issues! He decided to hold off on his other pet crusades. He had hoped to sponsor a bill that would outlaw "gerrymandering" by enacting a federal statute allowing all the residents of each state to cast a vote for all of the U. S. Representatives that state was allotted. In other words, if there were thirty candidates running for a seat in the House of Representatives in a state that was allotted seven Representatives, then every voter could vote for seven candidates of their choice. That would somewhat eliminate the locked-in advantage for incumbents and level the playing field. However, Christopher ran into such near-violent resistance on his credit card protection bill that he decided to allow a "cooling-off" period for his colleagues before introducing a bill that would be even more controversial.

As Christopher was approaching the fifth year of his senatorial term and preparing for his re-election campaign the following year, he was stunned to be approached by his party leadership in a bid to recruit him for entry into the presidential election. He was unaware of the real reason that he was being approached — an effort to divide the competition for the nomination. Since he was already known for his controversial positions on hot-button issues, the governor, who was planning to run for the party's nomination, knew that splitting the competition would likely insure his nomination.

Christopher's constituents loved that he was willing to go to bat for them against the corporate and banking behemoths; but there was no love lost regarding his position on other issues that struck passionately negative chords in some groups — gay rights, affirmative action, decriminalization of drugs that had medical potential, and other controversial social issues.

"Controversial" did not begin to describe the good Senator Bennington. For that reason, the governor's supporters felt that he was perfect for splitting the competition and diluting it. The governor was heavily bankrolled by the corporations — the banking and credit card institutions most of all. Once he won the party's nomination, he could run roughshod over the other party's likely nominee, a very unpopular incumbent who had increased taxes, increased pork-barrel spending, and increased the national debt to historic proportions.

Christopher was stunned to be asked to consider a presidential run, and his first response was a resounding "NO!" He loved his state constituents, and had no desire to go beyond helping them. However, before his answer was accepted by the party leaders — they told him to "think about it" for awhile — tragedy struck again. Christopher and his second wife, Carrie, were on their way home from a visit to Indonesia, where he had gone to learn more about their excellent comprehensive healthcare system. Carrie had a gallbladder attack and it ruptured mid-flight; before they were able to land and get proper medical care for her, she died.

Christopher was sixty-two years old. He had loved Carrie, although nothing like his first, brief, passionate marriage to Dana — nothing could have matched that — but he did love her, and he felt disconnected after she died. He decided to accept the request to run for president.

The supporters and financial backers of the governor were stunned and in complete disarray when the news broke about his indictment on fraud and conspiracy charges. The charges were of such a grand scale, involving the most prominent figures in banking, insurance, sports betting, and known or highly suspected mob connections, that he had no choice but to drop out of the race. The strongest and most popular candidate behind him was Senator Christopher Bennington, who easily won the party nomination. He chose as his running mate — with advice from the national party consultants — Jared Todd Davis, a prominent politician from the south, where Christopher's lack of recognition and popularity was most in need of a boost. Jared claimed to be a "direct" descendant of Jefferson Finis Davis, President of the Confederate States of America (Jared's great-great-great uncle claimed to be a half-brother of the Confederate President Davis, whose father had passed before he showed up to make the claim) highly popular in the south, but too parochial for national consideration. Not as tall as Christopher, but good-looking in his own right, Jared flashed a huge smile with professionally whitened-teeth, a full head of hair swept neatly to the side so that the transplanted plugs were not noticeable, and tinted a medium brown that covered the gray nicely and looked very natural. The perfect vice-presidential candidate. They won handily.

After his inauguration, President Bennington ran into problems early on regarding his more liberal and controversial stands. In addition to the aforementioned issues, he espoused a doctrine of freedom for women to obtain very early abortions without question, but allowed in later months only for documented health-threatening medical circumstances. Everyone came out against him on that. The pro-choice faction wanted no restrictions at all, and the pro-lifers wanted no abortions at all, regardless of the circumstances. Even members of Christopher's adopted church rallied against him.

A swing through Vice President Davis' home state was planned by the President's advisors, in order to gain support for his more controversial positions. Davis pushed for it, too. Christopher actually pleaded with the Secret Service team to allow him to ride in a top-down convertible, but he was reluctantly reminded that there were too many people in that state — and elsewhere — who would love to see a remake of the JFK assassination. He agreed to ride in the Presidential limousine to the auditorium where he would be speaking, and allow the Service to conduct their normal security procedures for such an event.

The limousine was, of course, bullet-proof, and they had staked out armed surveillance teams all along the route. What they were not prepared for, however, was a massive improvised explosive device of the kind favored by terrorists, solidly packed into a mailbox on the side of the street allegedly by a disgruntled postal worker who was allegedly recruited into this shadowy foreign group allegedly dedicated to the destruction of the American government.

The limousine blew thirty feet into the air, and into hundreds of pieces, killing fourteen bystanders who had collected along the streets to wave at the President and his entourage, and wounding nearly a hundred others. Christopher and the other passengers in the limousine were killed, except the driver, who landed on top of a canopy over a restaurant and slid down to the street, miraculously sustaining only a slight concussion and a few minor broken bones and teeth.

Vice President Jared Todd Davis was sworn in as President of the United States on Air Force One, on the way back from his home state to Washington, D. C.

Chapter 8: Jared Todd Davis

President Jared T. Davis, or "Todd," as he was called by his family according to the plan to differentiate him from his father, Jared Daniel "Danny" Davis, a former U. S. Senator; and his grandfather, Jared Neal Brett Davis, called by the dual designation of "Jared Neal," who had been Speaker of the House four decades before his grandson moved into the White House. That is, Todd moved into the *other* White House, as his family called it, as opposed to the Confederate White House in Richmond, Virginia, where his (alleged) great-great-great uncle, Jefferson Finis Davis, presided during the glorious years of the Confederacy. Now Todd brought the family tradition around full circle, to the Presidency of the (Old) Union, and there was much celebration in his home over the accomplishment — after, of course, a respectful show of mourning for the tragic and untimely death of Christopher Bennington.

There was a lot to do now. Many of the bills which his predecessor had passed had to be reversed or quashed. These changes would have to be done cautiously and subtly, however, as Todd Davis had spent many years carefully painting himself to appear to be a moderate. He had a savvy staff of advisors who could help him to accomplish these tasks without immediately alerting the public to his radical agenda. This staff was, as it happened, the same that had efficiently arranged the presidential visit to Todd's home state, where Bennington was tragically assassinated by foreign radical elements. (Todd couldn't help but smile when he thought about that.) Now Todd was free to emphasize how those foreign elements were the supporters and promoters of radical extremism which was destroying the country, such as being pro-abortion, and trying to destabilize the economy by penalizing business that hired sorely needed immigrant workers who were unfortunate enough not to have proper documentation to display at their fingertips. These were hard workers, willing to do menial jobs without complaining about "working conditions" or demand "minimum wages." The entire national economy could collapse without them. Did the country want to start paying ten dollars for an orange? The banks, insurance corporations, pharmaceutical and oil companies, not to mention the great financial stocks and bond houses — all those institutions which made this country the greatest in the world — were all hurting from Bennington's fanatical and destructive leadership.

Todd's first order of business as President would be to give back to those institutions that had enabled the citizens of this fine country to amass the wealth and reputation they had so painstakingly built over many decades, the tax breaks they had earned and deserved. Taxes, regulations, restrictions — all of these had chipped away at the foundation of freedom for which this country stood.

President Davis quickly gained in popularity as the people were thrilled with the tax cuts passed within the first few months of his new administration. Even though the national debt soared to record heights within the first few months, President Davis' approval rating soared along with it, and the country moved on past the dark cloud of despair that had taken hold immediately following the assassination. The stock market steadily turned upward, from the precipitous drop which took place following the tragedy, and within six months it had reached a new high. The only "bad" news was in the old Soviet Union, whose economy had never quite stabilized after the dissolution of the Iron Curtain in 1989. There were skirmishes across old borders, renewed saber-rattling and threats by the newly-elected Russian President Yevdokiya Shargorodsky to send in armed troops to maintain peace. She sent fully armed brigades right up to the border in a show of force with one wayward former Soviet satellite.

President Shargorodsky had a more personal motive for this action, of course — to let it be known in no uncertain terms that the first woman President of Russia would not be a pushover for anyone nor any country. She still remembered when Margaret Thatcher — some years even before she was elected as Prime Minister of the United Kingdom — was dubbed the "Iron Lady" by the Soviet Defence Ministry newspaper *Krasnaya Zvezda* (*Red Star*), after giving a speech with a scathing attack on the Soviet Union.

"The Russians are bent on world dominance!" Ms. Thatcher had inveighed. "They put guns before butter, while we put just about everything before guns!"

Well, President Yevdokiya Shargorodsky was just as tough. She would be known as *Zhenshtina Stali* ("Woman of Steel"). She threw that tidbit around until it was picked up and attributed as a name given to her by the Americans. Perfect.

Yevdokiya — or "Dokya" as she was affectionately known by her constituents — was also descended from heads-of-state. She was the great-great-great-granddaughter of Nikolai I, Emperor of Russia, and Alexandra Fedorovna of Prussia; which made her a cousin, several times removed, from the present-day royals of England. Except that — somewhat like the new President Davis — her lineage was not "official," as a wedding that would have to have been performed two generations back did not actually take place. However, the bloodline was satisfactorily established for the Russians who elected her — and the idea of electing a descendent of royalty was very exciting.

President Davis was brought up in the old antebellum tradition of showing great respect for the ladies, who required kid glove care, attention, protection, and of course, guidance. Dokya, he felt, would be a pushover. And as the former Soviet Union was the second largest producer of oil in the world, encroaching on Dokya's power base would be a worthwhile endeavor.

The 73-story U.S. Bank Tower, or Library Tower, sits across the street from, and was built as part of, a billion-dollar redevelopment of the Los Angeles Central Library, following two disastrous fires in 1986. It is the seventh tallest building in the United States, the tallest North American skyscraper west of Chicago, the tallest building in California, and the tallest building with a helipad on the roof. The building was also known for a time as First Interstate World Center after being bought by First Interstate Bank, and after First Interstate merged with Wells Fargo Bank, the name Library Tower was restored. In March of 2003, the property was bought by U.S. Bancorp and the building was renamed U.S. Bank Tower. L.A. residents in the know, however, continue to refer to it affectionately as "Library Tower."

Todd sat back and cackled out loud, rubbing his hands together in the sheer delight he felt. A bank building, another "world center," smack in the heart of the most sinful place in the country, Los Angeles, with its Hollywood liberals, gays and other smut-mongers, and the tallest building on the West Coast — what better target for another terrorist attack? Todd was still laughing as he picked up the phone and started to make calls.

When a Russian MiG47 jet fighter flew out of the Far Eastern Military Command at Khabarovsk, and headed across the icy waters of the Sea of Okhotsk, the Bering Sea, and approached United States territory, there was an amazing amount of confusion, as agonizing efforts were made to get word from the Commander-in-Chief about what action to take. But he was far away in the southern hemisphere, in the company of several heads-of-state on a fishing trip, leisurely discussing a new South American free trade agreement, munching on *po de queijo*, *feijoada* and sipping tall, frosted glasses of *caipirinha* garnished with lime wedges. When the administrators who had been left in charge of Homeland Security finally got President Davis on the phone, and explained what was going on, he responded in as casual a manner as though he had just been told the neighborhood Cub Scout was at the door selling geraniums, guaranteed delivery by Mother's Day.

"Okay, don't get too bent outta shape 'bout this now," Todd responded the frantic caller, "Least not 'til I get a chance to find out what it's all about." The staff surrounding him was dumbfounded. "Get little Dokya on the phone for me."

Less than ten minutes later, and before anyone on the staff was able to raise the Russian President on the phone, who at the same time was lunching with her counterpart, the recently-elected Angela Dorothea Merkel, Chancellor of Germany (they enjoyed great camaraderie, both being the first elected female heads of their countries), a salvo of bombs was released and struck the Library Tower, in a chilling repeat of the '01 World Trade Center attack in New York City. Then the MiG47 did a u-turn and headed back toward the Pacific, directly toward the Hawaiian Islands, and perhaps planning a reprise of the previous century's '41 attack on Pearl Harbor. However, before that could take place, President Davis gave the order to scramble our jet fighters, which shot down the Russian fighter jet. The pilot was rescued from the Pacific waters.

President Davis expressed great remorse over the thousands of people who lost their lives that day. Little Dokya — President Shargorodsky — insisted that she knew nothing of the rogue pilot who attacked the Library Tower. The entire world was skeptical, however. President Davis vowed to get revenge on whoever was responsible, and President Shargorodsky had no choice but to express her desire to find out as well. She was chagrined and embarrassed by the attack, so much so that she did not object when President Davis wanted to send troops and advisers onto Russian soil. When they began taking over the smaller, outlying Russian villages, and the oil fields therein, President Shargorodsky realized that she had made a terrible mistake. She tried to order the American troops out, but President Davis refused. Both held back from declaring all-out war, but the citizens of Russia were taking matters into their own hands. They began attacking the American soldiers, advisers, and contractors who were sent to the oil fields. The number of disappearances, kidnappings and murders of Americans rose, as did the impatience of the American public. Half wanted to declare all-out war on Russia, and the other half just wanted to bring our soldiers home and avoid any more bloodshed.

A purportedly fictional movie by a notoriously anti-establishment director depicted the Library Tower attack as a conspiracy by the fictitious U. S. President, "William James ('Billy Jim') Thackery" and his cronies, in a secret cabal to take over the oil fields of eastern Russia. The movie also depicted this same group as having planned the assassination of the previous President, which enabled "Vice President Thackery" to be sworn in as President. Half the country was supportive of President Davis, and vehemently protested the movie, feeling it was a thinly veiled repudiation of him and his administration. They felt the country was safer for his stewardship. The other half of the population believed the movie to be an accurate depiction of the events. A handful of people knew it *was* accurate.

President Davis' popularity waned, and eventually nose-dived, as the undeclared war in Russia and the increasing number of casualties took its toll on the populace's confidence in him and his goals. Even the people who had scoffed out loud and mocked the movie's alleged conspiracy theory started to believe it might have contained more fact than fiction.

When his term ended — not with a bang, but a whimper — Todd retired to his home state. A statue of him on a mighty steed was erected in the capital. (Some thought it resembled a little too closely the statue of Robert E. Lee in Lee Park in Charlottesville, Virginia.) He gave a guest lecture at the state and private universities from time to time, but he stayed out of the public eye for the most part, until another two decades went by. Then, gradually, his counsel was sought out as an elder statesman, and he wrote (with the help of several ghost writers) a series of books and memoirs, which brought him not only fortune, but a newly polished image in which he was held in high esteem, in this country and around the world. He died in his sleep at the age of eighty-three, surrounded by his family, and there were speeches and praises worthy of the most revered head of state given at his funeral. The newspapers wrote of little else; stories of the great deeds of President Jared Todd Davis were on the front pages for weeks; and everyone who ever knew the man personally was interviewed on Larry King Live.

Part II: The Path

Chapter 9: Charlie

Charlie looked around to see if he could recognize anyone. The line was very long, stretching up and over a grassy hill in the distance, as far as he could see. Off to one side, perhaps a quarter-mile down a softly sloping hill covered with grass and wildflowers in bloom, was a little lake. It was surrounded by what looked like apple trees. He saw some stone benches there among the trees, and he would have liked to sit there for awhile, but he did not want to lose his place in line. After awhile, when he was sure several hours had passed, he was somewhat surprised to note that he was not the least bit tired. He turned around to look at the person behind him. A very elderly gentleman, with thick white hair, neatly combed and parted on the side was dressed in what appeared to be a hospital gown. Charlie noticed a plastic bracelet band on his wrist, with some typing on it. The man smiled at him, and something about his face was serene and familiar — even though he did not know the man at all.

"Excuse me, Sir?" he asked the man, who was looking at him with a slight smile.

"Yes, Charlie?"

"Oh! Uh … How did you know my … uh … Have we met?"

"We met on the way up here," the elderly man responded, still smiling. He turned and gestured behind them. "Down there."

Charlie looked back down the long line of people still waiting behind them on the hill, assuming the old man meant they had met somewhere in the line earlier. He could not recall the meeting momentarily, but then something happened:

He was no longer standing in the line on the grassy slope. He was in a hospital … in another line. Shirley had just given birth to Jamie, and a hospital administrator had asked him to come down to the cashier's office to straighten out their insurance. The man in front of him at the cashier was obviously distraught — flushed, sweating, tugging at his collar and looking around frequently. He was dressed somewhat shabbily, in a rumpled suit and tie, as though he had slept in it. There was a shadow of white stubble on his chin. The left temple of his glasses had been reattached with a small safety pin where a tiny screw used to be. His shoes were very worn, but seemed to have been polished.

The old man pressed his face closer to the glass barrier in front of the cashier and dropped his voice so that only the man behind it (and Charlie, as it happened) could hear him.

"But we *have* coverage, I tell you! I've been paying on that supplemental policy for ten years, since I retired! How can you say we are not covered?"

"Well, that may be the case, Sir," the man behind the glass said, loud enough for the old man, Charlie, and the four people in back of them to hear. "But until we can get confirmation, we need six hundred dollars."

"But ..."

"Or we'll have to ship your wife out to the state facility."

"Please!" the old man implored, now with both hands against the glass, "Please can't you call the company? We ..."

"I'm sorry, Sir! We have called and faxed them, but we have not received any answer." the cashier said, even more loudly, it seemed. "You have to pay us now, or we must initiate the transfer. There's nothing else we can do!"

Charlie couldn't understand why he did what he did. Even as he did it, he told himself he was nuts. All he could think of was all the foolish financial moves he and Shirley had made in the past — leasing a car and trying to turn it in a few months early, discovering they owed the entire balance of the lease (the finance manager at the dealership specifically told them the opposite); forgetting to deposit a single paycheck and being charged with hundreds of dollars of insufficient-fund penalties (his own bank, all the recipients' banks, and the companies and utilities themselves all had their own penalty charges for the bounced checks. After that, he began to have his check direct-deposited every month); and many other stupid or unlucky moves that cost them so much unnecessary expense over the years. He thought of all this as he reached around the old man and slid his credit card under the glass window.

"Take six hundred dollars out of this, Sir," he said, as the cashier nodded and the old man just gaped at him.

"Certainly," said the cashier, nodding, "I'll apply it to your father's account."

Charlie just smiled. Let him think the old guy is my father. I would do it for my father if he were still around.

The old man grabbed Charlie's sleeve and a small pool of tears began to collect in his red-rimmed eyes. "Why? I'm just ... Do I know you?" He wiped at his eyes and adjusted his glasses in an effort to see Charlie more clearly.

"No, Sir," he answered, putting the credit card back in his wallet, and taking out a business card. "I'm Charlie Miller. It's nice to meet you. My address is on here. Whenever you are able you can send the money back to me."

"Oh, my," said the old man ... and Charlie worried that he might faint, but he stood fast, still holding onto Charlie's sleeve. "I shall send it back to you as soon as possible! I can't begin to ..."

"*When you can,*" Charlie emphasized, "*Not* 'as soon as possible' … When you *can.*"

The man just kept staring at him, not knowing what to say. So Charlie told him to go see his wife. He let go of Charlie's sleeve, slowly, and turned and started to walk away, turning back once more to look at his benefactor, who was now taking care of his own business at the window.

That's who this is, he thought, now recognizing the man in line. *That's where we met.*

"Go ahead," said the elderly man now, waving Charlie toward the grove of trees some distance from the line. "I'll save your place in line."

The old man seemed to know where Charlie wanted to go. He headed down the grassy slope toward the little oasis. When he got there, he noticed that the trees did indeed look like apple trees. He picked up one of the pieces of fruit that had fallen from the tree, and noted that it did not look bruised at all. He polished it on his shirt, and took a bite. Stunned by the incredible sweetness of it, his mouth watered as he ate it. He had never tasted an apple so intensely sweet and delicious.

After finishing the apple, with a second already in hand, he felt completely full and satiated, and — pleasantly drowsy. He felt like lying down and taking a little nap — very unusual for him. But then he thought about the old man holding his place in line, so he started walking back up the hill. He was sure it was not any farther than a few hundred yards — the line was hardly moving that he could tell.

But he could not find the man. He walked up the hill, which was the direction they had been going when he left the line; but after walking for at least a mile or more, he was sure the man could not have moved that far. He must have missed him. He started to walk back down the hill. He walked for a long time, looking carefully over the line of people, at each face, so as not to miss the man again. He continued walking down the hill until it began to get a little dark. Clouds were rolling in overhead, and a shadow deepened the color of the grass from Kelly green to dark forest green, and eventually a drab muddy color. That is when he saw a young girl a short distance back in the line, looking to the side. By her profile, he thought she looked familiar.

Charlie walked down to the girl and tapped her on the shoulder. When she turned around, he was both shocked and revolted. It was the young woman who had been about to jump over the Second Street bridge before he intercepted her and sent her home in a taxi.

What was her name? Patty… Penny. That was it. Penny.

He was shocked at her appearance: her skin was a sickly yellowish-blue; her beautiful brown eyes were now a cloudy gray, red-rimmed and wet with drainage, and sunken into the bluish-purple bony orbits around her eyes. Her hair was matted and filthy. Something was moving in it.

"P-P-Penny?" he stammered, wondering if it were really the same person — what could possibly have caused such a devastating change in her appearance. "Is that you?"

Penny looked up at Charlie and squinted her eyes, as though she had difficulty seeing him, even though he was standing right in front of her. Then she started to answer him, but muddy water dribbled out of the sides of her mouth, and she started to cough and then heave with great wracking spasms. More filthy water spewed out of her mouth, and then a fish and another fish came out. Charlie started to back away; but when she stopped heaving, he moved back closer to her.

"You're sick ... Can I get you some help?" he asked.

The ravaged girl wiped her mouth with the stained sleeve of her thin coat — the same one she was wearing on the bridge, he recalled. She looked up at him with the rheumy eyes of a person decades older. She did not try to answer again — perhaps fearful of another coughing spasm — but just looked away and shook her head. Then she turned her back, remaining in her place in line but facing the other way.

Charlie said, "I'll get you some help." He looked at the others in the line behind and in front of Penny ... Many looked nearly as sickly as she did.

None would answer him about getting some help. None would even make eye contact with him.

Walking farther up the hill — he wasn't sure at first, but the farther he went, the more the sun seemed to come out and the sky brightened. He saw an elderly woman, who returned his gaze with a friendly smile — the first one to do so since he left Penny to get help. Charlie noticed that she was wearing a lacy blue nightgown and matching penoir. She, too, had a hospital identification wristband on.

"Excuse me, Miss," he said to the woman — and was struck by her sparkling blue eyes, crinkling with her smile. She had rosy cheeks, and her hair was shining silver.

"Yes, dear?" she responded.

"There's a girl down there who needs some help," Charlie said, pointing down the hill. "She is ill ... Do you know where I can get some help?"

"Well, dear, I'm not sure," said the lady, "but you might try going up the hill to the top of the line, and see if someone there can help."

"Thank you." Charlie walked for what seemed like at least a mile, he estimated, but never seemed to get any closer to the top of the hill. He stopped and asked a couple of more times, and each time, he received the same answer: "Try going up the hill to the head of the line."

Finally, he felt — well, not exactly frustrated, he still had a very positive mood — but he felt that he was not really getting anywhere. He was worried about Penny. He stopped and looked back, to see if he could spot her back in the line and see if she were all right. When he turned around, there was someone sitting on a bench. That was odd, because he had not noticed the bench before, as he approached this spot on the hill.

The lady sitting on the bench looked sort of like a nurse. She was wearing a white dress, with a wide white belt, and shiny white slippers on her feet. She had a small white lace doily pinned to the back of her hair, which was a rich brown, and so shiny that it almost seemed to glow in the sunlight. She looked up at him. Her face was exquisite, with skin that looked as soft as silk.

"Do you need some help?"

"Yes, yes," he answered. "There's a girl back there," pointing down the hill. "She's ill, she needs medical attention. Can you get someone to help her?"

"Yes, we'll take care of it," said the woman, and her voice was so sweet and musical that it had an immediate calming effect on Charlie.

He thanked her, and started back down the hill, but not before the woman reached out and touched his sleeve. It gave him a pleasant tingling feeling, and he turned back to her.

"You do not need to go back down the hill, Charlie. You may stay here in line." Then she got up and began walking down the hill toward where he left Penny.

Charlie wondered how she knew his name ... but he was so glad she was going to help Penny, he did not want to delay her by asking any questions. He turned back to the line and looked at the person standing there.

A young girl, perhaps only ten or eleven years old, stood there looking at him. She was in play clothes — white shorts with pink and blue checkered cuffs and a little halter top with ruffles around the sleeves that had a matching checkerboard pattern. She had a delicate little gold chain necklace, with a puppy-dog pendant on it; a big green plastic ring — the adjustable kind that you get in gumball machines, with prongs that can be squeezed to make it smaller — and a picture of a "Powerpuff" girl on it. She had two barrettes in her hair, with Powerpuff girls on them, too, holding up two shiny pigtails. The child smiled and two deep little dimples appeared on each side of her mouth. She took a step back and motioned for Charlie to join the line in front of her.

He bent down so that his face was closer to her level. "Hi, what's your name?"

"Vallery," the little girl replied.

"Are your parents here?" he asked, concerned that the little girl was by herself.

"Yes, I saw them a little while ago," she replied. "I expect they will come and get me soon." She did not seem particularly upset, and Charlie wondered about that. But before he could ask her any more questions, he was tapped on the shoulder. He turned around and was surprised to see — his own parents.

"Mom! Dad!" he said, holding out his arms to them.

They looked wonderful — more youthful and vibrant than he had ever recalled. Tears came to his eyes. They embraced him, all at once. Then his mother slipped her hand into Charlie's, and his father wrapped his son's free arm around his own. They led him away from the line.

The three of them walked together, and Charlie was surprised by his own lack of pressing curiosity about how they came to find him, what they were doing there, and where they were going — but he felt such an overwhelming joy and peacefulness that he did not really care about those questions. It was unlike any feeling he could recall. Well, actually, now that he thought about it — he did feel this way once before — when his darling son Jamie was born.

He thought about the moment when the nurse put that tiny little human being in his arms. Jamie's face was soft and pink, his eyelids so delicate and tiny, Charlie bent down to kiss him and was overwhelmed with joy. Then he sat down next to Shirley, who was smiling and glowing in her own happy feeling, and reached over — not to take the baby, but to hold Charlie's hand. They sat there together, Charlie holding tiny Jamie in one arm and Shirley's hand in his other. He felt a similar peaceful joy now, walking across the grassy hillside, emerald green under the bright blue sky, together with his parents.

They came to a grove of trees surrounding a little pond. Charlie was playfully surprised when a goldfish swam up to the top of the pond. It looked as though it were made of real gold, the sunlight glinting off of it through the trees. His parents motioned for him to sit down, between them, on another bench like the ones he had seen before in the apple grove. This one looked like marble, and was intricately carved with birds and other little animals and landscapes.

"Mom, Dad," he said, turning from one to the other. "You both look so wonderful!"

His parents smiled softly, but did not say anything. It was at that moment that Charlie began to look around in earnest, and tried to place where they were, and how he got there. He looked down at his clothing. His pants were torn and dirty. Dried brownish stains were all over. And those black marks — they almost resembled tire tracks? His parents just continued to smile softly, without speaking.

Charlie wracked his brains trying to figure this out. He looked down at his torn and dirty clothes again. Bloodstained. Then the trees in the grove and the pond and the goldfish started to fade; his mother and father started to fade and soon became only translucent shadows. The bright sunshine dimmed, and darkness soon fell around him.

He looked up and saw the sidewalk ahead of him, as he approached the corner. He heard the sound of the truck horn as the eighteen-wheeler came barreling around the corner in front of him, its rear double-tires bumping up onto the curb, coming at him, pulling him down under them. He felt the terrible pain for only a fraction of an instant — although he did not feel any pain now, even as the eighteen-wheeler came over him again, crushing his chest. He closed his eyes.

When Charlie opened his eyes, he was still sitting on the beautiful marble bench, by the pond, with goldfish swimming to the top and back down again, surrounded by the tall trees and their shading leaves. His parents were gone. Someone else was standing beside the bench.

"I'm dead, aren't I?" he asked the figure, in a matter-of-fact way that surprised him in his own lack of sadness or anxiety about it. He had not lost his feeling of warm, lingering joy.

"Yes, that's right," responded the figure. Now Charlie felt a little curious because he was not sure if he were talking to a man or a woman! The figure was tall and slender, but with broad shoulders and a beautifully sculpted face. The skin was so radiant as to seem lit by candlelight; the nose was slender and the eyes large and shaded by long, delicate lashes. Shining silver hair cascaded down beyond the beautiful creature's shoulders. A bright white silken toga was belted at the narrow waist with a length of golden hemp, and soft white trousers under the hem of the toga billowed in the breeze around them. Beneath them, long, slender feet were bare.

"Who … who …" Charlie was afraid to ask or say anything that might be misperceived.

"I am Gabriel," said the creature, whose voice was both sonorous and musical.

Stunned, Charlie was unable to take his eyes off this large and beautiful creature. Suddenly struck by an overwhelming feeling of reverence, he began to kneel — but Gabriel reached down and took his hand and gently pulled him back up. The hand that gripped him was soft and delicate, and yet so strong that Charlie could not resist the pull if he had tried.

"It is not necessary to kneel," said Gabriel, with ... was that a wink?

"Oh ... of course!" said Charlie, with a meek little chuckle — not altogether sure if he should laugh. "Heh ... uh ... I wasn't quite sure ... I'm still not sure ... uh ... Sir? ... or ..."

"I am neither man nor woman," said Gabriel. "The Creator bestowed upon me a *soupçon* of all his anthropomorphic ideas ... Something of a prototype, you might say."

"Well," said, Charlie, "Glad to meet you, uh, Sir ... er ... or ... I mean ... uh ..."

"'Sir' is fine," said Gabriel, smiling. "Or Gabe. Whatever."

Charlie stood up and reached down to dust off his knees. Then he noticed, first, that there was no dust; and second, that he was no longer wearing his torn and soiled clothing. He was wearing a silken white tunic and pants exactly like Gabriel's — except that his belt was just plain hemp-colored rope.

"You have to earn your way up to a gold belt," said Gabriel, with a little chuckle. "Sort of like in *karate*."

"Heh, heh," said Charlie, weakly, still too unsure of himself to laugh heartily.

Gabriel turned away but did not let go of Charlie's hand. He started to walk away, and Charlie fell into step with him. Then he slipped — or felt as though he slipped — but when he looked down, he saw that the ground was falling away beneath him. They were rising up together.

Charlie felt as light as a feather, and so happy that he was afraid he would start giggling. Gabriel turned to look at him and said, "Giggling is completely acceptable. We have a lot of fun up here."

At that, Charlie burst out laughing, and it seemed as though the laughter was dancing around him and through him, like ribbons in the wind.

Chapter 10: Penny

Penny felt horrible — worse than any hangover she had ever had. A dull, pressing ache felt like a thick elastic band around her head, and an acid taste in her throat presaged a need to vomit, but it never came. She couldn't see anyone or anything very clearly — everything looked as though she were underwater — dark, filth-laden water. She felt her eyes squinting, but when she tried to open them more, they felt swollen. She was sure there were people around her — in a line of some sort — but she could not clearly make out anyone. For a minute, she thought someone was talking to her — that man, Charlie? Who was he? She couldn't remember. When she tried to speak to him, her mouth was filled water, and she couldn't say anything except to make a choking sound.

What is happening to me??

Penny reached forward to see if she could feel someone there. She did — she felt something hot and slimy, with very rough places on its skin — scales?

Oh, God, what is this??

The person in front of her turned around at her touch. She could barely make out his face, except for the light coming from his eyes, which had a purpleish quality, like the "black" lights that emitted ultraviolet light that made anything white look fluorescent. He or *it* — whatever it was — made a horrifying screech, and Penny stumbled backward into someone else. This one grabbed at her with claws so sharp they felt like scalpel incisions into her skin. She tried to scream, but only filthy water poured out of her mouth and she started choking again. She pulled away from the creature, away from the line of people or whatever they were, and started to run, but she may as well have been trying to run underwater, as she could barely sustain any forward motion. Finally, she gave up, standing where she was, and started to cry.

It was a strange feeling, because Penny could not recall the last time she cried about anything. She had been empty inside for so long that she forgot what grief felt like. Now real tears were rolling down her face, and even though it caused great stabbing pain in her eyes, somehow it felt good. When she looked up, someone was standing there. She could not identify the person, who was grayed-out by the thickness of the atmosphere around them.

"Who … Who's there?" She asked, frightened now, and yet feeling a comfortable vibration from the person.

"It's me, dear …"

"*Grandma??* Is that *you??*" asked Penny, and watched as Sadie's appearance became more clearly visible.

"Yes, dear, it's me," answered Sadie, and she walked toward Penny and put her arms around her. Penny felt a warmth and sheer goodness at the touch of this embrace that she could only start to cry again.

Suddenly she realized that she was able to speak now, without choking.

"Grandma, what's happening," she cried, still feeling the safe warmth and comfort of Sadie's embrace. "Where are we?"

"Don't you remember, Penny?" asked Sadie, quietly, and still with great love in her voice.

Penny felt a rush of nausea wash over her as she suddenly saw the door to her old bedroom, as clearly as though she were right back there.

She heard the lock snap open, and she saw her boyfriend jump off the bed. She saw her grandmother standing there and the frightened look on her face when her boyfriend started walking toward her. She saw her grandmother backing up to the stairs, and she looked down at her own feet, walking to the side and slipping one foot behind her grandmother.

"NO!!" screamed Penny, as she saw the entire sickening scenario unfolding again, "NO, Grandma! Watch out! Watch out!" But she realized it was Penny herself that her grandmother needed to watch out for. It was Penny herself who tripped her and caused her to fall down the stairs. Penny had caused her grandmother's death.

She put her hands up to her ears to drown out her own screams, *"NO, GRANDMA, NO! I DIDN'T WANT THAT TO HAPPEN! PLEASE DON'T FALL, GRANDMA!!"*

Sadie's image began to fade into a rippling grayness again, and Penny could feel the warmth of her embrace fading to a cold emptiness. But she heard the most beautiful words she had ever heard before, as her grandmother's countenance slowly disappeared, "I love you, Penny ... I love you ... and I forgive you ... I forgive you." Penny felt a lifting sensation in her chest.

The atmosphere around Penny remained dark, and she stood there for what seemed like hours, hoping that her Grandmother would come back again. Finally, she thought she would walk around and perhaps find her. She started to try and make her way through the dense thickness around her, and after walking only ten or fifteen laboriously difficult steps, she began to see the outline of someone standing ahead of her.

"Grandma? Is that you?" she asked, attempting to run to the person, but held back by the same oppressive weight of the atmosphere that surrounded her.

"Grandma!" The figure seemed to be moving, but not toward her. It was stroking something.

As she got closer, the figure appeared to be that of a slender young woman, holding something ... petting it ... or ... cuddling it. It was a baby ... a young woman holding a baby. The woman looked up at her when she came within a couple of feet, but she did not say anything. She just kept stroking her baby, and rocking it, and looking at it with the sadness of one who had lost everything they held dear.

Penny began to feel an icy coldness settling around her as she came closer to the woman and her baby.

"Who are you? Do I know you?"

The girl looked up at Penny and nodded her head to answer "yes" but did not speak.

"I'm sorry," said Penny, "I can't remember where I know you from. What's your name?"

The girl still said nothing, but just kept rocking and caressing her baby. Then she stopped suddenly and slowly grasped the blanket that was covering the baby's face. Carefully, and painstakingly slowly, she pulled it down. Penny bent forward to see. The baby inside the blanket was so tiny that it barely reached halfway up the girl's forearm. Its skin was blue and mottled, its mouth open and stiff, the eyes clouded over. The baby was dead. Penny was shocked and revolted. She felt sick.

Now she recognized the woman. This was the fifteen-year-old whom she had pressed into her prostitution ring. She had come to Penny, pregnant and begging for help. Penny and her high school henchmen drove her into the woods and forced her to drink a bottle of whiskey, then left her there. She was found dead, drowned in a ravine that she stumbled into in her drunken stupor. Now the girl just stared up at Penny, with her excruciatingly sad eyes, and held the dead child out to her.

"No, no!" protested Penny, stepping backward and holding her hands up in front of her, rejecting the girl's effort to give her the baby. "NO! I don't want ... I'm sorry! ... *I'M SORRY!!*" She kept stepping backward, and although the girl was not stepping forward, she somehow could not put any distance between them. The girl kept offering the baby, closer and closer, until Penny finally dropped to her knees in the slime and filth beneath her. She grabbed the girl's legs and hugged her.

"Please ... forgive me ... forgive me," she pleaded, over and over again, tears stinging her eyes like soapy water.

She felt the girl's hand rest on top of her head, and then begin stroking her hair. The tears stopped, and Penny felt herself being lifted up, even though there was nothing pulling on her. Soon she was face to face with the girl.

"We forgive you," said the girl, so softly that Penny was not sure she heard correctly. The girl was now holding the baby back against her breast. "We forgive you," she repeated.

Penny was standing now, and she saw the girl's face soften from sadness to a sweet, contented look.

"We forgive you," she said again, and now Penny felt her chest lighten again. The girl and her baby began to fade, and soon disappeared into the haze around them.

Many hours passed, and Penny had no way of knowing just how much time had passed in the murky haze that surrounded her. It could have been days. She had managed to take only a few steps before she gave up and merely stood where she was, sensing the vague images of a line of people around her once more. Then a sound came out of nowhere — a rumbling like a thunder storm, and the atmosphere darkened even more. She felt a terrible tightening in her stomach, and the acid taste of fear. So frightened did she now feel that she looked around for someplace to escape from wherever she was ... but where?

As blackness ascended — seeming to rise up from below — shadowy visibility turned to total blindness. As the thunder rolled in on louder and louder peals, a hand was suddenly on her shoulder. Penny was roughly pulled around to face ... a man she did not recognize.

His hair was thick and matted, and his skin was covered with sores. Lightening crashed through the blackness and she could see the shapes of others behind him — a woman here, another man over there, some more behind those. She could not tell how many there were, but it was at least two dozen or more.

All of them seemed to be craning their necks to look at ... *her*.

Penny pulled away from the man who had held her shoulder, turned away from the group and started to run. But again it was as though she were running on a treadmill, unable to make any forward progress. She began to panic from sheer fright, and tried to scream, but her mouth felt as though it were stuffed with cotton. She could make no sound at all.

The man took her shoulder and again pulled her around to face him. Now the faces in the crowd were much more clearly visible. They all looked horribly sick, with open, weeping sores and peeling patches of dead skin, sweating as though fevered; or pale, with whitish countenances and shivering with chills.

"WHO ARE YOU?" Penny tried to shout, but nothing came out. "I DON'T KNOW ANY OF YOU!!" She started to choke again as she tried to force the words to come out.

The man who still gripped her by the shoulder answered, even though no sound had come from her lips: *"You know us,"* he said, in a raspy, phlegmatic voice. *"You brought us here."*

His face began to redden with anger, and he repeated louder, "YOU BROUGHT US HERE!!" Then he bent backward in a shaking seizure, and pieces of dead flesh fell off with each spasm.

A young woman, so emaciated that her arms and elbows resembled wire coat hangers, stepped forward. Penny could see her ribcage poking through her thin dress.

"You know us. You infected us with HIV."

Penny reeled backward as the vision in front of her faded.

She saw herself sitting in her apartment. The room was very dim, lit only by candles placed around the room, and heavy metal rock music played loudly. She could hear the banging on the walls by the neighbors who wanted the music turned down, and she remembered thinking how funny that was.

"Did you disinfect it?" the young boy was asking her in the memory, and she had said, "Yes, that's Clorox bleach over there — don't worry!" Then she helped him pull the rubber tourniquet around his arm and find a vein to inject the "junk," as they affectionately called their heroin. Penny had enticed this fourteen-year-old boy into her circle with sex, and then turned him on to drugs. She had done so many like that. Boys and girls. Some thought it would be safe to be with another woman. But it was not. Not with this woman. Not with Penny.

There was no bleach, nor any kind of disinfectant in the container she had pointed to. There was nothing but tap water in there. Penny had learned that she was HIV-positive, and she wanted to pass it around to as many others as she could. If she had to suffer, she would not suffer alone!

The memory faded, and the young emaciated woman in front of her now reached out for her hands, and grasped them softly. "I believe you did not mean to infect me," she said. "My boyfriend had been doing drugs with you, and he did not know that he had been infected."

Penny started to turn away from her, as she did not want to face this girl, but the girl held her firmly in her grasp — and the girl's hands somehow exuded a warmth and comfort that Penny wanted to keep holding onto.

"It was not your fault," the girl went on. "It was my own fault. I knew my boyfriend had been doing intravenous drugs. And even when he promised to stop — and he did stop for awhile — I knew about the possible consequences."

Penny felt tears pushing sharply, painfully out of her eyes and the wetness rolled slowly over her cheeks and lips.

"I had sex with him, you see?" the girl went on, pulling Penny closer. Her face was so thin that she could see the sharp ridges of her cheek bones and the rims of bone around her sunken eyes. And yet she did not look unpleasant. Penny could still see a beauty — a soft light that seemed to be radiating from inside her.

"I was only sixteen, I should not have been having sex yet," the girl went on, "I was impatient — immature. I lied to my parents about my whereabouts, about my friends. I gave in to my impulses. *It was not your fault.*"

The girl dropped Penny's hands then and dropped her gaze downward. Penny did not think she was going to say anymore, so she tried to think of something appropriate to say to her. But the girl suddenly looked up with her lovely, sad eyes and said, "So, you see? I forgive you — I forgive you, because it was not your fault — I forgive you."

Penny felt the tightness in her chest release a little bit again. It felt so wonderful. She took a breath. The girl turned around to walk away.

The words came out softly at first: "Thank you." Then more strongly, "Thank you! *THANK YOU!*" And with each breath, the tightness in her chest diminished a little more. But the girl had already disappeared into the crowd behind her.

The man who first spoke stepped forward again. He was frightening to look at — not just because of the horrible lesions all over his skin, but because of the terrifying look in his eyes. They seemed to bulge from their sockets as he spoke, and the tiny red veins crisscrossing the whites of his eyes got larger and redder, as his eyes bulged forward and then receded as though they were breathing with him. When he spoke, Penny could feel the heat from his breath, and the noxious odor that he emitted.

She tried to back away from him, but again the ground felt slimy, slippery, and seemed to move underneath her with each step so that she never was able to get away from this man. He grasped her hands, just as the young girl had done, but his hands were so freezing cold that they actually burned her; and when she tried to pull free of them, she was scratched by the sharp scaly lesions that covered his hands.

"You did this to us," he spat out in his raspy voice. Blackish phlegm dribbled out from the sides of his mouth. "YOU DID THIS TO ME!!" Suddenly he was overtaken by another jarring seizure that first bent him over backward and then forward, until he fell to his knees.

But he did not let go of Penny's hands, and she could not pull free of him. Instead, he pulled her down to her knees along with him. She felt the wet slime penetrating through her thin jeans, and some *things* were crawling onto her legs. She opened her mouth to scream, but the man covered her mouth with his own, and she started to gag and wretch. She could not breathe, and she could feel her chest tightening and contracting as her lungs strained to get air, but the man held her tightly in his repulsive kiss. Finally, blackness descended as she was about to lose consciousness.

She heard her tormenter's last words to her before she passed out: *"I do not forgive you. I DO NOT!!"*

When Penny opened her eyes, she was in the same place. The man who had kissed her was still there, but he was standing off to the side now, arms crossed. The girl who had spoken to her was gone. But she faced another dozen people who still stood in the group, staring at her.

One by one, each person in the group approached Penny, and expressed either forgiveness or anger. They either spoke kindly, reverently absolving her of whatever part she played in their having contracted HIV and eventual demise; or they shouted curses, furiously blaming her for what she did to them. Each one in turn approached her, and afterward she always felt the same way: If the person had forgiven her, she felt a lifting of her heart, a rising comfort and peacefulness; calmness, a relief, a shedding of anxiety and fear.

But if the person expressed anger and fury, and could not forgive her for the pain and suffering she had caused them in their life, she felt tormented, frightened, and a great fear pressed down on her like a smothering pillow — an overwhelming paranoia, an irrational certainty that she was to be locked away and tortured. The fear was so intense as to be torture itself, and she felt that she was dying over and over again, until she wished she could pass out, lose consciousness, die forever.

After all the people in the group had spoken their piece with Penny, she looked around and realized that a smaller group was still standing off to the side. As her eyes adjusted more, she was able to identify the people standing there. This group consisted of all those who had expressed their fury and vehemence toward her with curses and castigation. The others — those who took the blame on themselves and expressed forgiveness — were gone.

Penny started to walk away, gingerly, testing the ground under her to see whether she would be able to make any forward progress. Surprisingly, she did, and she stepped more quickly, to leave that area and those horrible people behind as fast as she could. She did not have any idea where she was going, but she was going. It was not easy, though, as the thick, clammy atmosphere was still very difficult to negotiate through, and she could see very little.

Penny walked for what seemed like days, stopping occasionally to look around and see if she could make out anything in the nebulous dimness — a path, a road, a sign of any kind — anything that would show her some direction. After trudging hopelessly, endlessly it seemed, she thought she heard a rustling noise. When she looked over her shoulder, she was startled to see ... the same group of people that she had left behind!

They were standing together, just as they had been when she had left them. She kept looking at them as she took another step forward, and watched with a sickening sinking in her stomach that they, too, took a step forward. She took a step back away from them, and they in turn took a step toward her.

Penny dropped her head into her hands and felt herself trembling, her shoulders heaving as she felt like crying, to release her fear, her indescribable sadness. But now no tears came. When she looked up, she saw what looked like a grove of trees through the grimy air, and she turned in that direction. The air seemed to clear a little as she approached the grove, and she could make out what looked like a small pond or lake beyond the trees. There was a stone bench and — yes, she was sure — someone was sitting there. There was a radiance about the person, she thought, and that may have been where the light was coming from that lit up the grove of trees.

As she approached the grove, the group of people who were following her seemed to hang back. They were not moving toward the grove of trees. Penny felt a surge of hopefulness, and pushed on with all her energy to get to the person on the bench. As she got closer, she saw a lady, about fortyish, dressed in a neat pantsuit and sensible shoes. Her hair was short and curly, brown with glints of gold; and it shone with such beauty that it seemed to light up her face. Penny recognized the little social worker who had been so good to her back in the women's prison. It was Marion Wilson.

As Penny got closer to Marion, she froze. She recalled with a wave of shame how mean she had been to Marion — cursing her for not delivering her illicit letter, spitting in her face. And she began to feel afraid.

"Come on, dear ... it's okay," Marion said, as she turned to look at the fearful girl a few feet away. She patted the bench next to her and said, "Sit down here with me."

Penny moved forward until she was next to Marion. She started to sit down on the bench, but she just kept bending her knees until she was kneeling in front of Marion, and laid her head down on her lap. Then the tears flowed, and Penny heard herself wailing in grief and guilt, as Marion gently stroked her hair. "It's okay, dear — It's okay."

Penny started to feel a rising comfort, a release of anxiety, and the clear air that filled her lungs with a lightness replacing the constricted feeling in her chest. She already knew that Marion forgave her — she could feel it. And Marion knew that Penny knew, so she just said, "That's right, dear — that's right — But do you know something else?"

Penny lifted her face, which was still wet with tears, and looked up into Marion's large, sparkling eyes, and the twinkling smile on her lips.

"Wh-what else?"

"I love you, Penny." Marion pulled her up from her kneeling position, guided her onto the bench next to her, and slipped her arms around her. She pressed Penny's head gently down to her shoulder, and said, "I'm one of many people who love you, Penny — you need to know that — you need to keep that knowledge in your head and your heart."

Penny lifted her head up from Marion's shoulder and felt such a sweetness emanating from her that she thought she would start crying again and never stop.

"I've always loved you, Penny."

Marion took the other's face in her hands. She looked in her eyes and reaffirmed her statement to the perplexed girl: "Yes ... I've always loved you."

She brushed her lips lightly against Penny's, who felt an immediate joyful rush of pleasure in a wave from her lips down through her whole body.

Marion began to stand up.

"NO! Please, Marion! Don't go! DON'T GO!"

Penny reached out to try and stop her, but she grasped only air. Marion's countenance faded away quickly as she walked into the dusky fog surrounding the grove.

Penny lay on the bench and covered her face. She could still feel the sweetness and warmth of Marion's kiss, and she never wanted to get up. She would just stay there forever, she thought.

A sound rustled behind her and suddenly Penny remembered the hateful group that had been following her. She sat up and started to leave the bench when a hand closed around her arm and held her fast. She looked up and found herself staring into the face of possibly the most exquisitely handsome man she had ever seen. He was a large man, well over six-and-a-half feet tall. His skin was bronze in color and had a satiny glow and burnished cheeks. His hair was coal black, and sleek, like the fur of a panther, rippling in sensuous waves down to his shoulders. His eyes were a deep sea green, shaded by thick dark lashes and perfectly sculpted eyebrows. His shoulders were broad and his muscular arms strained against the white silky shirt he wore, opened at the collar, revealing a smooth, clean, muscular chest. His waist was narrow, and his pure white linen slacks were belted with a shining gold belt, the large buckle having the man's own likeness carved into it. The face on the buckle almost seemed to stare out with a life of its own.

As Penny's gaze dropped down she saw on the man's feet gleaming red patent-leather Nike cross-trainers with an iridescent pink-and-silver *swoosh* by the heel. She started to giggle, but held it back. She looked up at his gorgeous face, wanting to ask who he was — but he was so strikingly handsome that she was afraid her voice would tremble. The man reached down and deftly stroked Penny's hair, and she felt electric shocks zing through every inch of her body. It was painful, to be sure, and yet she wanted him to do it again and again. Finally, she found her voice.

"Who — who are you??"

"My name is Lucifer. But you can call me Lou."

Chapter 11: Marion

Marion did not know what happened. She saw the line of people in front of her, climbing up and over a beautiful grassy hilltop. When she turned around and looked back she saw the rest of the line of people, extending for miles behind her, as far as she could see. She turned forward again, and asked the person in front of her, and then one or two people behind her, where the line was going. No one was able to answer with more than a shrug and a smile.

When she got to the head of the line — hopefully not too far beyond that beautiful hilltop up ahead — she was sure she would get some answers. She hoped she would, anyway.

She continued to wait, at some point marveling at the fact that her legs did not seem to be getting tired at all — and she did not feel impatient at all, for some reason — even though she surely must have been standing in that line for hours already. She did seem to be getting closer to the hilltop, and that was good. Besides, there were lovely bushes and flowering grasses along the way, some with colors so vivid that they almost seemed to radiate a light from within, like incandescence. A small bush some distance from the line seemed to bear fruit of some kind. She wanted to take a closer look, but did not want to lose her place in line.

Just then she was tapped on the shoulder. She turned around to see a very elderly man, wearing crisply pressed peacock-blue pajamas with yellow piping around the collar and cuffs. He looked quite lively and very healthy, with rosy cheeks and sparkling blue eyes. He was holding onto an IV pole on rollers with an intravenous bag hung on the hook at the top, and a tube leading from the bag down around the pole and under his sleeve.

"Go ahead, Miss," he said, and pointed over toward the small bush with the fruit on it. "I'll keep your place in line." Marion thanked him and started walking over toward the bush before she realized that she had never mentioned anything about wanting to go there! How did he know?

At the same time that she asked herself this question, she felt satisfied — not curious at all — as though there were nothing strange about it! Of course he knew that she wanted to go to the bush, and of course he would save her place!

Marion walked over to the bush and noted that it was much larger when she approached it — more like a tree, thick with leaves and branches that reached all the way from the top down to the ground. The fruit resembled apples, but they were more pinkish in color, with silvery speckles. As she reached for one, it seemed to fall off into her hand. She was unsure whether to peel it or not — but as she held the fruit, the peel softened and seemed to melt into the fruit. She took a bite. It was both intensely tart and sugary sweet, and her mouth watered with delight as she ate it. The leaves of the bush were so soft that she used one for a napkin and wiped her lips. She barely had eaten two mouthfuls when she felt completely full and satiated. Then even more miraculously, she watched as another fruit grew and ripened in place of the one she had plucked!

Walking back toward the line of people, Marion looked for the nice gentleman who had held her place. Even though he should have been easy to spot in his brightly colored pajamas and IV pole, she could not find him. She walked up and down the line, certain that she was in the right vicinity, but she could not spot him anywhere.

As she walked farther down the hill, thinking she might have to go to the end of the line, she saw a familiar figure. She was not sure, but she thought it looked like ... Dr. Harrison? Dr. Douglas Harrison? The doctor who treated her in the hospital for a severe infection and fever after her father had driven her into the mountains and arranged for the abortion of — her father's baby. Dr. Harrison had not been kind to her. He called her degrading names. But most hurtful of all was the fact that he surgically sterilized her without her knowledge, so that she could never become pregnant again.

Marion had long since forgiven the doctor in her heart, though — just as she had forgiven her father for his misguided cruelty, and her brothers, who merely succumbed to their father's influence. She forgave her mother, too, whose loyalty to — and abject fear of — her husband eliminated any possibility of her being able to help Marion, even if she wanted to.

Yes, that *did* look like Dr. Harrison. He was quite some distance away, down the hill. She could just make out his face, the rest of him blocked by the other people in line. Marion walked down the hill toward him. She looked up when a large shadow darkened the landscape around her, and saw that the wispy white clouds were rapidly being replaced by cumulonimbus storm clouds. She picked up her pace, but the atmospheric roiling seemed to do the same. She hoped it would let up by the time she reached the doctor. It did not.

The weather turned even more violent as a supercell thunderstorm formed, and a tornado could be seen in the distance, heading in this direction. Marion took cover under an area on the side of the hill that jutted out, forming a shallow protective awning. She trembled with fright as giant hail stones and brilliant lightening soon crashed all around her.

When the lightning and hail finally let up, Marion timorously ventured out from under her hillside awning. The sky was still dark, with only the barest suggestion of daylight at the edges of the storm clouds. The wind continued to whip at her and blow dead leaves and other detritus about her face. It was at least twenty degrees colder than it was before she walked down the hill. The people down at this end of the line did not seem to notice, though — none had made any attempt to take cover. She looked for Dr. Harrison again, and spotted him a short distance farther down the hill.

When she approached within a few feet of the doctor, she was mortified to see that he was completely naked! He must have felt embarrassed, because his hands were covering his private parts; but he was otherwise standing in line as though nothing were wrong. Marion looked around to see if there was anyone who might have a coat or shirt to offer him — but no one responded to her. They did not even seem to notice the naked man among them. She looked down then and realized that she was still wearing the scarf she had worn to work that day.

Marion loved that scarf, because it had been given to her by the wife of the Dean of Admissions at the state university where she had received her undergraduate degree. The Dean and his wife had been so kind and understanding of her, extending her scholarship to cover dormitory expenses as well as tuition, and inviting her to join them often for dinner on all the holidays — Thanksgiving, Fourth of July, Passover, Hanukah (she was Jewish), Christmas and Easter (he was Catholic). They were wonderful surrogate parents to her. The scarf she wore today was a graduation gift from the Dean's wife. It had been a family heirloom, made of pure raw silk, printed in beautiful pastels of watercolor scenes from the Chinese province where it had been hand-loomed. And since they had no children of their own, she wanted Marion to have it. Marion had always treasured it above any other item she owned.

Now she took off the beautiful scarf and walked up to the naked man, shivering in the icy wind. She held it out to him. Dr. Harrison looked down at her and the scarf she was offering. He made no move to take it, though, and Marion thought he must be horribly embarrassed.

"Please, Dr. Harrison — I think you will be more comfortable if you take this — borrow this for awhile? Just until you get ... uh ... some clothing issued? I ... uh ... I'm sure that someone will provide ... "

Dr. Harrison continued to cover himself with one hand while he raised the other up, snatching the scarf from Marion's outstretched hand. He started to wrap it around himself, but could not do it with one hand, so he turned away from Marion. He slipped the scarf around his buttocks, and was adjusting it somehow in front of him. Then she heard a loud ripping noise, and her stomach sank as she knew the beautiful scarf had been torn apart. She felt a tendril of anger rising, but then reminded herself of how humiliated Dr. Harrison must have felt to be standing there in that line in all his nakedness. He needed the scarf far more than she.

Marion then watched as Dr. Harrison spread his legs slightly and threaded the ripped-off portion of the scarf between his legs and up around the back of the wrap, so that it functioned as a loincloth. Then he turned back toward the front of the line, looking straight ahead, and took no notice of Marion still standing there.

"Dr. Harrison?" she asked, unsure why he would not at least acknowledge that she supplied him with a covering. The wind was still howling around them, but she was sure that he heard her.

He turned toward her and looked intensely at her as his face contorted into something resembling a grotesque gargoyle. He opened his mouth, apparently to speak, and a thick black foul-smelling cloud mushroomed out and spread across the doctor's face. As it got larger and larger, completely covering his head and sliding down over his neck, Marion could make out small movements within the cloud. She heard a buzzing sound, which got louder as the cloud enlarged, and soon she could see tiny legs with sawtooth hairs sticking out here and there. It was a cloud of insects, and Dr. Harrison's screams were garbled as his mouth became filled with them. He fell to his knees, slapping and clawing at the scourge around him, until he began to convulse in great spasms.

Then, almost as quickly as it had appeared, the cloud of insects withdrew back into the orifices of the doctor's face and disappeared. Marion had backed away from the horrible sight, but when the doctor seemed to have recovered from his spasms, and stood back up looking placid once again, she moved back toward him. He stood as though nothing had happened.

"Dr. Harrison? Do you need some help? Shall I go look for help?"

The doctor would not look at her.

Marion decided that she had better go and get some help anyway. Although she didn't understand what had happened, it was clear that the man was suffering from some horrible affliction, which might recur. She would walk up toward the top of the grassy hill, and thought perhaps she might yet find the man in the peacock pajamas and her original place in line, as well as getting some help for Dr. Harrison.

Marion walked up the hill and noticed shortly that the dark storm clouds were beginning to part, moving back toward the lower part of the hill. As she continued walking up the hill, the sky gradually brightened and the fierce wind died down to a soft, warm breeze. She walked for what seemed like another hour, until she spotted a small path going off to the side. She looked beyond the path, to see if she could see where it led. Was that a small building in the distance?

Wonderful! she thought. *There must be someone there who can help!* She turned down the little path.

It was difficult to stay on the path, as Marion noticed bushes and trees everywhere around it that appeared to be laden with gorgeous fruit of one kind or another. Aromatic flowers bloomed everywhere, dizzying in their perfume. The colors were even more vibrant and appeared almost fluorescent — somehow emanating a brightness that seemed to come from within. It was difficult to stay on the path without stopping to breathe in the tantalizing array of scents and aromas, or to resist picking and tasting the beautiful and unusual fruits. But she did resist, and kept her mission in focus — to get some help for poor Dr. Harrison.

When she arrived at the building, she was stunned by the intricate paintings in the gilded door. It seemed to tell a story, with vast clouds and stars scattered at one end, birds and fish and other animals that she could not identify, and then human figures — first only one or two, and then more and more as the vast painted mural moved around the door, until the end, where there were painted huge hordes of people and only a small tree or a lone animal here or there. A gleaming brass ring sat in the middle of the door, and Marion reached up to rap on it. Just as her fingertips touched it, the door swept open.

The day outside had been as bright and sunny as a perfect spring day, but when the door opened, a light so brilliant shone through that she covered her eyes. She expected to feel the kind of pain that stabs one's eyes when walking from a darkened theatre into the bright sunlight. But although the contrast was just as extreme, she felt no pain at all. She uncovered her eyes and reveled in the brightness.

Inside, the light had the brilliance of a diamond. Marion looked around in awe. The floor was marble, and had swirls of color that gave a rainbow effect — that appeared to rise above the tiles, like a true rainbow. A magnificent stairwell led upward in a slightly curving pattern, and there must have been more lights above because it got brighter the higher one looked. As Marion looked up to see where it led, she had to shield her eyes, as the stairwell disappeared into the brilliance of light. She was too awe-struck even to consider trying to climb the stairs.

Marion looked around and saw two chairs on either side of a small table. The chairs were carved of a rich dark mahogany wood, which had patterns in the grain that seemed to be dipping down and then up again as she watched. It was almost as though the patterns were dancing within the wood.

Marion walked over to the chairs to look more closely, and then felt drawn to it, as though the chair itself were beckoning her to sit down. She did so. As she rested her arms along the large bare wooden armrests she was surprised at how smooth and soft they felt, as though they were covered in velvet. She heard a slight scrape, and when she looked up, someone was sitting in the other chair. It was a beautiful person, tall and strong, and yet with a delicate grace that befitted a ballet dancer. The creature was almost regal in its commanding presence.

"Who … uh, who … ?" Marion was afraid to ask any questions that might seem insulting. Perhaps she should have known who … or what … it was?

"Gabriel," responded the figure, in a voice as harmonious as a chamber orchestra.

Marion fell silent, feeling an intense joy in this Gabriel's presence, and not wanting to hinder the continuation of it by speaking. But after a few minutes of silence, she began to look around again, and now she felt a curiosity about what this was all about. No sooner did the question come to her, than the surrounding scene began to fade and change.

Marion saw herself as if in a movie. She was on a concrete floor. A deranged woman wearing the drab blue dress of the inmate uniform was above her, pressing down on her neck. Marion recalled the moment when she felt her head exploding with pain, seeing stars and flashes of light — and then finally darkness, as the last molecule of oxygen and life drained from her body. The feeling came back now — the terror, the pain — and she felt herself pulling away, pulling free of the crazed woman, pulling out of her own body — and what a tremendous relief it was when she did! The crushing weight was immediately gone from her throat, and her entire body felt as light as the air around her! And then she was surrounded by the star-filled night — clear and beautiful, sparkling like diamonds on black velvet. Then the light came, and then — she was standing in the line.

Marion reached up now and could still feel the place where the woman had pressed down on her neck with all of her weight, crushing her windpipe — but it did not hurt anymore. Now she knew what had happened.

"I … I died, didn't I?" she asked, and Gabriel nodded his head in assent. *How interesting,* she thought, *that a rainbow-like swirl of light trailed in the air as he moved his head.*

Then he spoke. "You may go up if you would like," he said, gesturing with a long, graceful hand toward the marble staircase.

Marion was fearful of asking questions as it had been ingrained —
beaten — into her by her parents not to question them. But she felt so
safe now, so — loved, somehow — that she realized she did not need to
fear anything from this beautiful creature.

"If … If I would … like … ?" she asked, tentatively, hoping that
Gabriel would fill in more information for her without her having to ask
outright.

Gabriel sighed. "Marion … You may go up to Heaven now …
Paradise … Nirvana … the Next Plane of Existence … There are lots of
names for it, but it's there for you now."

Marion thought for a minute and weighed her next question
carefully. Then she said, "You said 'If I would like' … What did you
mean? That is … Do I have a choice?"

"Yes, of course you do, Marion!" Gabriel chuckled and it sounded
like a carillon of bells. "You have choices in life, and you have choices
after life, too, dear girl." He looked up and laughed again. Marion
followed his gaze upward to see what he was looking at. But she saw only
the brilliance of the light coming down in rays, one brighter than the
next..

"Well … How nice," she said, when it was apparent that Gabriel
was not going to say anything else. "Can you … uh … tell me more
about these 'choices'? Wh-what are they … uh … Is it okay to ask?"

"Yes, of course, Marion," he said, reaching over and touching her
hand. She felt an intense tingling pleasure and comfort at his touch. "You
have two choices ... for now. You will have many more at a later time."
Then he added, almost as an afterthought, "Much later."

"Well … Okay," said Marion, now feeling more confident in her
ability to question her host. But she also wanted to draw out the visit as
long as possible, and hoped he would never take his sweet hand away
from hers. As though he had read her thoughts, Gabriel turned toward
her, reached over and clasped her hand between both of his. The
pleasure of his touch traveled throughout her body and covered her like a
warm velvet cloak.

"Your two choices are these: You may go up; or you may go
down."

Marion snapped out of her sensual reverie. "D-down? Wh-what do
you mean? Wh-where is 'down'?" It sounded so ominous that Marion
suddenly felt a small finger of fear scrape across her gut.

"Don't be afraid, Marion," said Gabriel, again seeming to
anticipate exactly what was on her mind; and her momentary anxiety
disappeared like so much vapor. "*Down* is simply where you go if you
don't go *up*."

Marion somehow expected that Gabriel would laugh again after saying that, but he did not. She decided that she had better get to the point here. "Is that ... *Hell?* Is that what 'down' is?"

Gabriel sighed again, and once more looked upward as though he were seeing something or someone. Again, Marion followed his gaze but saw nothing. He shrugged his shoulders, and said, "Really, you don't have to call it that ... We don't ... And it's not exactly what you think, either."

Marion started to flash back to her encounter with the naked Dr. Harrison back in the line. But her memory did not stop there. She thought about her father, the constant assaults she suffered at his hands, the pregnancy with his child and the forced abortion. She remembered the women she met in the prison — Penny Jackson, the young woman whom she tried so hard to help, and thought for so long that she was accomplishing something until the incident with the letter, and Penny spitting on her when she tried to resume their therapy sessions. Now she was happy that she had had the opportunity to see Penny again, here in this place, and to sit on the bench with her for a few minutes. The brief encounter had seemed to provide some comfort for her. And finally, she thought again about the woman who crushed the life out of her.

She looked up at Gabriel, who was staring intently into her eyes, and she felt so happy and peaceful, that she did not want to think about any of those people who had hurt her so much in life. But she felt compelled to ask: "Are they ..."

"Yes," Gabriel answered, not needing for her to ask the whole question. "Yes, except for the last woman, they will all be going down."

"Not the woman who ... who ..."

"Who killed you?" supplied Gabriel. "She was mentally ill, you know. She thought you were a demon. She was tormented by a constant flood of voices in her head, and truly thought she was defending herself—and saving the world. We take that into consideration, you know."

Marion felt surprisingly relieved to hear that. But then she thought about her parents.

"They have not finished their earthly lives, you know," said Gabriel. "They have some years to go before they will come over. Let's not speculate here, okay?"

"Okay," said Marion, now feeling terribly serious and not wanting to enjoy the pleasures of Gabriel's touch on her hand, when she felt so worried about the others. Gabriel wordlessly acknowledged her thoughts and slipped his hands away.

Marion became anxious and surprised at how upset she felt about all those people who had been so unkind to her. She looked up at Gabriel, and said, "They need help! Who will help them if they go ... *down*?"

Gabriel did not answer, but just raised his eyebrows and opened his hands. Then he said, "Who, indeed?"

Marion's mind was racing. *Should she ... could she ... possibly ... ?*

"Can I ... *May* I ... help them?"

Gabriel barely hesitated before answering, "Yes, of course you can, Marion. We anticipated that would be your choice."

And at that, he stood up and swept his arms wide in a grand gesture, moving in gliding steps around the room. As he did, the stairwell began to vibrate — Marion thought it felt the same as when she visited California once and experienced one of their temblors. The stairwell began to glow, first bright yellow, then orange, then blood red ... and it began to sink ... down, down, down, until it was completely reversed in orientation, the steps all spiraling downward now. And the brilliant white light from above had faded to a dim pink mist.

Marion got up from her chair — feeling a pang of sorrow to leave the supreme comfort of it, much as she felt when Gabriel let go of her hand a few minutes earlier — and cautiously approached the now-descending stairwell. As she looked over the edge, she saw that the bright red glow became softer, and then darker, and completely dark some distance down, beyond which she could see — nothing but blackness.

"Go ahead, dear," said Gabriel, gesturing for Marion to approach the re-oriented stairway. She hesitated for a moment and looked up at him; he answered her apprehension: "Don't be afraid. You don't have to do this, you know? But if you do — don't be afraid."

And she was not afraid. She grasped the handrail and gingerly stepped down the stairs.

Chapter 12: Dr. Harrison

It was dark and misty, but Dr. Harrison could tell that he was standing in some sort of line. He felt a rising anger at having to do this. He was a wealthy and powerful man, why should he have to stand in this line at all? He stepped out of the line and felt a cold draft of air — that was when he realized that he was completely naked. He covered himself with his hands and quickly stepped back into the relative protection of the line.

Oh, Jesus, what the hell is going on here??? It was just then that the young woman approached him, coming from somewhere out in the darkness. He turned his body to face the other direction from her, so that she would not see his frontal nakedness.

"Dr. Harrison? Is that you?" she asked, apparently oblivious to his humiliating condition.

He turned his head to look at her. She looked vaguely familiar, and he wracked his memory to try and place her.

"It's me, Dr. Harrison — Marion Wilson."

Wilson. Oh, Jesus. Sheriff Wilson's daughter? The little whore whose ass I saved after she had a botched abortion? What the hell does she want?

Douglas Harrison got his answer just then, as Marion held out her beautiful heirloom scarf to him. He looked at the scarf and then, unsure whether it was a joke she was playing on him, snatched it out of her hand. He turned back away from her and wrapped the scarf around his lower parts, and then tore a length off the end to wrap underneath him.

Ha, ha! he chuckled to himself, *I always wanted to be a Sumo wrestler!*

Marion was still standing there when he turned back. He would just ignore the little wretch, and she'll go away. But when she still stood there, and spoke to him again, he decided he would have to tell her in no uncertain terms to get lost. He started to speak, but suddenly he felt his mouth exploding with something — something moving, filling up his mouth explosively and then forcing its way out. Tiny, skittering, buzzing fleas flew up and across his face, filling his nostrils, his eyes, crawling through his hair, covering his neck, forcing their way into his ear canals so he could hear nothing but their insane buzzing, louder and louder, until it was like a freight train inside his head. He clawed at the swarm and tried to scream, but they went down his throat, gagging him until he couldn't breathe. He fell to his knees and then started to convulse on the ground.

He gave up trying to fight, and as soon as he did, the fleas seemed to relax and quiet down, withdrawing back into his mouth. In a few seconds they were gone. It was as though they had never come.

Marion had stepped away, but when Douglas finally stopped his spasms and the infestation disappeared, she came back. Douglas stood up and looked at her in disgust.

What is it with this stupid bitch?

"Do you need some help, Dr. Harrison?" she asked — and Douglas found the question surprisingly comforting — but he could still feel the residual taste of the foul bile in his throat, and was fearful that it would come back up again. He just stood fast, looking away, ignoring her question. When she said she would go look for help, he was so overwhelmed with gratitude that it brought a painful congestion to his eyes as he tried to refrain from weeping. He could not recall when he felt such benevolence before in his life. Marion was going to try and get help for him.

Thank you, Jesus. He felt an ever-so-slight lifting of his heart, as he watched her, out of the corner of his eye, disappear into the murky darkness.

After a short while, Douglas began to wonder just where Marion had gone to get help. He realized that he was confused. Where was he, anyway? What is this place, this line? The questions formed in his mind, but his attention was diverted when he thought he heard a little sniffling sound beside him. He looked around, but visibility was steadily worsening and he could no longer see the person in front or in back of him in line — he was no longer sure there was even anyone there. The air seemed to have gotten denser, and the little available light was much dimmer. He swung his hand out tentatively, in front and then behind him, but if anyone was still in the line, they had moved farther away.

Douglas stepped out of the line, toward where he thought the sound was coming from. He heard it again — a little sniffle — coming from below him. He looked down. There was a small child, a little girl, perhaps four or five years old. She was looking up at him with large, expectant eyes. A little clear dribble exuded from her nose and she sniffled it back in again. After a second or two, the clear little drip slowly oozed out of her nose once more, coming to rest at the edge of her tiny cupid's bow lip. The child was completely naked.

Douglas stared at her and suddenly began to feel an old familiar sensation. He was getting an erection. But as soon as the pleasurable feeling began to build, an acute piercing pain lanced through his groin, doubling him over. As his erection grew, so did the pain, until it was so excruciating that it was as though a carving knife were being thrust up between his legs. He held himself and screamed, but he could not stop it. The erection kept increasing until the pain was so unbearable he thought he would surely pass out — but he did not. He cried and gasped, dropping to his knees, screaming for the pain to stop. He prayed for his pain to stop. He pleaded with God to make it stop. He prayed for death. He prayed for the devil to put him out of his misery.

Slowly the blood receded and as he became flaccid again, the pain finally abated. He fell over onto the ground, still holding himself, praying that it would never happen again.

Finally, when he was sure the pain was gone, and it wasn't coming back, he got back up. But when he was only halfway up, still on one knee, he found himself staring into the face of the little girl. He looked into her eyes — large and beautiful, clear and perfect, with little delicate eyebrows and lashes; the tiny nose with its little dribble; the perfect butterfly lips; and then he looked down at her young little body. He felt the tingling again, the beginning of the same pleasurable stimulation — and the first spark of pain in his groin. But this time he shut his eyes tightly and wrenched his thoughts away from the girl. He began reciting what he could recall of his Hail Mary's. Thankfully, he did not get another erection, and the pain that started to return subsided.

When he opened his eyes, he looked around, but he did not see the little girl anymore. He decided to put more distance between them and avoid running into her again. He started walking away from the direction of the line, stepping carefully, testing the ground in front of him, since visibility was still very poor. He saw the outline of many rocks and tree roots. He saw the trunks of large, nearly dead trees as he passed them, their crooked and gnarly branches extending up into the murky darkness above, like so many arthritic fingers.

Douglas traveled only a short distance, perhaps thirty feet, before he heard a sound that frightened him to the core. He began trembling with fear, and tears welled up in his eyes and he did not even try to restrain them. He heard the sound again, and dropped down to his knees. He had heard another sniffle. He began to cry, covering his eyes tightly with both hands, not wanting to open them and see the little girl again.

It was only a few minutes later that Douglas could cry no more. He did not want to see the little naked girl again — so as he got back up, he dropped his gaze and shielded his eyes with his hands, like blinders. In that way he could only see the path directly beneath him. He started walking. Shortly, he heard the soft crunching of leaves — small footsteps beside him. Another sniffle.

Now Douglas found himself getting angry. He whipped around to where the little girl was walking next to him, and leaned down into her face.

"WHO ARE YOU?!! STOP FOLLOWING ME!!" he bellowed, grabbing her shoulders and shaking her roughly. But she did not flinch at all; nor change her melancholy expression.

When Douglas stopped shaking her, the little girl spoke. "I'm Colleen, Sir."

Colleen. Colleen O'Gready.

Douglas saw the little girl running out of her house, turning around to wave at her mother, smiling as she approached the Lexus. Douglas opened the door for her. She joined the other two children in the back seat, laughing and giggling together. He drove to his house. He had a cartoon video already going on the big screen plasma television set in the basement playroom. He sat all three children down on beanbag chairs, each having picked the color they liked best, and went upstairs to pour some punch and put some cookies and candies on a tray. Then he reached up to the topmost cupboard and took down the bottle of Gilbey's gin, and poured a shot into each cup of punch. He poured two shots into the little boy's cup. Then he unwrapped three pieces of sourball candy and dropped one into each cup.

When the children were all sufficiently intoxicated, drowsy and confused, he undressed each one, and then himself. He carried Colleen over to the daybed first. She protested and tried to pull away from him, but he covered her mouth with his shoulder, drowning out her screams as he tore into her. As he felt his pleasure building, his heart pounded faster and faster, and that is when he felt the crushing pain in his chest. He started to get up, fearful of what his medical knowledge told him was a probable heart attack. Before he could rise from the bed, the pain exploded in his chest and he lost consciousness, falling back down onto Colleen. His chest covered her face. When he opened his eyes again, he was standing in the line. Now he knew. He was dead. Colleen was, too.

Douglas continued to hold onto the little girl's shoulders, looking into her eyes and watching the little dribble of snot make its way down toward her mouth, sniffled back in, and sliding back out again. A tear welled up in each eye, and slowly spilled over and down her cheeks. Douglas felt a little stab in his own eyes, and then felt the wetness of tears on his own cheeks.

Douglas looked around but did not see anyone to turn to … to help … to find out what he should do … to find out what was going to happen to them. The little girl shivered slightly. Douglas turned his back to her and unfastened the briefs he had fashioned for himself out of Marion's scarf. He took the smaller piece and wrapped it once around his hips, which just barely covered his privates — if he didn't move around too much. He took the larger piece and fashioned it toga-style around the little girl. Then suddenly the fog lifted a little, and the air around him became a little brighter. Now Douglas could make out a path between the trees. A single tiny flower with pink petals grew on a small bush by the path, and he plucked it and handed it to Colleen. Then he took her other little hand in his, and started walking along the path.

They walked for what seemed like several hours, slowly, so that the little girl could keep up easily. Douglas was worried about what would happen if she got tired — he did not want to pick her up and then fall to temptation again. But surprisingly, she never seemed to get tired. She just walked along quietly with him, holding onto his hand, the little pink flower in her other hand.

Douglas thought he saw a light up ahead — but it was still foggy and relatively dim, so he was not sure. As they walked around a bend in the path, though, there was definitely a light coming from somewhere up ahead. The closer they walked, the brighter it got, and Douglas found himself wanting to run toward it. He reached down and wrapped his arm around the little girl's waist, hoisting her up onto his hip, and then breaking into a sprint toward the light source. As he jogged around the bend in the path, the light became very bright, and the air around him cleared completely. It was as though the sun had come out from behind a heavy black storm cloud. He put his hand up to shield his eyes from the brightness, and set the little girl down.

When he took his hand down from his eyes, he saw a beautiful woman standing there. She was youthful and vibrant — perhaps no older than her late teens — but her hair was pure white. It shone like polished porcelain, parted in the middle and pulled back by a lacy ribbon that had bright blue sapphire gems woven through it. She wore a white tunic intricately embroidered around the collar and belt, with threads of brilliant combinations of colors, some of which Douglas could not identify. She held out her hands, with long, youthful, delicate fingers, toward the little girl.

"Come, Colleen!" she uttered in a voice of flute-like sweetness. Colleen ran to her, and was folded into the woman's arms, who lifted her effortlessly, gently hugging and rocking the little girl.

Suddenly Douglas felt a rush of embarrassment as he remembered the scanty loincloth he was wearing that covered him so inadequately. He looked down and was even more shocked at what he saw — he was wearing a rather decent pair of slacks.

Wh-what ... Where the ... ?

"Haggar Classic Fit, thirty-eight-thirty-two, right?" the woman asked, head tilted to the side. "I sent an assistant down to Kohl's ... These were on sale ... I hope they're okay."

Douglas was speechless. Then the woman giggled a little, which sounded like raindrops on crystal, and added, "Sorry — No returns!" She turned and started to walk away — or rather, float away.

"No ... No, WAIT!" said Douglas, when he found his voice.

The woman turned back around, and raised her eyebrows. "Yes?"

"Please ... Can you tell me what ... what's going to happen? Where I'm — "

"All will be revealed to you soon enough," she answered, not waiting for him to finish his question. "At the right time." With that, she turned and once again started to leave.

"No, wait, PLEASE!" Douglas took a few steps toward the woman, and reached out to her. Before he made contact, though, he hesitated, unsure of whether it would be appropriate even to touch her. He gave a little wave of his hand instead.

"I ... uh ... I ... Can I ... uh, may I ..." he stammered.

"Ask my name?" she supplied, somehow knowing what he needed at that moment. "Certainly. I am Agnes."

"Oh ... is that ... uh ... the same Agnes ... the Agnes who ..." Douglas was beside himself with frustration, as he could not recall ever before being so flustered and unable to articulate his thoughts, uncharacteristically lacking confidence in his own recollection of his many years of parochial school studies.

"Yes, yes," answered the woman, "Saint Agnes. That's what they call me. *Down there.*" Then she rolled her eyes and gave another little musical giggle. "So! Any more questions now?"

Douglas just shook his head, unable to take his eyes from the beauty of the woman, and wishing desperately that he could think of something else to say to keep her from leaving. He wracked his brains, but nothing rational emerged. As the woman turned to leave once more, he thought he would try a delaying tactic. He stepped forward and opened his mouth to say that he had one more question — but the woman with the girl in her arms faded from solidity to translucence, finally disappearing into a cloud of sparkling colors. The cloud itself dissipated seconds after that.

Douglas felt a gaping emptiness inside his chest. He hung his head and wrapped his arms around himself, rocking back and forth in his sorrow. When he looked up, he saw that the thick storm clouds that had been blocking out the light before were back. Darkness had descended once again, and the path he had followed seemed to have been swallowed up in it. He felt … frightened … but he didn't know why. He had never been afraid of the dark before.

He started to walk away, in the direction he had been going before, he thought — but soon tripped over a large rock and fell painfully to his knees. That is when he realized that the slacks he had been wearing had disappeared. He once again found himself barely covered in the torn piece of scarf. His knees were raw and bleeding, and the ground had become slimy with a kind of loose muck that stung his open wounds. When he tried to get up, he kept slipping and sinking down, and he realized with horror that he was being sucked into some kind of thick, fluid-filled pit. He called out for help, hoping that someone would hear him. He screamed into the darkness around him, but only heard the echo of his own screams coming back to him. He screamed until his throat was raw and raspy, and he could scream no more.

Douglas looked up when he felt — more than heard or saw — someone standing there. It was a small person — another child? He tried to speak again, but he only slid further into the quicksand-like slime, and the pain from his raw throat started him in a fit of coughing that wracked his body.

"Please!" he finally gasped out between coughs. "Please help me!"

A girl stepped closer. She was a little older than the one he had just left — perhaps nine years old. Her eyes were not melancholy, as Colleen's had been — but instead flashed with the searing anger of a much more mature person.

"You hurt me!" she said, in a little girl's voice laced with a fury of agelessness. "*YOU KILLED ME!!*" She sat down and started to cry; and then she looked so much more childlike. He remembered now.

Her name was Mikayla and her parents had emigrated here from Haiti. They both worked at the church, her mother cleaning and cooking, and her father doing maintenance and groundskeeping. Mikayla was a little older than the children that Dr. Douglas Harrison usually targeted — but her parents were "not the type of people to make trouble," as he put it. He suspected that they were illegal immigrants; that made them much easier to take advantage of — or intimidate — if necessary.

And Dr. Harrison was quite taken with Mikayla. Her brown skin was exotic and enticing to him; and although she was not yet ten years old, she was starting to show a slight budding underneath her dresses. He felt very confident in his plan to bring her home — no need to bring along other children or pretend that he was throwing a party or anything. He could tell her whatever, and she would be easily frightened into submission and silence, he thought.

He was wrong.

Dr. Harrison cruised by Mikayla's school as it was just letting out for the day, and waited until he saw her. He drove up slowly by her as she walked toward her home, and told her that her mother wanted him to take her home. Mikayla was suspicious, and had no hesitation about questioning Dr. Harrison. That irritated him, but he continued to smile and convinced her that she was supposed to come home with him and her parents would call for her later. She knew him from the church, so she agreed to get in the car with him. When they got to his house, he sent her down to the playroom and told her to make herself at home, turn on the TV, play with the video games, or just do whatever she wanted to do. He would bring her some cookies and punch.

Mikayla was very happy to do so, especially when she saw the playroom. There were dolls and toys of all kinds, and a Playstation 3! She sat down in front of it, but wondered whether she should ask before using it. She went over to the Barbie doll collection, and marveled at all the different ones he had, dressed in all kinds of outfits — Capri pants with halter tops, bouffant evening gowns with rhinestones and fancy hairdos, business suits (including briefcase and cellphone accessories), and costumes from many different countries. One Barbie had brown skin and a skirt with many multicolored layers. Mikayla decided she was Haitian, too. She started to dance with it around the room. Then Dr. Harrison came down the stairs. He had a glass of punch and a plate of cookies for her.

The punch tasted funny ... Mikayla did not want to drink it. But Dr. Harrison wanted her to finish it, and when she said no, he started to get angry. Then she said she wanted to go home, now. That's when he told her to take her clothes off. She bolted for the stairs, but the man caught her easily. He pulled her by the hair and dragged/carried her to the daybed. She started to scream, and he put his hand over her mouth. He said he would slash her throat if she screamed, and then he would go to her parents' house and slash their throats. She stopped screaming. She stayed perfectly still. She watched as Dr. Harrison unbuckled his pants and slid them down. That is when she bolted for the stairs again, and this time, with his pants down, he was unable to catch her right away. She made it out the door and down the street. She ran until she was out of breath, and then she slowed down to a walk.

Mikayla was not familiar with this part of town, with its huge houses tucked in behind sentinel hedges of emerald green arborvitae and sculptured juniper trees. She looked through the gated driveways and at the stately mansion-like homes she saw beyond. She was the top student in her elementary class, and she thought if she kept up her studies and went to college, she could live in a house like one of these some day.

Then she heard a car's engine down the street, and turned to look, but did not see anything — not until the Lexus, with its headlights off, got closer and began rapidly accelerating toward her. Mikayla started to run, but the big car was coming directly at her. She looked for an opening in the hedge along the sidewalk, but could not find one. The car smashed into her, pinning her into the hedge. The pain seared through her body for only a second, as a branch pierced her heart, and the life quickly slipped out of her.

Now Mikayla sat next to Dr. Douglas Harrison, weeping softly into her hands, as he was sucked down, slowly, another inch every few minutes, into this vile suffocating pit.

She won't help me ... Why would she? he thought. *I'll die here.*

Then he wondered at the thought of *how he could possibly die when he was already dead??* Suddenly a much more horrifying possibility crossed his mind: *What if I am to remain here, choking and gagging, suffocating in this vile, putrid stinking pit, for — for — FOREVER??!!!*

He started to cry. He wailed loudly, choking and coughing and keening in his grief and terror and pity for himself.

Mikayla stopped crying and looked over at him. He stopped his crying then, too. Mikayla quietly got up and started to walk away.

Resigned to his horrible fate, Douglas just followed her with his gaze. As she walked away from him, he watched the receding smallness of her, and thought of the sadness of her lost future, her lost hopes, her dreams that would never be realized. He said softly, barely mouthing the words, "I'm sorry ... I'm so sorry, Mikayla ... I'm sorry ..."

He did not expect the girl to hear him. He did not expect that at all. So he was surprised when she stopped, turned around, and came back to where he was stuck, now up to his chin, head tilted backward to keep his mouth from sinking in the fetid pit.

"What?" she asked, "What did you say?"

He looked at her now, and the tears flowed freely down his face and mixed with the muck around his chin. "I'm sorry, little girl ... little Mikayla ... I'm sorry I hurt you ... I'm so sorry."

"Oh," she said. "Oh, that's what I thought you said." Then she got up and walked away.

Douglas continued to sink, very slowly, and now the muck was up to his nostrils. He was too terrified to cry any more. He felt completely hopeless. *Now,* he thought, *now ... I abandon all hope.*

Just then he heard the crunching sound of footsteps coming toward him, but he could not move his head to see who it was. Only his forehead down to his nose remained above the muck. If he moved, he would likely sink farther down; and although he was resigned to his fate of being completely submerged in the vile pit, he did not want to bring it on any sooner.

The footsteps came around the side of the pit, and then to the front, and then stopped. Douglas could only see a pair of black shoes and black trousers. The rest of the creature was shrouded in murky darkness.

Chapter 13: Father Bryan

Father Bryan couldn't believe what he saw — could that really be a *face* in the middle of that mud puddle? He crouched down to look more closely. Yes, that's exactly what it was!

Holy Mother of God!

Just then a dazzlingly bright light shone over his shoulder, and a most exquisite woman appeared to him.

"Yes, my child?"

Father Bryan looked around, bowed deeply to the beautiful apparition, and said, "Oh, I'm sorry, Mother ... I did not mean to call you just now ..." He gave a little nervous laugh and added, "Old habits are hard to break, you know?"

"Yes, I do," sighed the beautiful apparition, who had become momentarily more solid, but still hovered slightly above the ground. "I had one myself, once." Then she added, "Well, don't hesitate to call if you really do need me!" and disappeared into a dazzling cloud of scintillating silver light.

Father Bryan recalled his last days in bed in the rectory. There had been calls for him to go into a hospice, but he wanted to die at home, and knew the time was very short. He tried not to take any of the pain medication offered to him, feeling that any suffering he endured was God's will; but the pain grew so great near the end that his doctor finally convinced him it would be no sin to take it.

"You stubborn old fool," said his physician and colleague in the priesthood, Father Doc, as they called him. "Who put these medications on earth to ease our suffering, eh? *You* didn't! *I* didn't! That leaves God! God put them here! How can it be a sin to take them? Have you gone nuts in your old age?"

The older priest had to smile at that, though even that small movement brought on more pain.

"Okay, shoot me!" he said. "I suspect you've wanted to do that for years!"

"You ain't just whistlin' Dixie, you old fool!" answered the younger man, as he pulled the syringe out of his black bag and quickly poked it into the tiny vial of narcotic liquid. He gently rubbed an alcohol pad over a small area on Father Bryan's arm — and felt a pull in his gut as he saw Father Bryan wince with pain even at that slight touch. He inserted the needle, pulled back on the plunger slightly to make sure he was in a muscle and not a blood vessel; then pushed the soothing liquid into the limb. He gently wiped off the area with another alcohol pad, and pulled two band-aids out of his black bag. He held them up for Father Bryan to inspect. "Mickey Mouse or Sponge Bob?"

That was a mistake, because Father Bryan started to laugh and then went into a violent coughing spasm that was excruciatingly painful for him. Father Doc could almost watch the narcotic work, however, because within a few minutes the older man quieted down and was drifting off to sleep.

When he woke up, Father Bryan was standing in some sort of line. The weather was gorgeous, the sun shining brightly in a crystal clear blue sky, and a cool soft breeze occasionally blew a flower petal across the grass. He felt good. He had no pain at all. Father Bryan stretched out his arms to test them, and felt strong and healthy. He wondered for a minute about the Sponge Bob band-aid, though. Then he recalled Father Doc. He closed his eyes and said a prayer of thanks to God, and a blessing for Father Doc for all his help at the end.

"The end" — that sounded so ... so ... *final!* And yet, he never felt better in his life than he did right now! He wondered if he might look around, but thought it best to remain in the line. He must be there for some reason! He craned his neck to the side to look up the line and see what he could see.

Was that ... Yes! Derek McCarthy! He was about thirty places up in the line. Father Bryan had performed last rites on him a couple of months ago ... he was still well enough to work then. He craned his neck to the other side, to look over the line, which was curving off farther up the hill. Oh, my, yes! There was the beautiful Megan Flynn ... the poor darling was hit by a drunken driver and killed at the age of only twenty-five! It did not seem fair, really, although Father Bryan was comforted by the belief that God must have had his reasons. Besides, he reminded himself, "Only the good die young," which was probably why he had lived to be ninety-two! The thought amused him.

Father Bryan was startled by a tap on the shoulder, and whirled around. He felt guilty — perhaps he was not supposed to be looking at others in the line?

Then he saw her.

"Welcome, Bryan," she said, in a voice so lustrous that it seemed to fall around him like a silken robe. Bryan was so stunned by her beauty and luminescence that he could only stand there, frozen with the vision. Her skin was a dark pearl, her eyes large and shaded by long delicate lashes. Her hair cascaded down to her shoulders, a rainbow of golds and silvers, coppers, burgandies, browns and onyx black. A small crown encrusted with diamonds sat atop her head, encircled by a sheen of light. After a few seconds, Bryan came to the reality of who this might be, and he dropped to his knees.

"Are you ... are you ... are you?" He could hardly bring him self to say her name.

"Yes," she responded when it was apparent he might never complete his question. "I am Mary." He started to reach for the hem of her robe, wanting to kiss it, but then quickly drew his hand back, not knowing whether it would be acceptable for him to touch it.

"Go ahead, dear man," she said, reading his very thoughts.

Bryan reached out gingerly and touched the hem of her robe with the tip of one index finger. A rush of pleasure washed over his body, tingling everywhere, down to his toes and up to the very ends of his hair. He took the hem of her robe in both hands and brought it to his lips. The pleasure buzzing through him was even more intense, and he saw rainbows of sparkling colors and lights. He thought he would lose consciousness. He dropped the hem and his head cleared. He looked up. The beautiful woman was smiling at him.

"Come with me," she said, and walked away from the line. Bryan got up from his kneeling posture and followed a few steps behind. She stopped and looked back at him, and he stopped in his tracks. "Walk next to me," she directed. He hesitated only for a second, and then strode up to where she stood. She then hooked her arm through his elbow, and they began to rise.

The feeling was seismic. Father Bryan had experienced some orgasms in his early life (for which he copiously and frequently confessed, not just for the act but for the pleasure he took when he recalled it. He did this so often that his bishop early on told him he heard all that already, and to please move on). But what he experienced now was infinitely more pleasureable.

They flew together over the top of the grassy hill, and Bryan did not know what to look at first — the magnificent landscape beneath him, with flowers and trees so luxuriant and richly colored, magenta mountains in the distance, covered with silvery snow caps — or the ineffable beauty of the woman with whom he flew arm-in-arm.

Soon, he could see a structure up ahead, and that is where the line of people below seemed to be going. As they got closer, the structure loomed larger before them. It looked as though it were made of marble, a pure white marble, with silver and gold veins running through it. Their flight began to slow, and as they alighted at the foot of the building Bryan began to shield his eyes from the brightness of it, but soon realized that he was able to look at it with no discomfort at all. He looked up and saw hundreds of steps leading up to the entrance, with massive columns interspersed at different places along the steps. Some of the columns looked to be made of pure gold, some of the brightest silver, and some of the same white marble as the walls of the building, each with fine, intricate carvings along every inch.

"I want you to meet someone now," said Mary, as they walked up to head of the line, at the bottom of the steps. The people at the front of the line parted for them, with smiles or looks of sheer awe, many bowing or dropping to their knees. As they reached the head of the line, Bryan saw another beautiful creature who seemed to be illuminated by his own inner light.

"Gabriel, this is Bryan. Bryan, Gabriel."

Bryan just stood there, nodding his head, speechless at the overwhelming joy he felt at meeting this divine being.

Gabriel smiled, and looked down at a massive book on a lectern in front of him. He flipped through a few pages, and tiny lights, like fireflies, flickered above the pages as he turned them. When he stopped turning the pages, he ran a thin silver pointer down one side and then the other, reading something for a minute. Then he nodded to Mary.

She looked at Bryan and said, "Let us enter the Hall now." She turned and started to ascend the first steps. Bryan started to follow her, but then looked around and saw all the people in the line who had stepped back to allow them passage.

"Wait ... " he said to Mary, pulling back slightly on her arm that was still hooked in his. Then he felt a sudden rush of embarrassment at having spoken to her like that — where did he come off telling the Mother of God to wait???

But she sensed his concern and stopped climbing the steps. She turned back to him.

"Yes, my son, what is it?"

"What about ... " he gulped loudly, still uncertain about questioning what was happening.

"What about what?" she answered, sensing his anxiety, and patting his hand in a reassuring gesture.

"What about all these people?" he said, with a sweeping gesture of his free arm, encompassing the miles and miles of people waiting in line behind them.

"What about them?" answered Mary, still speaking in her soft musical voice, showing no impatience at his questioning.

"Well ..." said Bryan, clearing his throat and feeling a little more confident now that no chastisement seemed to be forthcoming for his impertinence, "Well, they were here first! Why am *I* going in front of them?"

Mary smiled, and Bryan could see Gabriel next to her, raising his eyebrows in a gesture that he could not quite read — but he seemed to be amused. Or surprised? Annoyed? He could not be sure which it was.

Mary answered, "My dear son, you have lived a life of such goodness — such simple purity, such generosity of your time, willingness to put aside your own needs and desires, such uncompromising sacrifice for the least of all those among you — you are One for whom our Lord does not wish to wait." Then she turned and started up the steps again. But Bryan pulled back on her arm again, feeling a bit bolder now that he had not been chastised — but praised, yet!

"No, I can't!" he said, and then kneeled on the step below Mary, bowing his head deeply, nearly touching the steps. "Forgive me! Please! But I cannot do this! All of those people deserve to keep their place in line — it's only fair!"

Mary bent down and touched his head, and said, "Rise up, my son." Bryan slowly got to his feet, but kept his gaze downcast. He could not help but feel alarmed and ashamed at his brazenness to express opposition toward this Holiest Woman of heaven and earth. He was surprised by her response.

"Understandable," she said, rubbing her chin. He looked up at her now. "Go, my blessed son. Go back to your place in line. We shall see you again — in much less than an eternity."

Bryan bowed to her again, and said, "Thank you ... thank you." Then he turned and quickly skipped down the steps and back along the line of people.

When Father Bryan was out of sight, Mary held out her hand, palm up, to Gabriel. He lightly slapped it and said, "You sure called that one."

Bryan looked ahead to see what direction the line was taking, and whether he might try a shortcut. The line seemed to be snaking around a wooded area, and he wondered if he could not just cut through the woods, and get back to his place a little more quickly. He hesitated, not wanting to end up lost somehow — then thought that was ridiculous! How could he get lost? He was in Heaven! Or somewhere around there. He saw what looked like the beginning of a footpath into the woods, and headed for it.

It wasn't long before Bryan accepted the fact that he was completely lost. The woods had grown dark and misty so quickly that he could no longer even see the path beneath his feet, nor the tops of the trees overhead. He did not know which way to go; and when he decided to backtrack, he had no idea from which direction he had come. He started to kneel down, hoping that he could send up a prayer and Mary might come back and help him. But the ground was slimy and there was a foul-smelling vapor coming up from it that forced him to stand back up. He looked up, closed his eyes, folded his hands together, and prayed.

No one came, and after what seemed like an hour, Bryan decided to start walking again. After all, he thought, he was not the only child they had to look after. He was sure that Mary would come for him in due time. He walked onward slowly, but it wasn't long before he tripped over a large rock, and again over a tree root that was completely hidden by the mist on the ground. He fell to his hands and knees in the muck more than once.

Bryan began to berate himself for questioning the decision not to cut in front of the line and accept his Heavenly Reward when it was offered. He had refused, and ended up in Hell! Then he laughed to himself and decided this punishment was entirely appropriate! But he could not believe that Mary had arranged or even approved of it. Gabriel? Well, he didn't really know him as well. But, no! It was his own idea to return to his place in line, and then foolishly take an unknown "shortcut" through the woods. So no one was responsible for his present plight save himself.

And wasn't that the way it was in life, too? You make your bed and you sleep in it.

But tears welled up in his eyes against all his effort to make the best of the situation. He kept walking, wiping his eyes and his nose on areas of his sleeve that did not have any muck on them; feeling a momentary burst of joy at a glimmer of light he thought he saw through the trees, only to realize, when he got closer, that it was a mirage. That was when he nestled his face into the crook of his arm and allowed himself to cry out loud, which he could not recall doing since he was a little boy. It failed to bring any help, but it made him feel better.

Then he saw it.

At first, Bryan thought for sure it was another mirage — but as he got closer, it became clearer. How could it be? Was he losing his mind now? He walked closer, stepping very carefully. As the mist swirling around his feet blew to the side, he could see now that it was — yes, it was a face! In the middle of a mud puddle! The forehead, eyes and nose were clearly visible, but the mouth was submerged. The eyes were pleading!

Bryan looked around, and then he spotted, lying right beside him, a large, sturdy tree branch. It was smooth, thick and very solid-looking, about six feet long.

"Don't worry, my son!" he said to the face. "Just grab onto this!" He wondered at that point whether there was any more to the person —

did he even have arms? Well, he would find out. He slowly, cautiously slid the branch into the pit, trying to make sure that he did not injure the man by pushing it too forcefully. As he disturbed the muck, a strong fetid odor rose off of it, and he felt a wave of nausea. But he could not abandon the man — or whoever or whatever it was.

Finally, Bryan felt a slight tug on the branch, as though the man had grabbed onto it. He leaned back, pulling slowly, so as not to pull the branch out of the man's grip, and backed up one step at a time. Yes! The man was coming out! He had to stop several times, as it took great strength to pull against the resistance of the thick mud, and the stench was overwhelming at times, sapping his strength. He had hoped the man would speak to him, once his head was free of the pit — and it seemed that the man had tried to speak — but bilge poured from his mouth when he opened it, and he could only make a sickening, gurgling sound.

Slowly, painstakingly, with great effort, Bryan managed to pull the man free of the pit, who then laid down on the ground next to the pit, gasping for breath. Finally, he was able to get up to his knees, and shakily to his feet. The man tried to speak again, but it was useless. He extended his hand to Bryan, but then pulled it back when he realized he was still covered with slime from the pit. But Bryan reached over and took his hand anyway, grasping it tightly. He heard the man start to sob, and he pulled him close and hugged him, suppressing the need to gag from the overpowering stench.

A flicker of light came through the trees from above, getting brighter and brighter. Both men turned to look, and Bryan wondered with a depressing feeling whether that was just another mirage. But then he saw Mary's luminescent form descending to the ground. She reached out with both hands and placed them on Dr. Douglas Harrison's head. The muck and slime covering him from head to toe began to thin out, as though a light rain were falling on him alone; and within a few seconds, all of the soil was gone — and so was the stench that had hung in the air.

Bryan looked at the man whom he now recognized from his church, and was stunned. "D-Dr. H-Harrison? Douglas?? Is that *you*???"

"Yes, Father Bryan," he answered, tentatively, unsure whether he would be able to speak at all. But his voice came out clearly. "And I don't know how to thank you for helping me." He started to tremble, looking back and forth at Mary and the priest. Large tears rolled down his cheeks.

Bryan looked at Douglas, and then again at Mary, who was standing quietly off to the side.

"I don't understand!" he said, looking back at Douglas. "You passed away ... You died of a heart attack, wasn't it?.. Years ... no, *decades* before I came here!!" Bryan held his hands out in a gesture of complete bewilderment.

Mary reached out and touched him gently on the arm, and said, "*Time* ... Well, my son, *time* is not the same here ... It does not work the same way *here*." Then she added, "You will see ... eventually."

Douglas grasped Bryan's other arm, then, and looked pleadingly into his eyes. "Father Bryan? Father, would you take my confession now? Is it too late?"

Bryan looked over at Mary, who took a small step backward and nodded her head.

"Yes, my son ... Go ahead."

Douglas grasped Bryan's hands and fell to his knees. He proceeded to describe a litany of sinful acts nothing like Father Bryan had ever heard before in his confessional booth, even into his tenth decade. He recalled his own shock at learning of the "good doctor's" pedophilic activities when he was found dead in his basement playroom, and the tragedy of the children; little Mikayla's torn clothing found in his garage; and his own feeling of failure as a priest — failing to recognize what was going on, failing to protect the most vulnerable in his flock — and his thwarted effort to resign from the priesthood. He recalled the feeling of salvation that followed, and his desire to live as generously and unselfishly, as purely and simply, and as charitably as he possibly could. He felt in a strange, distorted way, *grateful* to Dr. Douglas Harrison for presenting that turning point in his life.

All of these thoughts ran through his mind as Dr. Harrison continued his extensive and shocking recitation of evil deeds, the magnitude of which was beyond anything Father Bryan could have imagined. So many children — and not just children, but women of all ages, who came to him for medical care and ended up humiliated and abused, even sterilized without their knowledge.

"*Ego te absolvo a peccatis tuis in nomine Patris et Filii et Spiritus Sancti,*" Father Bryan recited, when the doctor finally finished his confession. Conferring forgiveness was his duty ... but then he looked over at Mary, still standing placidly to the side, seemingly unaffected by the litany of evil acts she must have heard, too. He hoped she would say something now, because he had no idea what possible Penance he could offer this man for salvation. Ten million Hail Mary's? Ten billion? The pathetic soul had already spent grueling days, weeks — how long, he did not know — almost completely buried in a noxious putrescence. Was that not Penance enough?

"It was a start," said Mary, answering Bryan's question before he asked it out loud.

As she finished speaking, a soft pink light glimmered through the trees beside them. It shone brighter and then turned yellow and then to a flame-orange spotlight. A form began to emerge under the spotlight, and Bryan suddenly felt anxious ... frightened. He had a sudden urge to step backward, away from it.

Dr. Harrison, on the other hand, felt somehow drawn to it, attracted ... like rubber-neckers passing a highway accident ... and stepped forward to get a closer look.

A huge man with gleaming bronze skin, satiny black hair slicked back to his collar, dressed in a red paisley silk shirt and strawberry colored corduroy pants, with a huge golden belt that had an engraving of his own countenance on the buckle, stepped forward. The firey red spotlight moved with him. He wore shiny red calfskin Faro Gancini loafers. Douglas and Bryan could only gape at this vision.

"Hello, Lou," said Mary, with a somewhat enigmatic smile.

Lucifer bowed slightly, but kept his eyes on Mary, as he reached out to kiss her hand. She discreetly drew it back, however, wiggling her fingers, before he could touch it. Then, turning to look at Douglas and Bryan, she said, "Gentlemen, meet my Esteemed Colleague."

Douglas immediately reached out to shake hands, but Bryan felt a sense of fear and revulsion that held him back. Then he thought perhaps he *should* shake hands, and not be rude — but he did not get a chance to do so.

As soon as Dr. Harrison clasped Lucifer's hand, a bolt of blazing orange-red lightning crashed down through the two of them; the ground opened up, emitting a brilliant ruby red glow, and both the doctor and the devil dropped into the gaping maw. The ground closed up and it was as though no one had ever been standing in that spot!

Father Bryan was both dumbfounded and horrified. He looked over at Mary.

"Not to worry, my son. My colleague will handle the Penance." She smiled and held out her hand to Bryan. He took it, gratefully once more, feeling a bit faint, and allowed her to lift him softly up above the trees and the mist.

The sun shone brightly above as soon as they cleared the treetops, and they flew in silence for awhile. Finally, Bryan spotted the line of people again, coming up from over a hill and down through the lush green valley. They dropped to a lower altitude, and as the individuals in the line began to be more clearly visible, Bryan thought he saw a familiar face.

"Why, there's Mrs. Bennington!" he said, excitedly, to his Hostess. "Carrie Barley Bennington! I married her to both of her husbands!" He looked over at Mary and added, "Can you drop me off here?"

They slowly, gently descended to the ground, right next to the line of people — but no one in the line seemed to notice them.

"Carrie?" Bryan said to the plump little woman in the pink dress, "Mrs. Bennington?" But she did not seem to hear him at all. He tapped her lightly on the shoulder, but she did not respond.

"My son," said Mary, and he turned to look at her, "You really need to come with me now."

"But you said ... You agreed ... I could go back to my place in line!" Then he looked over at Mrs. Bennington, and said, "Why doesn't she answer me?"

"You wanted to get back in line, yes, my son — but you did not succeed — and there was a reason for that."

"Wh-what do you mean?" asked Bryan. "A reason that I got lost? I was just looking for a shortcut, you know." He felt a little miffed that he was — well somehow being blamed, or accused of being remiss in some manner for losing his way.

"Yes, we know that. You were not to blame. The fact is, you were drawn into the woods because someone needed you to be there."

Bryan hung his head. It all made sense now. He was sent to help Dr. Harrison out of his desperate predicament. The pathetic man needed to be found by someone he could trust, someone to whom he could confess and unburden his soul. Well, he helped him all right — right into the arms of the Devil himself!

Perceiving his thoughts again, Mary said, "I told you not to worry, my son. God's love encompasses all; His mercy is boundless."

"Yes, but that was *not* God!" he retorted, wondering why she could not see the problem.

"No," Mary agreed, "He is ... ah ... an Employee, though. Sort of." Then she added, "Do you think I would tell you not to worry if things were not as they should be?"

Bryan hung his head in shame. Mary gently cupped his chin in her hand and lifted it up. "You should come with us now, my son," she said. "Gabriel and I need you."

Bryan was almost too stunned to answer. "Need ... *me?* You and Gabriel? *Need me?*"

Mary sighed. "Yes, my dear ... We need an extra pair of hands to help us with our work."

"Yes, I can see that," said Bryan, "But *me?* There are so many bishops and cardinals and…"

"Yes, yes, there certainly are," she responded, "They're all over the place. But none here now can come within eons of your purity and goodness ... It's no contest."

Bryan bowed his head. He was speechless. He was also defeated. He would give up trying to get back into the line. He was filled with a joy so keen that he could hardly bear it. He hooked his arm in Mary's, and rose upward with her, as his heart rose upward in joy.

Chapter 14: Carrie

Carrie stood in the seemingly endless line, and wondered if it were going to rain, or if the sun would stay out. It was fairly nice out, but there were storm clouds on the horizon. She did not know how long she had been standing in line, but it seemed like forever already. She did not see anyone she knew, and when she tried to talk to the person in front of or behind her, it was apparent that they were not interested in engaging in conversation. Frankly, it bordered on rudeness, and she wondered how they could just stand there and not want to talk.

The storm clouds had been gathering for as long as she had been standing there. The sun shone through them from time to time, but then was blocked by the rolling clouds again, sending large cold shadows sliding over the land. Carrie wondered whether she would be able to find some shelter if it started to rain. No one else in the line seemed concerned, though.

Finally, her patience gave out. She stepped out of the line a few paces, and surveyed the rest of it as far as she could see in either direction, trying to see anyone she might know, or at least might figure out what they were waiting for. Or how long they would expect to wait. Or where they would go if it started to rain.

Who was that? Could it possibly be … No!! Up ahead, perhaps a few dozen people ahead in the line, was … *Jules??* Her first husband?? He was almost turned the other way, but she recognized his stature, his haircut, the way he swayed a little and hung his hands in his pockets when standing for awhile. Carrie started to walk in his direction, faster and faster, to get a better look.

Yes! She was sure of it now! It was definitely Jules!! *Oh, happy day!* She could not believe her eyes. She started to run toward him, but got winded rather quickly, and slowed her pace back down.

When she got up to him, she threw her arms around him and cried, "Jules! Jules! It's so wonderful to see you again!!"

The man turned around to look at Carrie. He had open, weeping sores all over his face. He raised his hands to return Carrie's embrace, but she backed away in revulsion. She knew that Jules had died of AIDS — but she did not remember him looking like *this!*

Carrie had not gone to see him at all during those last painful months in the hospice. She said she could not visit because she was worried about getting infected. Besides, she had so much work to do for the church, she had little time for anything else. But she called on the telephone nearly every day — at first. Jules had said that he understood and agreed that she should not come to visit; and that he greatly appreciated her telephone calls. After the first few weeks, though, the phone calls diminished in frequency; and in the two months before he died she had not spoken to him at all.

Seeing him face-to-face now, as horrible as he looked, Carrie was glad that she had not visited him. It was the right decision, she realized, in not wanting to see him like this, and heaven forbid, ending up like this herself.

Carrie and Jules had married after he dropped out of the seminary, and they had five children in the first six years of their marriage. Although Carrie had a strong, almost insatiable libido before they were married, it diminished following all of her childbirths until she found the very idea repugnant. She decided to become celibate, and insisted that Jules should, too, for the sake of the church.

Carrie felt that celibacy would insure a special place in Heaven for them both, somewhere around where the saints resided — although she was not so presumptuous as to think they would reside exactly in the same palace with them — but close. Carrie believed that for all her work and devotion to the church during her lifetime, she would be entitled to something just beneath the saints' accommodations — a slightly lesser level of glory and luxury — but glorious and luxurious still! And her husband Jules would be entitled to come along with her.

Jules was not at all happy about the idea of celibacy. Although he was on course to be a priest when he first met Carrie at a church picnic, her aggressive sexuality put an end to that — right in back of the church on the very first day they met. Jules had occasional regrets and guilt feelings for failing in his goal to become a priest — but he was also thrilled at being able to partake in the joy of sexuality. But through Carrie's pregnancies, her increasing discomfort and pushing him away more and more consistently, there was eventually no physical relationship between them at all.

Jules felt bad for Carrie, and tried to be understanding — but eventually he gave in to his basal yearnings. He slipped out when he could, to places lit by buzzing neon lights in rough neighborhoods where he could have his needs met with anonymity.

In spite of his efforts to be extremely careful at first, Jules became more and more depressed and guilt-ridden by his inability to conquer his physical longings. He became careless, subconsciously allowing the environment to exact its retribution, and he contracted the AIDS virus. Shame and fear kept him from getting the medical help that may have prolonged his health and life. He died alone in the hospice.

When Carrie met Christopher Bennington and married him a few months after Jules' death, she indulged his sexual desires with well-rehearsed enthusiasm. She felt that was necessary to secure her future, and that Jesus would surely understand why she had to set her personal vow of celibacy aside. For awhile, anyway. Besides, she thought, it was just a personal choice — it wasn't like she took any formal vows to become a nun or anything. So it was not difficult to feel justified about it, and not guilty.

When Christopher was elected to a state congressional office, he was required to travel frequently and spend much of his time in the state capital. Carrie was relieved to be free of her "wifely duty" and have her time all to herself, as well as the great financial comfort of Christopher's considerable income. She felt it was her earned reward, since she had struggled to make ends meet on Jules' meager paycheck working in the furniture factory all those years. She felt that she had truly been a martyr in those days.

When she did go on trips with her new husband, they were treated like royalty! How she loved those junkets to faraway places that she had never heard of! She could hardly wait to get home and show off all of her new exotic finery — clothing, bed linens, jewelry, tablecloths, silverware — to her church ladies' group. How they gawked and fawned over her fabulous new possessions! That last trip, that was ...

Wait ... What happened? Carrie thought. Her abdomen hurt. She had the most horrible cramping pain. They were on the airplane. *What happened?* They were flying back from — where was that? Indonesia? Singapore? Someplace like that — she had purchased a beautiful silver clock with rubies embedded in each of the numerals — she was going to put it over the mantle piece. Whatever happened to that clock? Her belly really started to hurt ... Now she remembered the drilling, tearing pain she felt, like a sword going straight through from her belly to her back ... It became so severe, so quickly, she felt as if she were being sliced open ... Then it exploded in a shower of pain so exquisite that she saw stars, and then they faded to blackness, and then the pain was gone, and then ... and then ...

Carrie was standing in this line. *I must be ... I can't be! ... How can I be dead? There's so much more I want to do, to see, to buy!!*

Before Carrie could really absorb the idea, there was a stirring in the line. People were craning their necks to see something ... someone coming. Carrie stepped to the side so that she could see past the people in front of her who were leaning out to the side, each one trying to see past the one in front of him.

A smallish man was walking along the line towards them. He was dressed in a plain, inexpensive looking brown suit; a light blue shirt with a button-down collar, and a blue bow-tie with gold polka dots. The polka dots were different sizes. He had a fringe of springy gray curls popping out from beneath a brown fedora; and the hat band around the brim exactly matched his bow-tie, blue with gold polka dots. A pair of pince-nez spectacles were situated at the end of his nose. He carried a small, palm-sized brown leather case, open to reveal a stack of white 3x5 note cards. On the top card there was a numbered list of some sort, in neat, tiny handwriting.

The man stopped a few steps before getting to Carrie. "Barley?" he said, and looked around at the people in line.

Carrie eagerly stepped forward, elbowing her way past several people in the line who were standing between her and the little man. She thought he must not have known that she took her second husband's name, "Bennington."

"Here!" she heard someone say in a scratchy voice, followed by coughing. Carrie was mortified to see Jules stepping out of the line toward the man. She quickened her pace and reached the man, stepping between him and Jules.

"*Here*, Mister! *I'm* Carrie Barley! Mrs. Carrie Barley Bennington!"

The little man looked up at her and adjusted his pince-nez on the end of his nose. Then he looked back down at his little note card and back up at Carrie.

"Uh, no, I don't think so," he said. "I am looking for a gentleman — Jules Michael Barley." Then he leaned to the side so that he could see Jules, who was standing behind Carrie. "Your name, Sir?"

"Jules Michael Barley," he responded, stepping up next to Carrie, and starting to cough again. Carrie quickly moved several steps away when she saw the fearsome lesions on Jules' skin again.

"Yes, Mr. Barley, I believe you are the individual whom I am seeking," said the little man, as he took a small pen from its band in the center of the note case and carefully drew a line through a name on the note card. "Come with me, please, Sir."

Jules waited for the man to take a step forward so that he could fall in behind and follow him — he was still coughing — but the man did not move before Jules. Instead, after he put the little pen back into the notebook, and slipped the notebook into his inside coat pocket, he turned to face Jules. Then he placed one hand on each side of Jules' head, as though he were measuring him for a hat.

All of the people standing in line around them gasped in unison, drawing in their collective breaths, as they watched what happened next:

Jules' lesions began to heal and diminish in size, and then they disappeared altogether.

Jules stopped coughing and stood up straight. His appearance changed before their very eyes. In the space of a moment, he was back to the tall, strong, healthy and robust man that he was before he fell ill.

Carrie was flabbergasted by the sight of her husband looking as handsome and youthful as the day they first met. She smoothed out her skirt and patted her hair, and walked quickly back toward the pair.

But they were already leaving. The two men slowly rose upward together, as the man in the brown suit held Jules' arm in his. They floated upward, swaying gently as they ascended higher and higher. Their smooth climb broke only once, when the little man tugged Jules backward to avoid colliding with a small flock of white doves crossing their flight path. Soon they were out of sight.

"Well," said Carrie, looking around at the other people who had witnessed this, "Wherever they are going, that is probably not where *we* would want to go!" Several others nodded their heads; some did not respond. All fell back into their places in the line.

Hours passed, and then days went by. Darkness fell, and the sun came out, and darkness fell again, and then again and again, until Carrie lost count of how many days or weeks she had been standing in line. Progress was so slow that it seemed non-existent most of the time. Estimating the distance between trees that grew nearby, she thought they were moving forward somewhat; but then occasionally she realized she had only been looking at the same tree again.

Strangely enough, she did not feel tired. There was no pain in her legs or back, as she expected there would be if she stood in that line for so long. Nor did anyone seem to be complaining. But then again, no one really spoke to one another, and Carrie could not tell how anyone else felt about being in the line.

When she felt herself getting frustrated, she pictured Jules again, and envisioned him in torment, as would be the fate of anyone who contracted that terrible illness. Just contracting AIDS was a sign that God was unhappy with him, she thought. It was understandable that the weird little man who picked him up would clear up Jules' skin. Why, the devil himself would not want someone in such terrible shape to sully his lair! Carrie was glad she was not picked to go with him. And then she was more comfortable standing in this line. At least it was better than whatever Jules' fate was!

Eventually, her body and her spirit began to droop. She looked over at a succulent fruit tree just down the hill from her. She had only moved a few feet in at least three days and nights already, and although she had not felt any hunger at all — strangely like the lack of any pain from standing for so long — the fruit looked so delicious she could feel her mouth watering for it. She was sure she could walk down the hill and back up again in only ten or fifteen minutes — but she worried about losing her place in line.

No one was very friendly here, it seemed. She tried to strike up a conversation with the person in front of her and in back; and although they were polite enough, they simply would not engage in any meaningful conversation with her. They would listen for awhile, and nod their heads, or shrug their shoulders — perhaps answer with a word or two — then eventually just turn back to their own thoughts. She could not understand why they would not be eager to talk with someone — especially someone like herself, since people always told her what a good conversationalist she was.

Weeks passed. Months. The line was painfully slow, but definitely edging closer to the top of the hill. Every day Carrie would crane her neck, this way and that, trying to see what might be up ahead. Every few weeks she saw the little man in the brown suit and fedora come and go with another person he plucked from the line, somewhere ahead of her or behind her. Sometimes she felt jealous, wishing he would come and get her so that she could just get out of this line already. But a couple of times, when she recognized a man or woman she had known in life, it reaffirmed her feeling that she did not want to be picked to go with him. If she had any doubts about where Jules would be going, she had no doubts about the others she knew.

One man she knew from church was a homosexual — of that she felt certain. He never married, just lived by himself in a house left to him after his mother died. And he had this feminine way of gesturing with his hands when he talked. Everyone in church knew he was perverted that way. He came to church every Sunday, and all of her friends agreed that he sullied the place with his presence. They would stop talking when he came by, and give him icy stares, but he just did not seem to understand how his lifestyle — as they were sure it was — defiled God's house. Often in the sisterhood groups they discussed him, and they all wished he would just stay away from the church, but no one had the nerve to step forward and confront him. Well, not *all* of the sisterhood expressed those feelings — but the important ones did. The others didn't say anything. They shared their concerns with Father Bryan, but he just came back with all these platitudes about being "tolerant" and "inclusive."

Carrie had hoped that Jules would be willing to tell the man how the congregation felt about his presence there; but Jules actually *defended* him! He said the same thing Father Bryan did, that everyone is welcome in church! Well, Jules was never able to think for himself. And obviously *that* was exactly why both he and the homosexual man were headed to the *same place* now!

Carrie also saw the little man in the brown suit flying off with a woman who had been in the line somewhere far behind Carrie. She knew her, too — she was some kind of a loose woman who dressed like a prostitute! She came to church every Sunday wearing short skirts and high heels, with huge earrings hanging down to her chin. And the eye makeup — oh, really! — and that glossy lipstick like they wore on TV. Carrie was sure that the woman was wearing false eyelashes, too. But worse than that was the fact that she lived by herself with her illegitimate daughter. What kind of upbringing could she give the child? Did she think she was a movie star or something, having a child out of wedlock, and going to church as though there was nothing wrong with that? Disgraceful!

But the biggest shock of all came when Carrie saw the man in the brown suit and fedora drop down to the line some distance behind her, and rise up with ... with ... could it really be?? ... *Christopher??* Carrie simply could not believe her eyes! Christopher Bennington, her second husband, was ... well, she was so sure that he was a good and decent man — apparently he was not! So, he would be going where Jules, and the homosexual man, and the trampy woman, and ... and only the devil knew who else ... would be going. Well, good riddance!

Time dragged on. Day followed endless day, night after endless night. Carrie fanned herself with her hat and dabbed at her neck with the handkerchief she always kept tucked in her bodice. Even though it was hot, the storm clouds always seemed not to be far away, rolling in and out, sometimes turning black as night, but never quite reaching the threatened cloudburst stage they seemed to portend. At night a cold wind would blow in with no warning, and Carrie would hug herself, trying to keep warm, and turn her face away from the dry leaves and other debris that blew her way.

One morning, the sun came up, after a particularly bad night. It was sunny and bright, and the temperature just perfect, even though the night had been terrible. It had been freezing cold, and the wind had whipped dirt up into little whirling dervishes that stung Carrie's face. No matter which way she turned, it would smack her in the face, the eyes, the mouth, and on her bare arms and legs below her skirt. But now the sun came up, and Carrie was thrilled beyond description when she saw the sparkling marble building with gorgeous columns, rising up just beyond the next hilltop.

Heaven! Carrie thought, *Heaven! Dear Jesus, thank you! I should see you any minute now, shan't I!*

Several more days and nights later, Carrie did indeed reach the front of the line. There she saw Gabriel, behind his lectern, with his large golden book in front of him. She could not tell if the sun was shining behind him, or if the light she saw actually radiated from him; but she curtsied deeply and bowed her head. Gabriel looked over the lectern, and tapped on the edge of it with a small shining silver pointer. It had a tiny hand carved at the tip of it, the index finger pointing upward.

"Up, up, my dear," he said, looking over the lectern to see Carrie. "There is no need to bow! We're all rather informal here."

Carrie stood up slowly, speechless, smoothing out her skirt and patting her hair, and then folding her hands together into a prayerful arch.

"Am I ... Am I ... ?"

Gabriel raised his eyebrows, and waited patiently for Carrie to ask what he already knew she was going to ask.

"Am I ... g-going to s-see Jesus now?"

Well, he was still occasionally wrong. He thought she was going to ask if she were dead. Anyway, he reminded himself, that is why it is always best to wait for the question to be articulated before answering.

"Oh, in due time, my dear Carrie! In due time," Gabriel chuckled, shaking his head a little at his own near error, and looking down at the large gilt-edged book in front of him. He turned a few pages, then stopped and ran the silver pointer down the page. When it stopped, a little cloud of sparks rose up from the page.

"There you are!" he said, with another little chuckle. He looked up at Carrie and set the pointer down. He stepped around the lectern and took Carrie's arm. Carrie's knees began to buckle at the tremendous warmth and energy radiating from this wonderful being. He was pointing to an area a few hundred yards away, where some people were standing and talking, and some were sitting on the steps that led up into the magnificent building. Gabriel started walking toward them, still holding Carrie by the arm.

When they came closer, within a few hundred feet, Carrie recognized the little man in the brown suit and the brown fedora hat. She stopped walking and tugged back on Gabriel's sleeve.

"W-wait ... Who is *that?* Why is *he* ... "

But before she could ask her next question, she recognized others in the group. Jules was there, youthful, tanned and healthy! And Christopher! And the gay man, and the trampy woman from church —

all of whom had been flown away by the man in the brown suit and polka dot tie and fedora!

Carrie also spotted in the group a couple of others whom she had known before — the ratty little black man with one leg who always sat begging on the street downtown, getting in everyone's way; and ... *No! Could it be?* Maria, her old housekeeper! She had cleaned and cooked and helped take care of Carrie's five children while they were growing up. Of course, Carrie knew Maria was an illegal immigrant, so she didn't need to pay her minimum wage; and of course she didn't pay any employee taxes — she would just be giving away Maria's illegal status. But that was the way it worked, if you wanted the opportunity to work in this country, she thought. As soon as the children were old enough that Carrie didn't need help with them anymore, she fired Maria. After all, it was a crime for her to have snuck into this country in the first place, so she should have been glad that Carrie hired her at all!

Everyone in the group was dressed in glistening silver robes with beautifully embroidered sashes. They all looked so *healthy* and ... and ... *so happy!* Even the black beggar was — *whole!* He was no longer missing a leg, but was standing on two strong legs, tall and robust! Surely these people did not realize that they were destined for ... well, *not* for Heaven! They *couldn't* be — not with their lifestyles!

Gabriel had stopped when Carrie hesitated to go on, and said, "Come, dear, there is nothing to be afraid of." His voice was so sweet and rich and soothing, Carrie knew he would never leave her with this group of misfits. He would be taking her past them to somewhere else.

But he did not. He stopped right in front of the little man in the brown suit. Carrie kept walking, though, trying not to look at anyone in the group. She tugged on Gabriel's sleeve to keep walking with her. He held her arm fast, though, and she could not budge him to go any farther.

"I would like to introduce you to someone," he said, when Carrie finally stopped trying to pull away, and looked up at him. He stood in front of the little man in the brown suit and fedora. "Rabbi Moshe Mendelson, meet Mrs. Carrie Barley Bennington."

"R-rabbi?" She looked up at Gabriel, confused, "You want me to meet a *rabbi*?" And, dropping her voice to a whisper, *"Aren't they Jewish?"*

The little rabbi smiled. Was the sun shining behind him, too? Or was there a soft radiance coming *from* him, just as there was from Gabriel?

No, Carrie decided — *it must be a reflection off of Gabriel!*

"Yes, my dear," said the rabbi, with a slight bow to Carrie, "Forgive me for not taking my hat off or shaking your hand ... Tradition, you know ... "

Carrie was aghast, unsure why Gabriel introduced her to this man. She was at a loss for words — but both Gabriel and the rabbi seemed to raise their eyebrows, in expectation that she would say something.

"Rab- Rabbi, did you say?" she stammered, "Mendel- What?"

"Mendelson," He repeated, bowing again slightly, and then straightening up. "Moshe Mendelson! But you can call me Moe!"

Carrie curtsied slightly, and then turned back to Gabriel. But he was gone.

"Carrie!" called someone from the group, and she saw Christopher walking toward her, silver robes flowing out behind him. "It's so good to see you again!" Carrie smiled, and wanted to embrace him, but the others — the gay man, the tramp from church, the beggar — and now this Jew! She turned to Christopher with a befuddled look.

"Christopher, what are you doing here? You ... We ... don't belong here with these ... people!"

"Oh, yes, we do!" answered Christopher, taking her hands in his and then turning to the Rabbi, "Tell her, Moe!"

"Yes, dear Carrie," he said, "You may come with us. I think you will enjoy ..."

"NO!" said Carrie, stepping backward and pushing Christopher's hands away. "No, *you* may belong here, but *I* do not!" Then, turning to the rabbi, and drawing herself up to her full five feet in height, she said, "*I am a Christian!*"

The rabbi sighed, and pushed his hat back on his head, allowing more little silver curls to spill out, and said, "Yes, we know that, my dear. We are all the same here, though, in a sense, Christians ..."

Carrie looked at him, frowning. She drew in a deep breath to interrupt and set him straight, but he went on, "... and Jews, and Muslims, and some who don't know what they ..."

"Well, *whatever* you are," she interrupted, "it is definitely *not* a Christian!" she sputtered, "And I definitely *do not belong* with the likes of this group!" She turned on her heel and started walking away in the direction from which Gabriel had brought her.

The little rabbi was not going to give up, though. He appeared to drop down in front of Carrie, and she stopped in her tracks. "Please, dear Carrie! Have faith in Gabriel, if not me, will you? He has assigned you to come with us, and I'm sure you will be extremely glad if ..."

"I'm sorry, Rabbi ... Moe ... Whoever or *whatever* you are! Now, please get out of my way!"

The rabbi dropped his eyes downward and nodded slightly. "You do have that choice, my dear. The choice is yours." Then he looked up at her once more. His eyes were so clear and sparklingly blue, his skin so flush and radiant -- for a moment, Carrie wanted very much to go with him.

But it passed. He stepped aside.

Suddenly thunder clapped in the distance, and the sky began to darken. Clouds rolled in, and the sun disappeared completely. An icy wind blew over, and bits of dust and flaking leaves raked across Carrie's face so that she had to shut her eyes tightly. When the wind died down, and she opened her eyes, she immediately recognized, with a sickening feeling in her gut, where she was. She was back in the line — where she had started.

Chapter 15: Christopher

Christopher watched as the little rabbi had flown after Carrie and tried to convince her to come with them. He watched as Carrie rebuffed his efforts; and then she seemed to faint or fall unconscious, her knees buckling under her. The rabbi caught her and gently lifted her up in his arms and flew off with her, over the grassy hilltops, until they disappeared into the blue skies.

Christopher turned to the beautiful young woman next to him and said, "Dana, I'm sorry." His first wife, whom he had loved so fiercely, and who died so young, was standing by his side, and squeezed his hand gently.

"Don't be sorry, Chris!" she said. "I know you wanted to introduce me to Carrie, but maybe I'll get another chance to meet her. Anyway," she added, "I guess it just wasn't her time to be with us."

Jules walked over to them and nodded his head. "I think you are right, Dana — It just wasn't her time yet. She was a good person."

Christopher nodded in agreement, and said, "She did a lot of good work, you know — for the church, especially. But she just needs more time to sort things out, I guess."

Maria walked over to the three, and they parted to make a space for her. "*Señora* Barley was a good woman," she said. "I enjoyed working for her — she was not unkind to me — and for you, *Señor* Barley," she said, turning to Jules. "*Los niños* — I mean, your children — they were *muy agradable* — very sweet."

"They missed you a lot after you left, Maria," said Jules. "You did a wonderful job taking care of them."

"You were *muy amable y generoso*" Maria said, "so kind and generous to me, I am always very appreciate you."

Jules smiled at her still-imperfect English. He remembered how she taught all of their children to speak Spanish — and the kids helped her with her English. He thought the kids definitely got the better deal! But his good feeling faded when he recalled how abruptly Carrie had fired Maria, without a single day's notice, when she decided she didn't need her anymore.

Jules had taken issue with Carrie about it; after all, Maria was sixty-three years old and had worked for them for eighteen years, raising their five children, cooking all of their meals (even keeping track of the special dishes that each liked best), and keeping the house as neat as a pin. But when the youngest turned twelve, and began babysitting for their own neighbor's youngsters, Carrie insisted they let Maria go. Jules tried to avoid arguing with her, as she would continue relentlessly on about it until he agreed; so he acquiesced to her wishes. But then — without Carrie's knowledge — he went to the bank and arranged for them to continue paying Maria's salary plus her health insurance premium until the day she died.

Reading Jules' face and guessing what he was thinking about, Maria said, "*Señora* did what she thought was right, *Señor* Barley — she put *los niños* first, before anyone. She was *una buena mujer* — a good woman!" Then she added, "I wished to thank her for being good to me for so many years — Did I say that right, *sí?* — She took good care of me." A dark shadow seemed to pass over Maria's countenance as she recalled that which she had never spoken about to anyone: the terrible abuse she had experienced at the hands of her previous employer, before going to work for the Barleys. "*Sí* ... The *Señora* was very good to me. *Es muy importante recordar eso, sí?*"

"*Sí,*" replied Jules. "It is important to remember."

"I hope to get chance to tell her thank you," said Maria.

"Maybe one day."

What neither Jules nor Maria knew was that Christopher Bennington had taken over the accounts when he married Carrie after Jules died. The banker handling Jules' account — which he had set up for the sole purpose of seeing to Maria's welfare — had personally contacted Christopher to advise him about it. He knew that Carrie was unaware of the arrangement and would be incensed to find out about it. He also knew of Christopher Bennington's political and business reputation as a very caring and generous individual. Now there was not much money left in the account Jules had set up from which to send the payments. The banker was not entirely surprised when Christopher instructed him to set up a new trust account for Maria using the remaining funds, plus whatever additional funds were needed from his own personal account.

The scene on the street had been utter chaos, with blood and body parts strewn along two city blocks — the kind of sight only seen in the movies (fictional) and on television (actual). A shiny, heavy black car door with the Seal of the President of the United States was the only identifiable article among all the wreckage and carnage. Christopher stood on the side of the road, in front of a delicatessen which served, in the Southern tradition, "bagles" (spelled like that) and "smoked salmon" (not "lox"). Jewish fare was not familiar to very many folks in that part of the country, but the small congregation of Jews who lived in the area knew what to ask for. (Those who kept strictly kosher would order weekly shipments from an online company based in New York.)

Christopher surveyed the situation with no small amount of confusion. He was not sure where he was, but the horrific accident that took place must have occurred only minutes earlier. People were still screaming and running in all directions, and pieces of clothing and other bits of material were still on fire. More puzzling were the people who were standing around near Christopher, or across the street, calmly surveying the situation, seemingly unfazed by it all. He tried to stop one young man who was running toward him, clothing in shreds, blood spattered all over his face and shirt, but the man seemed to run right past him. Christopher had reached out for the man's arm, and thought he had caught hold of it, but the man kept running somehow.

Christopher turned to a woman who was calm, standing near him, looking out around the place. "Miss — Pardon me, Miss?"

The woman looked over at Christopher and opened her mouth to speak, but no words came out. As she turned toward him, though, he saw a huge gash on the side of her neck, with a deep path of blood splashed down the whole side of her body.

"Oh, no! Oh, my God!" he said, moving closer to the woman, and reaching out to keep her from falling. But she did not fall. She looked at him and then turned away, taking a few steps farther down the block. Then she calmly continued to observe the horrifying scene in front of them, which was still unfolding.

Christopher turned around and tried to get his bearings. The window of the delicatessen was completely blown in. Shattered glass covered prepared meats and bowls of coleslaw and potato salad. On the counter lay the upper torso of someone who used to be a whole person, and blood dripped down into the beds of ice making them glimmer like bins of rubies. He began walking down the street, looking into one shattered storefront after another.

In the next block, a *haute couture* shoe store display window was intact. And there, in the window between the two-hundred-dollar Moschino moccasins and the five-hundred-dollar Sigerson Morrison suede wedges was Christopher's reflection. He first noticed that his left arm was missing, and then realized, so was the entire left side of his head. Before he could comprehend what he was seeing, he heard footsteps behind him, and then a tap on the shoulder — the right one, which was still intact. He whirled around and saw Dana.

"Christopher! My darling Christopher! I've been waiting for you!" she said, as she embraced him. A scintillating light came slowly over them, brighter and brighter. Christopher wanted to return Dana's embrace, but feared he could not do so with his missing left arm. He was surprised, then, when he reached around her slender waist and felt both of his arms cross over each other. He backed away and stared at both of his hands and arms, now fully intact, muscular and healthy. He reached up and patted his face and skull, which were also completely whole again. He turned to look in the shoe store window again, but it was no longer there. Anyway, he didn't care — he could hardly believe that he had his beautiful Dana here with him once again!

"My darling, my sweetheart, my Dana! Words can't describe ... How wonderful to see you again!" Tears came to his eyes and trickled down his cheeks, and he could taste their sweet saltiness on Dana's lips as they pressed against his own. Their bodies seemed to blend together, and he felt a rising flush of joy and pleasure beyond description. It was almost as though he was more "alive" now than he had been before the accident.

After what seemed like hours of pleasure, but in reality was only a few seconds, the brilliant light began to fade into a soft, rosy glow around them. Dana took Christopher's hand in hers and stepped lightly toward the source of the glow. Christopher followed.

Soon they were walking over a soft, grassy plain, and in the distance were trees, thick with leaves of emerald green. They came to a set of fences, woven thickly with vines that tumbled over each other, laden with shining bunches of grapes.

The grapes were huge, some as big as walnuts, and Dana and Christopher stopped to eat. The grapes were strangely colored — some were peacock-blue, or turquoise, and so sweet that Christopher could feel the sugar melting on his tongue. Some were deep purple with a pinkish glow, and they had a rich, nutty flavor. A bright orange bunch had a tangy lemony-peppermint taste.

They walked on, hand in hand, tasting the fruits, and as they did, the light around them became brighter, as on a clear, perfect spring morning.

What was that ... a line of people? Over the ridge, in the distance? Christopher was not sure.

"They are waiting," Dana answered, before he asked.

"Waiting?" Christopher looked at Dana, expecting her to say more, but she just kept walking, holding onto his hand, and smiling her enigmatic smile that would have challenged *Mona Lisa*.

"They are waiting to be called," said Dana, just before Christopher drew a breath to ask for more information.

"Oh. I see." He looked over at Dana again, and this time she anticipated his next question without any delay.

"We have been called." She turned away, still holding his hand, and leading him on toward the queue. But when they got there, they did not join it, but rather turned parallel to the line, and continued to walk by.

Some of the people turned to look at them, and Christopher expected that some were bound to be resentful, assuming that he and Dana were line-jumping. However, most did not even seem to notice them at all. Those who did just smiled; others nodded slightly. That was all.

Christopher scanned their faces, looking ahead, trying to see where the line led, but it went on as far as he could see, and then disappeared over a grassy hill in the far distance. There seemed to be a bright light emanating from beyond the hill. He shaded his eyes from the brilliance of it to see if there were anything beyond the hill that he could identify, but finally he gave up. Then he turned toward the back end of the line to see where it started. It seemed to be coming up from an area of thick woods, far in the distance, up from a valley. He could not see where the line began.

Christopher started to turn back to Dana, when suddenly he thought he saw a familiar figure. It was far down the line, toward the wooded area from which the line emerged.

"Wait!" he said, craning his neck to see as far as he could, "I think I see someone I know ... knew!" He looked at Dana. "Can we go down there and take a look?"

"Go," said Dana. "I'll wait for you."

"Come with me!" Christopher pleaded, "I don't ever want to be apart from you again! Not even for a moment. Never!"

Dana smiled. Her love for Christopher radiated toward him like a rippling aura. "I can't go with you — you have to go by yourself. I'll be waiting here for you."

Christopher knew somehow that he could not argue about it — that he *had* to go by himself. He also felt a sense of certainty that he would not be separated from Dana again. He kissed her lightly and turned toward the line as it snaked back toward the woods.

Christopher walked for what seemed like miles. He was not tired, or out of breath — or even hungry! He marveled at how really good he felt — even more energetic and ... *alive* ... than he had in years. But as he walked along the line of people, which seemed to be dipping downward at a slight incline, he wondered if the walk back would be as easy.

Now he was unsure about what he had seen. He could no longer see the person he thought he had recognized from the distance farther up the hill. The weather around him seemed to have changed, too. The sunshine had dimmed, and there were gray clouds gathering in the sky, sending long shadows across the ground, and a slight chilling of the air. The grass was no longer as green, but showed dried and brown spots, and there were rocks and ruts in the ground that he nearly tripped on at times. He looked back once and felt a surge of panic when he did not see Dana anymore, and started to turn around and go back. But the feeling was quickly allayed when he felt a little rush of warmth that calmed him, and he knew somehow that Dana was waiting for him. He did not have to worry.

Finally, after what seemed like hours, the sky had darkened to such a degree that Christopher could no longer make out the features of the people in the line. A cold wind had stirred up, and leaves and bits of dust were blown around him. When the wind turned to an icy cold that whipped at his face, he knew he might as well turn back.

That was when he saw him.

Jared Todd Davis. The Vice President. Christopher's running mate. He was completely naked, shivering, hugging himself with one arm and cupping his other hand over his privates, trying to shield himself and keep warm. His eyes were squeezed tightly shut against the wind, and his face was contorted in a grimace of pain.

"Todd?" said Christopher, coming closer. "Todd? Is that you?"

At the sound of the familiar voice, Todd immediately turned toward him. Christopher was repulsed by what he saw. Todd had no eyes at all. His lids hung over empty black caverns, flapping against the empty orbs like awnings in the wind.

"Todd, oh my God!" Christopher said, taking a step backward, but at the same time, not wanting to insult the man he had worked so closely with, and whom he had considered to be a good friend. "Oh, oh, my God, what happened?"

Todd opened his mouth to speak, and a black cloud with a wretched odor wafted out. He made a sickening, groaning sound -- he had no tongue. Again, Christopher tried not to show his revulsion, but the odor and the horror of what he saw made him feel so nauseated that he was afraid he would start retching.

But he managed to stay composed. He watched as the naked man crouched down on the ground, moving his open hand along over the ground. He was apparently groping for small rocks his vacant eyes could not see. He picked up each one he located, and moved it to a different place on the ground. He kept his other hand on top of the newly moved stones, to keep track of where they were, and moved other stones next to them.

Christopher crouched down next to him and watched, as the little stones began to form letters.

I'm sorry.

"Sorry?" said Christopher, looking back up at Todd. "For what?"

He watched as Todd's shoulders began to tremble — at first he thought it was because of the icy coldness — but then he saw little streams of dark liquid spilling out of the gaping holes that once held Todd's eyes. Then his lips began to tremble, and a terrible piercing wail came forth from the tongueless mouth. He covered his face with his hands, and his body shook violently, as he cried with all the force of the damned.

Christopher felt a gentle tug on his sleeve, and he turned around to see Dana. The warmth in her touch was as comforting as a cup of cocoa by the fireside on a wintry night. She started to lead him away from Todd, away from the line of people.

"Dana, we have to help him!" Christopher said, resisting her effort.

She stopped and looked at him with a sadness and a kindness in her eyes that, without any words, told him the answer. There was nothing they could do to help Todd. Nothing. As he looked back at him, Christopher's heart wrenched in his chest at the pitiful sight of the man's naked vulnerability, pathetically crouching on the ground, shaking from the cold and quietly sobbing. Christopher took off his jacket, walked the few steps back to Todd, draped the jacket over his shoulders and buttoned the top button under his chin.

When he walked back to her, Dana took hold of Christopher's hand and squeezed it gently. She started to lead him away from the line, and this time he did not resist. As they walked back up the hill, the cold wind died down and became a soft breeze; the dark clouds began to part, and glimmers of light formed halos behind them. Before long, they were replaced completely by wisps of white clouds in a sparkling blue sky.

They walked on in the sunshine, passing the fruit trees and grape vines, but this time they did not stop to eat. Although they were walking at a slightly uphill incline for what seemed like many hours, they felt no strain on their legs at all, and no tiredness. After a while, Christopher saw a small grove of trees a short distance away from them, down a gentle slope. Little benches were interspersed between the trees. Some were built around the trees, with intricate designs — gentle scrolls, flower and leaf-shaped details that gave the appearance the benches had grown right out from the trees and were one with them. Dana and Christopher stepped quickly as they went down the slope and sat down on one of the beautifully carved benches. The trees were tall and thick with leaves that swayed in the light breeze, and seemed to emanate a perfume scent that floated in the air around them.

"Hello, there!"

Christopher was startled momentarily to see a man sitting beside them on the bench. He had not been there when they sat down!

Dana turned to the man and said, "This is Christopher."

"Yes, I know," said the man. "He is just as you described — very handsome!"

Christopher blushed, but before he could think of anything to say, Dana turned to him and said, "Chris, I'd like you to meet Rabbi Moshe Mendelson. We call him Moe."

Christopher swallowed hard, and sat up straight. "M-m-m ... uh, Ra-rab ... uh ... " he stammered. Then he cleared his throat and boldly extended his hand. "Hello, Moe! Nice to meet you!"

The little rabbi chuckled. He clasped Christopher's outstretched hand and shook it firmly, with more strength than Christopher would have expected from the little guy.

"Welcome, Son."

He got up off the bench, turned around to face the two of them, and extended his arms out to his sides. He crooked his fingers, signaling that they should get up and come to him, which they did. He wrapped an arm around each of them, and they felt weightless as the three slowly rose up into the bluest of skies.

Chapter 16: Todd

He was standing in some sort of a line. He could not see very well, because it was pitch dark. He could sense the movement of people, someone in front of him and someone in back of him. It was hot, and he started to sweat.

Where the hell am I?

He could hear the sounds of people breathing heavily, coughing, scratching, pissing, farting; and he could smell the pungent odors of them filling up his nostrils.

A memory kept coming back to him, running through his head:

His hand was on a Bible and he was swearing to uphold the Constitution of the United States of America, and blah, blah, blah. He looked over at his best friend, his Chief-of-Staff-to-be and winked. Everything had gone as planned. Bennington had been assassinated by "foreign elements" and now the world would belong to President Jared Todd Davis!

That flashback kept recurring over and over. He could not stop it, seeing it as though he were actually there again, *winking again, winking again, winking again,* over and over, like a scratched CD. He tried to think of something else, but his mind would not obey. He could only see the face of the old man, the Chief Justice of the Supreme Court, holding the Bible under his hand, looking at it so solemnly, so sadly — were those tears in his eyes, or were they just rheumy from old age? Todd remembered thinking how funny that was, and since the old man was not looking at him, he winked at his pal.

He winked at his pal.

He winked at his pal.

He —

Stop it! Stop it! I don't want to think about it any more!

He tried to cry out, but no sound came.

Todd shivered violently, in spite of the oppressive heat, when an icy wind suddenly blew over. His sweat evaporated instantly, causing him to feel freezing. A minute later, the wind died down and he was again sweating as though in an oven. He couldn't see anything at all. Where was he now? What was this line of people all about?

He reached out to tap the person in front of him, to ask him where they were and what this was all about. He felt some kind of bumps on its flesh—open tumors, oozing some substance that burned his fingers—and he quickly withdrew his hand and jumped backward. Then he felt fingernails as sharp as razors on his back, slicing into his skin; and at the same time the creature who owned them emitted a deafening, hollow roar that sounded like a trainload of gravel falling down a well.

Frightened to the depth of his bones, Todd stepped out of the line, and started sprinting quickly away. Almost immediately he slammed into a wall that he could not see, because it was still pitch black. He was now sweating profusely. He reached down to his back pocket, where he always kept a handkerchief — and that's when he realized he had no clothes on.

Todd cupped his hands over his genitals. He felt along the wall, walking sideways, hoping to find a door or an opening, or a corner around which he could keep going. But the wall was intact. He turned back around, thinking he would go back to the line, a different part of the line, and perhaps find a real person, someone to explain things to him. But now he was blocked by another wall, parallel to the first, on the other side of him.

Did he walk into an alleyway? He backtracked along the wall, but after he had retraced his steps much farther, he was certain, than he originally came, the wall behind him was still there. Well, he would just keep walking down this alleyway between the walls until it opened out somewhere. Surely it would. But just as the thought came, he immediately bumped into a third wall, connecting the two.

Now he was scared. Really scared. He put his hands up to the wall and pressed, thinking perhaps he could push his way out. It felt like solid concrete. Hot concrete. He began to sweat profusely, so much so that he could feel it streaming down his face and dripping off his chin onto his chest, and another stream trickling down his back. He was afraid — too afraid to turn around — would there be a fourth wall there? Would he be completely walled in? Was there any way out of this? Where was he?

He rested his forehead against the wall, trying to gain the courage to turn around, nearly paralyzed by the fear of what he would find. He turned slowly. He still saw nothing but blackness. He moved his toe forward an inch, two, three inches, wondering if he would feel another wall.

He did not.

Now he had moved his foot six inches forward, and he shifted his weight forward. Could he take another step forward? He lifted his hands and slowly, painfully, and reached out in front of him.

No wall.

He stepped forward, still keeping his hands out in front of him, waving them slowly, unable to see them in the total darkness. Sweat poured down his chest and freely ran down his back. The ground felt slippery underneath him, and he realized it was wet with his own sweat.

He took another step forward.

Then another and another.

Then he was walking — slowly, but walking.

Forward.

There was no wall.

Todd picked up his pace, stepping quickly now, having no idea where he was going, still unable to see anything at all in the blackness — but at least he was moving — between the two walls.

This corridor must lead somewhere.

As he walked, the heat seemed to die down and soon he felt a breeze blowing, which was a welcome change. His sweat was evaporating. He started walking more quickly, and then sprinting.

That made it infinitely more painful when he ran into the next wall.

He ignored the pain and turned around to run back in the direction he had come, but now he did indeed feel solid concrete completely surrounding him.

Four walls.

He could touch all four with his arms still bent.

Panic strangled him, and he tried to scream, but he was too choked by his own fear; only a low hissing sound came out.

He started to cry, sliding down the wall at his back, but the space began to narrow, and he could not bend his knees.

Now he did something in earnest that he had done in the past only for show — he put his hands together in front of him.

Oh, God, I beg you, help me ... dear Jesus, help me ... I'm so ... scared ... please ... God, Jesus, help me ... I beg you ...

He was sitting on a stage, and the presenter at the lectern was introducing him. "Now please welcome the former President of the United States, Mr. Jared Todd Davis!"

Applause. He stood up and slowly walked over to the lectern, puffing slightly for the exertion. He shook the extended hand of the presenter, who then went back to his own seat behind the lectern. Todd looked out over the audience where several hundred college students sat decked out in robes and mortar boards with tassels ready to flip to the other side as soon as the graduation ceremony was over. In the rows behind them sat their proud parents and siblings; and the grandparents lucky enough to get tickets from those who did not intend to use theirs.

"Ladies and gentlemen," Todd began, clearing his throat. "I am very proud to have been invited to speak to you here at the venerable Lincolnville College of the Arts on this momentous occasion." He cleared his throat again, and went on, "Lincolnville may be a small institution, but none could be more proud of ... of ... "

Todd began to feel warm, and his collar seemed too tight. He tugged at it, but it did not help. Then he felt as though he were suffocating, and his breath became ragged and uneven. He could not get any air. Everything went dark and he collapsed on the stage to loud gasps of shock from the audience.

The next thing he remembered was opening his eyes in his own bed at home. His wife, sister-in-law, oldest son, daughter-in-law, two of his grandchildren, and their baby surrounded his bed. Old Doc Sanders was sitting in a chair next to the bed. Everyone seemed surprised about something.

"He's opened his eyes!" someone said, and his wife started to cry. Then she leaned over and kissed him. Doc Sanders was slipping his stethoscope underneath Todd's pajama top, and asking him a question, which he couldn't quite make out. The stethoscope was so cold, it gave him a chill. A shiver went all through him. He closed his eyes again, and once again everything went dark.

When he regained consciousness again, he became aware of his surroundings. He was in a line of some sort.

Now the dreadful realization dawned on him, and he felt a terror so profound that he could not breathe. He could only think of the words.

"Our Father, who art in heaven, Hallowed be thy Name."

As the words came to him, he felt a subtle lifting of his fear. He realized then that his voice had come back. Now he spoke as loudly as he could, *"Thy kingdom come! Thy will be done! On earth as it is in heaven! Give us this day our daily bread. And forgive us our trespasses ... "*

He stopped suddenly, as he sensed a body nearby. He could feel the breath on his face. He extended his arm out in front of him, and was overjoyed to discover that the wall in front of him was no longer there. Or else, it had moved back some. He took a step forward and bumped into a mammoth living form.

A soft reddish glow began to rise from behind the form, and outlined whatever was there. Todd saw a man's chest in front of him, at his eye level. He looked up, and saw an exquisite creature, now more and more visible as the reddish light brightened to a pink and then a bright orange-yellow. The man was superhuman in size, at least nine feet tall, muscles glistening in the new light that surrounded him — but his face was not visible, still shadowed in darkness. He stood in a casual posture, one leg crossed over the other, one hand on his hip and the other resting against the wall next to them.

"Wh-who-who ... " Todd could not get the words out, he was so overwhelmed with fear of this mighty creature, as well as the relief he felt at no longer being imprisoned by the four walls.

In a voice as powerful and ominous as an oncoming avalanche, rising to a thunderous roar, the answer came: "I think you know, Jared Todd Davis — I think you *know who I am.*"

"Y-y-you-you're ... you're not ... Jesus?"

Lucifer threw his head back and laughed with such fury that blood-red lightning bolts slashed across the sky around them, and a sudden icy wind blew over, chilling Todd to the bone, his teeth chattering so hard that he bit his tongue. Now the lightning lit up the creature's face — and he was stunningly handsome. He had a smooth forehead, perfectly arched brows, beautiful eyes with long lashes, high carved cheekbones, a wide, sensual mouth and solidly square chin split by a deep dimple. His skin was perfect and had a rosy luster.

As abruptly as he started, Lucifer stopped laughing, and the wind died down and the lightning ceased just as quickly as it had begun.

"Poor boy," he said, showing his wide white teeth. "What *shall* we do with you?"

The realization of who the creature was began to dawn on Todd. Tears welled up in his eyes, and he clasped his hands together in front of his face and dropped heavily to his knees.

"Oh, no, please, *please*, I beg you, *please don't take me there!! Please don't send me to ... to ... to ... "*

"To Hell? My dear man, is *that* what you are afraid of?" Lucifer said, softening his voice so that it now came out as smooth as cream.

Todd nodded his head up and down rapidly, little squeaks coming from his throat. He thought he felt fear when he was trapped within the four walls — but that was miniscule compared to what he felt now.

"Don't worry, my dear man!" said Lucifer, in a comforting tone. He reached down and lifted Todd by the elbows, bringing him to his feet as easily as though he were picking up a Raggedy Ann doll. "Don't you worry about going to Hell, my son."

Todd unclasped his hands and looked up at the creature. "D-d-don't worry?" he repeated, "I don't have to worry? I-I-I'm n-n-not going to be sent to H-H-He ... *there?*" He still could not bring himself to say it.

"Hell, no!" said Lucifer, and then chuckled at his own little pun. An icy gust of wind and small branch of lightning whipped into the sky momentarily, punctuating Lucifer's chuckle, and then disappeared.

Tears again welled up in Todd's eyes, only these were tears of relief. He dropped to his knees again, an overwhelming feeling of gratitude compelling him to kiss the cloven hooves of the creature's feet.

But before he could do so, the creature uncurled the scale-layered claw of his index finger and pointed it at Todd. A blue-white bolt hit him squarely in the chest and spread in ripples that felt like red-hot waves of lava. Lucifer drew his finger upward and Todd rose up along with it to a standing position, grimacing in pain so unbearable that he could hardly breathe.

"Don't do that, Jared Todd Davis," Lucifer said, quietly, "I don't like people messing with my feet." He pointed at his hooves and threw a tiny ball of fire down — just like the one he had thrown at Todd, only smaller. A pair of shiny red patent leather Italian Baldinini dress boots appeared over his hooves. Lucifer smiled, turning each foot this way and that as he admired them.

"I-I-I'm s-s-sorry ... *Sir!*" Todd managed, when he could finally catch his breath. Then, fearful that he had heard wrong or misunderstood, he gathered his courage to confirm what he had hoped for. "Did you mean I am really *not* destined to go to *H-H-Hell?*"

Lucifer stopped admiring his new dress boots and looked back at Todd. "That's right, my dear man." As Todd smiled with relief, Lucifer added, "You see, Hell is *too good* for you. *Much* too good."

"Wh-wha-what?" Todd felt a stab of fear again, but then wondered whether the creature was just kidding. After all, he seemed to have something of a sense of humor; or at least he seemed to think he did.

"You heard me, Jared Todd Davis. You are *not good enough* to get into Hell."

Todd was speechless.

"Harvard isn't the only place with admission standards, you know."

Todd just stared at him for a moment, but then forced a weak laugh. What could this be, except a joke?

Lucifer was not laughing. He turned on his heel and signaled with a crooked finger for Todd to follow him. But Todd was frozen. His mind was racing so fast, trying to make sense of all this, that he failed to comprehend the signal to come along. Lucifer turned his head and looked back at Todd, still standing there, mystified and pathetic, naked, holding onto his privates.

Without breaking stride, Lucifer uncurled his claw again and pointed it back over his shoulder. He sent out another beam of powerful electrified energy, which hit Todd squarely in the neck and spread out like a painful choke collar of spikes. He began tugging Todd along behind him. Todd screamed for death to come and relieve him of this torture — all the while knowing that it already had.

They came to a clearing. There were trees which looked petrified in their deadness, with branches splayed out like grasping hands with gnarled fingers. Dried up leaves crackled on the ground underfoot, and thorny bushes, barren of foliage, scraped at Todd's knees as he was half-dragged along, jogging unsuccessfully to try and keep some slack in the painful electrified leash he was on. Finally, Lucifer stopped, and the bolt of energy disappeared. Todd fell backward from the sudden release. His fall was broken by a bench, of ice cold stone, jagged and rocky. It seemed to have materialized from nowhere. As he stumbled down onto the seat, it poked into his bare buttocks, but as he tried to move away from them, other sharp protrusions tore his skin. He started to stand up, but as he saw Lucifer's finger starting to uncurl toward him again, he quickly sat down. The stone bench was preferable to the beam of pain the creature could project. He hugged himself against the cold.

"Now," said Lucifer, exhaling on his claws and polishing them against his chest, "There are some people you need to meet."

Todd just stared at him, once again speechless for fear of saying the wrong thing and having the excruciating beam thrust at him again.

"These are people you should get to know." Then, seeing the look of fear and confusion on Todd's face, he added, "They can't hurt you."

Todd managed to stammer, "Th-they can't? A-a-are you s-s-sure?"

"Just get to know them. Listen to their stories."

"L-listen ... ? I don't understand ... "

"You will, my dear Jared Todd Davis. You will." Lucifer then faded into a beautiful sunset of color, darkening to a fiery red ball, then a flash of brilliant white light that sent spears of pain searing into Todd's eyes — and then the creature was gone.

Todd sat there in the darkness, trying to let his eyes get adjusted to it. Suddenly, he heard a crunching of footsteps on the dried leaves. He felt a shiver go down his spine. A soft greenish glow came toward him through the trees, and soon it took the shape of a man. Only the man was deformed.

As he came closer, Todd could see that the man had only one leg. He walked, though, with the same cadence as though he had two legs — but the other leg was not there, that was the only difference. He had no arms at all. He came closer to Todd, who started to get up from the bench to run, away, anywhere, get away from here. But he could not. The jagged rocks of the cold bench penetrated further into his skin the more he tried to pull away. Finally, he stopped trying to get away.

The triple-amputee stood before him. He was a young man, perhaps not out of his teens. His skin was the color of aged oak.

"I would salute, Mr. President, Sir — but I have no arms."

"I-I-I see ... " Todd felt a little glow of pride at being addressed like that. It had been a long time since he had been addressed as *Mr. President*. How long? He did not know. It seemed like yesterday that he was on stage, addressing the Lincolnville College graduating class. In fact, it was yesterday. But time did not exist for him anymore.

Todd looked at the man — unsure what was supposed to happen now — and then recalled the instructions. He was to *get to know* him. *Okay*, he thought. *I can do that!*

"What is your name, boy?" he asked.

The young man looked down at the bench. "May I sit down, Sir? It's hard standing on one leg like this."

"Why, of course!" said Todd, patting the bench beside him and thinking the fellow would change his mind as soon as he felt the jagged rocks.

"Ah, thank you, Sir," he said as he maneuvered himself around on his one foot and plopped down onto the bench. "That's a relief!"

Todd looked down and saw that the bench under the young man seemed to be different ... It was ... soft ... velvety-looking! He reached over and patted the seat next to the man and, indeed, the bench was plush and cushiony there.

"Stand up, boy!" he barked to the amputee. "I want you to change places with me!"

"Yes, Sir!" said the amputee, struggling to stand up on his one leg without the help of any arms. When he found his balance, Todd slid over to the space just vacated, wincing as the jagged rocks sliced his skin. The amputee maneuvered around him and sat down on the bench where Todd had just been.

"Is that better, Sir?"

Todd realized, with tears of pain and frustration coming to his eyes, that his new seat was even colder, like icy steel, and far more rocky and jagged than it had been in the spot where he sat before. He looked askance at the bench under the amputee, and saw that it had become as soft and velvety looking as this side had been just a moment ago!

"Sir?" the young man asked again. "Is everything all right?"

Todd felt utterly beaten. He sat there, saying nothing, hanging his head, not wanting to speak with this deformed youngster, not giving a damn about him or whatever his story was.

Finally, without looking up, he said, "Go away."

The greenish light gradually faded and dissolved into darkness, as he heard, from far away, *"Yes, Sir, Mr. President. Thank you, Sir."*

The wind blew colder, and Todd started to shiver. He did not know how long he sat there, alone, in the darkness. He was afraid to try and get up from the bench, fearful of the intensified pain he had felt when he tried to get up before.

After what seemed like hours, Todd again heard footsteps crunching on the dead leaves. He looked up to see the same soft greenish glow coming from behind the trees. It came closer, and Todd felt the same icy shiver go down his spine. Soon he saw the features of the same young man walking toward him, somehow doing that on one leg. No arms.

"It's an honor, Mr. President, Sir!" said the young man, "But I still can't salute, Sir!" He stared straight ahead, standing at attention as best he could.

The words he had heard flashed through his head, like a lancing blow: *Get to know them. Listen to their stories.* Todd patted the bench beside him. "Sit down, boy. Tell me about yourself."

"Thank you, Mr. President, Sir!" He flopped down onto the bench, and Todd saw the bench give like a cushion as the young man sat down again, just as before. "It's a real privilege to meet you, Sir!"

"Uh ... Thank you, son." Todd was pleased in spite of himself to see how enthralled the young man was to be in his presence. They both fell silent, just staring at each other for a minute, until Todd spoke: "So ... Tell me about yourself."

"Yes, Sir! I'm Lance Corporal Hunter Sanchez, U.S. Marine Corps, Sir!" Then, after a few seconds of silence, "Uh ... What else would you like to know, Sir?"

"Uh ... Well ... Where are you from?"

"Carver City, Oklahoma ... Sir!"

Todd was uncomfortable with the young man's obvious deformities, but he supposed he should ask about them. After all, how else was he supposed to "get to know" this kid without asking about his obvious amputations? He cleared his throat. "How did you lose your ... uh ... your leg?"

"In Russia, Sir!" answered young Sanchez.

A feeling of devastating despair began tugging at Todd, and he did not want to ask any more questions of this young Marine. But, Sanchez went on without being asked.

"You sent us there, Sir, remember? I fought for my country ... Like you said, Sir. Those Russians attacked us ... they destroyed the Liberty Tower ... and we had to fight for the freedom of America before they took it away from us! Sir! I was proud to serve!"

"*Library* Tower," mumbled Todd, wishing the young man would just go away. "It was the *Library* Tower."

"Yes, Sir!" said Lance Corporal Sanchez, "But we called it the *Liberty* Tower, since that was what we were fighting for, Sir."

"I see ... How clever." Todd hoped the conversation was over, and the man would leave the way he came, but he kept talking.

"I lost my arms there, too. Our helicopter was shot down over the Kamchatka Peninsula. Only two of the ten of us in the chopper survived." Sanchez looked down at his one foot. A single shining tear squeezed out of one eye and trickled down his cheek.

"And you?" asked Todd.

"No, Sir," responded Sanchez, sitting up straighter now. "I'm *here*, Sir."

Todd recoiled from his own stupidity. "Yes, of course. I'm sorry. You have my deepest sympathy." He slowly, cautiously rocked back and forth, trying to find a comfortable — or less painful — position on the bench. He looked over longingly at the cushiony side that Sanchez was sitting on.

What was he supposed to do now? Oh, yes — *"Get to know them."* Now he wondered who "they" were. Perhaps he would meet another one of Sanchez' buddies who was on the helicopter with him?

Sanchez continued to sit, staring down at his foot, and Todd became increasingly impatient. Finally, he decided to keep asking inane questions. "So you're from Oklahoma, eh, Sanchez?"

"Yes, Sir!" he responded, brightening up again. "Carver City. It's not too far from Norman."

"Who's Norman?"

"Norman, Oklahoma, Sir."

"Oh, yes, of course. Norman." Silence descended upon them again. Then, "Sanchez? Let's see — uh, Mexican-American, isn't it?" *Probably an illegal,* Todd thought. *Are they allowed in the military?*

"Oh, no, Sir, we're not from Mexico," the young Marine responded, straightening up as he spoke. "My family emigrated here from Spain in the 1700's. I am descended from one of the first Sanchez families listed in the California census of 1790 — Joaquín and María Sanchez of San Francisco, Sir."

"Oh ... I see," said Todd, somewhat chagrined by the error, but not really interested. "Well, I'm sure you know *my* family tree, do you not?"

"Yes, Sir! Everyone knows that you are a direct descendant of Jefferson Davis."

"*President* Jefferson Davis."

"Oh, sorry, Sir ... *President* Davis ... of the Confederacy, right?"

"Uh ... that's right, son." Todd decided to direct the conversation elsewhere. "So, tell me more about yourself."

"Well, I left my wife back in Oklahoma ... and my son," Sanchez said, and dropped his head down again, an acute sadness in his eyes.

"You ... have a son?"

"Yes," said Sanchez, without looking up, "He was born while I was in Russia. I never saw him."

"Oh. That's terrible. Didn't you get to see a picture of him?"

"No, Sir. He was only two days old when I died. Rosita — that's my wife — she sent a picture, but I died before I got back to the base. I didn't get a chance to check my email." He looked up at Todd, and then back down at the ground. "I only learned about him after I got here."

Todd was silent. He didn't know what to say. Back when he was President, someone would have written a little speech for him — a few thoughtful words, memorable phrases — but he couldn't remember them now. This young Marine was just pathetic.

A glimmer of light shone through the barren trees surrounding Todd and Lance Corporal Sanchez, and both looked up. The light became brighter — first a soft blue glow, turning to white, and then a crystal-like brilliance. Todd had to shield his eyes, but Sanchez seemed perfectly comfortable as the light grew brighter and nearer. When it was within a few feet of them, it began to shimmer, and Todd could hear little crinkling sounds, like a gift being unwrapped from foil paper. A man's figure began to emerge from the light.

His hair was longish, copper-blonde, and curled under at his neckline. He wore a short white toga — like those of the ancient Greek warriors — with a breastplate of highly polished silver, crossed with belts of gold. He carried a sword, the handle of which was encrusted with brilliant jewels of every kind. As he became more solid and visible, two magnificent wings of the softest, whitest feathers unfolded from his shoulders. His face was exquisite, with perfect features and a tawny, flawless complexion.

As Todd and Sanchez watched in awe, the angel-warrior extended the sword. He pointed it at Sanchez, who said, "Wh-who ...? Sir, who are ...?"

In a deep, flowing voice, the angel-warrior said, "I am Michael. Come with me now."

Sanchez started to get up, but Todd reached over and pushed him back, saying, "I believe he means *me*, boy."

At that, Michael moved the sword so that it pointed directly at Todd, and a white hot flame streaked out from it. Todd put up his hands to shield himself; but it was no use. The pain penetrated through his hands and encased his entire body. For what seemed like an eternity,

Todd writhed in pain as though every nerve were set on fire. Finally, Michael lifted his sword and the flaming stream disappeared.

Todd fell backward over the bench, onto the ground, the frigid coldness of it only intensifying the pain in his sore and burning body. Tears came to his eyes, and he sobbed loudly for help, from someone, anyone.

But no one heard him. The angel and Sanchez were gone.

When the pain had subsided somewhat, and he was able to stop sobbing, Todd remained on the ground, curled up, hugging himself against the cold. He was grateful that he was no longer on the bench of jagged stones.

It was pitch dark again, and the surroundings were no longer lit by the brilliant white light of the warrior angel nor the soft glow from Lance Corporal Sanchez. But soon a rosy glow outlined the rocks and dead leaves on the ground around him, and Todd had a sinking feeling, along with a curious feeling of relief. It might be Lucifer; but then again, it might be somebody else. Another angel, perhaps? This time coming for him?

The heat from the massive crimson form preceded him, and Todd was afraid to get up. He turned his head and peered underneath the rocky bench. He saw two massive, bright tomato red Sanita Viktor Aniline oilskin leather clogs, size twenty-seven. Ruddy ankles the size of small tree trunks rose out of them, meeting the cuffs of a dark purple linen leisure suit. Todd did not want to look any farther.

"You may get up now, Jared Todd Davis," he heard, in a voice as deep and foreboding as a death knell. Todd uncurled himself, slowly, still feeling the raw pain of the burning and the ice and the jagged rocks. As he stood up, and looked into the formidable face of Lucifer once more, he took a few ragged breaths, tried to maintain control, but gave up and started crying again.

"There, there," said Lucifer, patting Todd on the shoulder with shocking gentleness. "No need to cry, Mr. President!"

The sarcasm was not lost on Todd, and he started crying even harder.

Lucifer waited for him to compose himself, which he did after a few minutes. Then he lifted Todd's chin with a perfectly manicured index finger, and dabbed at Todd's eyes with a black silk handkerchief he had pulled from his breast pocket.

"Is that better now, little fella'? Hmmm?"

Todd nodded his head, feeling comforted for the first time since this ordeal began.

"Okay, then," said Lucifer, stuffing the hanky back in his suit pocket and meticulously arranging the folds to form a fan. "Time to meet your next visitor."

Todd looked up at him, now, wiping the last residual tears from his cheeks with his hand. "Wh-who is it? Is it that Michael guy who came for the kid?"

"Sanchez," said Lucifer, clucking his tongue softly, a signal of chastisement at Todd for not even remembering the young man's name. "Lance Corporal Hunter Sanchez."

"Yeah, okay, whatever," said Todd, "But who ... "

"Say his name, Jared Todd Davis. Say it."

"Oh ... uh ... Lance Corporal Hunter Sanchez ... Okay?"

Lucifer sighed. "You are going to get to know these people, Jared Todd Davis. Pay attention."

"Oh, I will, I will!" said Todd, enthusiastically, "You can take that to the bank!"

Lucifer rolled his eyes. "We don't have banks here."

"Oh, sure, I knew that ..."

"All of our financial institutions are in New York and Chicago."

Todd did not know how to respond.

"And the Cayman Islands."

"Uh ... I see." Todd waited to see whether Lucifer was going to say anything else, but he did not. Todd actually felt a bit more confident now, since Lucifer had comforted him and wiped his tears away. Things obviously were going to get better. "So who was that guy? With the wings?"

Lucifer sighed again. This was going to be more difficult than he anticipated.

"That was Saint Michael, Patron Saint of Warriors — but in the Old Testament he is known as Micah, Champion of the Jewish people, Defender of Israel." He stopped for a minute, rubbed his chin, and then added, "He is also known as the Special Patron of sick people, mariners, and grocers. If you ask me, he's stretched a little too thin. But I don't do the canonizing."

Todd felt a little deflated. He never went into the military himself, so he probably wouldn't be called to go off with St. Michael, the Warrior, like that Mexican kid was.

"He *wasn't Mexican*," corrected Lucifer, showing his irritation. Todd became frightened at the sudden realization that Lucifer could read his thoughts!

"You really need to *listen* better, Jared Todd Davis — *if you ever want to get out of here*," he added, the last part too soft for Todd to hear.

"Yes, Sir!" said Todd, standing up straighter. "I'm listening!"

Lucifer opened his hand toward the bench, and Todd realized that he was signaling for him to sit down again. He didn't want to, and he started shaking his head, squeezing his eyes open and shut, hoping to produce some tears which had seemed to soften Lucifer's attitude a few minutes before. But Lucifer just raised his forefinger which now uncurled into the same hideous claw he had seen before and pointed it at Todd's chest. Todd scrambled over the bench and took his seat, knowing all too well what that finger was capable of.

Lucifer's form dissolved into the fiery red ball of brilliance that hurt Todd's eyes, as it had the last time. It was pitch dark again. But he was glad he was gone. The bench seemed as jagged as ever, but Todd thought it wasn't quite as bad as it was the last time he sat there. Perhaps his buttocks were getting calloused?

Shortly, another soft green light could be glimpsed, outlining the scraggly trees. The small figure of a woman gradually became visible. She was wearing a light pink chiffon smock and a matching pink scarf around her neck. She stepped toward him tentatively, leaning backward a little, as though she had some trouble standing straight up. She stopped in front of Todd, seemingly oblivious of his nakedness, and saluted smartly.

"Petty Officer First Class Blair Morton, Sir!"

Todd looked her over and noticed the bulge in her midsection. But he set his curiosity aside. He had learned his lesson. He patted the bench next to him, and watched longingly as the jagged rocks softened into a velvety cushion just as the girl sat down.

"Uh ... Tell me about yourself ... uh, Blair ... er, *Miss* Morton is it?"

"Yes, Sir. Well," she looked down at her belly and tears started to form, making little pools in her lower lids before spilling over and down her cheeks. "I ... I'm pregnant, Sir."

Todd had no idea what to say to this wayward girl. She obviously had been screwing around, not doing her job. Was he supposed to sympathize with her? A promiscuous little slacker? Well, he would just *get to know her*, as the Big Red Hulk had said. He chuckled to himself at the designation, and then froze with fear, glancing around furtively, remembering that Lucifer could read his thoughts! He looked all around, but saw no rosy glow anywhere. He looked back at the girl.

"Well, *Miss* Morton," he said, ignoring her rank, "What happened to you?"

She looked up at him, eyes still moist, but her voice was cool and clear. "I was in the Navy for six years, Sir. I joined for the schooling — communications technology — so when I got out, I could afford to go to college. I had just finished my first semester when the Liberty Tower was attacked. I was in the reserves, so I got called back to active duty after you declared war on the Russians, Sir."

Todd swallowed hard, recalling how he planned all that with his cronies, to oust that silly little President Dokya and take control of the Russian oil fields. The girl continued:

"I was a shipboard radio technician. We were crossing the Bering Strait, just between the Diomede Islands, when we took a torpedo to the port bow. Hundreds died, but some of us were rescued by a Russian-sympathizing merchant boat." She stopped and looked down at her belly again, and laid her hand across it. "They ... they raped me."

Todd was still speechless, not wanting to hear any more of her story, but unable to stop her. The girl composed herself, wiping another tear away with her hand. "They kept us for seven months ... The baby was growing, and they gave me plenty to eat, but they still kept me locked up ... Every now and then someone came by to question me ... they kept slapping me if I couldn't answer ... sometimes they raped me again."

The girl fell silent, and Todd did not think she was going to say anymore. But before he could think of something to say, she took a deep breath and started talking again.

"There was a rumor that we were going to be rescued ... A Navy SEALs team was supposed to have located the island where we were being kept, and they were going to storm the place and rescue us." She tugged at the pink chiffon scarf around her neck, until it loosened. She unwrapped it slowly, carefully. When it fell to her lap, Todd saw the huge gaping bloody slash across her throat. "The SEALs never made it. It was just a rumor. But our captors thought it might be true, so they killed all of us. Cut our throats."

The girl hung her head down, making an oddly acute angle over the slash in her throat. She slowly — and lovingly — rubbed her hand over her protruding belly, and sobbed quietly. Todd just sat there, having no idea what else to say to this silly creature. Why, she caressed her swollen belly carrying her little Russian bastard, as though she really cared about it! What a pathetic little nymph.

A rustling caught their attention, and they both looked up. A light shimmered through the trees and golden sparks began to shower down. In only a few seconds, the grove was completely lit up once again with the brilliance of St. Michael's presence. He alighted before them and spread his magnificent white wings open, producing a blessedly warm breeze and a sound like a flute. He pointed his bejeweled sword at the young woman, a beam of golden light emanating from its tip.

Todd watched as Petty Officer First Class Blair Morton floated up from the bench, rising gently along the golden beam toward the sword, her pink chiffon dress floating around her and shimmering in the light. The warrior angel took her under his wing. Then, to his horror, he watched as the warrior angel raised his sword and drew it across the woman's throat! Todd recoiled in shock until he saw that the bloody gash in her throat was now completely healed — the skin smooth and unbroken!

Then in one more graceful motion, the angel raised his sword and brought it down, slicing through the dome of the woman's rounded belly. Todd was too horrified to watch, and covered his eyes. He could understand Michael's wanting to get rid of the bastard child — but the way he did it seemed so ... so ... barbaric!

He only looked up when he heard the soft little sounds of a baby cooing. There was no blood, no gash — only a beautiful young mother holding her newborn child to her breast, smiling with the joy of ecstasy.

The mother and baby continued to rise up in St. Michael's arms until they disappeared into the shimmering clouds above.

Todd sat in the darkness for a long time. He could not stop thinking about the beautiful young Blair Morton. And Sanchez. He tried not to feel guilty. He sent them into combat. But isn't that why kids like that join the military? They want money for college — but they also want to fight! Kids play cowboys-and-Indians because they want to grow up and fight! Of course, it was hard to apply that to Blair Morton. But she joined for the money, to pay for college — and she got what she wanted, didn't she? And the possibility of going into combat goes along with the pricetag. So he did *not* have to feel guilty!

"Guilt is a strange animal," said Lucifer, startling Todd to see that he was sitting beside him. Todd looked down to see whether the bench under Lucifer was cushion or rocks. But he saw that Lucifer only *looked* like he was seated, while he was actually floating an inch or so above the bench. "It is born of the ... uh ... *goodness (yecch)* in one that begins to encroach on the *evil*," Lucifer continued, gagging slightly on the word *goodness*. "It is *goodness (yecch)* that brings forth guilt; but *not without evil first.*"

"Okay," said Todd, not really understanding the purpose of all this. "So what now?"

"So now you have to finish the task before you."

"And ... What is the task?"

"You have to meet the rest. You have to get to know all of them before you can move on."

"*All ... who?*" asked Todd, now feeling irritated, unsure what Lucifer meant by his little *goodness* and *evil* speech, or by his assigning Todd some kind of *task*.

"All of those for whose death you are responsible." Lucifer's glaring look began to make Todd feel very warm, and then hot. Todd began to catch his drift.

"I'm ... I'm not ... *I'm not responsible* for those kids!" He began to sweat freely again. "They joined the military of their own accord!"

"And the occupants of the Library Tower? And the Russian citizens who were caught in the war you wanted?"

"I didn't want a war!" Todd sputtered, "I just wanted to take over the oil fields! After all, that would be good for the economy! *I did it for the United States of America ... For the good of the country!!*" Now an icy gust of wind blew by and cooled the sweat on Todd's body until he started to shiver. Between chattering teeth, he repeated, *"For ... the ... good ... "*

Lucifer sighed and subtly shook his head from side to side. "I know you feel that way, Jared Todd Davis. I know you sincerely believe what you are saying." He stood up from the bench, his nine-foot height towering over Todd. "After you meet all of them, perhaps you will feel differently."

"Wait!" Todd cried, reaching out to Lucifer, grabbing his arm but pulling back rapidly after burning his finger.

Lucifer did not wait. He disappeared into the darkness again.

Todd met twenty-nine more casualties before he saw Lucifer again: Young men with missing limbs, missing faces, throats cut open, chests destroyed, genitals slashed. He met older men and women who had been working in the fields, or going about their business, until they were blown to kingdom come. He met children, some still holding a toy trumpet or a doll that had been beheaded in the explosion that took their lives.

Todd kept telling himself he was *not* responsible for these mishaps. He was tired of listening to their stories. He wanted to put some clothes on. He was cold and thirsty and hungry. His buttocks were in constant pain. When Lucifer came back, he would tell him: Enough is enough!

Lucifer appeared on the bench as suddenly as he had the last time, startling Todd.

"I really wish you wouldn't do that," Todd said, then wondered if he should have said that.

"Oh, sorry old chum!" Lucifer replied, "Here, let me make it up to you." He produced a polished silver tray with a teapot and a steaming cup of tea, and a small plate of little cakes.

Todd couldn't believe his eyes. He looked at the tray, only now realizing how terribly hungry and thirsty he was, aching to eat and drink. He couldn't help but wonder, though, if this were not a trick. Would snakes come out of the teapot, or would the cakes turn into rats?

"Of course not!" assured Lucifer, reading his thoughts. "That would be crude." He pushed the tray a little closer to Todd and smiled, adding, "I'm a vegetarian myself."

Todd could not resist. He took the cup up to his lips and drank — the sweetest, most delicious tea he had ever tasted. He hungrily gulped it down, and poured himself another cup, while reaching for a cake with the other hand. The cake was rich and heavy with vanilla cream, sweet berries and nuts. He stuffed it into his mouth and washed it down with more tea. When he had finished all the cakes, he sat back and belched. Then he started to cry again.

"Why the tears, my dear man?" asked Lucifer, balancing the empty tray on his lap.

"I ... I ... I'm just so *happy!*" cried Todd, bawling unabashedly.

"That's nice," said Lucifer, reaching down and placing the tray under the bench. "Now, the tray will refill itself, and it will be there for you while you work on your task."

"T-t-task? What task?" asked Todd, wiping his face with the back of his hand and eyeing the ground under the bench to try and see if the tray had really replenished itself.

Lucifer sighed again. *Can this man learn anything?*

"My dear man. The twenty-nine people you have just met are just the tip of the iceberg."

"Iceberg?" He could not see the tray without bending over more and looking too obvious.

"Right. And the tray won't refill itself until you need it."

"Oh ... Okay," Todd said, sitting back upright. "So, the 'task' is ... what? Something about an iceberg?"

"Two thousand, eight hundred and forty-seven people were killed in the Library Tower attack, Jared Todd Davis." Now Todd stopped thinking about the tray under the bench and actually started listening to Lucifer. "One thousand, six hundred and thirty-two military men and women died in combat and accidents."

Todd was beginning to see where this was going. "Do the accidents count against me? They shouldn't, you know. Accidents can happen ..."

"They *do*, my dear man. They *do*." Lucifer stopped for a second to let that sink in. Then, "Three thousand, four hundred and fifty-one Russian soldiers have been killed. Nine thousand, six hundred and thirty-two Russian civilians."

"Okay, Sir, I get the point," Todd interrupted, seeing where this was going. He wouldn't be able to talk to thousands of people here — so what was he supposed to do?

"You will have to talk to every one of them, Jared Todd Davis. You will have to *get to know* every one of them. You will learn their stories, how they lived, how they di — "

"Now just a darn minute!" Todd said, secretly congratulating himself that he avoided using the word *damn*. "That would take *forever!*"

Lucifer looked at him but did not speak. Todd kept waiting for a response, but none came.

"That would take *years ... decades!*"

Lucifer stared at him, but remained silent.

"I don't want to talk to all these people!"

Still no response.

"Damn it, I don't want to see these people, and I don't want to talk to them!" Todd turned away from Lucifer and crossed his arms across his chest in defiance.

After more silence, Todd turned back to see if Lucifer were still sitting there. He was.

"And you can't make me! You can't make me talk to these people!"

"You are right, Jared Todd Davis," said Lucifer, calmly and in a voice softer than Todd had imagined he could speak. "You are right. I cannot make you speak to these people if you do not want to."

He leaned over closer, and Todd felt the burning heat radiating from Lucifer's mass.

"Are you sure that's what you want? Not to have to see or speak to your victims?"

Todd was shaken by the term. He still did not think of these people as *victims*. Certainly not *his* victims. They were merely *casualties*. Or — what was that term the generals used? — *collateral damage.*

"No," he responded, calmly. He felt somewhat powerful, having the opportunity to tell this creature what he did and did not want. "They are not *victims* — certainly not *my* victims — and I do not want to *see* nor *speak* to them."

Darkness fell again, and the bench disappeared from under Todd. Everything disappeared. There was complete blackness around him. But he could hear people — a shuffling of feet, a passing of gas, someone choking, vomiting. The buzzing and skittering of insects.

He listened carefully to try and determine the distance and direction of the sounds. He heard a cough that sounded like it was some distance to the left of him. He turned in that direction.

The ground under his feet was slimy and slippery, strewn with rocks. He felt something crawl over his foot, but he kicked it off and kept moving in the direction of the coughing he had heard. He stopped and listened again — yes, he heard the cough again. He was going in the right direction. When he heard the cough for the third time, he was sure it was a regular human like himself. He was within a few feet of it — him or her — now, so he would call out and see what kind of a response he would get.

Todd opened his mouth to say hello. Nothing came out except for a hollow, breathy sound. He reached up to his mouth and discovered that he had no mouth. No lips, no teeth, no tongue. Just a gaping hole.

You did not want to speak to them. The words rang in his head. Then he heard, *You did not want to see them, either.*

With shaking hands, Todd reached up to his eyes. He felt only limp lids hanging over the hollow caverns where his eyes had been. Before he could fully react to the horror of this discovery, he heard someone calling him.

"Todd? Is that you? Oh, oh, my God, what happened?"

Todd recognized the voice of Christopher Bennington. President Christopher Bennington. The man that Vice President Jared Todd Davis had conspired to assassinate so that he could ascend to the Presidency himself.

Now he understood. Now it was clear. He dropped to his knees in the rocks and the slime. *I'm sorry*, he spelled out in little rocks on the ground.

Part III:
The Beginning

Chapter 17:   Charlie

Charlie flew with Gabriel, over the beautiful hillsides and valleys, reveling in the gorgeous colors of the countryside, unable to take it all in. The colors of everything were more intense and varied than the rainbows he had seen. The greens of trees, the reds of apples, and the blue of the sky — each single color seemed to reflect a whole multitude of new shades. No landscape he had ever seen could compare to this.

It made him think about a time when he was very young — five years old, perhaps — and he lived with his parents in a small efficiency apartment in the northeast, in an old part of town. There was only a living room and a small kitchen-dinette area, which was really part of the living room, too. At night they pulled out the convertible sofa bed in the living room, and the three of them went to sleep there. Often there was too little heat, and they huddled together for warmth. He recalls having fun, even on those nights when it was too cold, because his parents would sing songs together softly, until he fell asleep. Later, when his father got a promotion at work, he remembers how they danced together around the kitchen table, singing and laughing. His mother had gone out and bought steaks — the first he had ever tasted — and a bottle of champagne. He thought they poured him a glass, too, but — he found out much later — it was ginger ale! Two years later they moved into a much larger apartment. He never knew they had been poor.

Charlie thought of all this now because in that first tiny apartment they only had a small black-and-white television with a "rabbit-ears" antenna. His father had fashioned tin foil around the ends to get better reception, which didn't really help much. There was always "snow" on the screen; or the picture rolled up horizontally, over and over. His dad could fiddle around with the control knobs, and slow down the horizontal roll until they were sure it had stopped. For a minute. Then it rolled again. Some time later, perhaps a year or two after they moved to the larger apartment, his father brought home a color television set. He could still remember how stunned he was to see the programs he loved in color; how much more *three-dimensional* things were; how *real* everything looked.

Now, as he flew along the countryside in this amazing place — he felt exactly the same way. He felt as though he had never seen colors or depth before — not like this! He felt a giggle welling up inside him, and put his hand up to his mouth to suppress it.

Soon they glided over a hilltop, and Charlie could see where the line of people was heading. The people at the front of the line looked so happy and relieved to be there; and yet those behind them seemed to wait so patiently, so serenely.

Gabriel alighted with him onto the ground in front of a massive marble building of exquisite workmanship. Charlie had had the opportunity to see some of the most beautiful buildings in the world during his brief stint in the Air Force. It was peacetime, and he grabbed every opportunity to take "hops" to all the exotic places he had only read about. The Taj Mahal and the Akshardham Temple in India; the Parthenon in Greece; the Cathedral of Pisa in Italy; the Chateau de Fontainebleau in France; all paled in the shadow of this exquisite structure.

"Sir ... uh, Gabriel? May I ask," he started politely, tentatively, "what is this place?"

"This is Heaven's Portal," responded Gabriel, looking up at the building himself. He smiled, but did not look proud. "Something of a misnomer, though — in my humble opinion."

" 'Misnomer?' "

"Well ... It's not exactly the 'Entrance to Heaven' as the name implies."

"Oh, I see," said Charlie, not seeing at all what Gabriel was getting at. "Well, is it ... is it the entrance to ... somewhere else?"

Gabriel smiled more broadly, rubbing his chin with his hand, "Um ... Actually ... I like to think of it as the 'Portal to Life.' But that's just my take on it."

Still mystified, but not wanting to press him any farther, Charlie decided to let it go.

Gabriel sensed his confusion, and added, "You'll see shortly."

They walked over to the lectern at the head of the line.

"Excuse me ... Excuse me," Gabriel apologized politely to the people standing there. They quickly opened a pathway for the two of them. Gabriel walked behind the lectern and opened the massive gilt-edged tome reposing there. He flipped over a section of pages, then flipped back a few more, finally stopping at one. "Yes, here you are."

Charlie craned his neck a little — trying not to be too imposing — to look over the lectern and see what was on the page. He saw, from his upside-down vantage point, his own name, in bold letters at the top of the page.

CHARLES ALEXANDER MILLER

The rest of the pages were filled with a tiny, finely printed script. The letters were completely unfamiliar, and Charlie could not even guess what kind of an alphabet it was. Gabriel picked up the little silver pointer with the tiny hand and upright index finger, and started running it down the page. After a few seconds, he turned the page, which continued in tiny print covering the next two pages. Then he looked up.

"Yes, just as I thought," said Gabriel, tapping the little silver pointer at a certain spot on the page. It reminded Charlie of the time his mother had taken him to the doctor, when he tried to feign a sore throat and stay home from school.

"Yes... Just as I thought," the doctor said, looking over the thermometer poised close to his spectacles. "Did you do your homework?" Charlie slumped down and admitted that, no, he did not do his homework, and that's why he wanted to stay home from school.

"Wh-what is it, Sir?" he now asked, feeling the same sense of surrender and guilt as he had at that long-ago doctor's visit.

"Gabriel. Please. Call me Gabriel. Or Gabe. 'Sir' makes me feel so ... well ... *ancient.*"

"Sorry ... What is it ... uh ... Gabriel?"

Gabriel set down the pointer and looked over the lectern at Charlie. Then he turned on his heel and said, "Come with me." They were going to the Principal's office. He knew it.

Together they walked up the hundreds of steps that led into the majestic building. Gabriel walked so fluidly that he seemed to be floating over the steps. Somehow, though, for Charlie, it was easy, too — he kept up easily. When they got to the top, Gabriel stopped at two huge oaken doors, polished to a gleaming luster. The doors opened before them as they approached.

Inside, Charlie was uncomfortably surprised by what he saw. There was nothing there. Nothing. They were standing in a plain, small room, with white walls and a high ceiling that seemed to go up several stories, but there were no stairs or landings. Just the open, empty, bare high walls. The room was bright, even though there were no lights that Charlie could see anywhere — and only one lone window sat high up on one wall, covered by a simple white shade. Two plain wooden doors, unadorned with any carving or design, faced them.

"You have a choice, Charlie," said Gabriel, turning to face him. "You lived a very good life. You were kind to people you liked and charitable with those you did not like. You withheld your anger more often than not — that may account for your chronic indigestion, but nevertheless, it was a virtuous thing. You sacrificed your time and energy and personal wants when there was not enough to take care of others and satisfy yourself, too."

Seeing where this was going, Charlie suddenly felt awash in a feeling he could only identify as ... guilt.

"But, Sir, you don't know..."

"Gabriel. Please."

"Sorry ... Gabriel ... I did some bad things, you know ..." Charlie trailed off, wondering why Gabriel didn't seem to know about those incidents.

"Yes, we know about those," said Gabriel, smiling his radiantly comforting smile which eased all of the other's anxieties in a flash. "You're not a saint, okay?"

"But I ... I ..." Charlie gulped, not sure he could say what Gabriel obviously *did not* know.

Gabriel looked calmly at him, eyebrows slightly elevated, waiting patiently for him to finish.

"I ... *I didn't believe in God!* I went to church, but ... *I never really believed in God!*" He trailed off, filled with shame and remorse at his own words.

Gabriel was silent for a moment that seemed like an eternity to Charlie. Finally he spoke, in a quiet voice, "Well, my dear man, it's like this: God believed in *you.*"

He put one arm around Charlie's shoulders and raised the other in a swooping motion in the air underneath the lone window. The shade went up slowly, and as it did, the window widened and lengthened, until it filled the entire wall. The beautiful landscape and the line of people outside were visible for a second, but then faded to a cloudy mist.

Charlie saw himself as if he were in a movie...

He was at the doctor's office. The doctor was taking the thermometer out of his mouth, studying it for a minute and then saying, "Yes ... Just as I thought ... You didn't do your homework, did you, son?" From there he saw himself with a couple of friends from school — the ones his mother didn't want him to hang around with. They were in a music store. One slipped a CD into his coat pocket and handed another one to Charlie, which he slipped into his own coat pocket.

The scene merged into another...

He was an older teenager here — he couldn't quite place the scene — but he was walking down a sidewalk. There was snow shoveled to the side, and he was looking down to be sure he wouldn't slip on any ice. Then he looked up and saw all the Christmas decorations in the store windows. He stood there for a minute, enjoying the decorations — a display of moving puppets depicting Santa Claus putting gifts under a tree, and two small children watching him from the stairway, clapping their hands together after Santa went back into the chimney. Charlie pulled some bills out of his pocket. There were four five-dollar bills and several ones. He put the money back in his pocket and walked toward the store entrance. Just inside the doorway, a filthy man in rags sat on his haunches. He pushed a hat toward Charlie. The man was so dirty that he could hardly tell if he were black or white. Then a store manager came out and yanked the beggar's arm, cursing at him and roughly pushing him away from the store entrance. Charlie pulled a one-dollar bill out of his pocket and held it for an instant.

Then he looked in the store window again. He slid the bill back into his pocket and went into the store.

Charlie felt tears beginning to well up in his eyes. But the scene quickly faded and another moved into its place like a gust of wind blowing smoke away from a chimney.

He was a young man. He was driving rapidly down the highway. The weather was nice, and he could see the beginning of a pink-and-gold sunset reflected around the clouds like a halo. A car was stopped on the side of the road and a middle-aged woman was standing next to it, looking down at a flattened tire. Charlie looked at his watch — he was late. Shirley was coming home from college for the weekend, and he was supposed to pick her up at the airport, but road construction had slowed the highway traffic to a crawl. He had barely enough time to make it. He felt he had no choice. He drove on. Someone else was bound to stop and help the woman.

Now Charlie recalled, with that how-did-we-ever-manage? feeling, that this incident had taken place several years B.C. — before cellphones!

Suddenly, he turned off the highway at the next exit, circled around and got back onto the highway, pulling up behind the woman whose car was disabled. He remembered worrying about how some predator-type might stop and take advantage of her — and how he'd feel if that were his mom or Shirley stranded there. He got out and changed the woman's tire. She tried to shove a twenty-dollar bill into his hand, but he just waved her off, got back in his car, and raced off to the airport. How he laughed when he arrived and learned that Shirley's plane had been delayed for two hours!

The "movie" went on for several hours, showing every incident in Charlie's life wherein he either did something unkind or unlawful; or very unselfish and generous. The movie ended with Charlie's near-suicide from a devastating depression; and how his spirits were lifted after saving the woman on the bridge. The final scene showed the semi-tractor-trailer running him down, causing his own premature demise.

The window shrank back to its original size, high up on the wall, and the shade came down.

Gabriel turned to look at him, and said, "Well, let's see what you would like to do now, Charlie."

Charlie just shook his head and raised up his shoulders. "What do you mean?"

"You have earned two choices, Charlie," said Gabriel. "You may have more choices later on — but for now there are two." He spread one hand open, palm facing outward, and waved it toward the two doors opposite the entrance through which they had come.

The first one opened slowly, and Charlie's parents came out. They walked over to him, beaming with excitement, and each hugged and kissed him.

"We've missed you, son," said his father.

"We're so proud of your accomplishments," said his mother.

Before he could respond to either of them, the other door slowly opened. Through it he saw — like the previous "movie" of his life — his house, and his wife Shirley, in a black dress. Her eyes were swollen from crying. Their young son Jamie was standing at her knee, holding onto her hands. He was sad, too, but appeared to be trying to comfort his mother.

Charlie looked at Gabriel. "Does this mean ... Do you mean that I can ... *go back*? I can be ... with them again ... *alive?*"

Gabriel shook his head, "No, Charlie. But you may follow them ... follow along in their lives ... maybe even help them out from time to time ... when the need and the opportunity coincide." Then he added, "They would not be able to see you. They may — no, they *will* — speak to you as though you are there sometimes ... But they will not hear you if you try to answer ... although ... they may sense your presence at times."

Charlie was trying to assimilate what that meant, but Gabriel continued: "Your other option is to remain here. You are entitled to move up to a higher level, a higher plane of activity, which can be very exciting and ... *fun,* even! It is more like the 'heaven' you conceptualize in earthly life — but a lot more fun, believe me!"

His parents were smiling and nodding. His father spoke, "Gabe is so right, Chucky! It's terrific here! Your mother and I are having a ball! We're like teenagers again!" He gave Charlie's mother a squeeze, and wiggled his eyebrows at her. She blushed a rosy pink and giggled.

Charlie looked back through the doorway that showed his wife and son, apparently mourning over Charlie's own death. He watched for awhile, and then made up his mind. But before he could speak, his parents came over and hugged him together.

"We knew what you would choose, darling boy," said his mother.

"Go take care of your family," said his father. "You can always join us later."

They released him from their hug and went back through the door from which they had entered. Charlie looked over at Gabriel, who nodded to him. Then he walked through the door to his wife and son.

Chapter 18: Penny

"Lou." *He said I could call him that.*

Penny knew who he was — but as she looked up at this gorgeous creature in his white silken outfit and golden belt, all she felt was a strong tingling of pleasurable desire. She felt an intense heat radiating from him, as though she were standing too close to a fireplace. He looked at her and smiled a knowing smile. Then he reached out and took her hand, enclosing it completely within his own massive hand. It burned her as though she had touched the handle of a simmering skillet. He held onto it for a minute, watching her squirming under the heat; then reached his other hand around her back and pulled her roughly toward him.

When she saw it — it shocked her, and struck both fear and awe in her — but at the same time, excited her so acutely that she felt physical pain in her loins. A massive flaming red projectile beyond any human size arose from beneath his belt like a nuclear missile from an underground silo.

Lucifer pulled Penny roughly onto his lap, and thrust himself so hugely inside her that she thought she would split apart. Her insides were on fire, and electrical shocks crackled through her body from head to toe. This went on and on, unceasing torment, until she felt white-hot molten lava searing into her. Every muscle in her body contracted at once, and the pain was excruciating and yet so powerfully orgasmic that even as she screamed at the top of her lungs, she did not want it to stop. And still it went on for hours, torture and pleasure beyond endurance.

When he finally withdrew, Lucifer pushed her from him, and she fell backward onto the slimy ground. Every nerve ending in her body felt raw and inflamed, spent completely, and yet still craving more.

Penny lay there for several minutes, unable to move. Lucifer leaned forward with his hands on his thighs, watching her. When Penny was able to move again, she slowly raised herself up onto her elbows, and then pulled her knees up, one at a time, testing each movement, unsure if her body still worked at all. But when she tried to stand up, Lucifer slapped her with the back of his hand so that she fell back into the muck and slime.

Tears came to her eyes as she rubbed her stinging cheek. "Wh-why did you do that?"

"You need to stay down there for awhile," he said. "That's where you belong. For now."

"For n-now? What do you mean?"

"Until you make a decision about where you want to go." Lucifer sat back on the bench, crossing his arms over his chest and inspecting his polished nails.

"Wh-what do you mean, 'where I want to go?' I thought ..."

"You thought you were there already? Here?"

Penny nodded her head.

"Ah ... no." Lucifer laughed, and it sounded hollow, as though coming from a deep cave. "You're not anywhere yet, my dear girl."

"Where then ... where ..."

"Okay, sweetcakes, let me explain this to you." Lucifer leaned forward, arms resting on his thighs. "You have two choices about where you go from here." He raised an index finger. "One: You can go over there and convince that crowd to forgive you. *And make them care about you.*"

He turned his upraised finger so that it pointed at the angry crowd of people who had continued to follow Penny since she arrived. Those were the people whom she had deliberately, or accidentally, infected with the HIV virus, contributing to their deaths — the unforgiving ones. The ones who said they forgave her had already moved on. Somewhere.

"But they'll never ... I can't make them ... What if they won't ever forgive me?"

"*And care about you.* Don't forget that part."

"But that's im*poss*- ..." Penny stopped in mid-sentence. "You said I had *two choices* about where I go from here?"

Lucifer nodded, "You do."

"What's the other one?"

"You can go back."

"B-back?"

"Back. You may go back where you came from. It will be very difficult — more difficult than the life you came from — but you can earn the opportunity for more choices after that."

As he spoke, Lucifer pointed toward a huge moss-laden rock formation among the trees. Penny followed his finger and looked toward where he was pointing. She watched as the rock formation began to dissolve into a cloudy mass, and then flattened out into a large white screen. A scene began to appear on the screen, like a movie:

It was a small house — an apartment, or maybe a trailer — and there was trash strewn all around. There were broken toys, broken garbage bags dripping onto the floor, dishes caked with dried food stacked up in a filthy, food-encrusted sink and spilling over onto every counter. Small dark things skittered across the counter and into the sink. Penny could hear the sound of children fighting, yelling at one another; a baby was crying somewhere. The scene moved into a bathroom, and Penny felt queasy looking at the dried excrement everywhere, in the toilet and even in the bathtub, which looked as though it had never been used to bathe. Black mold was everywhere. A rat ran across the floor, its nails clicking on the old linoleum, and a thin, mangy dog came running into the bathroom after it, barking a raspy bark.

The scene moved into a bedroom, where a woman was lying on the bed, propped up against a pillow, with a can of beer in her hand. Crude, homemade tattoos were etched into both arms. Cigarette butts were everywhere, and there were burn marks on the furniture and the carpet. The sheets on the bed were grimy and torn. A game show was playing on the large plasma television set across from the bed, but no one was watching. The woman seemed to have passed out, drunk. She was in her late forties — but looked much older — with prematurely craggy lines on her face. Her hair was uncombed, a flaming orange color with an inch of gray-black roots at the scalp. She was wearing a sleeveless pink blouse and shorts that were much too tight, with a safety pin holding the zipper together over her obese belly.

No, not obese — pregnant.

"Wh-who is *that?*" Penny asked Lucifer, tentatively. "Why are you showing this to me?"

"That's your other choice."

She stared at the screen, which was now fading to a cloudy mass, and then taking its original shape of the rock formation.

"I don't want to go there," said Penny, starting to feel tears well up in her eyes, "That's not a good choice."

Lucifer pointed back to the angry mob. "Well, then, there's you're other choice, kiddo. Make them forgive you. *Make them care about you.*"

She looked over at the mob. They still showed signs of the disease she had spread to them. But ... she had manipulated people easily in the past ... some of *these very same* people. Perhaps ... perhaps she could do so again ... perhaps ... she could do this. She could convince them ... change their minds about her.

Penny stood up and dusted the dirt off her knees. They remained soiled, though, so she smoothed her tattered clothes, and turned toward the angry crowd. She held her head up high and pasted a big smile on her face. She took a step forward in their direction.

A rock came at her, grazing the side of her head. She stopped in her tracks and the smile fell from her face ... but she put it back on immediately. Raising her hand in a gesture of "peace" or "halt", she took another step in the direction of the mob.

More rocks flew at her, stinging where they hit. But she remained resolute. As she continued her approach, slow but unbroken, the barrage of rocks stopped. The angry people quieted down and just stared at her.

They seemed to be ... confused ... by the fact that she was unfazed by their assault.

Continuing her gingerly approach, Penny soon came face-to-face with the man at the front of the mob. She broadened her smile and extended her hand to shake the man's hand. But he did not move to accept the gesture. He stared at her outstretched hand. The others were all silent, watching, waiting. It was clear that they viewed the man at the front as their leader of sorts, and they were waiting to take a cue from him. But he seemed somewhat taken aback — unsure of what to do next.

"What's your name, Sir?" Penny asked. She did not recognize him, possibly due the distortion of his face from all the disease lesions. She kept smiling, hiding her revulsion as she dropped her hand slowly back down. She folded her hands in front of her. She kept smiling.

The man did not answer. He stood there, staring, saying nothing.

"I ... I want you to know," Penny began, trying to find just the right words for an apology. (She knew how effective apologies could be in helping her to be spared from punishment. Starting with her grandmother, and later, judges, probation and parole officers, wardens and other prison administrators — were all so ready to accept an apology and give a lighter punishment or dismiss charges altogether. They always said, "I believe you are sincere in showing remorse for what you did." She always had to stifle the urge to laugh when she heard that.)

"...that I am really, truly sorry for..."

She did not finish her sentence before the man suddenly wrapped his hands around her neck and began choking her. The others behind him roared their approval, and rocks flew again. Pain stung her as one hit her squarely in the eye, but she was already seeing stars from the choking. Then a club came down on her shoulder and she felt her bone crack. A branch whipped at her back, tearing through the thin clothing, and flayed her skin open again and again.

Unable to speak, she mouthed the words, "Help me ... please ... help me ..."

Instantly, the crowd stopped their assault and retreated several yards back. Penny lay on the ground, gasping for breath. When she looked up she saw Lucifer sitting on a bench beside her.

"Well, that didn't go so well, did it?"

As he spoke, the rock formation began to light up once again. The filthy trailer came back into view. The pregnant woman was still there, still passed out with empty beer cans next to her on the bed, the nightstand, the floor.

Penny started to cry. She leaned forward, grabbing onto Lucifer's knees, pulling herself up.

"Listen! Please!" she pleaded, "I don't want either choice! I want *you!* I want to stay here with *you!*" She reached up to his belt and began fumbling with the buckle.

Lucifer reached down, arresting her movement as he encircled her wrists in his sizzling grip. He leaned forward, inches from her face, breathing his hot fetid breath on her.

"You cannot stay with me, babe — I'm strictly a loner."

"B-but I'll work for you!" cried Penny, "I'll do anything you want! *Anything!* I'll be your assistant — *your slave* — I'll do whatever you want!"

Lucifer sat back and smiled. "Oh, you have been watching too many movies, kid!"

He swiftly placed one hand around Penny's neck, digging into her flesh like a choke collar. He rose up from the bench, pulling her to her feet. He continued to rise, growing from the six-foot stature up to a full nine feet tall. His white silk clothing dissolved to reveal his massive fiery-red musculature, all the way down to his cloven hooves. His neatly manicured fingernails grew into thick curved claws, and they sliced into Penny's neck as she dangled from his outstretched hand.

"Now — *choose.*"

Penny could see the angry mob of people behind Lucifer. He was signaling for them to approach, and they were rapidly advancing toward them. The leader was slamming his fist into the palm of his other hand, over and over. Others held even larger rocks and thick branches that they held like clubs.

"Perhaps you want to try again, sweetcakes? Make them forgive you — *make them care about you* — or choose your wonderful new family!"

He pointed to the scene on the rock formation, which now seemed to be ... materializing ... becoming more real ... almost like a 3-D projection.

"No! No!" she tried to cry, but it only came out as a whisper under Lucifer's grasp.

"*Choose* — or *they* will make your decision for you!"

Lucifer pulled Penny's face closer and covered her lips with his, mashing against her mouth, feeling like a branding iron, searing into her flesh and cutting off her air entirely. Blackness swirled in her head and her lungs strained for air, feeling as though they would explode.

She felt the first rock hit her forehead, and blood trickled down into her eye; then a tree branch whipped at her back, tearing the flesh open again and again and again.

The family! The family! I choose the family! she thought ... but she was unable to speak.

"I figured as much," said Lucifer, winding up like a big league pitcher, preparing to fling Penny toward the rock formation.

"Go back to your family ... your mother ... the twenty-year-old woman you were taken away from when you were five ..."

Penny slammed into the rocks and slid down, down, down, into a spiraling darkness.

The woman on the bed awoke from her drunken stupor and grasped at her belly, which was contracting in pain. She reached for the cellphone on the table next to her, and cursed when she realized the battery was dead. She stumbled out of bed and walked, wobbly from the pain, into the filthy kitchen. She reached for the telephone on the wall, and dialed a number. A trail of blood traced her route.

"Nicky! NICKY!" she screamed into the telephone, "Get home *now!* The baby's coming! Hurry!"

A contraction came that was so fierce, the woman doubled over in pain and then passed out on the floor, dropping the telephone receiver, banging against the wall. A few minutes later, the cries of a newborn baby could be heard as it tore from the woman's body.

Lucifer watched as the baby girl was born.

Welcome to hell, sweetcakes.

Chapter 19: Marion

The farther down the stairwell Marion went, the darker it got. She looked back up to get one more reassuring glance from Gabriel; but even though she had only gone down a short distance, she could no longer see him. She took a deep breath and continued descending down the spiral staircase. It grew considerably warmer as she went. The lighting had changed from the diamond-like brilliance of the room where she had met Gabriel, to a foggy pink mist that was getting murkier and darker as she descended. Soon it was almost completely dark, and she clung tightly to the railing, testing each step below the next before shifting her weight onto it. Now she could feel a more intense heat rising up from below, and she could feel beads of sweat on her forehead and face trickling down her neck. An acrid odor suffused the place and seemed to get more intense the farther she descended.

Suddenly she heard a horrible screech somewhere in the distance that sent her stomach churning. She looked around and tried to get her eyes adjusted to the darkness, but could see nothing. When she looked down now, she could no longer even see her feet. She held out her hand in front of her and it was just barely visible in the surrounding blackness. She felt cautiously with her toe to see where the next step was. Then she heard an even more blood-curdling scream which seemed to come out from the very wall next to her. She put out her hand to touch it. She felt … a hand. It was hot and sticky with a gritty substance. Before she could pull away, it grasped her hand and tightened around it so that she could not pull free. Its nails were long and sharp, and began to dig into the palm of her hand. She could feel it slicing into her skin. She beat at it with her other hand, finally biting the fingers that clawed her, the gritty substance tasting like bile. As her teeth bit through the sickening flesh, another horrifying scream pealed out from the wall, and the hand released her.

Marion turned on her heel with only the thought of going back up the steps to where she was before. Only there were no steps there anymore. She could only feel a smooth solid surface, with a slight upward incline, impossible to scale. Even if it were less steep, she was already damp with sweat and could feel her hands slipping on the polished surface. Then she realized that she could not even see her hands in front of her face anymore. All light was extinguished. Solid blackness surrounded her like a coffin.

Slowly, turning back around, trembling with fear, Marion inched one foot forward to the edge of the step she was on. *What if there are no more steps going down, either?* She slid her foot gingerly over the edge of the step, holding her breath as it hovered in the air for a second, and then exhaled with great relief as she felt the step below. Now, if she could just keep going in the pitch blackness. She closed her eyes and began to recite out loud:

Yea, though I walk through the valley of the shadow of death, I will fear no evil ... for Thou art with me ...

As she recited these verses, her courage seemed to return, and she was able to continue the descent. With painstaking slowness, she stepped down another step. The darkness was so complete that she was unsure whether her eyes were open or closed. She felt momentarily disoriented, and reached out to steady herself against the wall. She felt — a foot?

No sooner did she touch it than an ear-splitting scream blasted through the wall. Before she could react, two legs extruded from the wall and clamped around her, pinning her arms to her sides. She heard another anguished scream and realized, to her horror, that it was coming from herself.

The legs were hot and wet with the same gritty sludge as the hand that had attacked her. She could feel the burn through her thin dress. The legs were thin and bony — almost skeletal — but squeezed her so tightly that she could hardly breathe. They were crossed at the ankles, and Marion could not move at all. She could not grab at them in any way because they were clamped right around her waist, pinning her elbows so that she could not even bend her arms. She was filled with a terror that froze a massive iceberg in her throat.

Drenched with sweat, Marion struggled with her corporeal shackle. She tried to slide out of its hold — but like the children's "Chinese handcuffs" toy, the more she struggled, the tighter it got. She bent forward and tried to bite at the limbs but it was impossible to reach down to her waist. As the sludge-laden ankles kept twisting over each other, the legs tightened and compressed around her. She could feel the intense pressure building inside until her head was pounding and she thought her eyes would pop out of their sockets. Her face was becoming congested with blood pumped in that could not go back down, and trickles of blood from her nose ran down over her lips and chin.

Bending sideways, trying to reach the feet with her teeth — impossible. Marion watched, rapidly becoming overwhelmed with a deep, sickening sense of hopelessness, as a few drops of her blood fell onto the bottoms of the locked feet. As the ruby droplets splashed onto them, the toes curled, wiggled, and momentarily loosened. A low bubbling sound — a giggle? — came from within the wall. In a second, the feet tightened around her again. Marion shook her head over the feet, releasing a shower of sweat and blood. A loud screaming laugh howled through the wall and reverberated through the darkness with resounding echoes. The feet released their hold and withdrew back into the wall.

Overwhelmed with relief, Marion was still so shaken that she could not bring herself to move. When she finally felt composed enough to get going again, she looked back, hoping perhaps that there was some light or some stair steps on which she could retreat. She still could see nothing in the pitch darkness, however — and now she was afraid to reach out and feel anything at all. She did not want to take any chance of disturbing anything else that might be laying in wait behind — or within — the walls around her.

She moved one foot forward, agonizingly slowly, until she reached the edge of the step; and then slid her foot down to the next step. She tapped it with her toe to be sure it was solid and secure before transferring her weight onto it. When she did, she thought she heard a low moaning sound. She made the same tentative move, testing the next step before putting her weight on it. And each time she stepped onto the next step she heard the same low, human groan. Slowly, holding her breath each time until her foot reached the next step below, she tested it for security, and then transferred her weight — only then could she exhale. All the while she kept reminding herself … *Don't touch the walls … Don't touch anything.*

Painstakingly, and with deliberate slowness, Marion descended the stairs. Hours passed, and then she was sure, days on end. In the total darkness there was no way to keep track of time. She kept her eyes closed and thought about the good things that happened to her in life: Her dog Sniff, who was her "best friend" all the while she was growing up. She was not allowed to visit or invite friends home from school — but she always had Sniff, always there for her, wonderful to play with and keep her company. When she finally got away from home and went to college, besides meeting the wonderful dean and his wife — her "surrogate parents" — Marion made many more friends. And when she received her degree in sociology and went on to become a clinical social worker, it was infinitely rewarding to be able to help so many people — especially the women in prison. Their lives were so chaotic and they needed help so desperately. Although the pay was nominal, her reward was far more than money could have provided, when a woman she worked with was successful in turning her life around. And when she did not succeed — well, even just meeting Penny had been a gift. In the darkness, Marion could picture her — and it made her want to keep going.

The darkness began to recede so subtly that Marion was not really sure it was happening. Her eyes were closed, and she had been imagining so many things that she had visions and hallucinations at times. So she could not tell that it was getting lighter immediately. When she finally opened her eyes, a murky red glow was coming up from somewhere below. As she walked, it became brighter, and she could now see a handrail next to the steps. It took the shape of snakes, one entwined around the next. She didn't touch it. The steps became more visible, too, and Marion saw that they were carved in the shape of naked men and women bent over on folded knees, their hands covering their heads. She was stepping on their backs. And from these pitiable creatures came the distinct, low groans she heard as she stepped on them.

Wondering whether she might help these wretched souls, doomed to serve as stepping-stones for — eternity? — Marion bent down and gently touched the one beneath her on one thin bare shoulder. A tormented screech, earsplitting in volume, filled the stairwell around her, and the step began to tremble violently. She feared being thrown off balance, but even more, she feared reaching out to steady herself against the wall and being attacked again by creatures, whole or part. She rode the trembling stair step with her feet apart and her knees bent for maximum stability. Finally it calmed down and the movement stopped, although a pathetic whimpering continued. She continued down the creature-steps.

As the light from below intensified, the heat was also increasing, becoming more intense, and Marion was sweating even more profusely. A noxious, sulfurous odor wafted up from somewhere below. After a time, the light in the stairwell brightened to a clear red, and she could now see the ground beyond the steps. Glimmering in the low light, here and there, a shining stone or brick was set between the steps. But she could not examine them, because as she descended the odor got worse, and she was afraid of retching from disgust. She stepped down the last step, onto the ground, which was rocky and covered with the same gritty sludge as on the hands and legs that had attacked her from within the walls.

At first Marion could see nothing in front of her; but then noticed a small white light coming from somewhere behind her that was illuminating her surroundings. She turned around to see where the light was coming from, but it still seemed to be radiating from behind her. She turned around again, but the light source always seemed to remain behind her.

"It's coming from you, Marion," said a deep stentorian voice that made her jump backward, nearly tripping on a rock. She looked in the direction of the voice, and then took a few tentative steps toward it. As she walked, a figure — nearly invisible in the red light of the surroundings

— became more visible as the white light around Marion lit it up. The massive figure of Lucifer became visible, and Marion was both amazed and filled with terror.

The Lord is my shepherd, I ... she began again, silently — she thought.

"Will you stop that, please?" said Lucifer, "I find it extremely annoying — if you don't mind."

Marion stopped thinking about the Psalm, and started trying to think of something appropriate to say to this creature. Again, he read her thoughts:

"I am Lucifer, my dear — there is nothing appropriate that you can possibly say to me."

Marion just stared at him. He was tall and extremely handsome, in a blood-red tuxedo and tails over a burgundy silk shirt. A flame-orange cummerbund matched his bow-tie; and on his feet were Adua calfskin loafers. Crimson.

Noticing how she gazed at his shoes, Lucifer said, "Contrary to popular belief, I do *not* wear Prada — that's for the Pope." Then, as an afterthought, he added, "I wouldn't want anyone to get us confused," and threw back his head and laughed. The walls shook.

Marion smiled, and gave a weak "heh-heh." She did not want to insult this creature's effort at humor.

Lucifer's smile faded to a serious demeanor, and he stepped closer.

She stood frozen to the spot.

"Now, my dear Marion," he began, with an earnest expression. "Tell me. What can I do for you?"

Marion swallowed hard, her throat dry, sweat trickling down her back. "I — I'm," she began, but then the glimmer of one of those oddly shining bricks from the stairwell caught her eye. She pointed to it. "What are those?"

Lucifer followed the direction of her index finger to the spot at which she was pointing, then turned back to Marion and smiled. "Good intentions... They were."

His smile faded as rapidly as it had appeared, and he said, "Now, my dear Marion, I know you did not come all the way down here to confirm that little adage. May I ask what you *did* come here for?"

"P-Penny Jackson," she answered. "I'm looking for Penny Jackson."

Lucifer stood back and looked Marion up and down. He knew good from evil.

"She's not at all your type, my dear. Why would you be looking for her?"

"I — I think she needs me. I think I might be able to help her."

Lucifer threw back his handsome head and laughed again. Thunder shook the ground they stood on and pebbles rattled down the walls of the cavern.

"Help her? You cannot help her. Besides, she has already gone."

"G-gone? Where? Can you tell me?" Marion asked, anxiety and fear now closing in on her.

"Nope. Can't tell you," he said.

Marion felt herself getting angry now, at his flippant attitude. She expected *some* kind of answer from him, after all her trouble to get here.

"But since you went to all the trouble to get here, I'll *show* you where your little friend is."

Lucifer raised a massive arm and uncurled his fist to reveal his hideous claws. He pointed to a rock formation nearby. Bolts shot out, and the rocks melted into a large screen onto which was projected the same scene of the pregnant woman in the filthy trailer home. Only now, there was a screaming, red-faced baby lying in a pool of blood next to the woman, whose clothing was covered with blood. The woman was unconscious underneath the telephone receiver, which hung down lazily banging against the wall.

"There's your friend." said Lucifer.

"I — I don't understand!" said Marion, "Where is she?"

Lucifer lowered his gaze, sending a red laser-like beam from his eyes onto the baby's image. The baby screamed even more loudly — but more like panic than pain.

"Th-that's P-Penny??" said Marion, dumbfounded by the knowledge that was dawning on her. "That little baby?"

"In the flesh."

They both watched the screen, the screaming baby still tethered to the motionless woman.

Marion turned to Lucifer and said, "Please! *Please!* I have to help her! How can I get to her?"

She reached out to touch Lucifer on the arm in a pleading gesture, but he drew back —almost as though out of fear — as if her touch would be painful to him.

"*Social workers!*" he spat, "*You're all alike!* You think you can save all the wretched misfits and morally defective miscreants of the world! You think you can barge into Hell and turn it into Sesame Street!"

Marion was momentarily put off by this tirade — but then she drew herself up to her own five-foot-three-inch height, put her hands on her hips and surprised herself by saying, "You're damn right!"

Lucifer shook his head as he raised his hand up and uncurled a ghastly claw toward her. Fire streamed from it and hit Marion squarely in the chest. She screamed in pain as it spread through her body, and then she rose upward, off the ground, the pain intensifying with each second, until she was sucked through a vortex of fire and into the scene before them.

The woman opened her eyes and screamed in agony as the second of the twins tore its way out of her body, to lie next to its new sister.

Lucifer watched until the scene faded and the screen melted back into its original rock formation.

Good luck, kid. Take your best shot.

Chapter 20:   Dr. Harrison

Douglas hit the ground hard and felt every bone in his body fracture. He was confused — one minute ago he was talking with Father Bryan and St. Mary herself, wasn't he? What happened?

He looked up at the handsome man whose hand he shook moments ago, and recalled how the ground had suddenly split open and swallowed them both. Then he watched in horror as the man ... changed ... slowly transformed into ... *something else.*

It grew to a giant's size, clothing ripping away, and its skin turned from a smooth tanned bronze to a scaly blood-red color. It's hair was thick and black, with an oily sheen. Two small protrusions extruded from the scalp underneath on each side. A long, pencil-thin mustache curled up from under the nose and a sharply pointed goatee jutted from the chin. Most frightening was the thick tail with a large pointed barb at the end that snaked around from the creature's hind quarters, moving as though it had a mind of its own. It snaked through the air toward Douglas and poked at him, who still lay on the ground in great pain from all the broken bones. Each jab felt like a red-hot needle, and Douglas tried to crawl backward out of its range; but the tail just grew longer and continued its jabbing. It almost seemed to be teasing him, moving to the left and then whipping to the right to catch him with yet another jab. The creature to whom the tail belonged was snickering — apparently enjoying the entertainment.

"Please! *Please, stop! Can't you stop it!*" he pleaded, succeeding only in drawing thunderous peals of laughter from the creature, which became louder with each pathetic plea. Finally the doctor just began to sob, resigned to the torture he had to endure. He stopped trying to avoid the jabbing tail. That is when it stopped and withdrew behind the creature. The laughter stopped, too.

The doctor looked up into the purple-red eyes of the creature and quietly said, "Thank you ... God bless you." The creature drew back as though something had been thrown at his face.

"*Do not say that again!*" it bellowed, with the force of a turbine engine — so strong that Douglas felt his cheeks blown backward toward his scalp.

Perhaps, he thought, he should try to show deference to the creature — to bow, or kiss his hand, or something. He tried to get up, but each movement was excruciatingly painful. He wondered whether any of his bones were *not* broken.

"I-I'm sorry ... I didn't mean to ... uh, insult you, or anything." He stopped trying to move at all.

"Apology accepted," said the creature. All anger seemed to have dissipated. But then, to Douglas's horror, the thick tail came out and began snaking its way toward him again. He started to sob loudly, anticipating the needle-like jabs again.

To his utter surprise, when the tail poked at him this time ... there was no pain. Indeed, the bruised and broken areas where the tail now poked seemed to be — *healing*? He moved an arm in which the bone had surely been shattered, but now it moved easily, with no discomfort at all. The tail poked at his dislocated kneecap, which had slid off to the side, and he watched in amazement as it moved back into its proper place. Then he was able to bend his leg freely. So went his other injuries.

He looked up at the creature, who now had something of a disgusted expression on his face. His arms were folded over his chest, and he was tapping his toe, as though impatient for this restorative process to end. Douglas was afraid to ask him what was happening.

"You'll know soon enough," the creature responded out loud to the other's thoughts.

"M-may I ... uh, get up?" asked Douglas, meekly, when he felt no more pain anywhere. He propped himself up on his elbows.

"Of course," said the creature, and his thick red tail whipped out again, wrapping itself around Douglas' chest and jerking him up to his feet. He wobbled for a minute, and then spun around like a top, as the tail rapidly pulled away.

When he got his bearings again, still slightly dizzy, he looked around and saw that they were in a darkened rocky cavern of sorts, lit only by a reddish light coming from somewhere. He immediately thought of the darkroom he had built in the basement of his house, lit only by red light, where he developed the photos he took of the children he had — *oh, no, no!* He pictured the little naked boys and girls and began to feel a painful stab in his groin again. *No! NO!! I won't think about that anymore! I won't! God help me, never again!*

The creature cringed, his features contorting suddenly as though he had just heard some terrible profanity. But he composed himself quickly, and moved toward an opening in the rocky walls that surrounded them. He crooked his clawed finger toward Douglas, signaling that he should follow. They moved quickly and silently down the passage, Douglas jogging to keep up with the creature's giant stride.

Terrible, frightening sounds emanated from the walls around them: the cawing of birds, the skittering of rats' claws on stone, the hissing and rattling of snakes, and the low growling of predators he did not even want to try and imagine. He heard teeth tearing at wet flesh. He could see none of these creatures, until he nearly ran into a huge bat, the size of a

German shepherd, hanging upside-down from above. Its eyes flashed bright red, fangs bared, and its wingspread blocked Douglas's passage. As he bent forward to try and get by without disturbing it, the horrible winged rodent suddenly dropped down and wrapped itself around his face and shoulders, tightly covering him. Douglas's scream was muffled by the animal's body.

"Down, Rupert!" Lucifer commanded, and the bat released Douglas and flew off down the passageway, with a shriek so piercing that Douglas had to cover his ears from the pain. Lucifer laughed and said, "Don't mind him — he just likes to play."

When they finally got to the end of the passageway, Lucifer stopped in front of what looked like a set of elevator doors. They glistened in the low light, and Douglas saw that the doors were covered with huge multifaceted blood red rubies — and from them emanated the red light that illuminated the cavern.

Lucifer turned toward Douglas, and said, "I could have had you for eons, you know." He had a strangely frustrated look on his face. "Now it can only be for one year. And that's only if you choose me over your other option."

"Other — ?"

"That's right, Mr. — oh, pardon me — *Doctor* Harrison. You have two choices."

"Wh-what are they?" he stammered, then feared that he may have overstepped his bounds in the view of this frightening creature. "Uh, that is… if it's all right to ask?"

"Yes, of course. Are you stupid? How could you make a choice without knowing what they are?" Lucifer looked up and stroked his goatee, "On second thought … It would be fun to have you make a blind choice!"

Lucifer's laughter stopped short and he tipped his head sideways, as though hearing something from somewhere. "Okay, okay … I'll give him his choices," he muttered.

He turned toward Douglas, and at the same time, placed his finger on a magnificent ruby in the shape of a starburst, just to the right of the elevator doors.

"You already know what you have to face here, and for how long," Lucifer said, staring into Douglas's eyes, reading his every thought and response. "You will remain here — yes, *here*, in this cavern — making friends with all the sweet lovely creatures who dwell here — or *fighting them off*, as the case may be!"

Lucifer indulged himself in a thunderous belly laugh that caught on like a contagion among the multitude of unseen creatures, who laughed and roared and screeched along with him. Douglas could hear water sloshing from somewhere behind or within the cavern walls.

"And ... and ... You said ... I have *another* choice?" he asked, fear raising goose bumps under every inch of his skin.

"Yes — But I don't know why you would take it," Lucifer answered, pressing the ruby starburst under his thumb. The elevator doors instantly and noiselessly swooped open.

The scene beyond was shocking.

Douglas beheld the African country of Darfur, an area in the center of the country, an arid plateau with the Marrah Mountain range of volcanic peaks rising up to ten thousand feet. He could see a multitude of licorice-skinned people — adults in bright colorful garb tending their fields and meager animals; and many, many children, playing about. As he looked closer, he saw that there were mostly women and children, many with distended bellies — the children's from poor nutrition, and the women from carrying yet more babies. When he spied an adult male, he often had a limb missing, or some other severe disfigurement. There were no young men or boys there — they had all been recruited or kidnapped into the patchwork of warring militias.

Lucifer went on, "If you choose this fate, you will spend many decades here — a minimum of seven, I can assure you, maybe more — growing up among them, working as a physician and caring for the population — especially the children." He looked over at Douglas, who seemed mesmerized — not at all repulsed — by the sight in front of him.

Lucifer gave a disgusted cluck of his tongue, and then went on: "However, if you stay here in this warm and lovely cavern with me, remember, it will only be for *one* year — one teeny, tiny, little year! Pretty good deal, eh?" Lucifer smiled broadly, showing two rows of jagged black teeth, gleaming like onyx.

"But I ... I can go *there* if I choose?" asked Douglas, pointing to the vista revealed behind the ruby doors. "I can help care for them?"

"For a lifetime! A l-o-o-o-o-o-ng, long lifetime! Like, the better part of a *century*, even!" Then he added, "And you would be subject to the same suffering as *they* are! You would be born of those people and minister to them, but you would experience starvation, attacks from hostile tribes, pestilence, disease — all of those Biblical shenanigans — and more!"

Douglas just stared at the vision. He saw desperately poor, hardworking people. He stared at the little children among them. He was shocked to discover that he did not feel any sexual stimulation at all.

And suddenly he was overwhelmed by a huge, unexpected joy — he felt so happy when he realized that — the children no longer stimulated any prurient feelings in him! He swallowed hard to keep from crying.

Then he recalled something. He looked up at Lucifer, staring him straight in the eyes for the first time since being there.

"You said ... Didn't you say something about ... Didn't you say you *'could have* had me for eons,' but *now* I have a choice? What did you mean by that?"

Lucifer was becoming impatient; and it was infuriating to him to be questioned by this insignificant footslogger. He began to turn even redder, inflating his chest, heat rising into his face and gnashing his teeth together. He raised one huge hand, spreading the hideous claws — and Douglas shrank back in fear.

But nothing happened. He suddenly stopped, closed his fist and dropped his hand back down. Once again he cocked his head to the side as though listening to something which Douglas could not hear.

"Okay, OKAY! DAMN ALL OF YOU!" He visibly deflated, and the temperature dropped around them. He smiled at Douglas.

"Yes, dear Doctor, I could have had you for eons — here in my cozy little abode — for hundreds of years, maybe a thousand! And in that time, you would be my slave, my whipping boy, my plaything; and my *pets'* plaything." At that, he swept his massive arm around the place, and the sounds of the creatures which had receded as they came to the ruby doors now increased in a great screaming cacophony.

Lucifer snapped his fingers sharply, and the sounds instantly ceased.

"But n-o-o-o-o-o-o, you had to go and *feel sorry for what you did*! You had to go and *help that little girl*, you had to go and *give her your scarf to cover her nakedness;* then you went and carried her to safety in (yechh) Saint Agnes' arms." He seemed to choke a little on her name.

Lucifer looked as though ... he were about to cry. His lower lip trembled and his voice had risen to a squeak at the end. But he took a deep breath and composed himself. "You even *apologized to God* when you were sinking in my little sludge pit, *without so much as asking Him for mercy!*" A black velvet cloth materialized in Lucifer's hand, and he blew his nose into it with a noisy honk. "You ... you ... *redeemed yourself!*"

Still shaken and sniffling, but with more conviction, he added, "Partially."

After that, Lucifer became quiet, and looked so genuinely miserable that Douglas was tempted to say something ... something like ... *There, there, fella.*

Lucifer glared sideways at him and said, "Don't even try it!"

A minute passed, and the giant creature dabbed at his eyes with his black hanky, and said in a voice so quiet and calm that Douglas couldn't believe it was the same creature, "You see, on earth they say 'One bad apple can spoil the whole bushel.' But *here*, one *good* apple can cleanse and renew all the spoiled ones. So, when you expressed *true remorse* — abandoning all hope, *accepting* your punishment, requesting no mercy — you earned a much lesser penalty for your sins."

Then under his breath, barely audible, he added, "I was robbed."

Lucifer dabbed at his eyes again, and then balled up the black velvet handkerchief, and it disappeared into his palm.

"Now," he said, completely expressionless, "Choose."

Douglas stepped through the ruby doors.

Lucifer grimaced. *The agony of defeat.*

Chapter 21: *Father Bryan*

Everything had been so much fun, so enjoyable and so gratifying. Father Bryan had been spending his days helping to identify and transport the new flock of visitors from their place in line to "the Portal," helping to counsel them, taking last-minute (really overdue) confessions, and so forth. He occasionally met some old friends, and was especially thrilled to see Tom and Rachel Quadling again. Many decades earlier, he had advised Tom not to worry about being separated from his Jewish wife after they died, as Rachel would be "known by her work" — recognized for her inate goodness and kindness, and her selfless generosity toward others — and she would be reunited with Tom in heaven.

Bryan enjoyed his work here so much. His new colleagues were a lot of fun, too. Rabbi "Moe" Mendelson was a fountain of knowledge, but also a real stitch, who had a seemingly infinite supply of "a priest, a rabbi, and a lawyer" jokes. Gabriel was ever available with the most astute advice. There were others on their elite but humble team — Michael, who always had a kind word about every soul they engaged; Raphael, who was good at predicting the penances that would be assigned; Ishmael, who took it upon himself to collect and mend the body parts of the tragically misguided suicide bombers and minister to them. Mary could always be counted on to appear at the precise moment that her knowledge, support, or advice was needed to resolve seemingly unsolvable problems or debated issues.

Beyond the delightful company, Bryan had the opportunity to travel. He had flown to new and exciting places with one or the other of his new colleagues, or with old friends whom he was tasked to — or received permission to — pluck from the line and bring forward. He was always surprised when an old friend or parishioner he saw waiting in line did not recognize him, or even acknowledge his greeting ... such as the time he saw Carrie Barley Bennington. His new colleagues explained that not all those who had just crossed over were operating on the same mental and spiritual plane; and they would need more time before they were able to communicate with him.

Bryan's recreational excursions had taken him on a Tour of the Stars — not the Hollywood ones. He had visited Sol, the star that warmed and lit his home planet of earth; Alpha Centauri, the closest neighboring star; and many of the planets and moons in between. His own Moon, he was not surprised to learn, was *not* made of green cheese. Venus was. At least, it was in one particularly crater-filled region. He scooped up a handful and tasted it — very Swiss-like, actually, but more tangy.

Mars was teeming with life, not visible to the human eye at all. The Martians were tangerine-skinned with light blue or green eyes. Some of the anthropological experts in the group thought they resembled the native American Melungeon Indians, a tribe thought to be of Mediterranean — Spanish or Portuguese — descent who may have settled in the Appalachian wilderness in the sixteenth century. That provoked a lively discussion about the "Chariots of the Gods," and interplanetary cohabitation.

The inhabitants of Jupiter — the Jovials, as they liked to call themselves — looked more like mineral than animal. Indeed, they were huge, lumbering folk that required the equivalent strength of steel girders in their skeleton to remain standing upright against the massive gravitational pull of Jupiter. True to their nickname, they loved to joke and tease, frequently knocking themselves over with laughter. Moe visited them often, where he found both a great audience and a great source of material.

Saturn was the only somber place. Classes were held there for confused souls who were not innately evil, but had been deluded into false beliefs and manipulated by unscrupulous leaders.

Pluto was a surprise, since it was thought to be a barren chunk of ice, even losing its designation as a full-fledged "planet" by those who felt it failed to meet "true" planetary standards. Pluto, though, like Mars, was teeming with life. These were a slender, wiry breed of people, all of whom had big, hairy pets in their magnificent homes, which put our "McMansions" to shame. Every family not only had a house, but every family member and even each pet had its own suite of rooms in the house — a bedroom for sleeping, a lounge for reading, a study for working, a cleansing room and an evacuation room (the latter two separate, rather than one "bathroom"). The only place they all congregated was the single, cavernous kitchen/dining room. The Plutons could not fathom the term "homeless" and insisted it was some kind of a joke that Moe was working on.

But the most unusual inhabitants that Bryan met were on the planet closest to the sun, where no life could possibly have been expected to exist — Mercury. The Mercurials were pure liquid, and flowed through their cities and streets with a stream-like gait. They lived in bowl-shaped homes, and filled it up to the rim when the whole family was at home. Yet at the same time, each person kept his or her own individual identity — somewhat like the different colored bubbles in a lava lamp.

Other moons and planets and stars in other galaxies were just as amazing and exciting.

Bryan loved every minute of his recreational time, but he frequently cut the tours short so that he could return to his ministering at the Portal, and especially to the people in line farther back. That was where his heart was, and his thoughts were never far away from them no matter where in the universe he happened to be.

Now he found himself thinking about Dr. Douglas Harrison again. He had pulled him from the vile pit in which he had sunk up to his nose. Then he was snatched down into the bowels of the earth, or somewhere, by Lucifer. He wondered how he was doing now; and at the very moment he had that thought, he saw a red beam of light coming from somewhere. He felt a strong compulsion, as well as curiosity, to follow it to its source. He took only one step toward it when Mary appeared in a bright scintillating light that obscured the red beam. Her silken, silvery gown rippled softly in the cool breeze that seemed always to come along wherever she appeared.

"Let's not go there," she said to Bryan, before he had a chance to greet her.

"W-well," he stammered, not wanting to contradict her advice — but already knowing that it was only advice, and his decision would always be his own to make.

Actually, it *had* to be his own decision. He had already discovered that he would be impeded in doing anything that he was doing only because one of the Team recommended it, if in his heart he truly disagreed with it. So he told Mary his feelings. He wanted to see how Dr. Harrison was doing. He wanted to go.

"I knew that," she said. She hugged him gently and kissed his cheek. A sweet sense of joy settled around him. "Goodbye, my son."

The brilliant light faded with Mary's exit, and the cool breeze disappeared. The red beam was visible again; and the temperature began to rise.

Bryan followed the beam, which led back into the same wooded area where he first stumbled across Dr. Harrison in the muck pit. He walked for days, it seemed, and the rocks and slime increased as he went, as did the murkiness of the air, until he could no longer see anything that was not near enough to the unremitting red beam casting its meager light. The heat seemed to increase each day. He was sweating profusely, and felt desperate for a drink of water — but somehow he did not weaken at all. At some point the red beam began to get bigger and much, much hotter. Bryan felt as though he were swimming in his sweat. He tried taking his collar off and opening his shirt, but the heat seemed to singe his exposed skin, so he put them back on again.

After estimating that he had been walking for at least two weeks, Bryan seriously began to doubt whether he could or would succeed in his mission to find Dr. Harrison. As soon as these thoughts of disappointment and failure entered his mind, the red beam began to diffuse into a lighter color, until it finally suffused the whole atmosphere with a warm — but no longer hot — pink mist. It was lighter, and now Bryan thought he saw someone sitting in the distance. Yes, it *was* who he thought it would be.

Lucifer appeared eminently dashing in his red leather Dolce & Gabbana military jacket and matching studded jeans, with ostrich leather cranberry slip-ons.

"May I help you, Father Bryan?" Lucifer asked, in a tone so silky and seductive that Bryan felt a desire to walk over and hug him. Lucifer's face showed a momentary shadow of fury, but then melted back into his handsome and gracious appearance. Bryan was amazed at how sweet and kindly the creature could look and yet still emanate such a feeling of deadly foreboding.

"I'm checking on someone you ... someone who went off with you."

"Yes, I know," said the dandy, inspecting his perfectly manicured nails. "The good doctor. Douglas Harrison."

"Uh ... yes, actually ... that's right," said Bryan, still surprised when everyone around here seemed to know what he was thinking before he said it. "May I get an ... uh, update ... on his whereabouts?"

"No," Lucifer responded, without looking up, now picking up a small creature with grotesque scales on its back, that had started crawling up his pants leg. A trail of slime stained his shoes and was now beginning to stain his pants. The creature began to sizzle under Lucifer's two grasping fingers, and then a rapid flame shot up, disappearing under a puff of smoke. The creature and the trail of slime had turned to dust, and Lucifer tapped his toe, causing the dust to fall off, leaving a pristine pant leg and shoe. Then he looked up at Bryan.

"Any other requests?"

Bryan took a deep breath and pulled himself up to his full tall, thin height. He folded his arms across his chest. "*I want to know about Dr. Harrison. What happened to him?*"

Lucifer stared intensely at Bryan — which felt like standing in the path of a welding torch. The lanky priest started to tremble, unable to ignore the pain — but he stood his ground.

One corner of Lucifer's mouth twitched. How he enjoyed watching people squirm in pain!

"You want to know what happened to Dr. Harrison?" he said, raising one eyebrow and intensifying his stare, and in so doing, increasing Bryan's pain, "Are you sure — *absolutely sure* — that is what you want?"

"Y-y-yes," said Bryan, now sweating even more profusely, not just from the heat and the pain — but from a fear so overpowering that it almost seemed to paralyze him. He parted his lips to say a prayer; but before he could utter the first word, he watched as Lucifer began to rise up ... and up and up. His surging size continued until he reached nine feet in height, his skin darkening to the color of dried blood. The stylish clothing tore away to reveal his mountainous stature; the cloven hooves burst through his shoes.

Lucifer uncurled a huge claw, and hooked it into the priest's neck, causing excruciating pain. Bryan tried to scream, but he felt his breath cut off as they were both sucked down into a flaming whirlpool, the pain increasing beyond human endurance, spinning down, down, down.

He landed with a painful crash onto rock-hard ground, glistening from the heat that radiated from everywhere. He was dizzy and nauseated, and began retching, again and again, but there was nothing in him to come up.

When he could finally pull himself together, Bryan looked around and saw Lucifer standing some distance away, smiling.

"The doctor will see you now!" He started laughing; then abruptly stopped. "Well, this *is* what you wanted ... ain't it, my dear Father Bryan?"

He started laughing again even louder, and small creatures from all over began skittering around quickly and disappearing into hidden pockets, while others — much larger, from the sound of them — roared and snarled and howled.

Bryan stood up slowly, testing each limb to be sure it was intact. He took a handkerchief from his pocket and wiped at his grimy and sweat-drenched face. He renewed his resolve.

"That is correct, Sir!" he said, in a voice so strong and clear that it surprised even himself. Lucifer twitched slightly. "Now, if you don't mind, please show me where I can find Dr. Harrison."

Lucifer's face darkened with frustration and rage. It infuriated him when these do-gooders came around and thwarted his control. With one scaly claw he pointed toward a passageway in the rocky cavern.

Bryan turned and swiftly walked through the opening. He could see a bright red gleaming light coming from somewhere down the passageway. As he approached, he saw a large cylindrical extrusion, like a drainage pipe — encrusted with beautiful sparkling rubies. It extended straight up through the floor of the cavern, and had a handle mounted on each side ... and a set of eye-pieces?

A periscope? Coming up from ... below?

"Pretty cool, dont'cha think?" said Lucifer, who suddenly appeared next to Bryan.

The priest did not answer him, even though he did think, whatever it was, really was pretty cool.

"Where is Dr. Harrison?" he repeated.

"Oh, all right!" mumbled Lucifer, "Haven't you ever heard of just stopping to smell the roses?" And with that, he pointed toward the eye pieces of the device. Bryan looked into them.

Before him, the priest saw the hostile, scarred territory of Darfur, and the bedraggled and poverty-stricken peoples there. The scene moved to a tent-like structure, with beds and crude medical equipment. The beds were full, some with two patients in each, some with children, bandaged, delirious, arms tethered to IV poles. A slender man, his coal black skin sharply contrasted against the white smock he wore, bent over a woman in one of the beds. He gently held up each eyelid in turn and waved a pen light over her eyes. Then he adjusted her IV tubes and patted her shoulder gently. She looked at him with great compassion, smiling through obvious pain, and mumbled something. The doctor nodded and patted her again. Then he moved on to the next patient. He started to check that patient's IV, but looked startled momentarily. He pulled a stethoscope from inside his smock and placed it on the patient's chest. After a minute, he reached over and closed the man's eyelids, and gently pulled the sheet up to cover his face. Tears came to the doctor's eyes. He knelt down next to the bed and bowed his head, silently moving his lips.

Bryan looked over at Lucifer, who was looking away from the scene. He tried to suppress his impatience as he said, "Are you going to show me where Dr. Harrison is?"

Lucifer pointed toward the periscope. Then he crossed his arms over his chest and looked at Bryan with his lip curled up.

With a sudden shock, Bryan realized ... the black doctor he had been watching ... *That was Douglas Harrison!* It took a moment before he could fully grasp what he saw. Then he knew what he had to do.

"He ... He looks like he could use some help there ... " said Bryan, trailing off with uncertainty about how his request would be received.

"I suppose you would like to help him?" said Lucifer, leaning in toward Bryan, his red-purple eyes becoming bigger and bigger, extruding halfway out of their sockets. A more frightening sight Bryan had never beheld.

"I ... I would ... if I may ... If I could," Bryan answered.

"It can be arranged, you know," said Lucifer, leaning even closer now. Bryan could feel the heat and vile odor of his breath.

"Are ... you ... *sure? Absolutely ... sure?*"

Instantly, before Father Bryan could draw a breath to answer, a blindingly bright light and blessedly cool wind blew into the cavern. The sulfurous odor that permeated the place wafted away and was replaced with the sweet scent of lilacs. Mary appeared from within the light and hovered a few feet above the periscope. Her brilliance outshined all the glowing rubies and lit up the cavern like a bright spring day.

Lucifer stumbled backward into a corner and raised his hands to shield his eyes from the light.

"Bryan, my son," Mary said, her voice as lovely as a crystal wind chime. "Please think this through carefully."

From his corner, still holding his hand like a visor to shield him from the light, Lucifer shouted, "*Free will,* my dear Mary! *Free will* ... Remember? That little principle is from *your side!* Now you have to *stand by it!*"

He turned to Bryan and, dropping his voice to an ominous rasp, said, "It's your choice! You have earned this choice! You may have *whatever you wish!* Now, *CHOOSE!*"

The slender priest looked up at Mary.

"He is right, my son ... It is your choice," she said. Then she quickly added, "You do not have to do this, you know ... We can use your help ... The team misses you!" She hovered in her exquisite beauty, palms open and extended to him.

Turning slightly, Brian looked back into the periscope, at the heartbreaking scene in the pathetic hospital. Dr. Harrison needed help, no question about that. Those people desperately needed more help. He could help.

Bryan reached up and touched Mary's fingertips, which sent streams of energy and joy into him — but more importantly, what he needed at this moment — courage.

He had made up his mind. He was instantly sucked into the periscope.

Chapter 22: *Carrie*

Carrie cried often these days. She did not want to be back at the end of the line. It was moving as slowly as it had before. Day followed endless day, night followed night, and she was inching forward as best she could tell only by the estimated distance between the trees. She kept going over and over how good she had been in her lifetime — raising five children, active with the church, celibate after her last child, trying to save her first husband, Jules, by keeping him celibate, too — how could she not be whisked up to Jesus first and foremost? How could they stick her with those ... those ... miscreants? A Jew, a homosexual, a tramp — and Jules, who contracted that horrible disease. What were they thinking??? She started crying again.

Hoping to keep track of the time in some way, she started putting a tiny pebble in her pocket after each day and night; then when she had 30 pebbles in her pocket, she picked up a blade of grass. When she finally got to the head of the line once again, she had more than sixty blades of grass in her pocket. Even more depressing was the fact that she had hardly eaten anything in all this time, and yet she was still as plump as she was when she first got here.

Eventually she found herself once more standing in front of Gabriel at his lectern. She immediately dropped to her knees and began to cry. She was crying so hard that she could not find her voice. Gabriel tried to tell her that everything was all right, and she need not kneel before him again, but her wails drowned out his words. He waited patiently for her to get it all out of her system.

After a few minutes, she got the hiccups and stopped crying. She looked up at him, and he extended his hand to help her up. The gentle strength of it sent ripples of comfort coursing through her, and she started to cry all over again, sobs alternating with hiccups. When she was once again able to compose herself, she looked at Gabriel with puffy, reddened eyes.

"Now, Carrie — It's good to see you again, dear," he said, as kindly as he could. The woman whimpered a little, and her lip trembled, but she managed to refrain from crying again. She was really about all cried out.

Looking around, Carrie was relieved that she did not see the same silver-robed group of people that she saw last time. She was grateful for that, since she did not want to go with those low-lifes. Perhaps now she would be given her true place, a seat by — or somewhere near — Jesus. Or one of the saints. Preferably Mary. Surely she had earned that, with all her good work! But she was fearful of asking Gabriel about it, as she was still uncertain why her lifelong devotion to the church did not confer that position for her when she was here last time.

Anyway, any of the saints would do. She would not complain, even if it were one of the lesser saints. But hopefully not that Margaret of Castello, though … a deformed outcast … Surely she deserves better than that!

"Now, Carrie, let's see what we can do for you," said Gabriel, again flipping the pages of his massive golden book, and running the index finger of the tiny hand on his silver pointer down until it stopped.

"Ah, yes. Here you are." He looked up at her.

"Am I going to see Jesus now?" she blurted out, still picturing herself sitting next to him. She immediately clapped her hands over her mouth, as she had not intended to ask that again. More tears began to squeeze out of her tiny eyes and rolled down onto her hands.

"Ah … not just yet, my dear," said Gabriel.

Carrie's lower lip began to tremble again, and she was suddenly struck by a terrible thought. She grabbed onto the lectern so violently that it nearly tipped over, and Gabriel took a step backward.

"YOU'RE NOT GOING TO SEND ME BACK AGAIN, ARE YOU?? OH, PLEASE, NOT THE LINE AGAIN!! NOT THE LINE!!"

"No, no, my dear!" said Gabriel, patting her hands, which were still gripping the lectern, her knuckles turning white. "No, you are just not going to see Jesus *just yet* … But you will have that opportunity in the future."

That was true. The "future" could mean tomorrow or it could mean eons away, so he was being truthful. And it did succeed in calming her down.

"Oh, *thank you, thank you*, Mr. Gabriel, Sir!" Carrie said, nearly beside herself with joy. "I knew you would do the right thing this time!"

"Just *Gabriel*, my dear," he responded, ignoring the rest of her comments. "Now, come with me, please."

The archangel extended his arm to Carrie, and she was thrilled when together they lifted up into the air, softly gliding up the hundreds of massive marble steps to the entrance of the Portal. He stopped to open the doors for her, and ushered her into a plain, unadorned room. The walls were bare, except for one window high up on one wall. At the far corner of the room there was a man sitting in a chair next to a small table with some items on it. At least, she *thought* it was a man. She could not see his face. He was covered in a hooded robe that appeared to be made of sackcloth, with a plain piece of rope tied around the waist.

Gabriel put his arm around the little woman's shoulders and waved his other arm in a wide motion around the wall that had the window at the top. The window began to widen and lengthen, and soon it filled the entire wall. The beautiful landscape outside could be seen along with the line of people waiting for their turn to come forward. Then the scene faded and Carrie recognized the kitchen in her oldest daughter's home.

Kate was balancing a baby on her hip while she was stirring a pot on the stove. The baby's three-year-old brother was playing noisily with some pots and pans on the floor. The telephone rang, and the mother walked over to the other wall and picked up the telephone. Something disturbing must have been said, as she frowned and then appeared nervous and anxious. She set the baby down on the floor, and he immediately started crying loudly. Kate put her hand over her other ear to drown out the crying so she could hear what the other person was saying on the phone. The pot on the stove began to boil, but she did not seem to see it. The baby started to crawl in the direction of his three-year-old brother, who had stood up next to the stove to see what was in the pot.

The scene faded and a new one took its place. Carrie recognized her second son, apparently at his workplace.

Mike was in an office building, high up in a skyscraper somewhere, as there was a large picture window overlooking a beautiful view of the city. The office was expensively appointed. Mike was standing on a plush burgundy carpet in front of a massive mahogany desk with ornate brass fittings. His head was bowed, and his hands were clasped behind his back. A large man with a ruddy face and a heavy double chin was sitting behind the desk. He was yelling something. Then he picked up some papers from his desk and threw them at the younger man, who nodded, and then bent down to pick up the scattered papers. Then the man behind the desk turned his chair around and stared out of the window, no longer talking. When Mike collected all of the pages from the floor, he left, quietly closing the door behind him.

The scene changed again. Now Carrie saw her sixteen-year-old grandchild.

Brittney was looking out of a window. She was standing in a starkly barren room furnished only with a metal cot and a washbasin on a stand. There was a large crucifix hanging over the cot. The young girl looked despondent, her head hanging down. When she turned, her large protruding belly became visible. The girl was pregnant.

The scene faded. The window began to shrink back to its original tiny size and position at the top of the wall.

Gabriel was standing there looking at Carrie.

"Well, what can I do?" she asked, sensing the message in the scenarios. "I can't help them now, can I? I would if I could. But I can't, right?"

Gabriel did not say anything, so Carrie felt compelled to keep talking. "They are all adults, anyway, so they need to work out their own problems — isn't that right?"

"Well-l-l-l," said Gabriel, crossing his arms over his chest and rocking back on his heels. "That's partially correct. Actually, if you wanted to, we could arrange for you to go back there." He quickly added, "That is, if that would be your choice."

Carrie was stunned. "G-go back ... Th-there? Why ... How?"

Gabriel did not answer.

"Why would ... My choice? ... Why would I choose to go back there?" Now she felt herself getting angry. "You said I could meet Jesus!"

"Yes," said Gabriel, gently, without sighing or showing any impatience. "I said you could do that. That is a choice you will have, too. However, you would have to complete some tasks first."

"Tasks?" Carrie narrowed her eyes and looked askance at Gabriel. *"What tasks?"*

Turning toward the man in the robe sitting at the far end of the room, Gabriel said, "Come with me ... I want you to meet someone."

As they got closer, Carrie could not see the man's face, for his hood kept it in shadow. When they approached him, the man remained seated, and did not get up, as Carrie had thought he should. She found that a bit off-putting, but did not say anything.

Gabriel introduced them. "Lazarus, this is Carrie. Carrie, Lazarus."

The man extended his hand, but the woman drew back, horrified. Sores and chunks of skin were hanging, and fingers were missing from the hand.

"I'm sorry," said the man, withdrawing his hand back to his lap. "I'm sick, you see."

Carrie tried to restrain her revulsion and churning of her stomach. She looked away from the man and back up at Gabriel.

"Why do I have to meet this ... this ... creature?"

"You do wish to meet Jesus, do you not?" Gabriel answered.

Carried nodded, "Yes, of course! You said I could meet Him! Not this ... this ... sick person!"

"You must complete some tasks first, Carrie — do you remember my telling you that?"

"Yes, of course I do!" she answered, showing some irritation that he would think her memory was so short. "Please tell me what they are, and I shall complete them immediately, and then see our Lord!"

"This is your task, Carrie," said Gabriel. He reached over to the little table beside the man and where sat a plain porcelain bowl, a pitcher, a large sponge, and a bar of soap. He lifted the pitcher and poured water from it into the bowl, then set the bowl down on the floor next to the hem of the man's robe. When he lifted the hem, he exposed the man's sandaled feet, which were covered in weeping sores, bloody lesions and missing chunks of flesh.

Carrie was mortified and drew back in disgust; but Gabriel seemed to be unaffected by the sight. He gently grasped the man's feet, one at a time, and removed his sandals. Then he looked up at Carrie, who had turned slightly green with nausea.

"Your task," he said quietly, "is to wash his feet."

Carrie shook her head violently from side to side, unable to speak the words to reject the assignment. Then her knees buckled and she slowly slid down to the floor and lost consciousness.

When she came to and opened her eyes again, the afflicted man was still sitting there, his grotesque feet still awaiting her care. Gabriel stood off to the side. She looked away from the man and crawled over to Gabriel. Tugging at the hem of his robes, tears squeezed out of her eyes, and a pathetic, pleading look suffused her face.

"I-I can't do this! Please, Sir! Don't make me do this!"

Gabriel reached down and helped her to her feet. He spoke as gently as if he were addressing a hurt child. "I *can't* make you do this, Carrie. You *do not* have to do this. It is your choice. Do you understand? *It is your choice.*"

"M-my choice? Then … then I choose to meet Jesus! I-I'll wash *his* feet!!"

"No, Carrie. Washing the feet of Lazarus is your assigned task. But if you choose not to accept it …"

Carrie became terrified at that moment. What would be the option? Going back to the path again??? She couldn't touch that horrid man's feet, but she couldn't even imagine going through the line again either! She held tighter onto Gabriel's robe, hardly able to form her words.

"P-P-Please!! P-P-…"

"You do have another choice, my dear." Gabriel waved his hand at the window which had shown some of her family members in their present lives. "If you are not up to the tasks required to access a higher plane, then you may choose a little more time with your family on earth."

Carrie closed her eyes. After a minute, she slowly nodded her head.

The sixteen-year-old girl doubled over and grabbed onto the bed frame. She held her breath against the pain, and when she could finally let it out again, she started to shout.

"Sister Marguerite! Sister Marguerite! Help me! Help me, please!"

The nun came running into the room.

Soon the robust cries of a baby could be heard throughout the convent.

Brittney sat on the floor, cradling the tiny new baby girl in her arms, gently rocking her until her tiny eyes closed.

"I'm going to call her Caroline," she said to Sister Marguerite, as she nestled the baby in her arms. "It just came to me."

Chapter 23: Christopher

The group hugged and kissed goodbye as they knew each would be going on their own way. Christopher and Dana were leaving together. They both hugged Maria — Carrie and Jules' former housekeeper and nanny. Then Christopher hugged Jules and slapped him on the back.

"We'll see you guys again!" They all said their goodbyes: gay Jeremy; Andrea, the single mother, whom they knew from church; and Aaron, the African-American man who had lost a leg and begged for subsistence on the street. All were kind-hearted, gentle and generous souls who gave of themselves to others, and were destined for a multitude of choices.

Maria was forgiving of Carrie, who fired her at the age of sixty-three, after eighteen years of below-minimum wage service, with no advance notice and no provision for her welfare. But Jules secretly provided for her after she left; and after his death, when Christopher married Carrie and learned about it from the bank trustee, he continued paying her wages. Still in her heart, Maria held no animosity for Carrie, simply feeling sorry for the woman who was so spiritually destitute.

Jeremy felt equally sad for those who would not accept him for what he was — a hard worker, generous to a fault, and dedicated to the church in which he was raised in spite of their proscription of his lifestyle. He couldn't help it, he realized early on, and no longer tried to fight his natural leanings. He spent his adult life in a loving relationship with Eric, taking complete care of him during the last year of his life in a battle with cancer. But Eric's parents were the ones contacted to remove his life support at the end, even though they shunned his lifestyle and had nothing to do with him for years. Now Jeremy and Eric were together again, and stood arm-in-arm as the others came and hugged them and said goodbye.

Andrea had tried very hard to make friends with the other women of the church. She never thought that her single-parent status, as well as her flamboyant style of dress that accentuated her good figure made her the object of their resentment. She never stopped trying to be a good friend, a contributor to the church in spite of her meager income, and a volunteer, driving the older church members to their doctors' appointments, picking up groceries for them, and other necessities. Andrea always felt that her failure to be fully welcomed into the sisterhood was her own fault, though. She had a limited education, having dropped out of school when she got pregnant. After the baby was born, she enrolled in night school, first to get her high school equivalency degree, and hoping eventually to get certified as a teacher's aide. It was hard, taking one or two courses at a time, raising her daughter, and working eight- and ten-hour days in a convenience store. Her parents — who frequently reminded her how disappointed they were in her out-of-wedlock pregnancy — grudgingly helped out with childcare.

Andrea always felt she had let everyone down — her parents, her daughter, the church. No matter how hard she worked, no matter what she did for others, she always felt guilty. So when she died in a car accident at forty-two, what a surprise it was to be plucked out of the line by the little Rabbi and brought into this divine group of people! Secretly, in her heart, she thought they made a mistake — how could *she* be chosen for such a reward? But still, it was such a thrill to be *included!* Now these beautiful people were hugging and kissing her, and she felt a joy she had not known since her baby girl was born.

Aaron was born and raised in the housing projects. He managed to avoid the lure of drugs and the "security" of joining a gang, but did poorly in school. He dropped out and tried to join the military. That's when he discovered that he had diabetes. He worked at whatever job he could find, but could not take care of his health. Going to the free clinics meant hours of waiting to be seen — hours that translated to lost wages — and that time could double waiting to pick up a prescription. Eventually, a simple foot infection that would have been minor in a non-diabetic person became gangrenous. His leg had to be amputated. The doctors told him he was lucky to have survived at all. Alcohol was the most accessible drug to manage his constant pain, and along with his physical disability, he ended up homeless — sleeping in the street and begging for change. Aaron had nothing, and often wondered why he kept living at all. But he always seemed to find someone worse off than himself — and that gave him a strange sense of purpose. He would share his tattered blanket with someone sleeping in the cold. A discarded jacket with a zip-out lining made "two jackets," and he would give one away. He shared a precious pint of whiskey with the blind man who played the accordion on the opposite corner.

I'm lucky, he thought, *I have my eyesight.*

He passed away at fifty-three from liver disease. And he, like Andrea, was sure there was a mistake when he was plucked up by the little rabbi and taken to the head of the line.

They each went with Gabriel, alone or with their loved one, to the Portal. Christopher and Dana stood in front of the window, and watched as the different scenes were revealed to them. Christopher saw his parents, who were traversing the universe in a group tour. (He knew it was a group tour because they all carried the same tote bag — black velvet adorned with twinkling star-shaped crystals that spelled out "Elysian Excursions." The tour guide was holding up an umbrella of the same design.) Their tour guide was an electric flash who could change chameleon-like to resemble whatever creatures they encountered on other planets and stars. That enabled the group to be welcomed instantly and receive red-carpet treatment by the host inhabitants. When the tour guide appeared as a female of the species, he went by the name Marlena; when a male, Holden. Those names seemed to bring a favorable reception no matter where they went.

Another scene revealed in the window was the beautiful house in which Christopher and Dana had lived during the brief two years of their marriage, before Dana died. Since Christopher had also died prematurely, they were both given the option to return to their old neighborhood, to be born into kind, loving, well-endowed families, and they would meet each other again in that lifetime.

But — then they viewed another scene which excited both of them the moment they saw it. Simultaneously they agreed on going there. Gabriel motioned them through the window, and when they turned back around, the building was gone.

Looking around at their surroundings now, the landscape was just as beautiful as that in which they found themselves when they first arrived. The grass was a deep emerald green with a swirling opalescent sheen. The sky was bright neon blue, and the clouds were white with pink and gold tinges that gave them the beauty of a sunset in full daylight.

Christopher and Dana walked a little ways until they saw the first figure, sitting in a chaise lounge chair under a grove of what looked like pecan trees. There were two empty chaise lounges next to him, and he waved his hand, indicating they should sit down. The chairs were covered with the softest of velvet cushions, thick and plush, and so smooth that it almost felt as though they were touching air. When they sat down, a silent, almost imperceptible vibration gently massaged their legs and back. Pecans that had fallen to the ground slipped out of their shells at a mere touch, and tasted as sweet as honey.

"Hello, Miss Dana," said the man, reaching over to shake Dana's hand. Then he turned to Christopher. "Mr. President! It's an honor and a pleasure!" He shook Christopher's hand heartily.

"Oh, Mr. Twain," said Dana, "This is such an honor ... such a delight to get to meet you!"

"Call me Mark, dear," he said, and then added, "Or call me Sam if you like ... That's what my folks called me!"

"Oh, yes, Samuel Clemens," said Christopher. "Well, you can call me Chris. That's what my folks called me!

They all laughed. Then the famous author had so many questions to ask Christopher and Dana that they were not sure they would get to ask all of the questions they had for him. He wanted to know what the world was like at the end of the twentieth century and beginning of the twenty-first. He wanted to know all about computers and cellphones and iPods and DVD players. He wanted to know whether it was wiser to wait for the next model to come out, or buy the product when you wanted it.

Finally, when Sam took a breath, Dana was able to quickly interject a question: "Did you write *Jap Herron?*"

Sam's smile faded, and a frown crimped his forehead. Dana drew back, chagrined at having caused consternation for the man. She and Christopher exchanged glances, both worried that they had somehow overstepped the bounds of this amazing opportunity to sit and chat with the legendary Mark Twain. But he just looked upward, thinking about something while he twirled one end of his bushy mustache. "I'm not entirely sure," he said, when he finally answered.

"You're ... uh ... not ... sure?" asked Christopher.

"No. Uh ... that is ... Well, you see, this is what happened." Sam shifted a little and sat up straighter. "This woman ... Emily ... Emily Hutchings ... I met her and her husband ... in 1902, I think ... We had corresponded for a time ... She asked for advice about getting some works published, and later she did indeed publish many of her own works."

Sam stopped twirling a corner of his mustache, reached for one of his bushy eyebrows, and started twisting at the hairs poking out of it. "I died a bit later, as you know ... Then a few years later ... Well, she was fooling around with one of those *ouija* boards, you know ... where you try to get in touch with those of us over here. Well, I thought I would give it a try ... that is, see if I could spell out a message to her on the board. I didn't want to frighten her, or anything ... I just spelled out a few words."

Sam stopped then, and picked up one of the pecans from the ground and slipped the shell off. Then he popped it into his mouth and chewed slowly, thoughtfully, and went on with his story: "Well, I *did* have an idea for a story about a young boy in a little river village ... I think I called it 'Happy Hollow' ... and the boy's name was 'Jasper' or 'Jap' for short ... and he runs away after his father dies, and goes to work for a printer." He looked over at Dana, "Partially autobiographical, in a few respects."

"Then," Dana said, leaning forward a bit, "Then you *did* dictate the story to Emily Hutchings after your death? Through the *ouija* board, as she claimed?"

Sam frowned again. "Well, no ... Not quite ... I'm not exactly sure. You see, I had this idea for a story, but I don't recall actually *writing* it through that *ouija* board thing ... I don't really recall writing it at all."

He looked at Dana, and then at Christopher, and back to Dana again. "To tell you the truth, it's still a damn mystery to me!" He threw his head back and laughed heartily — then just as suddenly composed himself. He looked around anxiously. "I mean, uh, *darn* mystery!" Then he broke up laughing again, shoulders jiggling.

They spent the rest of the afternoon of that glorious day, eating pecans with Mark Twain, asking him questions, listening to jokes he never had a chance to write down, and getting his slightly jaundiced view of the political goings-on in his day — not too different from the skullduggery of more recent times.

After they parted, with plans to meet again, Dana and Christopher were able to spend wonderful days and evenings with other people whom they had only dreamed of meeting: Abraham Lincoln, Socrates, Will Rogers, Martin Luther King, Golda Meir, Marie Curie, Benjamin Franklin, Moss Hart, Isaac Newton, Cleopatra, Malcolm X, Thomas Jefferson, and an endless list of others. Both would have wanted to meet Jesus, but were afraid to ask.

One morning, the two were going over their meetings, talking about how quietly funny Abraham Lincoln was, how stunningly beautiful Cleopatra was, and how brilliant but kooky Isaac Newton was. Suddenly they noticed a light shining from beyond the little hill nearby.

Gabriel came walking over. When he got to them, he sat down on the empty lounge chair. Then he looked at each of the two in turn and said, "Are you ready to meet him?"

They looked at each other, too awestruck to answer.

"I'll take that as a *yes*."

Gabriel opened his arms and a brilliant light surrounded the three of them. Scintillating flashes and rainbows of spectacular colors danced around them. It was so bright that they could not see each other — only the light and the fabulous swimming colors.

The light slowly faded, and Gabriel was gone ... Someone else was sitting in the chair.

He wore a plain white linen robe and a plain white sash. His hair was bright gold, with silver, copper, and gleaming black onyx glinting through the soft movement of his locks. His eyes were the color of the sky, his skin tawny bronze and flawless. He smiled, and a great wave of energy crashed through the atmosphere like a Herculean symphony.

"Hello, Dana. Hello, Christopher."

Chapter 24: Todd

Todd was finally able to stop crying. He pulled the jacket tightly around his shoulders. He started to stand up, but then knelt back down and felt around the ground for the little stones that he had used to spell out *I'm sorry*, and carefully placed them in his pocket. He was so grateful to Christopher for taking off his own jacket and putting it around him. That was the first relief he had from the penetrating cold and from his humiliating nakedness. Yet that was the man whose assassination he had arranged.

To forgive a man for such a ... a monstrous deed ... How could he ever hope for ... He would live this way ... no eyes, no mouth ... forever blind and mute? Because he did not want to *see* nor *talk to* those pathetic ... *victims* ... yes, victims ... of the war that he started ... that he wanted.

This was his fate. He abandoned all hope.

"Well, I'm surprised it took you this long to come around," a thunderous voice spoke.

Todd looked up, but of course, he could see nothing. He tried to speak, but still could produce only the hollow hissing sound from the empty cavern that used to be a mouth with lips and teeth and tongue.

Suddenly a burning hot hand, massive in size and strength, gripped him completely around his neck. It pulled him upward as he tried to protest, choking and hissing, until he was lifted off the ground.

He was being carried somewhere. Soon he felt heat rising, and then flames licked at his feet. He started to panic, clawing at the hand which still held him by the neck, until it released him, and then he was falling, falling, falling, down into fire. Flames surrounded him and he choked from the smoke and pain as his flesh sizzled and huge blisters formed and then popped as he fell through the fire. He could smell his flesh burning.

He hit the ground. He no longer felt any fire. He was still wearing the jacket he had been given.

"He forgave you, you know?" said Lucifer, now somewhat more quietly.

"He ... Who ... forgave me?" said Todd, not even realizing for a minute that he was now able to speak. When he did, he grabbed his own throat and felt his mouth, his tongue and his teeth. He drew in his breath, so happy, that he could not speak now — from joy. He was too overwhelmed with emotion to speak.

"Bennington. The President you had assassinated. He forgave you."

Todd dropped his head into his hands and cried unabashedly.

"That's why you are here, Jared Todd Davis," said Lucifer. "You have a choice now — because you said you were sorry ... when you had no reason to expect anything from it ... it came from your heart ... No strings attached ... No entreaty for mercy. You said you were sorry ... spelled it out with pebbles, since you had no tongue ... and Bennington forgave you." *Damn him.*

Todd looked up, in Lucifer's direction. He could speak now, but he was still unable to see. "F-forgave ... *me?*" he repeated, "And I have a ... a ... second chance?"

"Not a second chance," corrected Lucifer. "A second *choice.* Now you have another choice ... because you asked for nothing ... and because he forgave you." *The killjoy.*

Todd sat up, still on the ground, and pulled his jacket closer around himself, in spite of the heat — he felt somehow *comforted* by the jacket, and wanted to keep it close to him. "Forgave me? How ... how did you know ...?"

"We *know*, Jared Todd Davis, *we know,*" responded Lucifer, bending down to Todd's level. "We know when a human is truthful about forgiving ... or about being sorry. We know when they are faking — paying lip service to avoid punishment — and we know when they are truly re*pent*ant."

Lucifer nearly choked on the last word, practically spitting out the "pent" syllable.

Lifting his trident above his head, he said, "*Up there* they can fool lots of folks — judges, priests — even their own victims." Then lowering his trident and jamming it into the ground, "Down here ... they don't fool anyone."

Todd swallowed hard before speaking again, carefully choosing his words. "You said ... something about ... 'another choice' ...?"

"Well," said Lucifer, walking around the half-naked man, forcing him to keep scooting around in a circle to follow his voice, "You know what your first choice is ... remember?"

Todd thought back to the painful, rocky bench that cut into his buttocks each time he moved the slightest bit. Lucifer told him to meet all the casualties ... *victims* ... of the Library Tower bombing ... which he also had engineered ... and the subsequent war with Russia. He was supposed to *get to know them ... listen to their stories.*

"Ah, you *do* remember!" said Lucifer, reading his thoughts, "Very good! So — do you want to take another crack at it? Hmmmm?"

Recalling the numbers involved, Todd winced. Lucifer mentioned at least fifteen thousand casualties, and there were probably many more.

"Right-o, Todd-a-o!" said Lucifer, reading his thoughts, "Many, many more! The sectarian violence and civil strife that broke out after you invaded and destabilized the country took a quarter of a million lives, by the time all was said and done."

Todd wished he could hide his thoughts from Lucifer and not be such an open book.

"Tough."

Todd thought back to the twenty-nine victims he did meet. Each took at least a half hour, some an hour or more. *No, no, no,* he thought. He could not see himself spending — a century? Two? — sitting on that torturous bench, listening to those wretched people.

He looked up to where Lucifer's voice had come from when he last spoke.

"Well, uh ... Mr. Lucifer ... Sir ... What is my other choice?"

Lucifer placed his massive hands on Todd's shoulders and spun him around. Todd saw a glimmer of reddish light, as though he were looking through is own eyelids. Then he realized that is exactly what he was doing. He opened his eyes, and realized, with a joy tainted only by the fear that this might not be real, that his eyes were really there again; he could see again.

Tears rushed out so quickly and copiously that he felt stabbing pain in his eyes. But it was good pain. Pain that let him know his eyes were truly back. He could see again.

Dropping down onto his knees and touching his head to the ground in front of Lucifer, he whispered, *"Thank you ... thank you ... God bless you ..."*

At that last comment, Lucifer recoiled in revulsion and blasted Todd with a fiery bolt of white-hot flame. *"Don't say that! Never say that!!"*

Todd ignored the searing pain of the bolt, only patting his eyes and his mouth to reassure himself that they were really there, intact and functional. They were. He was not dreaming.

Immediately Todd was plucked up by the neck again. It was painful, but he was held loosely enough now so that he was no longer choking for air. Lucifer carried him at arm's length — as one would hold a smelly bag of garbage — down a passageway. He stopped in front of what looked like ... an industrial size, ruby-encrusted, trash bin.

Still being held by the neck, Todd was too deliriously happy to have his sight and voice back to be worried about what came next — until Lucifer uncurled the clawed index finger of his free hand and pointed it at the lid of the bin. A greenish-yellow beam shot out from his claw; and the lid of the bin began slowly opening. As it did, a strong odor like rotten meat drifted out, worse even than the sulfurous odor that already hung in the place.

"Look."

Todd held his breath, now becoming filled with terror at what might be inside the bin. Snakes? Rats? No — Lucifer was far more depraved than to settle for anything so mundane. Knowing it was pointless to resist, Todd looked down into the depths of the huge receptacle.

He was dumbfounded, in utter disbelief at what he saw. It was a scene so beautiful that it rivaled a Paul Gauguin painting of a Tahitian paradise. He could hardly believe his eyes, and felt for them again, just to be sure they were still there.

They were. He started crying again.

Lucifer rolled his eyes. He waited patiently. After a few minutes, Todd composed himself. He blew his nose in the sleeve of his jacket, which Lucifer found surprisingly revolting.

"This is your other choice," he said, with a sweeping gesture toward the scene inside the trash bin.

Todd saw a vast panorama of lush green trees, a river flowing quietly among them, and snow-capped magenta mountains in the distance. But what really caught his eye were the beautiful coffee-hued native women washing colorful cloth on the rocks by the river. They seemed serenely happy, laughing and singing as they worked. They wore nothing above their colorful skirts except necklaces of stones and shells, and their naked well-sculpted breasts swayed as they washed their clothes. Children were dancing in a circle, and others seemed to be playing games around the trees. Farther down the river, men in loincloths and beaded jewelry were casting primitive nets over the water and pulling in large wriggling fish. The men, too, were singing as they worked, and seemed to be having a very good time.

Todd looked up at Lucifer. "*This* is my other choice?" he was mystified, certain that it was a cruel joke.

"It is not a joke," said Lucifer. He released the neck-hold he had Todd in, and carefully sat him down on the rim of the trash bin. He then proceeded to straighten and smooth down the lapels of the man's now-tattered and partially blackened jacket.

After a long minute of this fussing about, Lucifer said — so softly that it was almost as though he were talking to himself — "I can say anything I want ... but I must be accurate about choices of fate. So you may ask me any questions that you have. I shall answer ... *truthfully.*" The last word was nearly inaudible.

"Okay," said Todd, trying to reconcile the exquisite paradise before him with the hellacious experiences he had come to expect here. "So I can go *there* if I want? I can join those people there?"

"Yes. There. Right there," Lucifer confirmed. "As you see."

"Not somewhere else? Not somewhere farther down the river with a bunch of cannibals or alligators or something?"

"Not somewhere else, no. You can choose to live among the people you see. There."

"They are not cannibals?"

"They are not. They are, in fact, a very peace-loving people."

Todd thought for another minute, and then asked, "Would I still be white? Would I still be of the Caucasian race?"

"Ah, no," said Lucifer, smiling. "You would not be white; you would not be of the Caucasian race."

"Brown?"

"Yes, you would be brown."

Todd nodded. "And my other choice?"

Lucifer rolled his eyes and blew out his breath in a dramatic sigh. "You are beginning to try my patience, Jared Todd Davis."

"Okay, so I know — my other choice — the so-called victims ..."

"They are not *'so-called'* victims, Jared Todd Davis. They *are* victims. *Your* victims. You need to meet them. Talk to them. Get to know them. That is your other choice."

"Well, okay." He turned to look into the trash bin again, now getting somewhat acclimated to the stink that arose from it.

"I guess ... I think ... I choose *this!!*" and Todd abruptly placed his hands on the edge of the bin beside him, ready to push off.

He was stopped by Lucifer's hot claw, which was suddenly hooked into his shoulder.

"Ow-w-w-w! What did you do that for?"

"I must, as you recall, be forthright *(cough, cough)* about your choice of fates," Lucifer said. "Now you need to know that in choosing this option," he continued, uncurling his claw from Todd's shoulder and pointing it toward the scene inside the trash bin, "that you would *not* enjoy the same ..."

"I know! I know!" said Todd, impatiently, "I won't be rich or famous, like I was before! I'm not stupid!"

"That's right, exactly. Moreover, you would not ..."

"... be President! I won't be 'Chief' or whatever, either! *Okay!*" shouted Todd, and added, "I'll just be a poor muscle-bound native stud on a tropical island paradise surrounded by gorgeous babes with big tits! Po' li'l me! Ha-ha-ha!"

Lucifer bent down so that he was face to face with Todd. He grabbed at the lapels he had just smoothed over a few minutes earlier.

"There is one more thing you need to know before making your choice," he said, "and that is ..."

Todd held up his hand, and with two fingers of each hand he brazenly plucked Lucifer's claws off of his lapels. "Forget it! You think I'm stupid? You're not going to talk me into doing your bidding!"

He pushed off the edge of the trash bin and waved in a mocking manner to Lucifer as he dropped down, down, down.

Down in the village, two pregnant women walked back from the river with their baskets of freshly laundered clothes. As they stepped around a large rock that had been partially moved, they saw the *gewone slakvreter* — also known as the Southern Slug-eater, an entirely harmless brown snake found around the Limpopo River of Transvaal, in South Africa. It, too, was pregnant, and the two women watched excitedly as it gave birth to its twelve live young snakes. One was a bit smaller than the others.

~~~~~~~~~~~~~

Special Thanks to...

Joanne, for her wonderfully on-target editing suggestions and encouraging comments.

Janet, for her patience in standing outside for hours to get just the right photograph of the clouds; and for running interference through the crowds at *Le Louvre* to photograph *La Jeune Martyre* for the cover.

Joe, for his artistic skill which produced the award-winning "Fire-Dance" design for the Title page and back cover.